KILLING FURY

Dale Eaton was having troubles of his own in the federal penitentiary in Colorado. The trouble began when an inmate named Carl Inman Palmer was assigned to Dale's cell. Carl Palmer was in the common room, while Dale was back at the cell. Dale put a piece of cardboard in the window of the cell, signifying that he was using the toilet and wanted privacy.

Around 9:30 A.M. a message went out over the loudspeaker for all inmates to return to their cells. Palmer did as instructed, and either he didn't see the small piece of cardboard in the window, or he thought Dale had heard the message and knew he would be coming back to the cell. Whatever the circumstances, when Palmer entered the cell, Dale became extremely angry. Without a word he punched Palmer in the side of his head with all his might.

In shock and surprise, Palmer asked, "Why'd you hit me?"

Dale growled back, "I don't come in when you're on the toilet!"

Palmer didn't say another word; instead he collapsed to the floor. A guard called for help, and soon an ambulance was on its way. Palmer was rushed to Emergency. Knowing that he was in real trouble, Dale kept asking, "Is my roomie okay?"

Palmer wasn't okay, however, and he soon died from a ruptured vertebral artery. Now Dale Eaton had a new charge against him; manslaughter.

Also by Robert Scott

RIVERS OF
BLOOD

ROBERT SCOTT

PINNACLE BOOKS
Kensington Publishing Corp.
http://www.kensingtonbooks.com

Some names have been changed to protect the privacy of individuals connected to this story.

PINNACLE BOOKS are published by

Kensington Publishing Corp.
119 West 40th Street
New York, NY 10018

All Kensington Titles, Imprints, and Distributed Lines are available at special quantity discounts for bulk purchases for sales promotions, premiums, fund-raising, and educational or institutional use. Special book excerpts or customized printings can also be created to fit specific needs. For details, write or phone the office of the Kensington special sales manager: Kensington Publishing Corp., 119 West 40th Street, New York, NY 10018, attn: Special Sales Department, Phone: 1-800-221-2647.

Pinnacle and the P logo Reg. U.S. Pat. & TM Off.

ISBN-13: 978-0-7860-1996-0
ISBN-10: 0-7860-1996-4

First printing: December 2009

10 9 8 7 6 5 4 3 2 1

Printed in the United States of America

ACKNOWLEDGMENTS

I'd like to thank Greg Cooper, Detective Dennis Journigan, Investigator Eric Koss, Bobbette Jasmann, and Tony Howard for their help in gathering material for this book. I'd also like to thank my editor at Pinnacle Books, Michaela Hamilton.

I

RIVERS OF
NO RETURN

1

TERROR ON
THE HIGHWAY

Green River, Wyoming, September 1997

Newlyweds Scott and Shannon Breeden, of Santa Cruz, California, were taking a cross-country trip to visit Scott's family in Michigan. As they drove across the United States on Interstate 80, the Breedens basically lived in their old Ford van, which they'd rigged up with a sink, bed, and propane stove. One of the main reasons for their trip was to show off their four-and-a-half-month-old baby boy, Cody.

On September 11, 1997, the Breedens' van began to have trouble and the engine overheated as they drove along I-80 in Wyoming. They pulled off the highway between Wamsutter and Rawlins, onto a roadside strip sometimes used by truckers. The Breedens' van was indeed not capable of going any farther. The asphalt strip was really no more than a parking area, sometimes used by long-haul truckers, and there were no facilities or any habitations at all for miles around. At the time, the Breedens were the only ones stopped in a desolate area of sage and sand.

Unable to get the van started again, the couple decided to wait for help. Several truckers did pull off into the area and promised to relay a message about their distress to a town down the road. No help, however, arrived that day, so the Breedens decided to eat supper and bed down in the van for the night.

The next morning, they ate breakfast and began to realize they were heading into real trouble. Their water supply was running low and they had a baby to take care of. Then, around 9:00 A.M., another van pulled off the interstate onto the same parking strip. It was a faded green Dodge van, and the Breedens were sure help had arrived. Their joy was short-lived, however, when that van's owner stepped out and lifted his own hood and checked the engine. The Breedens wondered how a guy with engine problems of his own could help them.

The driver of the green Dodge van checked his engine for a while, seemed to think that everything was all right, and then closed the hood. He walked over toward the Breedens and asked if they needed any help. They were thrilled—it had been eighteen hours since they had pulled off the interstate.

The owner of the Dodge van introduced himself as Dale, and he was a stocky man, weighing around 250 pounds. The Breedens thought he was about forty-five years old, but he was actually older than that. Dale offered them a ride to the city of Green River, where he said his brother owned a repair shop and could help them with their van problems. The Breedens agreed to go with Dale and packed up a few belongings, along with baby Cody, a small kitten, and a three-legged dog they owned.

Shannon Breeden later said that she was uneasy about this "Dale" character. There was just something about him that set her on edge. She even related, "I thought he looked like a serial killer. But I'm kind of a hippie mom, and I told myself not to judge things like that." Besides, in their present situation, beggars couldn't be choosers.

Scott Breeden was less concerned about the man's looks, and his first impression was that Dale looked "normal." Dale was obviously some kind of welder, since he had welding equipment stashed in the back of his van, along with a bed and portable stove. As they drove off, Scott's first reaction of how "normal" the man was changed a bit. Dale seemed to mumble to himself a lot about something, and he was drinking one cup of coffee after another until he was completely wired. At other times, Dale was okay, and he talked about the gas fields and oil rigs in the region where he had worked.

Dale drove for a short while and then said he had to get out and urinate. Since Scott did too, that was no problem. Dale went off behind one set of sagebrush while Scott found another. Meanwhile, inside the van, Shannon opened her blouse and began to breast-feed Cody. Since she described herself as "kind of a hippie mom," this kind of activity did not embarrass her in front of strangers. When Dale got back in the van, however, he seemed to give her more glances than seemed appropriate.

It wasn't long before Dale announced that he was extremely tired and asked if one of them would drive while he crawled into the back of the van and took a nap. Since Scott had a suspended driver's license, Shannon said that she would drive. Shannon got behind the wheel, Scott and Cody scooted over to the passenger side of the van, and Dale crawled into the back. Shannon hadn't driven very far when both she and Scott heard a strange metallic clicking sound coming from behind them. They both turned around and were astonished to see Dale pointing a rifle at them. Dale growled, "This is a .30-30! Now drive down this dirt road, and I mean it!" He indicated a small dirt road that snaked off into the Red Desert.

Shannon did as Dale instructed, but she began to think, *If I'm going down, I'm going down right here!* She may have indicated to Scott that she was going to do something drastic, but in the ensuing chaos, neither one of them could remember the exact sequence of events. In any case, Shannon stepped on the accelerator and turned the steering wheel in violent motions, making the van swerve from side to side. The careening van caused Dale to lose his balance, and he fell backward with his rifle into the interior of the van. Shannon screamed at Scott, "Take Cody and jump!"

Scott vaulted out the door, with Cody in his arms. Miraculously, neither one of them was hurt as Scott landed and they tumbled into the dirt road. By this time, Shannon and Dale were struggling for control of the van, and Dale reached for the keys in the ignition. Shannon attempted to jump from the van, but Dale caught her by the back of her blouse and pulled her back inside. She said later, "It was a real struggle!"

Scott placed Cody beneath a sagebrush, then ran to where the van had now stopped. Shannon managed to get out of the van and started running, but Dale caught her from behind and they both tumbled to the ground. By this time, the rifle had fallen out of Dale's hands, so he grabbed a knife he carried with him and attempted to stab Shannon. Scott jumped on Dale's back, but was spun to the ground, and Dale placed the knife blade right up against Shannon's rib cage. He yelled at Scott, "Let go or I'll kill her!"

Scott wasn't about to let go, and he fought with all the strength of his 150-pound frame against 250-pound Dale. Luckily for Scott, Shannon was also fighting like a wildcat. Both of them knew they were fighting for their lives, and the life of Cody as well. Scott managed to grab the rifle; he hit Dale over the head with it so hard, the stock of the rifle broke. But Dale still kept on fighting.

Around and around they went, the knife somehow ending up in Scott's hands. He stabbed Dale in the chest, and still the man would not quit. Scott related later, "I said I was going to kill him, but somehow he still managed to get up!"

Dale angrily stumbled over to the van, grabbed a pipe wrench from the back of the van, and came at the couple again. Once more, the Breedens overpowered Dale and began beating him with his own wrench. And still he wouldn't stop fighting. At some point, Scott fired the rifle and the bullet kicked up dirt near Dale's feet. Dale shouted, "If you fire it again, it will blow up on you!" Scott didn't know if Dale was lying or not, but he didn't want to find out the hard way. Instead, he began beating Dale with the rifle barrel—on the head, on the shoulders, and on the back. And still the man fought on like a demon.

Scott related later, "I didn't expect him to get up after I stabbed him! The only thing I thought of was that I was going to stop him one way or another. He was insane! Crazy! He was not quitting!"

Hitting Dale in the head and back didn't seem to faze him, so Scott switched tactics and began hitting Dale in the knees with the rifle. This finally seemed to work, and after several blows, Dale went down and stayed down. As he lay on the ground, Dale even declared, "Okay, I'm done." And then, unexpectedly, he added, "Will you at least leave me a cigarette?"

Scott wasn't giving this madman a cigarette or anything else. Shannon stumbled back to the van; Scott picked up Cody; then they all climbed inside. Shannon fired up the engine, and as they squealed off, Scott shouted at Shannon, "Run his head over!" Shannon, however, wouldn't do it, and she peeled off back toward the main highway, leaving Dale looking like a bloody rag doll in the middle of the dirt road. Shannon had only one thought in mind—they had to get help.

Little did Shannon and Scott Breeden know at the time that Dale had kidnapped a young woman in Wyoming years before. He had kept her captive, sexually tortured her, and finally killed her. If the Breedens hadn't fought like tigers, they, too, might have ended up like Dale's victim from 1988, and possibly others he had killed as well.

Fremont County, Wyoming, March 1988

In Fremont County, Wyoming, the wind screams, howls, whispers, and moans. The wind is a living entity, always stirring, always blowing, a constant companion to travelers and locals alike. Whenever there is a momentary lull in the wind, people take notice because of its very absence. The wind sends tumbleweeds flying and dust devils swirling across the empty landscape. Vast distances, an arching sky, and floating clouds dominate the county, but prominently, and above all, there is the factor of wind.

A dynamic presence during daylight hours, the wind can take on a sinister aspect at night. That—and the empty landscape without a house, ranch, tree, or another vehicle upon the roads—lends an otherworldly feeling to the region. When a structure does finally loom upon the horizon in the headlights, it takes on the form of an island in a vast and empty sea. Small pools of light around the structure are minuscule in the ocean of darkness. There is a feeling of abandonment, as if the structure has been shipwrecked on some unseen reef—not pummeled by waves or breakers, but by wind.

Such an "island" in Fremont County is the Waltman Rest Stop on U.S. Highway 20/26. A modern building with solar panels and slanted roof, it appears like a bunker from some futuristic war, sitting in a desolate expanse of sage and sand hills that stretch on into infinity. Other than toilets, sinks, drinking water, and a few picnic tables, however, there is little else to tempt a motorist to stop at all. Yet, in a country so bereft of buildings, the rest stop seems like a beckoning oasis in an ocean of emptiness.

On March 25, 1988, eighteen-year-old Lisa Marie Kimmell arrived at the Waltman Rest Stop sometime around midnight, and it was indeed like an island on her long journey from Denver, Colorado, to the distant point of Cody, Wyoming, in the northwestern part of that state. Perhaps she needed to use the restroom, or wanted a drink of water, or only wanted to stretch her legs after so much driving. Whatever the circumstances, Lisa got out of her 1988 Honda Civic CRXsi and stepped into the night. Above her, a million stars sparkled in the vastness of the sky, and the wind wafted her blond shoulder-length hair around her neck. And despite having grown up in Montana's "Big Sky Country," it is not unlikely that she felt a shiver of fear as she stepped out into the darkness. She was, after all, a young woman alone on that long and desolate stretch of road.

Fear, coupled with apparitions, takes flight on such a night, and it must have come as a complete shock to Lisa when an apparition did take form and stepped out from the shadows and into the light. The apparition was no figment of her imagination, but rather a flesh-and-blood middle-aged man.

Did he speak to her? Did she respond? Was he friendly at first, or did he ask her a question? No one knows, except the man himself.

Whatever the circumstances, his intent soon became crystal clear. He wasn't there to engage her in conversation. He wasn't there to give her directions. He was there to abduct someone, and as misfortune would have it, that person turned out to be eighteen-year-old Lisa Kimmell.

With no one as a witness, except for her abductor, a man named Dale, Lisa Marie Kimmell and her vehicle simply disappeared as if they had never been there at all. Only the wind and darkness remained.

2

THE MISSING GIRL

Lisa Kimmell was working as a unit manager at an Arby's restaurant in Aurora, Colorado, near Denver, in 1988. At the time, she was living in a company-maintained apartment, while helping out her mother with the Denver-area restaurant. Lisa was well-liked by her fellow employees and general manager of the restaurant where she worked. She was always sweet and personable. There was a certain glow about her.

In the last week of March 1988, she and her mother, Sheila Kimmell, discussed their upcoming trip back to Billings, Montana. Sheila worked as a director of operations for the Arby's restaurant chain in the Denver area, although her home was in Billings. Sheila was, in essence, a regional manager and often commuted between Billings and Denver. During her stays in the Denver area, Sheila lived in the same apartment complex as Lisa. And even though Lisa had driven from

Denver to Billings on several occasions, this would be her first trip off the interstates.

The reason for that was that Lisa intended to pick up her new boyfriend, Ed Jaroch, who lived in Cody, Wyoming. Once Lisa picked up Ed, he would travel the rest of the way with her to Billings, where she would introduce him to her father and two sisters, Stacy and Sherry. Her mother, Sheila, had already met Ed. Lisa intended to arrive in Cody either later Saturday night or early Sunday morning after getting off her shift at Arby's.

On March 24, 1988, Sheila Kimmell was scheduled to fly home from Denver to Billings, because she intended to go skiing with her husband and daughters on the upcoming weekend. Sheila recalled about Ed Jaroch later: "He called the apartment on a number of occasions and I had the opportunity to speak with him and relay messages. They were becoming interested in each other." In Sheila's opinion, Ed seemed like a nice young man and well-suited for her daughter.

Ed Jaroch worked for the Marathon Oil Company in its Cody, Wyoming, office. He and Lisa had been introduced by mutual friends. When Ed and Lisa first met in person in Billings, they hit it off so well together that they spent Friday evening and Saturday, during the day, together. Both looked forward to meeting each other once again. In fact, in their absence, they phoned each other repeatedly and exchanged letters every three or four days.

In late March 1988, Ed and Lisa planned to meet again, and Ed recalled, "The arrangement originally was that we were going to meet in Casper, Wyoming, because it was the midway point between Cody and Denver. We were going to join up with two other friends there. A friend of mine by the name of Jim, and a friend of Lisa's, Karla. The four of us were going to listen to a country-western band at the Beacon Club. I was familiar with that band, but I didn't know the band members personally.

"But there were some things that came up. Lisa had a friend that was ill who lived in Billings. And I think Lisa was offered a position at Arby's in Billings. One thing after another happened. Karla couldn't make it, and this and that. We ultimately decided not to continue with those plans, and instead, Lisa decided to come up to Cody."

In fact, Ed and Lisa planned to get together a lot, and he purchased a plane ticket for later in April to come and visit her in the Denver area. As far as Lisa driving from Denver to Cody in March, Ed remembered, "I didn't especially like the idea of her driving all the way to Cody. I knew it would be late in the evening, after she got off work. The plans were for her to leave Denver after work, which would have been four or five o'clock in the afternoon. So I knew it would be late when she got to Cody. I was concerned about her safety, and tried to discourage her from making that trip that evening. I said I didn't like the idea, but she was pretty adamant that she could handle it."

As far as the route was supposed to be, Ed recalled, "I was very specific with her about the route. To the best of my recollection, she had never been to Cody, at least from the south. So I was very specific with her about the direction that I thought she should go. It was from Denver to Casper, on Interstate 25, and then from Casper to Shoshoni on Highway 20/26. Then north of Shoshoni to Thermopolis, then to Meeteetse, and then to Cody. I was very clear about the directions, because it was going to be in the middle of the night and I did not want her to get lost."

Ed and Lisa talked to each other on the phone after she got off work on March 25 and she indicated that she was running a little late. Lisa then told Ed that she would be leaving her apartment in about twenty minutes, which would have put the time around 5:00 P.M.

Sheila Kimmell recalled later, "When Lisa got off work, she was to take me to the airport. I was flying home for a four-day weekend. She talked at length about her trip, from Denver to Cody, to pick up Ed Jaroch and then travel to Billings. There [were] conversations about what her plans were to do in picking up Ed and meeting with friends. But in the meantime, knowing that her route would not be the typical route that she would take, the interstate directly from Denver to Billings, we got out an atlas, as I kept several, and we went over the route that would make the most sense for her to take. That was back roads from the Casper area to reach Cody. So we walked through that and looked at other possible alternate routes, and there really weren't any. We went over that, and I left my atlas with her. She then took me to the airport a little bit later that evening."

Sheila Kimmell recalled the route Lisa planned to take as being Highway 20/26 out of Casper that went by Moneta in Fremont County, then to Shoshoni, then up to Cody. Sheila also discussed going on the road trip with Lisa, rather than flying back to Billings. Sheila said later, "I told her, I didn't need to catch this airplane and that I was concerned about her traveling alone and not being familiar with the back roads. I could certainly cancel my plane, and I could drive with her. She, however, dismissed that as an option, explaining to me that her car was only a two-seater. She was going to pick up Ed. Then her plans were to visit friends in Billings. She wanted to have her car when I suggested that perhaps we take mine. So she found both of those alternatives not acceptable to her."

Among other items in Lisa's car, Sheila knew that her daughter was taking along some luggage. It was, in fact, one of Sheila's three-piece sets of luggage, small bags that were blue/silver in color. Also Sheila was aware that Lisa generally wore a flat gold necklace, a cross, a simple gold band, and stud earrings. The ring was one that her grandmother had given Lisa and was of white gold with laced filigree. It had a diamond marquise in the center of the ring.

At the airport parking lot, Lisa and Sheila shared a few more words, and then it was time for Sheila to go. Lisa gave her mom a long hug and said, "Mom, I can't tell you how much I really do love you and Dad."

Sheila replied that she loved Lisa as well. As Sheila headed for the plane, she turned around one more time and said, "You drive careful!"

Lisa responded, "Don't worry, Mom. I will."

Those were the last words Sheila Kimmell ever heard her daughter speak.

Lisa Kimmell's journey apparently took her up Interstate 25 through Colorado to Cheyenne, Wyoming, and on up to Casper. She owned a distinctive 1988 Honda CRXsi, which she had purchased herself. The Montana license plates read LIL MISS, which referred to a nickname given to Lisa by her paternal grandmother. This grandmother had often referred to Lisa as "my lil miss Lisa Marie." So the name "Lil Miss" stuck in reference to Lisa.

Lisa's father had instructed her to get gas at Cheyenne, before taking off on the two-lane roads across central Wyoming and on up to Cody. Sheila would comment upon this fact later by saying, "We would always stop in Cheyenne and get gas on the way up to Montana, and then also on return trips, we would also gas up in Cheyenne before we returned to Colorado. It was almost a requirement that my husband stipulated. He also had another stipulation. When you filled up with gas, you reset your odometer."

One thing was for certain. Lisa was driving at eighty-eight miles per hour in a 65 mph zone near Douglas, Wyoming, at 9:06 P.M. on March 25, when she was spotted by Highway Patrol officer Al Lesco. Lisa was soon pulled over and cited for speeding. Lisa, however, didn't have enough cash to pay for the speeding ticket, something that Wyoming required out-of-state drivers to do. So Officer Lesco led her to an ATM at a bank in the town of Douglas. This was 1988, however. Back then, one bank's ATM card would not work in a bank other than the one that had issued the card. That is exactly what occurred for Lisa; she couldn't get any cash out of the machine to pay her speeding ticket.

Officer Lesco had a decision to make at that point. He could put Lisa in jail until she came up with the cash, or let her go with the promise that she would send a check once she reached Billings, Montana. Since Lisa seemed like a nice young woman who would honor her commitment, Officer Lesco let her go with a promise that she send a check later.

From Douglas, Lisa most likely took the interstate to Casper, Wyoming, where there is one indication that she went into a grocery store between 10:00 and 10:30 P.M. This was just an unconfirmed sighting, however. From Casper, her most likely route to Cody would have been on U.S. 20/26, which becomes a two-lane road outside the city.

By going this route, Lisa would have been in the area of the Waltman Rest Stop around midnight on March 25. Even though it's not certain Lisa made it there, that remains the most likely scenario, due to some comments the abductor would later make. Other scenarios would be put forth later also, that she was run off the road or had a flat tire somewhere before the rest stop, or even stopped on the roadside shoulder near her abductor's property. But of all the scenarios, the Waltman Rest Stop seems most likely. The only one who knew for sure where she was stopped was her kidnapper, and he would only talk in riddles later.

Whatever the case, Lisa Kimmell was definitely abducted on the night of March 25, and her car was taken as well. The abductor apparently knew what he was doing. He had flex cuffs with him and handcuffs, items he kept in his 1979 Dodge pickup. The pickup was an extended-cab version and had dual rear wheels, making it both powerful and able to cross rough terrain. It also had a winch on the back. When the pretty young woman with shoulder-length hair came into view, the abductor could hardly believe his luck. He liked them young and pretty. And this one was alone.

The abductor generally kept one more item with him—a .30-30 rifle—and he most likely pointed it at Lisa, telling her to do everything he said or he would kill her. With almost no other options, Lisa must have done as instructed. He forced her into a compliant position and tied her arms and her legs with bindings. Once she was secured, the man placed the petite young woman into the extended-cab area of his pickup behind the front seat. When he raised the seat back in place, Lisa could not be seen from outside the vehicle. Then hurrying before anyone came along, the man most likely hitched up Lisa's vehicle, which sported the

Montana license plate LIL MISS onto his winch. His luck held. No one passed down the road at that hour of the night, and both Lisa and her car were driven away without any witnesses.

The man drove about twenty miles to his property, a weed patch of scrub and sage and sand. Even the buildings on the property didn't help its appearance much. They were a collection of weather-beaten sheds, jumbled car parts, and other piles of rusting junk on the property. Stashing Lisa's car in one of his sheds, the man took her into a dilapidated old school bus that he'd converted into his living area to fulfill his twisted sexual fantasies. What exactly he did to her can only be discerned in bits and pieces by mute evidence and a few things he would later relate. Lisa was apparently tied up with nylon rope most of the time, which was looped around her wrists and ankles. She may have been tied to an old bed frame. Early on, her abductor disrobed her. Fulfilling one of his fantasies, he shaved her pubic hair. He sexually assaulted her on numerous occasions, to the degree that detectives would later speak of her torment as being "violent sexual assaults." There would be reports of vaginal rape and sodomy. Trussed up tightly, she could not fend off her attacker.

Yet, there was something different this time compared to other occasions for the abductor. The sexual assault was not followed by an immediate murder and dumping of the body in some wild area. The abductor apparently grew attached to Lisa, and he kept her in his bus, day after day. He not only kept her to molest her sexually, but may have even formed some kind of twisted attachment to her as well. Almost certainly she spoke with him—he later claimed that she did. And though much of what was said was kept to himself, he did relate that she spoke about her family and that

Easter was coming up soon. If it was a means by Lisa to keep herself alive, it worked for a while. The man seemed to want to keep her alive, even though every day she was alive made things more dangerous for him. He knew she was being looked for by law enforcement agencies and the public. Newspaper articles he kept about her disappearance would later prove that he knew how wide the search area was, and that it did extend into his county.

What he would ultimately do with her became very problematic. In his mind, this was a young woman who was not like the rest. She wasn't just some "whore" or junkie or runaway that he abducted from the side of the road. She had good looks, spoke well, and had come from a good home. She was the kind of young woman he had often desired and had never possessed. As long as she remained tied up and kept out of sight, he could have a part of that dream. Maybe he even entertained visions that he could convince her to stay with him. His property was so isolated, and no one had seen the abduction. There was a good prospect that she wouldn't be discovered if he kept her tied up and out of sight. It wasn't like there were people who came to see him on a regular basis.

Yet, in the long run, he was a realist as well. He had just kidnapped a young woman and had sexually assaulted her. If he let her go or she somehow got away, and it was traced back to him, it would mean prison for the rest of his life. He had been incarcerated before and didn't like it. The thought of spending a lifetime behind bars was too much to contemplate. Even though he liked the young woman on various levels—especially the things he could do to her without her being able to refuse—the risks of keeping her around outweighed the pleasure he gained from her captivity.

He fed her on occasion, and on the evening of the sixth day, he apparently fed her a dinner of beef stew. Once night had fallen, the abductor forced Lisa into the back of his extended cab once again, her hands tied together as usual. He allowed her to dress only in socks and panties. Most likely, her ankles were tied as well, so that she could not run away. Whether he told her he was going to let her go somewhere out in the wilderness is unknown. What is known is that he drove about seventy miles to an area known as the Trapper's Route, on the North Fork of the Platte River. He may have used dirt back roads rather than the main highways to get there. And he probably knew this area from past travels. If, indeed, he took this route, it would have taken him by the Rattlesnake Range and Poison Spider Creek. He also would have crossed the old Oregon Trail, the most famous covered-wagon route of the nineteenth century. The man finally stopped his pickup near an unused bridge called the Old Government Bridge, which crossed the North Platte River. At that hour, there was no one else there.

The man took Lisa out of the cab and placed her on the roadway of the bridge. He either turned her facing away from him, or Lisa turned to try and escape. There were no bindings on her when she was found. Whatever the circumstances, once her head was turned, the man brought a lead pipe crashing down on the back of her head. He did it with such force that it fractured a four-inch area in her skull. Lisa fell to the bridge roadway unconscious, not yet dead, but she would have probably bled out if left unattended. The abductor did not wait for that to happen. He brought out a large knife and expertly stabbed her six times, piercing her vital organs. Each knife thrust missed her ribs, which might have deflected the stab wounds. Within less than a minute, Lisa Marie Kimmell was dead.

The man hoisted her up and dropped her body over the side of the bridge into shallow water, leaving a trail of her blood on the side of the bridge. Then he looked around. Once again, his luck was holding. There was no one around, and no witnesses to see that he or his vehicle had been there.

Ed Jaroch began to think something was wrong in the early-morning hours of March 26, 1988. He said later, "I expected Lisa about one A.M. I went to bed and woke up about three A.M., and she wasn't here. At that point, I began to become concerned. I fretted about it for a little while and then went back to bed. I got up the next morning, roughly at six, and didn't do anything immediately. But about seven-thirty A.M., I started to make some phone calls.

"First I tried to call her apartment in Denver, without any luck. I called my sister in Denver to get the phone number of the Colorado Highway Patrol, and I filed a missing persons report with them. Then I called the Wyoming Highway Patrol. Through the rest of the morning, I tried contacting Lisa at Karla's place in Billings. I eventually got ahold of Karla, who was working at Arby's." Ed also tried contacting Lisa's parents, but they were out skiing that morning.

On Saturday, March 26, 1988, Sheila Kimmell was skiing with her husband, Ron, and daughter Stacy at the Bridger Bowl in Wyoming. The other daughter, Sherry, had to work that day. When Sheila, Ron, and Stacy returned home, they received a phone call from Lisa's boss, Joe Morian, from the Arby's in Denver. Morian sounded worried and told Sheila, "Your daughter is missing!" Apparently, Ed Jaroch had phoned the Arby's in Denver wondering why Lisa had never showed up at his place.

Sheila recalled later, "We got home from skiing, about one or two in the afternoon, and I received a phone call from Lisa's direct supervisor, Joe Morian, telling me that Lisa was missing. I didn't, quite honestly, take him seriously when he originally told me this. I told him that Lisa had plans to see Ed and visit other friends, and that she would see us probably later that afternoon or the next day. I got a phone call following that, about fifteen minutes later, from one of the friends she was intending to meet, and [that person said], 'She really is missing! She didn't show up at Ed's, and I haven't heard from her!'"

Ed recalled, "I spent the rest of Saturday morning in Cody, essentially waiting for her. Then I went and picked up my friend Jim for someone to spend some time with. Roughly at one P.M., I drove up to Billings. I got ahold of Karla Kilham, who was working at Arby's, and tried contacting Lisa's parents again. By that time, they were home."

Ed and Karla arrived at the Kimmell residence around 4:30 P.M. on March 26. Once there, he discussed the situation with Ron and Sheila. They decided that the next day, Ron would drive on roads that Lisa might have taken, while Ed, who knew civil pilots, would have them look for Lisa's wrecked car somewhere along the routes she most likely would have taken through Wyoming. At the time, both Ed and the Kimmells were thinking Lisa had suffered an accident, not an abduction.

Ed remembered this chaotic day: "Lisa's father and I drove back to Cody and got there about ten P.M. We went to the Park County Sheriff's Office, and one of the deputies and Ron Kimmell and myself drove out to the county line and met an officer coming from the other direction. This was to no avail."

After Ed left, Sheila phoned the highway patrol and changed the status from "Overdue Arrival" to "Attempt to Locate." Under Montana law, she could not yet have the status become "Missing Person." That was because too many teenagers had run away from home overnight, only to come back the next day.

Around 8:30 P.M., the Wyoming Highway Patrol called Sheila and told her that Lisa had been cited for speeding near Douglas at 9:06 P.M. on March 25. At least the Kimmells now knew she had made it that far. It helped cut down on the territory they would have to search, and would eliminate all the roads in Colorado and parts of Wyoming, up to Douglas, Wyoming.

At 9:30 P.M., Sheila had a remarkable chance encounter. Nervous and anxious, she went to a grocery store for cigarettes. At the counter, she bumped into an old family friend named Al Ketterling. Ketterling had been a sheriff's deputy in Yellowstone County for many years, and was now a private investigator. He could see that Sheila had been crying and asked why. When he found out, Ketterling volunteered to help her.

In fact, Al Ketterling went over to the Kimmells' residence around ten-thirty that night and phoned Ron, who by that time was at Ed Jaroch's residence in Cody. After speaking with Ron, Ketterling decided to go to Cody as well. Sheila, meanwhile, stayed in Billings to answer the phone in case Lisa called. Sheila also contacted her sister-in-law who owned a typesetting shop in the area. Sheila's sister-in-law soon created a missing person poster of Lisa, and numerous copies were made.

On Sunday, March 27, Ron Kimmell and Al Ketterling drove along Wyoming highways searching every possible spot where Lisa's car might have run off the road. They also stopped at each county's sheriff's office along the way to report the girl as missing. At the same time, Ed Jaroch and Al Ketterling's stepfather flew in a chartered plane above the area where they hoped to spot Lisa's car. Particular attention was placed on the area from Douglas, where Officer Al Lesco had given Lisa a speeding ticket, to Cody. Both the ground and air searches, however, turned up no sightings of Lisa or her vehicle.

Ed recalled the flight: "The pilot, another person I don't recall, and I went up in the air in this plane, while Mr. Kimmell and another person searched the highway via the ground. We flew the route we expected. The one I had told her to take, which ran from Cody to Shoshoni, over to Casper, and as far south as Glenrock. At that point, we turned around, flew back essentially the same direction, except we flew on the Worland-to-Cody route." This route ran up the Wind River Canyon and then cross-country to Cody.

Ron Kimmell and Al Ketterling returned to Billings on Sunday night and filed an official missing persons report with the Yellowstone County Sheriff's Office (YCSO). Because Al Ketterling was a former deputy with that office, the authorities agreed to waive the seventy-two-hour waiting period. By Monday morning, March 28, the missing person posters were ready and Ron Kimmell loaded a batch of them into his vehicle for yet another trip on the roads of Wyoming. Ron distributed posters all along his route and stopped to inspect ditches, creeks, and ravines along the way. He also spoke with road crews, county sheriff's deputies, and truckers along the route. Almost all of them agreed to keep an eye out for the girl or her car, and to distribute flyers as well.

Sheila later said of the missing person flyers, "They were a picture of her, describing her and her car and offering a reward. They were eventually distributed nationwide, but most of the posters were distributed throughout Montana, Wyoming, very heavily, and Colorado. Some truck drivers promised to take them clear across the country. There were several thousand put out. I lost count after five thousand."

Meanwhile, Sheila Kimmell alerted the media about her missing daughter. It wasn't until March 29 that the regional newspapers started reporting about the missing girl. Under the headline TEEN DISAPPEARS FROM WYOMING, the *Billings Gazette* reported about Lisa's black Honda CRX and its distinctive Montana license plate, LIL MISS.

The article went on to state that around 4:00 P.M. on Friday, "a friend," who was obviously Ed Jaroch, stated that he had called Lisa in Denver to confirm that she was coming to pick him up for a ride to Billings. The article noted that Ron Kimmell had spent Sunday on a search all over northern Wyoming. The article went on to say, *Sheila Kimmell fears that her daughter, who was traveling alone, may be the victim of foul play. Yellowstone County Sheriff's Deputy Frank Dostal agreed that the young woman disappeared under "very suspicious circumstances."* Obviously, by this point, the Kimmells were starting to think abduction rather than accident.

By the next day, numerous "sightings" of Lisa and her vehicle popped up all around the area. Two witnesses placed Lisa driving through Buffalo, Wyoming, which would have taken her on Interstate 25, instead of her agreed-upon route. These two individuals placed Lisa at a 7-Eleven store in Buffalo, around noon on Saturday. Johnson County sheriff Larry Kirkpatrick related, "They made their reports independently. These two weren't together. We're checking around to see if anyone else has seen her."

The Kimmells tended to discount the reported sightings of Lisa in Buffalo. This route would have made no sense if she was driving to pick up Ed Jaroch in Cody. It would have taken her far out of her way. A more intriguing "sighting" occurred from someone who had "seen" Lisa's car between Shoshoni and Riverton on Friday night, March 25. This person noted an object hanging from the girl's Honda rearview mirror. This description matched a "crystal-faceted" teardrop ornament Lisa had hanging in her car.

Yellowstone County, Montana, undersheriff Chuck Maxwell reported that his office received fifteen phone calls of sightings of the Honda between Hardin and Riverton in the previous twenty-four hours. In another area, a man phoned the Bridger, Wyoming, town marshal to report a man driving Lisa's Honda. The Kimmells also received thirty phone calls about Lisa's Honda CRX. Ron Kimmell told a reporter, "Some of them were way off-base."

Before long, there was a stream of reporters making their way to the Kimmells' door, asking for information. Lisa's disappearance became a big story in the area, and numerous phone calls poured in about possible sightings of Lisa and her car. Because the Honda CRX was an unusual and distinct model, it gathered more attention than a more conventional model might have. Especially what stood out was Lisa's personalized license plate, which read LIL MISS.

Another air search was scheduled for Wednesday, but the weather turned stormy and the air search was canceled. When the weather was finally better on Thursday, March 31, another air search commenced, but with the same results as before. No sightings of Lisa, nor sightings of her vehicle.

By April 1, 1988, the *Billings Gazette* headline was SEARCHERS SUSPECT FOUL PLAY. They gave a reason for this by the fact that intensive ground and air searches had produced no actual sightings of the missing girl or her car. If she'd had an accident, it was assumed that her car would have been spotted by now. Especially if she had driven on the route that she planned to take.

Sheila Kimmell told reporters, "The search has been very intensive, both on the ground and in the air." Then she said that her husband was exhausted and returning from Casper, where he'd been putting up flyers at motels and convenience stores in the area. He'd been covering every base he could possibly think of, and decided he could be of more help in Billings than on the road.

By now, the Yellowstone County Sheriff's Office had sent teletypes to law enforcement agencies in Montana, Wyoming, and Nebraska. Meanwhile, Marilyn Fake, who worked with Lisa's aunt, started a fund to help defray some of the cost of printing posters and the expense of the extensive search. It was called the Help Find LIL MISS Fund, and was set up through the First Citizens Bank in Billings. Sheila Kimmell related, "The search has become very expensive, but I would sell my house, my car, anything to find my daughter." Even the Civil Air Patrol chipped in, volunteering to send out pilots to search at no cost. Once again, they flew flight patterns over Montana and Wyoming, but no sighting of the car turned up.

By now, Ron and Sheila Kimmell were beginning to believe that their daughter was dead. A reporter for the *Billings Gazette* went to the Kimmells' home and took photos and spoke with Ron and Sheila. The reporter got more information about Lisa's life than just her present circumstances. The reporter learned that Lisa had been a cheerleader and competed in a Miss Teen Pageant. In addition to being pretty, Lisa also had a keen, inquisitive mind and had done well in school. So well, in fact, that she had won an accounting scholarship to college. Lisa turned it down, however, saying that she liked working for Arby's so much, she wanted to stay in their system and work her way up the chain in business management. She preferred working in a more dynamic interchange of people, rather than just the more isolated realm of accounting. What was perfectly clear to everyone was that Lisa wasn't the kind of teenager to just run off and not tell anyone where she was going.

Then, during the afternoon, on April 2, 1988, a white Yellowstone County Sheriff's Office vehicle pulled up in front of the Kimmells' house. Looking out the window, Sheila saw two plainclothes Yellowstone County Sheriff's Office detectives get out of the car. Instinctively knowing that something very bad was going to be revealed, she called for her husband in another room of the house to join her. They both met the detectives at the door, ushered them in, and they all sat down at a dining-room table.

Detective George Jensen asked, "Would you like to have a family member or a clergyman join you? Maybe a friend?"

Sheila immediately said she would like Al Ketterling to join them and gave him a phone call. Within minutes, Ketterling was there.

Once they were all gathered, Sheila said, "Please tell us that you found Lisa!"

Jensen replied, "Well, Mrs. Kimmell, we have found a female that matches Lisa's general description. But we aren't certain if it's Lisa. We need physical details. Can you give us more information about her?"

The Kimmells told the detectives that Lisa had blue eyes and light brown/blond shoulder-length hair. She was five-three and weighed about 110 pounds. She also had a small scar on her left cheekbone and a permanent silver retainer on her lower teeth.

The detectives nodded and said that the description fit the girl that had been found.

In agony, Sheila Kimmell asked what had happened to her daughter.

Detective Jensen replied, "She's been murdered. She was found in the North Platte River this afternoon."

II

RIVER IN A LONELY LANDSCAPE

3

A BODY
IN THE RIVER

William Bradford was a fisherman who lived in Cheyenne, Wyoming. He knew the section of the North Platte River off the Trapper's Route and liked fishing there. On April 2, 1988, Bradford drove to the North Platte River with his son, a friend named Dick Rensch, and Rensch's daughter. They parked in an area not far from the Old Government Bridge, between 10:30 and 11:00 A.M. While the boy and girl headed off downriver in a southerly direction, Bradford and Rensch walked about a hundred yards north and started fishing.

Bradford recalled later, "We were there about an hour or so and it just wasn't any good. Nothing was biting. So we decided to work our way back upriver. And I was along the bank and got a lot of mud on my boots. So I stepped up onto a rise to clean off my boots, and I looked to the side, and I could see a body in the water."

Bradford hadn't seen the body on his original trip along the river, but because he stepped up onto the rise, he spotted it now. It was the body of a young woman, and because Bradford had seen stories on the news stations about Lisa Kimmell being missing, he immediately wondered if it was her body.

Bradford recalled, "I could pretty much see her whole body. It was a pretty shallow area. I went to get Dick and he came back with me. We walked out to verify that she was dead. Dick had hip waders on and he walked right up to her. We didn't touch her at all. We knew at that point that she was dead.

"Then we thought we'd better get the children and call the authorities as soon as possible. We went to get the children, because we were afraid they might be working their way down our way, and I didn't want them to see this. When we got to the children, we told them that we had to go down and notify the sheriff's office. We told them we thought we found the body of the missing girl. So we went to the Clark's Fork Store and called the sheriff's office. We told them we found the body of a young lady in the river. Then we told them where we were and that we would meet them at the Trapper's Route turnoff."

Natrona County Sheriff's Office (NCSO) investigator Mike Sandfort was at home on April 2, 1988, when he received a phone call that the body of a young woman had been discovered on the North Platte River beneath the Old Government Bridge. Sandfort had been with the Natrona County Sheriff's Office since 1975, and had seen his share of homicides and drownings. Investigator Sandfort knew from experience that the Old Government Bridge area was used a lot by fishermen and hunters. He said later, "It's a heavily used area nine months of the year, in the spring, summer, and fall. Used by fishermen, and hunters hunting waterfowl and white-tail deer."

Sandfort contacted Investigator Dan Tholson, and they went by the office, grabbed their mobile crime van, and together drove to the location about twenty-five miles southwest of Casper. They went south on Highway 220, to a road known as the Trapper's Route. Just before the more modern Highway 220 bridge crossed the North Platte River, two-lane Bolton Road veered off down toward the river, where the river made a wide bend. There was a large tree near the river, and Sandfort noticed that two Highway Patrol cars were already parked there, along with a sheriff's deputy vehicle and a civilian vehicle.

Upon arriving on scene, almost immediately, Sandfort and Tholson's gazes were directed toward a gravel bar in the river, about eight-tenths of a mile down below the Old Government Bridge. As they started walking that way, they could make out the form of a human body hung up on the gravel bar. It was facedown in the water, but not totally submerged.

Both Sandfort and Tholson waded out into the water, which was only about eighteen inches deep at that spot, and took photos of the body in place, not moving it at all. It was obviously the body of a young woman, and since Sandfort had already seen a missing person poster of Lisa Kimmell, he was becoming more and more certain that it was her. Sandfort noted that the body was still "fresh," as he later put it, and not someone who had been in the river a long time.

It didn't have a waxy appearance of a body that had been submerged in water for a period of time.

NCSO lieutenant Kinghorn arrived on the scene a short time later and took over the investigation. Along with him came Dr. James Thorpen, the county coroner. Dave Kinghorn put Sandfort in charge of certain aspects of the crime scene investigation, because Sandfort had taken an evidence kit along and was proficient in its use. In 1982, Sandfort had attended a homicide investigation class sponsored by the Northern Colorado–Southern Wyoming Investigators Association. Several instructors of that course were from the Wyoming State Crime Lab, and others were experts from around the country. At the class, Sandfort had learned crime scene management, how to block off an area, and how to grid an area. There were also classes in documentation, a method on how to collect evidence, and overall crime scene techniques.

Sandfort noted later, "It was a real nice day on April second, probably sixty-five degrees, and not a lot of wind. Six days previous to that, it had been typical Wyoming weather. It would be rainy and snowy one minute and sunshine the next. Two days before April second, there was a lot of rain, but on the day of the recovery, it was sunny and mild."

Lieutenant Kinghorn and the others finally took the young woman's body to shore, after nearly an hour of observing and photographing the scene. Once the body was on dry land, it was turned over and it became very apparent to them that it was the body of Lisa Kimmell. What was also apparent was that she had been stabbed in the chest five or six times by a sharp instrument. All she was wearing were pink panties, black socks, earrings, and a watch. The watch had stopped at nine-forty, but whether it was 9:40 A.M. or P.M. they couldn't say.

The water temperature was forty-four degrees and it had helped preserve the girl's body. It also had made it difficult for Dr. Thorpen to get a good reading of when she might have been killed. The girl's body still had some "color" to it, but that might have been because the water was so cold. While Kinghorn and Dr. Thorpen placed the body on a backboard and then into a body bag, Kinghorn had the others go check the main Highway 220 bridge and Old Government Bridge to see if either of those had been the initial dump site. The two bridges were the most likely locales for the killer to have dumped a body into the river.

Sandfort and the others set off for those locations, and also searched around Bolton Road for evidence. There was nothing on Bolton Road to indicate that a murder had happened there, so they soon focused on the bridge area. When the highway patrolmen drove across the Old Government Bridge and walked back in one direction, while Sandfort walked in the other, Wyoming Highway Patrol officer Means waved for Sandfort to come over to where he was standing. As soon as Sandfort got there, he saw why. There were two areas on the old bridge where blood had collected, and a large bloodstain ran down the side of the bridge. Some of the blood had actually puddled into two drains on the bridge. The blood in Sandfort's opinion was "fresh"—meaning that no significant amount of dirt or dust had collected on it since it had been deposited. Also, it had not "feathered out," which meant that no significant rainfall had made it wash away. Since Sandfort knew it had rained hard two days previously in Casper, he surmised it had rained some at the Old Government Bridge as well on that day. If the blood had been here then, it most likely would have "feathered out." So this seemed to indicate that whatever had happened here, had happened after the rainfall had occurred.

Because of the bloodstain down the side of the bridge, and the fact that Lisa's body had ended up midstream, Sandfort surmised she had been killed on the bridge and dumped over the side where the bloodstain ran. Her body may have even become caught up on a lower railing, before falling over into the river. Since there was not a lot of water volume in the river, as would have been the case when the spring runoff came, Lisa's body had only floated a short way downstream before becoming hung up on the gravel bar.

Investigator Sandfort and the others tried collecting evidence of tire tread marks on the bridge roadway, without any success. They also tried lifting latent fingerprints from the bridge metal areas, with no success. Despite looking around for a murder weapon, they found none, nor any other kind of evidence that could have been tied to the crime scene, such as cigarette butts, beer cans, and other relevant items. It was fairly clear the killer had been methodical enough not to leave telltale evidence behind. It also suggested that he felt comfortable at that time that the chances were slim that someone would suddenly come upon him during the murder and its aftermath.

After Lisa's body was placed into the coroner's vehicle, it was driven back to Bustard's funeral home in Casper. There it was photographed with what clothing she still wore, and then photographed completely nude. A sexual evidence kit was used upon her by means of swabs to her vaginal area, mouth, and anal area. This evidence was bagged and tagged, and turned over to Undersheriff Mark Benton for safekeeping. Lisa's clothing was also bagged and tagged and turned over to Benton to be kept in the sheriff's office evidence room. Once again, the time on Lisa's watch was noted as being nine-forty, but it was not a watch with A.M./P.M. readout or a calendar. There was an attempt to take blood from Lisa's body by both Dr. Thorpen and Tom Bustard that evening, but they were not able to do so, because almost all the blood had drained from her body. They decided to try again the next day when the official autopsy began.

The next day, Dr. Thorpen began his autopsy of the dead girl. He noted that she had earrings on one ear, a necklace with a cross, a gold ring, and a watch. She had been hit in the back of the head with a blunt instrument, possibly a hammer. The blow had been so severe as to cause a four-inch fracture to her skull. She had also been stabbed six times—five in the chest area and once in the abdomen. The killer had made small exploratory stab wounds prior to making deeper cuts. He apparently had been checking to see where her ribs were located. The six severe wounds measured from 5.5 to 6.5 inches in depth. They pierced her heart and left lung, and any of these would have caused death. The precision of the stab wounds to vital organs suggested that the killer was someone who knew what he was doing in regard to a knife. Possibly a hunter, or someone who had been in the military. From the girl's stomach contents, it appeared as if she had been fed some kind of beef stew a few hours before being killed.

Dr. Thorpen also noted that the girl's pubic hair area had been shaved about seven days prior to her death. He could estimate the time by the amount of hair that had grown back from that point until her death. Semen was eventually found on her panties, and the semen, along with samples of the girl's hair and an unidentified hair found on her abdomen, were collected and sent to the state crime lab in Cheyenne. Lieutenant Kinghorn took photographs of various segments of the autopsy and assisted Dr. Thorpen, when needed.

Even though there was the fact that the girl's body had been in cold water, throwing off any exact determination of time of death, Dr. Thorpen deduced that she had been killed thirty-six to forty-eight hours before being discovered. In his report, he listed cause of death as *death by stabbing*.

It wasn't until the next day, April 4, that something new turned up. Dr. Thorpen noticed bruising on the girl's wrists and ankles, and he asked Lieutenant Kinghorn to return and photograph what he had discovered. This was not totally unusual. Sometimes those kinds of bruises did not show up for a period of time. The bruising around the ankles and wrists appeared to have been made by nylon rope or some kind of binding material. It was surmised that Lisa had been trussed up while being sexually assaulted, and perhaps held captive for a period of time—possibly even six days—since she was last seen alive by Officer Lesco in Douglas. Her pubic hair growth, after being shaved, indicated about that amount of time. Just what sexual torture she had suffered couldn't be determined at present, but the deep binding marks from ligatures on her wrists and ankles suggested that she had suffered sexual torment over a prolonged period of time.

Since the murder appeared to have taken place at the Old Government Bridge in Natrona County—judging by the blood found there—it became a case for the NCSO to pursue as the primary agency.

Detectives Dan Tholson and Jim Broz were assigned
to the case as lead investigators and began to take in
what would eventually become a flood of phone calls
about possible sightings of Lisa and her car.

On April 3, 1988, the *Billings Gazette* published the
news of the body of a young woman being discovered
in the North Platte River, near Casper. It was not yet
verified in the media that the body was that of Lisa
Kimmell, although NCSO sheriff Ron Ketchum admitted that there were no other young women of that
description missing in Natrona County.

The newspaper also delved into another tragedy
that had befallen Ron and Sheila Kimmell years
before. Back in 1976, they had lost their three-year-old
son, Ricky, to a terrible accident. Ricky and a little girl
had been playing in the Kimmells' van, and somehow
slipped it out of gear. When it started to roll backward, Ricky panicked and jumped out the back of the
van, only to be run over by the rear wheels. Ricky was
rushed to a hospital, but soon died. Ron told the reporter he was thankful they had Ricky in their lives for
three years. He said he still pictured him playing with
his Tonka. trucks. To have this latest tragedy happen,
on top of the death of their son, was almost too much
to bear.

Getting back to what might have happened to Lisa,
the Kimmells were certain she had not deviated from
her planned route up to Cody. And they said they were
sure she would never have picked up a hitchhiker.
Even when she'd been in an accident before Christ-
mas, 1987, Lisa would not even open her car door
when a county road worker came to see what was
wrong and offer her assistance. She only rolled down

the window a crack and talked to him through the crack. "I don't know what went wrong this time!" Sheila told the reporter.

The April 4 edition of the *Casper Star-Tribune* finally alerted the public to the true nature of things, with the headline BODY IN RIVER IS IDENTIFIED AS MONTANA GIRL. Sheriff Ketchum stated that the autopsy performed on Sunday positively identified the body of the young woman as being that of Lisa Kimmell. Ketchum added, "It's a difficult case. We don't have any suspects at this point."

One bit of evidence did surface, however. Sheriff Ketchum said that a person positively identified Lisa as having stopped at a service station in Casper to fill her car tank with gas. This was somewhat odd, since her father always told her to get gas in Cheyenne. But perhaps, because she had been pulled over by Officer Lesco near Douglas, Lisa wanted another break near Casper to regain her composure.

Sheriff Ketchum told reporters that a weapon had been used to murder Kimmell, but he would not say at that time what he thought the weapon might have been. He also said she'd suffered numerous injuries, but would not relate what type of injuries or where on her body they had occurred. All he would say about the injuries was that "the wounds are explicit and clear."

Sheriff Ketchum had already let the cat out of the bag on one aspect of the crime, that her body had been partially clad when found. When asked about what she was wearing, Ketchum would only say that the killer would know what she was wearing. He would not elaborate on her items of clothing. Ketchum also revealed very little about the sexual assault, except to say that the river might have washed away evidence of that assault. Ketchum then related, "We don't know if the killing took place in her car or elsewhere."

Then Sheriff Ketchum turned to the matter of Lisa Kimmell's car and said that because of its unique style and license plate, it would be a significant factor in catching her killer. Ketchum related that supposed sightings of Lisa's Honda CRX had turned up in the neighboring states and even Canada. He added that he'd asked the FBI to help in the Canadian aspect of the case. Then he added, "The murderer may still be in the area and should be considered armed and dangerous."

By the next day, Sheriff Ron Ketchum, District Attorney (DA) Kevin Meenan, and Coroner James Thorpen were being more tight-lipped about the case. What was interesting was the fact that Casper police chief Dick Fields told reporters that his department would not be helping Natrona County in the investigation. To some observers, it seemed that the Casper Police Department (PD) and NCSO did not get along well together or share information.

By April 6, the *Billings Gazette* noted that law enforcement was sifting through three hundred possible sightings of Lisa's Honda CRX. Sheriff Ron Ketchum related that only a few black two-seat sports car editions of the Honda CRX had been sold in the Rocky Mountain states. Five "possible" sightings of Lisa's car turned up in the Kalispell, Montana, region alone. Two of these placed the car in a grocery store parking lot, being driven by a lone white male. One woman particularly was insistent that she had seen the girl's car. The woman said she remembered the license plate, LIL MISS, and wondered why someone from Mississippi would have a personalized Montana license plate. She mistook LIL MISS to mean someone from Mississippi. Two other reports placed the vehicle in Whitefish and Big Mountain, Montana, which fueled speculation that the driver had indeed taken the car north from Wyoming toward Canada.

For whatever reason, Sheriff Ketchum started releasing to the media more information about the sexual assault and stab wounds on the girl. Ketchum said that Lisa had been stabbed to death, but would not reveal in what pattern the stab wounds had been inflicted. He did note, however, that she had been stabbed in the chest area.

Now, not unlike Ron Kimmell had done, NCSO detectives began flying over northern Wyoming, seeking clues as to the disappearance of Lisa's car. There was always hope that it had been abandoned somewhere in an isolated area that could be seen more easily from the air. And the "Canada connection" would not die down as well. On two separate occasions, people in Regina, Saskatchewan, said that they had seen the black Honda CRX with its LIL MISS license plate.

Sheriff Ketchum noted that the Canadian police were not on the same computer system as American law enforcement agencies, and for that reason he was having the FBI deal with the Canadian agencies. One of the more intriguing things Ketchum added at this point was that there were "objects" found on the body of Lisa Kimmell after her death. He would not say what the objects were, fueling speculation on everything from bodily hairs to satanic symbols.

Soon the *Billings Gazette* quoted an unnamed law

enforcement official that it was very unlikely that Lisa
Kimmell had parked her car near the Old Government Bridge on the North Platte River and been attacked. It would have been hard enough for a local to
know that area, much less an outsider like Lisa.
Around this same time, Sheriff Ron Ketchum released
information that the blood found on the bridge did,
in fact, belong to Lisa Kimmell. There didn't seem to
be any of her attacker's blood anywhere in that area,
however. Then Ketchum added that he was considering the possibility that more than one person had abducted and then killed Lisa. He said he entertained
those thoughts because "of the injuries she received,
and things like that. And there have been sightings of
people seeing two men in her car after she was probably dead." Ketchum also revealed that Lisa did not
drown, but was already dead when her body was
dumped into the river. Ketchum noted, "She probably
didn't know she was being stabbed." This was in reference to the "other major wound" she had suffered, a
wound he would not name.

At least one thing was cleared up by April 8—the
black Honda CRX in the Kalispell, Montana, area actually belonged to a man who lived there. He had
been in a grocery store parking lot with his car, and
his wife resembled Lisa Kimmell. That was why so
many "witnesses" confused the car with Lisa Kimmell's
vehicle. As far as other sightings of the car went, Sheriff Ketchum said, "We still think some of the sightings
in Utah and Canada may be legitimate."

Lisa Kimmell's obituary came out in the *Billings Gazette*
and it noted that she had been born in Covington,
Tennessee. In 1972, she had moved with her parents

to Billings, Montana. She'd graduated from Billings Senior High School in 1987 with scholarships, but instead of going to college, she had become a unit supervisor at an Arby's in Aurora, Colorado. *She loved her family, friends, working, playing piano, cake decorating and animals, especially cats,* the obituary noted. She was survived by her parents, two sisters, and both sets of grandparents.

There were two memorial services for Lisa, one in Colorado and one in Billings, Montana. At the service in Denver, Gene Gruber, of the Non-Denominational Church of Denver, said, "When such a tragedy occurs in such an untimely way, our reaction is one of deep hurt and deep anger. The death of such a dear one just entering into adult life is almost beyond comprehension." Then Gruber said that such a tragedy would not escape God's righteous judgment, and that government agencies would be the instrument of God's judgment.

Up north in Billings, on the same day, Skip Orth of the Church of Billings, stated that Lisa would be remembered for her warm smile, loving personality, her devotion to life's challenges, and diligence in school and work. Orth said, "She was loved by the Lord, her family, her friends, and the community. She's now at rest. But her passing reminds us that we should not take for granted the gift of life."

Outside the chapel, friends embraced, and there was a mile-and-a-half-long procession of cars out to Sunset Memorial Park. At the cemetery, a brief graveside service was held as a chill wind blew across the city. Gathered around Lisa's grave, family and friends held hands and sang a hymn.

Soon thereafter, Ron and Sheila Kimmell thanked all their supporters of the last few harrowing weeks through an article in the *Billings Gazette*. By the time of Lisa's funeral, they had received hundreds of letters and cards from people who knew them and from others who had never met them. The Kimmells said they planned to answer each and every letter and card that they had received. Then they added, "Our biggest hope is that Billings knows what kind of a wonderful community we live in."

The Kimmells shared some of the letters with the *Billings Gazette*. A woman from Laurel, Montana, who didn't know the Kimmells, wrote, *Lisa Marie's tragic death has touched so many people. We just wanted to let you know that we care.* A family friend wrote, *We can only hope that this grieving process will soon pass, replacing with it the unity of love of family and friends.* A card from one of Lisa's former teachers at Billings Senior High stated, *She was a very beautiful girl and was always thinking of others with her kind heart.* Law enforcement officers sent in letters and cards as well, and one from a detective in Sheridan County, Wyoming, wrote, *Her loss is certainly felt by every member of our department. Our hearts and minds have been with you for the past week and are very much with you at this time.* Even people who had only been patrons of the Arby's where Lisa had worked sent cards and letters. One such person wrote, *We enjoyed Lisa very much. She really was unusual, and I always marveled at her spirit and her personal way with people, young and old.*

A day after the funeral, Sheriff Ketchum noted that at least fifteen people had supposedly seen Lisa in the Casper area just before her disappearance. A few of these people were hypnotized so as to try and elicit more details about what they had witnessed. One person was very specific about seeing Lisa in a Casper grocery store with two men.

* * *

As the days went by, however, a *Casper Star-Tribune* headline appeared: SHERIFF STILL STYMIED BY TEEN'S MURDER. Sheriff Ketchum said he had numerous composite drawings of possible suspects made from the descriptions by various witnesses. One of the sketches turned out to be a Casper man who drove a black car that looked a lot like Kimmell's. Then the newspaper reported about a man who had turned in information to the Casper Police Department very early in the proceedings, but the Casper PD had not passed this information on to the NCSO for a week. Sheriff Ketchum responded to an allegation that the NCSO and Casper PD were not working in tandem in what was turning out to be a difficult case. Ketchum said, "I've always gotten information from the police department. I've never felt that that was a difficulty. I've felt the flow of information between the two agencies was very good."

The "Canada connection" still seemed promising, and Regina police staff sergeant Mike Kelly related that officers there had checked every hotel and motel, day and night, for nearly a week. Kelly related, "The car was seen three times around April first. We didn't have any idea it was wanted at the time." Kelly revealed that the black Honda with unusual license plates had actually been seen by Regina police officers. They had noted the license plate because of its distinctive letters. As to this possible sighting, Sheriff Ketchum added, "There have been a lot of near misses in the Kimmell case, where circumstances have been beyond people's control."

Ketchum then defended the time, money, and effort spent by NCSO in its lengthy air operations searching for Lisa's car. He said, "We're covering all the bases from both ends (air and ground). I don't want to look back and say we should have done this or done that."

One man, who had supposedly seen the black Honda in the eastern end of Casper, was hypnotized, not once but twice. And still his hypnosis drew inconclusive results as to whether he had actually seen Lisa's car. Ketchum let it be known that NCSO's investigation would go on for some time to come. He related, "We'll evaluate the case weekly and go on from there. At some point, when the leads are becoming few or not productive, at that point we'll have to evaluate the number of people assigned to the case. But at this point, we have no intentions of closing the investigation."

FBI agent Robert Pence in Denver acknowledged that his office had helped in the initial stages of what appeared to have been an abduction of Lisa Kimmell. Once her body was found in the North Platte River, however, the FBI Denver Field Office was no longer involved in the case. Pence said, "Because there was no interstate travel, we had no jurisdiction. So we are not involved in that case any longer." The FBI, however, was still involved in the "Canada Connection" aspects of the case.

As far as the Wyoming Division of Criminal Investigation (WDCI) went, Director Kip Crofts stated that his agency was not and had never been involved in the investigation. When a reporter asked why not, Crofts answered, "Well, I don't know why. They (NCSO) didn't ask. We don't have any jurisdiction to get involved in those things without a request from the local authorities."

The fact that Sheriff Ron Ketchum had not asked the Wyoming Division of Criminal Investigation to help was not an issue in the first weeks of investigation. Soon, however, his decision would become a very contentious issue and come back to haunt him. It would seem more and more that Ketchum scorned all outside help on the case and only wanted NCSO personnel to deal with it.

In the beginning, the Kimmells' relations with Sheriff Ketchum had been okay, if not overly warm. His office seemed to be going about its business in the case in a productive manner. NCSO detectives spent numerous hours tracking down leads all over Wyoming and took appropriate actions. They asked ranchers to search their land for the missing car, found volunteer pilots to make air searches, and kept on using hypnosis of witnesses who thought they might have seen the Honda CRX.

One of the main problems on the case, however, was the jurisdictional boundaries involved. Since Lisa began her journey in Denver, Colorado, no one knew exactly where she had been abducted or her car had been taken. It could have happened on private land, county land, state land, or even federal land. If the latter, then the Feds needed to be a part of the process as well. All the jurisdictional issues tended to cloud an already murky case. And none of this was helped by Sheriff Ketchum's territorial mentality.

Some law enforcement agencies don't mind outside help, be it other police, sheriff's or federal agencies. Other law enforcement agencies hate it and discourage it as much as possible. They view it as outside interference that only tends to muddy the waters. There is also an undercurrent that when outside agencies become involved, there is an unspoken assumption that the lead agency is either too ill-equipped or incompetent to handle the matter. Sheriff Ketchum tended to look on matters in this fashion, as if the outside agencies were a threat, not only to himself but to his officers as well. Ketchum had his faults, but he did stick up for his officers.

Not helping matters was the fact that Ron and Sheila Kimmell had already set up a "liaison connection" to Detective George Jensen at the Yellowstone County Sheriff's Office in Billings, Montana. The only problem with that was Lisa Kimmell's murder was not a YCSO case. If an arrest was ever made, it was the Natrona County DA's Office that was going to have to bring the killer to trial. To Sheriff Ron Ketchum, it seemed that the Kimmells were interfering with his department's work; even though from their viewpoint, they were only trying to help. As far as they were concerned, the more people looking for the killer, the better. They knew that NCSO resources could only stretch so far.

The *Billings Gazette* started a reward fund for information that would lead to the arrest of Lisa's killer. Arby's also started a fund, and $5,589 was raised by the Arby's outlets in Billings and Casper. Soon the total amount of funds exceeded $10,000. Despite numerous possible vehicle sightings, and descriptions of Lisa and her vehicle in newspapers, radio, and television, the leads started dwindling dramatically as the weeks went by.

The Kimmells grew increasingly frustrated at Sheriff Ketchum's lack of enthusiasm about receiving outside help. Turning to a different avenue, Ron and Sheila contacted NBC's *Unsolved Mysteries,* and they agreed to film a segment about the case. In October 1988, filming commenced around the area. *Unsolved Mysteries* even made a mock-up to match the way Lisa's Honda CRX had looked. It had one unforeseen effect, however. New possible sightings of this car were confused by people who thought it was Lisa Kimmell's car, so quite a few false reports came in because of that.

Other avenues were less palatable. Rumors started surfacing that Lisa had run afoul of a Wyoming drug ring. One persistent rumor had it that she had unwittingly come upon a drug deal and been murdered to silence her. Another rumor spread that Lisa looked like another young woman, who had ratted on some drug dealers. In a case of mistaken identity, Lisa had been killed. Although these rumors were never proven, they seemed to have a life of their own and would not go away.

By December 1988, with no new solid leads, Hugh Duncan, a former assistant prosecutor in Casper, Wyoming, chipped in $5,000 of his own money toward the reward fund. He told a reporter, "Somebody has to do something, so I decided it might as well be me."

Despite the increase in money to the reward fund, little progress was made until March 15, 1989. That's when the segment about Lisa aired on *Unsolved Mysteries*. After the show, hundreds of phone calls came in that very evening. In the following days, the deluge from across the nation continued. Detective Dan Tholson said, "They flooded us! Literally flooded us with thousands of phone calls!" It wouldn't be admitted by the NCSO until later that they just didn't have the staff, time, or money to check out every possible sighting and every phone call.

When Ron and Sheila Kimmell read a headline in the March 19, 1989, *Billings Gazette*—NO CLUES—they were alarmed. Even more alarming to them was the fact that they knew that NCSO couldn't have possibly sifted through all the phone calls that had poured in during the last few days because of the television segment being aired nationally. When Sheriff Ron Ketchum told a reporter, "We have no solid leads in this brutal homicide," it seemed to confirm to the Kimmells that he was doing less than he could on the case. Their faith in him continued to diminish while their ire at his reluctance to seek outside help continued to grow. By March 1989, the Kimmells had grave doubts that Sheriff Ron Ketchum was doing all he could to solve the murder of their daughter.

4

STRINGFELLOW
HAWKE

A totally unexpected event occurred on March 28, 1989. Around 4:30 P.M., Sheila Kimmell received an "urgent" message on her pager while she was in Denver, Colorado. The page was from one of Lisa's friends, Terry Schlenker, in Billings. When Sheila phoned Schlenker back, she learned that Schlenker had just visited Lisa's grave to place flowers there. Once she reached Lisa's grave, however, Schlenker forgot all about leaving the flowers. Someone had placed a printed note on Lisa's marker at the cemetery.

Schlenker began reading the note and was so shocked by its content that she didn't finish, but rather went to page Sheila immediately. The note was so disturbing that Schlenker had not touched it, considering that it might be evidence of some sort. She couldn't recall everything of what she'd read, only that the content was "weird." When Sheila Kimmell finally reached Ron by phone, it was too dark for him to go out to the cemetery that night to investigate. The very next morning, he drove to the cemetery and was just as stunned by what he saw there as Schlenker had been.

Someone had taped a handwritten note to Lisa's gravestone and covered it with clear plastic to protect the writing from rain and mist. The note was dated 11-13-88, but Ron knew the date had to be a lie. He and many others had been to Lisa's grave since then and had never seen the note. The note stated: *Lisa— There aren't words to say how much you're missed The pain never leaves it's so hard without you You'll always believe in me Your death is my painful loss but heavens sweet gain. Love Always Stringfellow Hawke*

There were no periods after segments of the writing, nor an apostrophe in between heaven and the *s* at the end of the word. It was also strange that the note writer should have known exactly where Lisa's grave was. The grave site was not easy to find amongst all the others at Sunset Memorial Park, and it had to be wondered if at some point he had asked at the office where her grave was, or even watched the funeral of Lisa from some distance, in April 1988.

Since the cemetery was within Billings city limits, Ron phoned the Billings Police Department about the note. The dispatcher, however, did not understand the import of what Ron was saying and responded, "Sir, if it's a problem, take it off!"

That was the last thing Ron Kimmell was about to do—touch something that might be evidence from the killer or someone who knew the killer. Ron next phoned Detective George Jensen at YCSO, but Jensen was out of the office. In frustration, Ron finally contacted Al Ketterling. Ketterling advised Ron to take the note off himself, but to be careful and not touch it on the written portion. He told Ron to place it in an envelope or some other container and hand-deliver it to Detective Jensen.

Peeling the note off with a penknife, Ron only touched a corner of the note and placed it in an envelope from his vehicle's glove compartment. He then drove to YCSO and delivered the note to Detective Jensen, who had returned to the office. Jensen agreed the note was important, catalogued it, kept it as evidence, and wrote a report to the Natrona County Sheriff's Office about it.

The signature "Stringfellow Hawke" was obviously a pseudonym for whoever had written the note. Stringfellow Hawke was the main character in a television program entitled *Airwolf.* This program had first aired in 1984, and Hawke was played by actor Jan-Michael Vincent. Hawke was a Vietnam veteran who had flown helicopters in the war, but was now a reclusive "mountain man," living alone in a cabin in the wilderness. Called out of retirement by a secret government agency, he hunted down terrorists and bad guys by using a technologically cutting-edge attack helicopter. In part, Hawke had been convinced to join the team by a sexy and beautiful agent named Gabrielle.

There was a whole subtheme to the program about Hawke's background—how at age twelve he had lost his parents in a boating accident, his girlfriend had died in a car accident before he left for Vietnam, and his brother, a helicopter pilot, had been killed in that war. It gave Hawke a mournful, brooding antihero aspect. One particular plot was intriguing in light of the "Stringfellow Hawke" note pinned to Lisa Kimmell's grave. In that episode, Gabrielle had been living in Hawke's rustic cabin for six days—having sex with him and being fed by him. After the sixth day, Gabrielle was killed by "bad guys."

For anyone who was tracking such things, Lisa Kimmell had been kept by her abductor for six days, subjected to sexual torment, and fed by the abductor. After the sixth day, she had been taken, partially dressed, to the Old Government Bridge and murdered. The killer, not unlike Stringfellow Hawke, might then have incurred another round of living alone in the wilderness. As had been noted, the killer seemed to be someone familiar with knives and knew a certain amount about anatomy.

Boning up on *Airwolf* and the Sringfellow Hawke character, the Kimmells tried pointing out these similarities to Sheriff Ron Ketchum at NCSO. But Ketchum, however, had had his fill of wackos, loonies, and incredible rumors surrounding Lisa Kimmell. He'd had to deal with everything from supposed drug deals gone bad to Satanist rituals and sacrifice, to con man psychics and tales of alien abduction. And there were even rumors going around that Lisa had been into drug dealing herself and not the "good girl" she was supposed to be. These types of rumors floated amongst the "doper community" and, in fact, had no validity. To Sheriff Ketchum, this Stringfellow Hawke letter seemed like one more blind alley sent in by a kook who had too much time on his hands.

Unfortunately for the Kimmells, as time progressed, Sheriff Ketchum was less and less enthused about their involvement in the case, as they were angry at him about his seeming reluctance to try every available avenue. The main sticking point for the Kimmells was that Ketchum seemed dead set against accepting outside help from other agencies. The Kimmells felt that the NCSO detectives were doing the best they could, but they just didn't have the resources for a case of this magnitude, and were hampered by Sheriff Ketchum's own ego.

NCSO detectives Dan Tholson and Jim Broz liked the Kimmells, but found it increasingly difficult to communicate with them, due to their sheriff's directives. The last thing Ketchum wanted was some vital piece of evidence to be leaked to the Kimmells or anyone else— some bit of evidence that only the killer knew. Once that was out of the bottle, that key bit of evidence might very well be thrown out of court if things ever got that far. And with Lisa's case, it appeared by now that it was going to take some small bit of evidence to solve it.

The Kimmells understood that, but what they didn't understand was why Sheriff Ketchum and the medical examiner (ME) were keeping all details of how Lisa was murdered from them. Those were details they were not going to go blabbing to others. And the rumors and innuendos about how Lisa had died spread out in all directions, many of them outrageous. Sheila nearly came unglued when someone asked her if it was true about the rumor that Lisa's heart had been cut out.

Stymied by Sheriff Ketchum and at their wits' end, Sheila Kimmell phoned Rita Munzenrider, a reporter for the *Billings Gazette,* and asked her what to do, since the case seemed to be completely stalled as far as NCSO was concerned. Munzenrider suggested that Sheila contact the Wyoming Attorney General's Office about her concerns. Sheila eventually met with Wyoming attorney general Joe Myer and explained that she believed that

NCSO just wasn't equipped to handle such a far-ranging case, due to their lack of manpower and money. After the meeting, Myer tended to agree with her and said he would speak with Wyoming's governor Michael Sullivan. In essence, the Kimmells wanted someone to go over Sheriff Ketchum's head and order federal help to be allotted. They even got support for this idea from U.S. Attorneys Peter Dunbar and David Kubichek.

If Sheriff Ketchum was irritated by the Kimmells before, he was absolutely livid when these types of actions were discussed and he learned about them through the grapevine. In his opinion, a federal task force was not only a slap in the face to him and his department, but he tended to think they would muddy the waters if it ever came time to prosecute the case. When Sheriff Ketchum agreed to meet the Kimmells at his office on May 11, 1989, a confrontation was not long in brewing.

According to Sheila Kimmell, the meeting was chilly from its very inception. The Kimmells recorded the session, and so were able to maintain a record of the meeting. When the Kimmells told Sheriff Ketchum that they wanted a law enforcement task force to help on the case, Ketchum's reply was "Why do you feel that way?" The Kimmells repeated their arguments of how a task force would free NCSO to concentrate on certain things they could handle, and not spread themselves so thinly on all matters concerning the case.

Sheila started to speak, saying that both she and the attorney general—

Ron quickly jumped in, sensing Ketchum's displeasure at this revelation about the attorney general. Ron stressed that all of this was his and Sheila's idea, and no one else had put them up to it.

The cat was out of the bag, however. In Ketchum's perception, the Kimmells were alleging that he and his office were incompetent and not able to handle Lisa's case. (They didn't see it in that light—they just wanted outside help.) Ketchum, however, was not to be swayed on this point. His pride was hurt and he was angry. The mini–tape recorder revealed his response. Sheriff Ketchum said, "Do you know that in this county alone I have three other homicides that have not been solved? I have a competent staff in this office! We have dealt with one hundred ten different agencies around the United States, and we have followed up on over three thousand leads. We have talked to or looked at two hundred twenty-five suspects. I will agree with you that the case is limited in information only because of specifics of the crime. But the people I have working for me are competent!"

The argument went round and round in circles, accomplishing nothing except to make everyone angrier and more distrustful of the other side. Pressed once again on implementing a task force, Ketchum replied, "I'm not going to have a task force from here to Montana to down in Colorado that I do not have control over. Whether it's me or any administrator, and it only takes one, I'm not going to have this running all over. There is some information that is unique to this case. It has not been given to the media—I'm not going to give it to the media. Policemen are just as bad as anybody else in talking with anybody else about this information!"

There was the crux of it. Sheriff Ketchum did not trust other agencies to withhold vital information that only his office and the killer would know about the murder. On the other side of the coin, Ketchum's attitude flew in the face of modern law enforcement practices. This wasn't the Old West where a sheriff could send his deputies out on horseback to neighboring counties to try and bring in the "bad guy." This case required multiagency cooperation, and possibly even federal intervention. By the mere fact that Lisa had obviously crossed state lines on her journey meant that many districts were involved. She could have been abducted anywhere in Wyoming past the town of Douglas, and then dumped near the Old Government Bridge. If there had been any similar MOs in other counties, then those agencies were the ones to know about the similarities, since those were their cases.

Things only became uglier between the Kimmells and Ketchum when the sheriff strongly disapproved of Al Ketterling helping the Kimmells on the case. Sheila, in particular, was furious when Ketchum started to question Ketterling's qualifications. She strongly pointed out that Ketterling had been a YCSO deputy and knew what he was doing. Sheila told Ketchum that Ketterling was going to stay involved whether Ketchum liked it or not. Then she added, "I believe in this concept (the task force) and I'm going to pursue it."

Sheriff Ketchum's last angry words to the Kimmells were that if they kept interfering with his office's investigation of the case, he might have them arrested for obstruction of justice. Ironically, around the same time, Ketchum was named Law Enforcement Officer of the Year by a local American Legion Post. This put his name in contention for Wyoming State Lawman of the Year.

Not long after the disastrous meeting with Sheriff Ketchum, the Kimmells received a phone call from

Special Agent Don Flickinger, of the Bureau of Alcohol, Tobacco and Firearms (ATF). Agent Flickinger had been running an investigation about a drug ring in Wyoming and he wanted to ask the Kimmells a few questions. They agreed to a meeting and Flickinger went to their home.

Agent Flickinger revealed to the Kimmells that in the summer of 1988 a known drug dealer had told him that he'd seen Lisa's car parked near a cousin's home. As he and the parents discussed Lisa's information, it became apparent that her car had not been there at that time, and the two cases were unrelated. Nonetheless, the appearance of Agent Flickinger was very beneficial to the Kimmells. When he heard about Sheriff Ketchum's intransigence about interagency cooperation, he was irate. That was not the way to go about this case in his opinion. Flickinger sent a report about the matter to U.S. Attorney Dunbar at the U.S. Attorney's Office, and Dunbar was equally outraged, not only by the way Ketchum was handling the case, but by the way he was treating Ron and Sheila Kimmell as well. These, after all, were the victim's parents.

In May 1989, U.S. Attorney David Kubichek set up a meeting for the implementation of creating a task force on the Kimmell case. Although Agent Flickinger wanted NCSO to be invited, Kubichek was against it. He'd had it with Sheriff Ketchum's intransigence. The task force eventually met, and it was decided only later that they would send their findings to NCSO after the meeting. Agent Flickinger was made the head of the task force.

When Sheriff Ketchum learned that he and his office had purposely not been invited to the meeting, he was outraged. Ketchum held a press conference in Casper on May 24, and the results were in the next day's newspapers in the area. Ketchum said that the Feds were "deliberately" excluding him and NCSO from their investigation of the Kimmell murder. He was "very upset" that federal officials had met with Montana lawmen in Sheridan, Wyoming. Ketchum related, "I guess what they're saying is the Natrona County Sheriff's Office has fallen down on the investigation. I take exception to that. We have not. We've followed every lead, we've cooperated with any agency that has called us with information."

Then Ketchum added that he believed that the Kimmell family had "pressured" federal officials into creating their own task force to purposefully keep him and NCSO out of the loop. Ketchum said he only found out about the meeting in Sheridan through the grapevine and phoned the U.S. Attorney's Office in Wyoming to find out what had happened. According to Ketchum a lawyer there had told him that YSCO officials, U.S. Attorneys, and ATF agent Flickinger had met to discuss the case, and for Ketchum not to go public about the meeting. Of course, Ketchum did just the opposite by holding the press conference.

Ron Ketchum was so upset by the Kimmells that he once again stressed that he thought they had pressured the others not to invite NCSO to the Sheridan meeting. (In fact, the Kimmells had not done that.) Ketchum said that Natrona County residents should know that he and his office were doing everything possible to solve the case. They had received over four thousand possible sightings of Lisa's black Honda CRX and checked out 170 suspects. Then Ketchum added that he thought Ron and Sheila Kimmell were unhappy with him because he would not disclose the nature of one of the wounds Lisa had received. Ketchum vowed he was not going to release that information, even to outside law enforcement agencies. Ketchum added, "That's the only information that will eliminate or substantiate suspects." By his refusal to give this fact, even to federal agents, Ketchum was basically saying that he did not trust them not to leak the information.

Ketchum was particularly upset by the involvement with private investigator Al Ketterling, who was helping the Kimmells. He viewed this person as a loose cannon in the whole mix. And Ketchum reiterated that since there had been no interstate flight by a suspect, then no other agency except NCSO had jurisdiction in Lisa Kimmell's case. It was apparent that she had been murdered right at the Old Government Bridge over the North Platte River, and that made it a NCSO case, as far as he was concerned.

Sheriff Ketchum kept showing his irritation about the Kimmells at the press conference. He said to reporters that the Kimmells had told him that their lawyer would be contacting him. He surmised this might be in an attempt to "threaten me with a lawsuit."

Just how upset Ketchum was by the meeting that had occurred in Sheridan can be seen by his next statement. Once again, he stressed that NCSO should have been invited to the conference and "coming back now, saying 'We have somebody that went up to the meeting and we'll bring the information back down to you,' that's bullshit!"

County sheriffs generally do not use words like "bullshit" in a news conference attended by various members of the media.

A political cartoon was soon displayed on the editorial page of the *Casper Star-Tribune*. It depicted Sheriff Ketchum as a little boy dressed up in a Western outfit, with fringed jacket and chaps. He was riding a stick horse and wore a badge that stated, *Jr. Sheriff*. In his hand, he held a cap pistol, which he fired; a small flag came out the barrel declaring, *Bang!* Ketchum said in the cartoon, *"The Feds have got to learn that I'm the law in these here parts."*

A follow-up editorial in the *Casper Star-Tribune* on June 1, 1989, was GIGANTIC CRIME OVERSHADOWED BY SHERIFF'S EGO. The newspaper castigated Ketchum for his intransigence on the matter and his overriding ego. To them, it seemed as if Sheriff Ketchum's vanity and public image were more important to him than actually solving Lisa Kimmell's murder.

The federal investigation officially began on June 23, 1989, and they put their resources to work, looking at old tips and gathering new ones. Even though more than a year had now passed since Lisa Kimmell's murder, rumors and stories about her abduction and death still permeated the area.

Meanwhile, as best they could, NCSO detectives Dan Tholson and Jim Broz went about their business outside the loop of the federal investigation. They liked the Kimmells and tried not to let their boss's intransigence get in the way of a thorough investigation. In fact, the Kimmells would praise these two later for working diligently and competently on leads about the case, despite the ill feeling between themselves and Sheriff Ketchum.

Phone calls still drifted in to the Kimmells' home by people who supposedly knew something about Lisa's disappearance and murder. One of these phone calls came from a young woman who told Lisa's former boss at Arby's, Joe Morian, that her boyfriend had some information about the murder. The boyfriend was apparently given the Kimmells' phone number, and he made a series of collect phone calls from a county jail in Oregon, where he was incarcerated. This person wanted to set up a meeting between himself and the Kimmells, and Sheila was all ready to fly to Oregon, until Don Flickinger talked her out of it. Instead, Flickinger said he would fly there, and so would Detective Dan Tholson on a different flight.

Flickinger knew that the man in Oregon had a criminal history of petty crimes and drug abuse. Before he would say more, this man wanted to make a deal with law enforcement. Flickinger and Tholson met with the inmate in Oregon and quickly determined that the man knew almost nothing about Lisa's case. Tholson said later, "We flew all the way out there, went in, and talked to him, and were there maybe twenty minutes. He didn't know a thing. He was looking for a deal. But that was typical."

Agent Flickinger and Detective Tholson, however, stayed up late at a Portland hotel room that night and discussed the case and the evidence they had. They found that they liked each other and worked well together. They promised to share information in the future, despite Sheriff Ron Ketchum. Flickinger said, "There was a lot of ill feelings at the top between the federal agencies and the sheriff. It was never at our level."

Hardly had the Oregon trip been concluded when the Kimmells received a strange letter in the mail from a man in Las Vegas. This letter was similar in tone and style as the "Stringfellow Hawke" note—speaking of the person's deep feelings for Lisa and the sorrow at her loss. Since the Kimmells didn't know this person, they handed the letter over to Agent Flickinger.

Flickinger contacted ATF agents in Las Vegas about

the letter and return address of the sender. The very next day, he got an urgent phone call from one of the ATF agents. They had gone by the letter writer's house and sitting in that person's driveway was a black Honda CRXsi, just like Lisa's. It even had a sunroof of the same style. Excited by what seemed to be a huge break in the case, Flickinger asked the agents to contact the man and also get the identification number off the vehicle. Then Flickinger contacted Detective Tholson about making a trip down to Las Vegas. Tholson, in turn, contacted the crime lab and set up a flight to Las Vegas.

Before Tholson left Natrona County, however, one of the Las Vegas ATF agents called him and said that the Honda's identification number did not match that of Lisa Kimmell's. Tholson decided not to go to Nevada, but Flickinger made a trip there, anyway, to talk to the letter writer. As it turned out, the letter writer was a young man who had lived in Cody, Wyoming, at one time and had often taken trips to Billings, Montana. While visiting there, he had stopped many times at the Arby's restaurant where Lisa Kimmell worked and had developed a crush on her. He never worked up the nerve to ask her out on a date, but he was entranced by her "cool car." In response, he bought a black Honda CRXsi just like hers.

The young man claimed not to have murdered Lisa, and his story held up. He provided a DNA sample, which proved that his DNA did not match the semen or foreign hair found on her body. What had looked like a sure thing became one more dead end.

Always eager to learn about new techniques and law-enforcement-related information, Agent Flickinger met two FBI agents who were in Billings to give a seminar about serial killer Arthur Shawcross. Shawcross had made New York prostitutes his victims. Flickinger pumped the agents for all the information they could give him relating to Lisa Kimmell's case. The FBI agents told Flickinger that the unusual stab wound patterns formed what looked like a pentagram pattern on Lisa's chest, and one under the sternum. These stab wounds suggested a possible cult connection. The agents had seen similar stab wound patterns related to cult and satanic murders. The agents told Flickinger not to rule out an occult angle in Lisa's death.

Because of this knowledge, over the next six months, Flickinger interviewed more than twenty people in the Casper area alone who said they were members of a cult or knew people who were. Surprisingly, some of the members were professionals, and even housewives, who owned robes with designs similar to the stab wounds found on Lisa's body. The informants indicated that they held their meetings and covens out near some weird-shaped rocks that stood upon the exposed Wyoming plains. The area had a Stonehenge aspect to it.

These stories of a ritualized killing of Lisa came completely around once more when the rumors resurfaced that her heart had been cut out of her body. (This had not happened.) Detective Tholson said later, "I don't think we could ever track how that rumor started. It just went all over the place, to everybody. We got phone calls and tips on that all the time."

The other main focus of rumors was, of course, that Lisa had run afoul of drug dealers. One particular persistent story was that there was a local drug dealer named Jack who was in the Casper area when Lisa had been murdered. When Agent Flickinger finally went to see this Jack, he began to wonder if Jack really was involved in the abduction and killing of Lisa, or knew people who had been. Jack told Flickinger that he was in the Casper area one time and went to pick up a stolen snowmobile and take it to Montana. Jack met several people at a rustic cabin and noticed a suitcase and two stuffed animals in the cabin. The description Jack gave of the items matched items Lisa had in her car when abducted.

After several interviews, polygraph tests, and a DNA sample, Jack and several of his friends were ruled out as being responsible. And Flickinger learned later that the details of the suitcase and stuffed animals had been leaked by some law enforcement agent. Flickinger surmised that one of Jack's rivals in the drug trade had set him up to be a fall guy for the murder of Lisa Kimmell.

As 1989 ended, the detectives had followed leads about drug dealers, cultists, and just about everything and everyone else in Wyoming, and they still seemed no closer to solving who had kidnapped Lisa Kimmell, tortured her for six days, and then murdered her.

5

NEVER-NEVER LAND

As if Lisa Kimmell's case hadn't had enough twists, turns, and dead ends with Satanists and drug dealers, by the 1990s it started moving off into another unforeseen realm. Agent Flickinger began wondering if a law enforcement officer had kidnapped and murdered Lisa. The first such person to come up on his "radar" about this angle was a police officer in Texas who had lived in Casper in 1988 and had driven a taxi there. This officer became a viable suspect when several women spoke of the man as having driven young women in his taxi on much longer routes than necessary, just so he could spend more time with them. These women had felt "real strange vibes" about the man, and had commented to others about the man's strange behavior.

Flying down to Houston, Texas, Flickinger spoke to this man, who was now a police officer, and he was stunned by what others had said about him. He immediately volunteered to have his blood drawn so that he could be ruled out as Lisa's killer. The DNA profile that came back from the blood sample proved that he had not been the contributor of the semen or the foreign hair found on Lisa's body.

This foray with the Texas police officer was minor, however, compared to the brewing storm with NCSO and Sheriff Ron Ketchum. In the spring of 1990, an election was approaching for the sheriff's office, and Ketchum vowed to run again. Casper police lieutenant Bill Barnes decided to oppose Ketchum in the upcoming election and he made the Lisa Kimmell case part of his platform. Barnes said the Kimmell case was rife with incompetence under Ketchum's leadership.

One of Barnes's main themes was to create a better working relationship between the Casper PD and NCSO. Apparently, the Kimmells weren't the only ones who felt left out of the loop on law enforcement matters when it came to Sheriff Ketchum.

Then on March 25, 1990, the two-year anniversary of Lisa Kimmell's disappearance, something truly startling occurred. A headline in the *Casper Star-Tribune* declared KETCHUM IN CRITICAL CONDITION AT WMC. (WMC stood for Wyoming Medical Center.) Ketchum had been found unconscious in his home, and Undersheriff Mark Benton noted, "There were no signs of foul play, visible injuries, or drugs."

For some time, people within NCSO and some of Ketchum's friends had been worried about his mental health. Ketchum and his ex-wife had several arguments over the phone during the previous fall, and in one of those arguments, she thought Ron vowed to commit suicide. She was so concerned that she called a law enforcement person she knew to check up on him. The officer made a welfare check, and Ron said at the time that he was depressed, but not suicidal.

Then, on March 24, 1990, a friend of Ketchum's called him and became concerned about some statements that Ron had made. So concerned, in fact, that this friend contacted Lieutenant Dave Kinghorn, who was not home at the moment. Undersheriff Benton and his wife were visiting at Kinghorn's house at the time, however, and Benton phoned Ketchum to see if he was doing okay. According to Benton later, everything seemed fine.

When Lieutenant Kinghorn arrived home, however, he made several calls to Ron Ketchum's residence, but only got through to his answering machine. Finally, around 8:30 P.M., Kinghorn went over to Ketchum's place and found him sprawled out on the bed, unconscious. Ironically, it was a Casper Police Department officer who arrived on the scene along with an ambulance, since Ketchum lived within the city limits. Never a great fan of Ketchum's, Police Chief Fred Rainguet told a reporter that the officer did not check Ketchum's home for drugs or medication, "because it would have been illegal to do so without a warrant." Yet, in the article, there was an undertone of Police Chief Rainguet's less than admiring nature when it came to Sheriff Ketchum.

The next day, according to Undersheriff Benton, Ketchum was awake and talking to friends and family in the hospital, even though the hospital wouldn't even publicly admit that he was one of their patients. Benton said, "The family are not necessarily concerned about protecting Ron's public image, but in protecting his mental health." Then Benton once again admitted that Ketchum had suffered from depression in the past.

* * *

Ron Ketchum's "public image" may or may not have suffered, but his job as sheriff of the county brought him into the spotlight—whether he liked it or not. Police Chief Rainguet told a reporter, "We might invite a state body, such as the Division of Criminal Investigation, in to conduct an investigation because we are talking about a sheriff of a county." The unspoken word was the question of whether Ketchum had abused illegal drugs or was now too incapacitated to carry on as sheriff of Natrona County.

Two days after he was admitted to the hospital, Ron Ketchum checked out, and Undersheriff Benton related that Ketchum had left for an undisclosed location with his mother and stepfather. Benton added, "Ron Ketchum is following his doctor's orders and he is going away for a while to get away from the pressure of visitation and public inquiry. At the request of the doctor, I'm not going to disclose the location." Benton then added that Ketchum seemed embarrassed by all the attention the incident had received. Embarrassment or not, when Ketchum left the hospital, he left behind a firestorm of speculation on what had just occurred. And the Kimmells had to wonder what would ever become of their daughter's case under such a sheriff.

Just exactly what happened remained hidden. Obviously, Undersheriff Benton was picking his words very carefully, but the damage was already done. Many people would point to the fact that this supposed suicide attempt had fallen on the two-year anniversary of Lisa Kimmell's abduction and the failure to capture her killer under Sheriff Ketchum's tenure. Editorials filled the *Star-Tribune*. One letter writer complained,

There's a mystery going on in the Natrona County Sheriff's Office at the leadership level.

On April 12, another letter declared, *I feel that Sheriff Ketchum should step down from office since after the last three years that Sheriff Ketchum has held office, it has been nothing but disaster; ie, the Lisa Kimmell case, Sheriff Ketchum's refusal to cooperate with other law enforcement agencies, American Civil Liberties Union lawsuits, and his hush-hush methods of running an office.*

When Ketchum returned to his office on April 16, he admitted that he had suffered from depression, but denied abusing alcohol or drugs. He told a reporter, "What took place was strictly a medical issue."

On May 6, Deputy Sheriff David Dovala threw his hat into the ring for sheriff. Even though he was now running against Ketchum, Dovala said that he would keep Ketchum on in some capacity at NCSO. This was viewed by some as the "Good Ol' Boys" network, and by others as Dovala sticking up for his boss. Despite Ketchum's many faults, he did always stick up for his deputies at NCSO, and the officers who worked there appreciated that.

On May 18, the *Star-Tribune* ran an article, KETCHUM CHOOSES NOT TO RUN AGAIN. Ron Ketchum gave as a reason that he didn't want to explain about his hospitalization. In the back of his mind it may have been that he would not be elected once again, and might, in fact, lose in a humiliating referendum about how the public viewed his past job performance.

The Kimmells were not sitting on the sidelines concerning the race for a new sheriff in Natrona County, even if Sheriff Ketchum was no longer part of the race. In a press release, they reiterated their frustrations with NCSO and especially about Sheriff Ketchum and his direction of that office. They wanted whoever became the new sheriff to pay more attention to their concerns and work with outside agencies. The press release was picked up by local newspapers, radio stations, and television stations. After hearing the press statement, Lieutenant Dave Kinghorn phoned Sheila Kimmell and voiced his displeasure at the things the Kimmells were saying. Kinghorn said that he understood their grievances against Ketchum, but he also felt that NCSO had been unfairly tainted as well. Kinghorn pointed out that NCSO had spent thousands of hours on Lisa's case and had cooperated with numerous outside agencies. The Kimmells tried reassuring Kinghorn that they were not irritated at NCSO, and they thought that the detectives there had done a good job. All they wanted, they stated, was a new approach about how they were consulted when it came to their daughter's case.

Picking up on the Kimmells' press release, radio station KQLT asked the Kimmells to be on their radio show *Free for All,* and the Kimmells agreed. The radio host asked at one point, "Why would you make a statement now?" obviously relating to the upcoming election of a new sheriff. Sheila replied, "We have an interest in how the sheriff's department will be run in the future. Based on two and a half years of experience and our relationship with the sheriff's office, we feel compelled to share this with the citizens of Natrona County."

Ron added, "We're just here to give information as to how the department is being run and let the citizens of Natrona County decide for themselves how it should best be run."

Dave Dovala eventually won the race and became

elected as the new sheriff. He vowed to work more closely with the Casper Police Department and other law enforcement agencies around the state. Yet, Dovala's election was not the big news at the time. An item of bigger interest was the fact that by now Ron Ketchum was a suspect in Lisa Kimmell's abduction and murder.

It started when a reliable witness contacted Agent Flickinger and stated that Ron Ketchum had been in a sheriff's patrol car on the night of March 25, 1988, when Ketchum had been claiming all along that he had not done that. The witness said that Ketchum had pulled over a small black car with a young woman driver at the wheel. Ketchum denied working that night, but dispatch records proved that he had, in fact, been working.

Other reports began to surface of Ketchum pulling women over along lonely roads on other occasions, telling them that they had a problem with their taillights, when, in fact, there was nothing wrong with their taillights at all. One woman who lived in Casper was so upset by an incident like that occurring to her, she moved out of the area, clear to St. Louis, Missouri. She was absolutely shocked when one day out of the blue, Ron Ketchum showed up at her front door. When she threatened to call the local police, he left. It's not recorded if she ever filed an official complaint against him.

What really piqued Agent Flickinger's interest was the fact that Ketchum had chosen the two-year anniversary of Lisa Kimmell's abduction to make his "alleged" suicide attempt. That, coupled with the complaints by women drivers, made Flickinger make a special trip to see Ron Ketchum. Agent Flickinger asked Ketchum to give a blood sample so that he could be ruled out in Lisa's death. When Flickinger asked for the sample, Ketchum was furious and refused.

This refusal on Ketchum's part only added fuel to the fire, as far as suspicions and rumors surrounding him went. It threw his supposed noncooperation with other law enforcement agencies into a whole new light. And then another incident added to the already dark cloud hanging above Ketchum. An informant contacted Flickinger and said that he had seen Lisa's dark-colored Honda CRX parked near a car stereo store in Casper, right around the time of her abduction. It just so happened that the car stereo store was owned by a relative of Ron Ketchum.

With this latest revelation, the murky waters around Ketchum really began to swirl. Ketchum eventually agreed to give a blood sample, but he insisted upon certain conditions that had to be met before he would do so. Ketchum stated that it would have to be an NCSO employee who drew his blood, and he wanted the blood of Sheriff Dovala and Lieutenant Kinghorn drawn as well. Those two agreed, and instead of fighting this any further, Agent Flickinger agreed to the arrangement as well.

Yet, even this set off a new round of controversy and antagonism. The blood samples that NCSO took from Ketchum, Dovala, and Kinghorn were not labeled or packaged correctly. When Flickinger got the samples, there was no way of knowing whose blood was whose. Outraged by this new wrinkle in the case, Agent Flickinger almost sought a federal court order for Ron Ketchum to submit a new blood sample drawn by an agency other than NCSO. Eventually Ketchum did resubmit a blood sample, after much wrangling on his part, and he was ruled out as the contributor of the sperm or foreign hair connected to Lisa Kimmell.

The furor between Ketchum and Flickinger did not die down, however. Sticking up for his old sheriff, Sheriff Dovala requested that Agent Flickinger be reprimanded by his superiors at ATF for "his attitude." When Sheila Kimmell learned of this, she blew her stack. She phoned Sheriff Dovala and told him she wanted NCSO off Lisa's case. Thoroughly tired of what had been a "hot potato" for a long, long time, Dovala agreed to Sheila's demand. As far as Dovala and NCSO were concerned, some other agency could now do all future investigating on Lisa Kimmell. For their part, they were not sad to see the Kimmells go.

Tips and rumors continued to come in year after year about Lisa's missing Honda. One tip came in from as far away as Anchorage, Alaska. A police officer there was certain he had seen the stolen vehicle and informed Agent Flickinger about it. But when Flickinger flew all the way to Alaska, the black Honda CRXsi was not found. It was just one more long, tiring flight that led nowhere.

Still looking into rumors about Satanists and cops gone bad, Agent Flickinger expanded his investigation into the realm of known sex offenders in the area. One person, in particular, caught Flickinger's attention. This was a man who had been incarcerated for the rape of a young female college student in Billings, Montana, in 1989. What particularly made this a person of interest was the fact that he had shaved the young woman's pubic hair before raping her. And on top of all that, the man had told his ex-wife and girlfriend that he'd assaulted other women by hitting them in the head. When Flickinger learned that the man in question had not reported for work between March 23 and April 2, 1988, this person shot to the top of the list of suspects.

Flickinger interviewed the man's girlfriend and ex-wife and discovered the suspect sometimes bound them before having sex. He could also be rough at times. The girlfriend added that the man liked knives and seemed to know how to use them. He'd even threatened to "cut her up" at one point. Even though Flickinger thought this guy looked like a dead ringer for Lisa Kimmell's murderer, DNA evidence eventually ruled him out.

Another man, soon thereafter, also started looking "good" for the crime. The young man had held odd jobs and lived in a tent around Pathfinder Lake, not far from where Lisa's body had been found at the Old Government Bridge. One of this man's former girlfriends told Flickinger that he had once taken her out to the tent, bound her arms and legs, and sexually assaulted her. According to the girlfriend, he had also made small cuts around her breasts with a knife during sex. The woman said the man was definitely into Satanism and had once told her, "It's time for another sacrifice, like Lisa Kimmell."

When Flickinger spoke to this man, he denied everything his former girlfriend had said and took a polygraph test. He did not do well on the polygraph test, but DNA evidence eventually ruled him out.

By 1991, Flickinger had acquired the nickname "the Vampire," not only because he was drawing so much blood from suspects, but he was investigating so many cult members as well. By then, word had gotten out somehow about the strange knife pattern on Lisa's body. Just who in law enforcement leaked this is unknown, but plenty of occult members in the area seemed to know about it and its unusual pattern. For whatever reason, lots of people informed upon others as being into Satanism and cutting individuals during ceremonies. There was a miniature "Salem Witchcraft" scare going on in Natrona County, most of the rumors being bogus.

One of the most sensational stories that surfaced around that time was about an occult group in the Casper area, which had supposedly met in 1987 around the Old Government Bridge to practice Satanism, kill small animals, drink their blood, and dab animal blood on their bodies. According to an informant, the group disrobed a young woman in a Casper home one night, tied her up, suspended her from the ceiling, and the male members of the group raped her. They had also shaved her pubic hair. When they were done, the story went, they had told the girl never to tell anyone or they would kill her.

Flickinger was eventually able to track down one of the supposed cult members who had done this. This man and his girlfriend were in Denver by that point. Denying the incident of the "suspended/raped girl," they both took blood tests and were ruled out by DNA. Once again, a story that looked so promising petered out into nothing.

By now, Agent Flickinger was going ever further afield in his investigation. Willing to try almost anything, Flickinger listened to the Kimmells when they expressed their belief in the psychic powers of two elderly sisters from Great Falls, Montana. The Kimmells had been skeptical themselves about these sisters, Dolores and Darlene, until Ron's sister visited them and brought back an audiotape from them concerning the disappearance and murder of Lisa. Quite a few of the details the sisters mentioned had never been released by law enforcement to the press. The Kimmells agreed to give the sisters a try.

Sheila Kimmell drove to Great Falls and met with only Dolores, since Darlene was not available for a "session." Dolores held a glass of water before her eyes, which helped her to "see." Dolores then described the pattern of stab wounds inflicted upon Lisa and details about Lisa's car. The stab wounds had been mentioned in the media, but not the exact pattern at that point. Dolores would not accept money for the session, which, by itself, separated her from the con artists.

Sheila had tape-recorded this session and played it back to Agent Flickinger. Agreeing that there was something there, but still dubious, Flickinger checked the sisters' backgrounds and learned that they had a good relationship with various law enforcement agencies around the country. They had even helped to some degree on the Ted Bundy case.

Flickinger decided to ask the two sisters to come to Casper, and they agreed. Once they reached Casper, they told Flickinger that they had a very strong sense about the numerals 2 and 2—though they could not say why. Agent Flickinger later wrote in his report about the meeting: *They accurately described the patterns of the stab wounds and also remarked about Lisa Kimmell's head wound. The stab wounds have been mentioned in the press as simply being stab wounds, but were not described as to the pattern, and the head wound has not been publicized at all.* Flickinger went on to write that it was *somewhat remarkable* that the sisters spoke of Lisa as having been held against her will for a number of days. That fact had been withheld as well.

6

PROFILING

Not only did ATF show interest in the Kimmell case, but several individuals in the FBI did as well. This was especially true with those who practiced a relatively new method within the FBI known as profiling. One of the earliest to become involved with this aspect in Lisa Kimmell's case was Special Agent Ron Walker, a criminal profiler with the Violent Criminal Apprehension Program (VCAP). NCSO detective Dan Tholson initially had asked for the FBI's help, and Agent Walker drew up a report concerning Lisa's case. Walker analyzed all the information he knew about Lisa Kimmell's abduction and murder, and cited that her killer was probably a white male in his mid-twenties or older. The murderer had not been *overly sophisticated*, according to Walker: *The killer, however, did have the ability to think rationally and premeditate his offenses, methodically in a calculated fashion without panic.* The man most likely had unsatisfactory relationships with women and chose younger victims, *who he could dominate*. Walker thought the man had at least average intelligence and held a number of blue-collar jobs.

Walker believed the assailant had not known Lisa Kimmell, but rather came upon her by chance. The man had not initially thought of killing her for pleasure, but rather he killed her after the sexual assaults so that she would not be able to identify him. He wasn't in a category of sexual sadists who killed their victim while having sex with them. And while not overly sophisticated, the man knew enough to get rid of the ligatures before disposing of the body, because the ligatures could contain fingerprints or trace evidence. Walker wrote the man *knew how to think on his feet,* and was able to act methodically in a calculated fashion. And Walker did not believe that Lisa Kimmell had been the man's first crime victim of that nature. By the time he killed her, he seemed to be fairly at ease about what he was doing, with a plan to escape detection after the initial abduction and rape. In fact, he was so comfortable with the situation, he kept her for a number of days, although each passing day increased his risk of discovery.

The assailant was probably familiar with the area where he had first made contact with Lisa, and familiar with the body dump site as well. Walker thought the individual could interact with people when he had to, but he probably preferred being alone. And though he may have used alcohol or illegal drugs, he most likely was not addicted to either. The shaving of Lisa's pubic hair showed that he liked to dominate the female victim and fulfill his sexual fantasies in a manner in which he preferred. Agent Walker gave the "Stringfellow Hawke" note more weight than Sheriff Ketchum had. Walker even had a theory that the assailant may have idealized Stringfellow Hawke, and saw himself as someone of a similar type.

Walker believed that it was unlikely that Lisa had picked up a hitchhiker or a stranded motorist, because of the lateness of the hour, the isolated terrain, and being a young woman alone. With that in mind, Walker posited that the man may have spotted her somewhere, either at a mini-mart, grocery store, gas station, or the Waltman Rest Stop. At that point, the assailant may have followed her and bumped her car with his own vehicle, staging an accident when no one was around. When Lisa got out of her vehicle to check the damage and confront the person who had bumped her car, the assailant most likely threatened her immediately with a weapon. Because there were no defensive wounds on the hands of her body, Lisa most likely was taken without a struggle, because the man had used overwhelming threat capability with a gun. She most likely got into his vehicle without fighting back, and the man most likely tied her up early on in the abduction.

It was not known if she was later forced to disrobe herself, or the attacker tore off her clothes. When he had her at a secure location, it was known that he used ligatures on her ankles and wrists for prolonged periods of time. The fact that when her body was found, she was wearing socks and panties, suggested the man may have promised to let her go somewhere, and she had partially dressed herself before being taken to the Old Government Bridge and killed.

Because of the fact it would have been hard for one man to drive Lisa in his own vehicle and get rid of her car as well, Walker wondered if there may have been someone who helped the main assailant get rid of Lisa's car. Walker very much doubted that Lisa had picked up someone on foot, in which case that person could have taken control of her and her car. There was also the fact that she had been beaten in the head with a blunt instrument and also stabbed. This suggested to Walker that one person may have hit her in the head, and the main assailant stabbed her to death. Walker finished up by stating one chilling theory: the assailant would probably perpetrate more abductions and murders of young women until he was captured.

At the federal level, law enforcement began to wonder if some other murders of young women in Wyoming, in 1982 and 1983, were related to the abduction and murder of Lisa Kimmell in 1988. On August 5, 1982, the *Casper Star-Tribune* had run an article headlined, OFFICIALS REQUEST HELP TO IDENTIFY REMAINS. It was reported that the Sweetwater County Sheriff's Office asked for help about the body of a female discovered on April 26 in their county. There were only skeletal remains of a woman who had been between twenty-five and thirty-nine years of age. She had suffered injuries to her right upper arm, right rib cage, and left ankle. The Wyoming State Crime Lab team created a facial reconstruction because the woman's face had been so ravaged by the elements.

Sandra Mays, of that team, told a reporter, "The facial reconstruction is based upon general statistical measurements. An exact representation cannot be produced, but a general likeness is expected." Anyone who thought they recognized the woman was urged to contact the Sweetwater County Sheriff's Office (SCSO).

Then, on August 7, 1982, more than a hundred miles away in Converse County, Wyoming, the body of a young woman was found, dumped into the North Platte River, near Glenrock. The body was found around 6:30 P.M. by a bicyclist near a bridge on County Road 25. The next day's *Star-Tribune* reported that the woman's body was partially clad and there was no identification on her. Dr. James Thorpen did the autopsy, but the Converse County sheriff at the time said there would be no information released about the autopsy conclusions, other than to say it appeared to be a homicide. In fact, the next day's headline for an article was POLICE HUSH INFORMATION ON BODY IN PLATTE RIVER. The Converse County Sheriff's Office (CCSO) wouldn't even reveal the color of the victim's eyes or her hair color. An enterprising reporter, however, was able to talk to someone who had witnessed the body being pulled from the river. This person said that it appeared that the young woman had been strangled to death.

Somehow the reporter for the *Glenrock Independent* learned even more about the victim, stating that she had been between the ages of twenty and thirty-five, five-three, weighed between 115 and 130 pounds, with green eyes and shoulder-length dark brown hair. And by that time, the sheriff's office was a little more forthcoming as well. Sheriff Chuck Widick said that the body had been in the water for several days when discovered. She had indeed died from neck trauma, and a heavy rock had been tied to a rope, the rope looped around her neck, and the rock was used as a weight to keep her body down in the water.

Weeks went by and no one came forward to identify the victim's body. The *Star-Tribune* of August 22 reported, *Still no identity on body found in river.* Sheriff Widick admitted, "We really have no idea how long she was in the water. The coroner's report gave an estimate of three to seven days, but that is purely speculation." The CCSO submitted the victim's fingerprints to the Wyoming State Crime Lab and the FBI for identification purposes. No hits came back.

With still no pertinent information coming in about the young woman, the CCSO released a police forensic sketch of the victim's face. It depicted a young woman with dark brown hair and full lips. Undersheriff Jim Johnson said the woman had several tattoos. He would not specify what the tattoos looked like, because one, in particular, would be a giveaway as to who the woman was, and he wanted whoever came forward to be aware of what the actual tattoo looked like and describe it.

The release of the sketch and information that the victim had tattoos did the trick. A friend of the young woman came forward and positively identified her as twenty-year-old Belinda Grantham. Grantham had been a runaway from an early age, and been a ward of the state of Wyoming on several occasions. At the age of either seventeen or eighteen, she had moved down to New Mexico and had become part of a traveling carnival based out of Albuquerque. Eventually Belinda moved to Glenrock, Wyoming, where she lived with a boyfriend. In June 1982, she told friends she was going to visit people she knew in Kansas, and probably made that trip, returning to Wyoming sometime in late July.

Deputy Marvin Eaton, of the CCSO, who was one of the main investigators on the case, told a reporter, "The investigation is coming along real good. We have suspects and we have motive."

But the investigation was not coming along as "good" as Deputy Eaton may have supposed. The suspects and the motive did not pan out, and no arrests were made. A week later, there was an article in the *Star-Tribune* asking, *Can you solve the case?* It reported that CCSO was appealing to the public for information concerning the murder of Belinda Grantham. The case became a part of the new Crime Stoppers program in Wyoming, and a $1,000 reward was offered for information. This short article confirmed that Grantham had last been seen on August 1, 1982, at the Natrona County Fairgrounds.

Belinda Grantham stories were barely out of the news when the *Casper Star-Tribune* reported, *Cattlemen find body of a woman.* The article went on to say that cattlemen had stumbled upon the nude body of a young woman on 33 Mile Road, about eighteen miles north of Highway 20/26 in Natrona County. Sheriff William Estes thought the woman was in her twenties. A preliminary medical examination suggested that the woman had been strangled to death. The body was in a "mummified state" and could not immediately be identified.

Sheriff Estes said of the location where the body was found, "There wasn't much on the crime scene. The body was found facedown with the upper part of her body in what appeared to be a half-dug grave." A later pathologist report noted that the woman had been four-eleven, with medium-length dark brown hair, and weighed between one hundred and 110 pounds.

Not surprisingly, a local newspaper around this time ran a story that even though most crimes in Wyoming were down, the murder rate in the state had nearly doubled. There seemed to be a lot of young women's bodies being found in isolated parts of Wyoming that year. Dave Dovala, who had been a Casper police commander at the time, commented, "I've been hearing that crime is down nationwide. If it is down, I sure haven't noticed it."

It wasn't until later that more facts drifted in about

the body found out on 33 Mile Road. As it turned out, in June 1982, eighteen-year-old Naomi Kidder took a trip with some friends from Buffalo, Wyoming, to Rawlins. Naomi was a petite young woman, not even five feet tall, with long brown hair. When her friends returned to Buffalo, Naomi decided to stay longer in Rawlins. Starting her return trip to Buffalo on June 29, 1982, Naomi had by then run out of money for transportation. She started to hitchhike home and vanished somewhere along the road. Her mother reported her as a missing person on July 1.

On September 10, 1982, Naomi's body was discovered on 33 Mile Road, though law enforcement didn't know it at the time. A few more facts were out by now—she had been strangled to death with a wire ligature, which was still wrapped around her neck at the time. Naomi had been discovered nude, and a silver necklace, possibly belonging to her, was found nearby. Her remains unidentified at the time, she had been buried in the Natrona County Cemetery as a Jane Doe.

Somehow, Naomi's mother learned that her daughter's dental records were not in the computer system. Mrs. Kidder insisted that they should be, and it wasn't until March 14, 1994, that Natrona County's Jane Doe was positively identified as Naomi Kidder.

However, there were other murder victims found in isolated areas of Wyoming years before that. In February 1983, twenty-three-year-old Janelle Johnson left her home in Riverton, Wyoming, for an interview at the Vannoy Talent Training Center in Denver. Janelle was a pretty young woman with thick, curly brown hair. After completing her interview in Denver, Janelle was low on cash, so she hitchhiked as far as a truck stop in Sinclair, Wyoming, near Rawlins. A witness saw her there around 5:30 P.M. on February 17. When she didn't return to Riverton, her housemate became concerned, and a missing persons report was filed by the Riverton Police Department.

On March 1, 1983, Janelle's body was found by a county worker on Muskrat Creek Road, near Shoshoni, Wyoming. The county worker had seen a woman's legs protruding from a makeshift grave. Janelle had been buried, but storm runoff had unearthed part of her body. Her cause of death was listed as "mechanical strangulation" by the use of a "wide ligature," possibly a belt. She had been raped, and the attacker had left bite marks on her shoulder.

By 1996, a new profiler came on the scene concerning Lisa Kimmell's case. This was Greg Cooper, a former FBI special agent profiler. For such a young man, Cooper had a stellar and varied career in law enforcement. Starting as a police officer in Provo, Utah, at the age of twenty-seven, he was offered the job of police chief of Delta, Utah. Even though this was a very prestigious position for someone so young, Cooper had learned about the new field of criminal profiling at the Behavioral Science Unit of the FBI, as espoused by Special Agent John Douglas. Meeting Douglas at a seminar in Utah, Cooper joined the FBI in hopes of one day becoming part of the profiling unit.

Cooper had to wait a minimum of five years before being able to join the unit, so he put in his time as an FBI agent in Washington State and Los Angeles, California. When the five years were up, Cooper was admitted almost immediately as a profiler, the youngest man in the unit. Working alongside Douglas and others in the elite unit, Cooper served as national manager of the Violent Criminal Apprehension Program, supervisor of the Investigative Support Unit, and as an instructor at the FBI Academy in criminal psychology.

In 1992, he coauthored the *Crime Classification Manual,* a landmark book that classified aspects of homicide, arson, and sexual assault. He also consulted with law enforcement agencies from around the world in cases that included homicide, rapes, kidnapping, extortion, political corruption, arson, and bombings.

One particular case gave Cooper insights into the mind and habits of a serial killer. He provided expert testimony in a case that linked multiple homicides that had occurred in separate jurisdictions, and his testimony led to the conviction of that particular serial killer. The case was highlighted in John Douglas's best seller *Mind Hunter.*

By 1996, Cooper was out of the FBI, and serving as police chief of Provo, Utah, a city of one hundred thousand people. He still taught classes on the side at the Utah Police Academy, Utah Valley State College, and Salt Lake Community College, and was chairman of the board on the Utah County Major Crimes Task Force.

Looking at unsolved homicides of young women in his state and in Wyoming and Nevada as well, after 1996 Cooper started zeroing in on certain cases that had very dramatic similarities. He noted that the Lisa Kimmell case and Belinda Grantham case had certain characteristics in common, such as the killer of those young women had used rivers as the dumping grounds. Their bodies were also partially clothed when discovered. He also noted the similarities of the partially buried and mummified remains of Naomi Kidder in Natrona County and Janelle Johnson as well. Those cases had some similar characteristics to two cases in Utah and one in Nevada that had occurred in the early 1990s, especially as to isolated body-dumping sites.

There were also some differences, but then again, a specific killer will not always leave exactly similar evidence at different crime scenes.

In 1990, Patricia Candace Walsh, twenty-four, and her husband, Scott Zyskowski, of Seattle, Washington, had started hitchhiking to Texas. Somewhere along the way, they disappeared. Zyskowski's body was eventually found near El Paso, Texas, but Patricia's body was discovered by two hunters in rural Millard County, Utah. However, at the time, neither the hunters nor law enforcement had any idea who she was. The remains were listed as a Jane Doe. She had been sexually tortured, and her remains were so ravaged by sun and desert conditions that they were partially mummified, as Naomi Kidder's body and Janelle Johnson's body had been. One particularly noticeable aspect of her remains stood out—it was as if her body had been posed by the killer, her arms spread out in the form of a cross.

Then in neighboring Juab County, Utah, on March 22, 1991, the body of a young woman was discovered off an Interstate 5 exit near Mills Junction. Authorities there would not be able to ascertain who she was for many years. Once again, however, the young woman's body was partially mummified by the elements, and she had been posed, not unlike the body of Walsh, in the form of a cross.

Two years went by, and on November 16, 1993, in Elko County, Nevada, the body of a woman between the ages of twenty-eight and thirty-two years old was discovered. She was approximately five-eight and weighed about 140 pounds. Once again, the sun and desert conditions had worked upon her, making it difficult to even know what her face had looked like in life. She had been shot twice in the chest by a small-caliber weapon, one bullet piercing her heart. She might not have been discovered at all if a motorist had not stopped at that exit and walked off into the brush to urinate.

An autopsy found that the woman had a small amount of evidence of alcohol and marijuana in her system, but no hard drugs. She had blond hair, a small scar on her right calf area, and teeth in excellent condition. None of her clothing was found near her body, and she still had pink nail polish on her fingernails.

Detectives surmised that she had been beaten before being shot and killed in another area, and then driven to the freeway exit and dumped there. Tire tracks in the area suggested that the killer had used a midsize to large vehicle, possibly a pickup or van. And then something very interesting appeared in the detective's report. The investigator noted, *She was found lying on her back, her arms spread out to her side in the shape of a cross, legs slightly parted. Investigators believe her killer may have purposefully posed the body.*

Cooper teamed up with Utah Department of Public Safety law officer Mike King to create the Utah *criminal* Tracking and Analysis Project (UTAP). They wanted it to be like the FBI's VCAP system. Cooper and King began studying eleven unsolved murders in the region, which would eventually take on the name "the Great Basin Murders."

The Great Basin is a large section of the western United States, especially in Utah, Nevada, and parts of California, Oregon, Idaho, and Wyoming, where none of the streams and rivers reach the sea. All of the rivers and streams empty into desert areas, usually salt lakes, which may even dry out in certain months of the year.

Much of the Great Basin is noted for its series of valleys and mountains, one progressing after another for hundreds of miles. And much of the Great Basin is very sparsely populated.

Greg Cooper considered Lisa Kimmell's murder to be amongst this group. Over time, Cooper and King began to believe that two separate killers had been responsible for eleven murders. The Kimmell and Grantham cases had very similar characteristics, and even the Naomi Kidder and Janelle Johnson cases had similarities as well in conjunction with Kimmell and Grantham.

Sheila Kimmell eventually contacted Greg Cooper and he studied Lisa's murder. His report to Sheila was lengthy, and he was convinced that Lisa's killer had murdered other young women in the region. In one section, Cooper noted, *I have never witnessed a more disturbing anomaly of humanity than the serial killer. I suppose the most disconcerting aspect of this freak of nature is that the terrifying attributes generally associated with fictional monsters, have been transposed into human form, but they eat, sleep, talk, and walk just like you and me. The major difference is that they don't think or feel emotions like you and me, especially compassion or love.*

Cooper went on to say that a person can eventually understand how a loved one might have their life ended by an act of nature, or they can finally accept a death due to a car accident. Where they have problems is when a loved one's life is "snuffed out" by another human being. Because these perpetrators, especially serial killers, look and generally act in a manner similar to other human beings, it is hard for the loved one's family to accept the fact of the person's death. There is always the unanswerable questions of "what if?" What if the victim had not been at that location? What if they had arrived there at a different time of day? What if there had been more people around?

Once again, Cooper wrote, *They are not like us!* These individuals regarded other people as mere objects to be exploited, sexually abused, and discarded after the killer's needs had been satisfied. The killers often have certain distorted sexual fantasies they want to fulfill, by the use of pain and torture during sexual acts. They have no empathy for the victim—satisfying their own needs is paramount. Pain, grief, and the havoc they wreak is foreign to them.

Cooper related that Lisa's case had haunted him from the time he first became aware of it, because he had a daughter the same age who also liked adventure and independence, as Lisa had. Since Lisa was not a prostitute, runaway, or drug user, it was unlikely that she put herself into a dangerous situation in March 1988. Cooper surmised that Lisa probably was a victim of misfortune, crossing paths with an opportunistic psychopath who liked to sexually torture and murder young women. Even though Lisa was a "low-risk" individual, on March 25, 1988, she was a young woman alone at night in an isolated area on a road she didn't know. Cooper noted that if Lisa had car trouble or stopped for a quick break at a restroom somewhere, she might have become vulnerable at that moment. He summed up this portion: *She was in the wrong place at the wrong time.*

Cooper once again noted that he did not think Lisa's case was an isolated event. Speaking with a reporter later, he said, "From my perspective, this is a serial homicide. This would not be a case where you would look at this and suggest that it was a singular event, but one of a series by an individual who perpetrates these types of crimes over a period of time."

Cooper suggested several aspects of Lisa's murder that pointed to a sophisticated criminal. "Sophisticated" in the sense that he had done something like this before. Cooper noted the distinctive pattern of knife wounds, the amount of control the killer had over the victim, the dumping of Lisa's body in a river in a possible attempt to wash away physical evidence, and the complete disappearance of Lisa's vehicle. It was noted that the individual was able to keep Lisa in a hidden location for up to six days before killing her. This suggested someone living in an isolated area. Incredibly, it was the Elko Jane Doe case that would eventually have startling links to the Lisa Kimmell Wyoming case.

The Kimmells made one last effort to find Lisa's Honda CRXsi in October 2000. They had always wondered if the vehicle might have been dumped into Alcova Lake, not far from the Old Government Bridge, where Lisa's body had been discovered. NCSO had sent divers into the lake in 1991, but the waters were so murky that they had little success in their search.

By 2000, however, technology had improved and the Kimmells contacted Innerspace Exploration Team, a company in Washington State that used high-tech equipment to search areas of water for shipwrecks, downed airplanes, and human bodies. By this time, Mark Benton was sheriff of Natrona County, and he was on much better terms with the Kimmells than his predecessors had been. In fact, Sheriff Benton approved of the Kimmells using Innerspace Exploration Team for their search of Alcova Lake, and he sent along some officers to help on the project.

Investigator Lynn Cohee, of NCSO, was assigned to Lisa Kimmell's case, and she and Dr. James Thorpen accompanied the Innerspace Exploration Team on a boat, along with its tech crew, while the Kimmells and Sheriff Benton remained on shore. Despite a thorough search of the lake, the most that the boat crew found was an old tire and a picnic table. At least, however, Lake Alcova could now be scratched off the list of possible dump sites where Lisa's car had been deposited.

The Kimmells eventually moved to Denver, Colorado, after many years of living in Billings, Montana. But before their move, and before Lake Alcova was searched, another pretty young woman, two counties west of Natrona County in Wyoming, suddenly went missing in July 1997. Just like Lisa, she was a responsible young woman who was not apt to put herself in dangerous situations. And just like Lisa, she was, as Greg Cooper had noted, in the wrong place at the wrong time. He might have added, "She most likely came into contact with the wrong individual."

III

WHERE THE RIVERS DISAPPEAR

7

"SUDDENLY
SHE WAS GONE."

Amy Wroe Bechtel, of Lander, Wyoming, was a pretty twenty-four-year-old blonde, five-five, weighing 110 pounds, with blue eyes. Amy was the daughter of Duane and JoAnne Wroe, of Powell, Wyoming. Duane was a retired city administrator and former cop. Amy had gone to the University of Wyoming and was an outstanding runner on the school's team. In fact, she hoped to compete as a marathon runner in the 2000 Olympics. In 1996, Amy married Steve Bechtel, who was athletic in his own right, a very accomplished rock and mountain climber. They moved to Lander near the beautiful Wind River Mountains, where there was ample opportunity for rock climbing and outdoor sports.

The Lander area, unlike parts of Natrona County, was hemmed in by the spectacular Wind River Mountains to the west. This was "picture postcard" Wyoming, with lofty peaks, immense forests, and pristine mountain lakes. Many vacationers traveled there to picnic and camp in the summertime, and it was popular with fishermen, hunters, and winter sports enthusiasts. Amy and Steve lived in a small house on Lucky Lane, in Lander, next to other accomplished rock climbers. Next-door neighbor Todd Skinner had made difficult ascents on rock faces, from California's Sierra Nevada Mountains, to the Canadian Yukon, to cliffs in the Himalayas.

Amy began working part-time jobs at the Wind River Fitness Center and Sweetwater Grille. She also took photographs once in a while for a local newspaper, the *Wyoming State Journal.* Editor Bill Sniffin later wrote of Amy, *She is cute, with a beauty that is more than skin deep. She smiles a big shy smile that shows off her dimples. Amy loves Lander and our Big River Mountains.*

On Thursday, July 24, 1997, both Amy and Steve had a day off from their jobs at Wild Iris Mountain Sports in Lander. Amy told her husband, Steve, that she was setting off to run some errands around town. Since Amy and Steve were buying a new house across town from Lucky Lane, there were a lot of items on her to-do list. Meanwhile, Steve took off on a seventy-five-mile trip to the Dubois area, where he was going to scout a new climbing route with a friend, Sam Lightner, who would meet him there.

Amy stuck around Lander for a while, and taught a children's weight-lifting class at the Wind River Fitness Center. Later, she picked up the fitness center's recycling, then contacted the phone and electric companies about turning off power and the phone in her old residence. A short time later, Amy showed up at the Camera Connection on Main Street because she wanted to ask advice about some photos she was considering entering into a competition. Amy spoke with store owner John Strom, and he recalled that she was wearing a running outfit of a yellow shirt, black shorts, and running shoes.

After visiting the Camera Connection, Amy went to Gallery 331 and spoke with Greg Wagner there. He remembered her being in a hurry, as if she had a tight schedule. She kept glancing at her watch as she spoke with him. When she left, it was about 2:30 P.M.

Even though Amy didn't tell people where she was going next, she apparently headed up Loop Road, to the west of Lander, to check out a 10K route she intended to run in an upcoming event. This would have taken her from ten to fifteen miles outside of town on a two-lane blacktop road that eventually became a dirt road when it entered Shoshone National Forest. From the end of the pavement, it wound steeply up a mountainside toward Frye Lake.

Steve Bechtel came home around 4:30 P.M. and was not initially concerned by Amy's absence. They often did different activities without telling the other what the plan was for the afternoon. When Steve got home, he went next door and spoke with Todd Skinner and Amy Whisler for a while. Neither one of them had seen Amy Bechtel since midday. When Steve went home again, he noticed that Amy's rock-climbing gear and camera were still there, so she apparently was not out doing one of those activities. Since her running shoes were gone, Steve surmised that she was out running somewhere. She often went on five- or six-mile runs in the area.

When Amy didn't arrive home by 9:00 P.M., however, Steve began to be concerned. He phoned Amy's parents in Powell and asked if Amy had gone there on a spur-of-the-moment trip. She hadn't. When the parents asked if anything was wrong, Steve didn't want them to worry, so he said no.

He was worried, however; and around 10:30 P.M., Steve phoned the Fremont County Sheriff's Office (FCSO) and reported Amy missing. The FCSO sent two deputies to talk with Steve at his house, and the officers began to organize a search-and-rescue team that was slated to go out at first light.

Steve's friends Todd Skinner and Amy Whisler didn't wait that long, and they took off looking for Amy Bechtel's white Toyota Tercel. They drove through Lander, then turned west on Loop Road, past Sinks Canyon State Park, and on up into Shoshone National Forest. Around 1:00 A.M., Skinner and Whisler spotted Amy's vehicle parked off the road, near an area known as Burnt Gulch. Whisler phoned Steve on her cell phone and told him they had found Amy's car, but no sign of her. Whisler noted that the car was unlocked and there was a to-do list on the passenger seat of the vehicle. Nothing looked out of place, and it appeared as if Amy had just taken off running and not come back.

After Steve received Whisler's phone call, he and buddy Kirk Billings headed up Loop Road as well. Then he, Kirk, Todd, and Amy searched with flashlights in the forest for the missing friend. They called out her name, but received no response. Uppermost in their minds was that either Amy had fallen down somewhere and was now unconscious, or she had been attacked by a bear. In that rugged wilderness, that last scenario was a real possibility.

For whatever reason, the official search-and-rescue excursion began even earlier than planned. Sheriff's deputies arrived on scene around 2:00 A.M., and they discovered Amy's car keys underneath a to-do list on the front seat of her car. On the bottom of the list, Amy had written about milepost checkpoints along the Loop Road, in connection to the upcoming 10K race. One of Amy's pens was found on the road, about three-quarters of a mile from the vehicle. It was known to be her pen because it was a relatively expensive Zenith pen, and Steve recognized it as the one Amy always carried in her fanny pack. Her fanny pack and wallet were now missing.

By 3:00 A.M., a major search was under way, with more and more people showing up to look for the missing woman. At this point, it was termed a "search-and-rescue" mission, with the assumption she had become lost in the rugged terrain, or had injured herself and could not make it back to the car.

By the next day, search-and-rescue crews were using dogs to try and find Amy, and two private helicopters and one hundred volunteers were scouring the mountainous, forested, rocky terrain as well. By July 27, almost one thousand calls an hour were coming into the FCSO command post. A handheld infrared detection device was flown in from Cheyenne, and a helicopter arrived from the F.E. Warren Air Force Base. Searchers combed the areas around Frye, Fiddler, and Louis Lakes on horseback, and all-terrain vehicles (ATVs) set off cross-country on other search efforts. Another helicopter arrived from the Bureau of Indian Affairs (BIA), and volunteers scoured ravines, creeks, rivers, and rocky areas. The FCSO sheriff put in an appeal to Rock Springs and Green River, Wyoming, for help in the search. He told a reporter, "Since we haven't found a darn thing, foul play is a possibility."

In fact, by July 29, the authorities started searching places where a body might be hidden, such as abandoned mines, cabins, caves, and culverts. Duplicates of Amy's shoes and the clothing she had been wearing were purchased so as to give the searchers an idea of what to look for. By now, hundreds of ordinary citizens had volunteered to help out on the ground search and to distribute posters.

The volunteers were searching the area thoroughly in what was known as a "critical separation" search. That meant that each searcher was only far enough away from another that every square inch of terrain was covered. Every tree, every boulder, every nook and cranny, was searched and recorded. The search leader, section chief John Gookin, told a reporter for the *Lander Journal,* "We did a hasty search first, looking for obvious clues, and then a fine search." The reporter stated later in the article, "These guys are really organized. You can tell they've done this before." The main search area covered locations from Fossil Hill to Blue Ridge along the Loop Road.

One thing that was discovered was a shoe print similar in size to the shoes that Amy Bechtel wore. This shoe print was found in a rough drainage known as Canyon Creek. Just what she might have been doing there couldn't be surmised, or if it really was her shoe print at all. But since the finding of the Zenith pen on the Loop Road, this was the first tangible clue found in days. There were no signs of torn clothing, blood, or other evidence if Amy had been attacked by a bear.

The command center, which had been set up on Loop Road, was moved back to the FCSO office for better centralization, and twenty-five agents from the Wyoming Division of Criminal Investigation and FBI joined the sheriff's department deputies and detectives. With their aid, both ends of the Loop Road were blocked off, and all motorists who wanted to drive into the national forest by those routes had to check in at the roadblocks.

Dave King, the lead investigator for FCSO, told a reporter, "We're just continuing to do the same things, interview the people in Amy's life, the people who can possibly help us understand if someone abducted her. We're trying to analyze any possibilities, and we're trying to get a focus on this thing. She disappeared under circumstances not under her control."

Several people in the area were questioned, including a couple from Texas who were found at Sinks Canyon State Park in a stolen car. A Lander couple, Jim and Wendy Gibbon, contacted FCSO and told the investigators that they had been driving on the Loop Road on the day that Amy disappeared. They had passed a female runner along the road and noted it, because that was an unusual sight so far from town. Jim Gibbon said, "The odds are, it was her. She was on the stretch of road between the youth camp turnoff and Sawmill, heading toward Sawmill Creek at about five P.M."

Bill Sniffin, of the *Wyoming State Journal*, wrote of the volunteers searching for Amy, *There are tree huggers and tree cutters. There are mountain bike riders and mountain motorbike riders. There are horseback riders and ATV riders. There are ardent environmentalists and ardent multiple use advocates. They are all together, working together toward the common goal. That goal is to find one of our own.*

Amy's twenty-fifth birthday party was put on hold by her family, and a handmade birthday card and yellow ribbon were placed by her mom on the Wroes' front door. A framed print of an osprey, by artist Morten Solberg, from Duane and JoAnne to their daughter, remained in its packaging.

Because of his former occupation in law enforcement, Duane Wroe knew exactly what was happening with the task force committed to finding Amy. Duane agreed that the ground search had been carried out well, with up to twenty people abreast, combing the ground in a thorough manner for clues. They looked for anything that might be significant: a hair band, a credit card, a wallet, socks, or a sign of struggle. Despite all their effort, the most they came up with was the one shoe print that might have been Amy's.

Duane admitted, "This stage of the investigation is tedious. They hammer away at any leads. When they find one that's a blind alley, they drop it and go on. They're not bypassing anything."

Duane and JoAnne Wroe were constantly traveling back and forth between their home in Powell and Lander, almost two hundred miles away. When they arrived there one day, they were astounded by the sight greeting them—Main Street had become covered with yellow ribbons and yellow balloons. Duane said later, "We both lost it. Those people in the community have been wonderful." There were yellow ribbons on telephone poles, trees, and parking meters. Lander was a sea of yellow, all up and down Main Street.

On August 1, Steve Bechtel was in an interview with various agents between two and three hours, when one from the FBI suddenly spoke up. Out of the blue, according to Steve, the agent said, "I have evidence that proves you killed Amy. We would like to have you take a polygraph test right now to prove that you didn't."

Steve was floored, and terminated the interview. Whether the agent really did have evidence, or this was just standard procedure—because all spouses are high on the list when a mate goes missing and is considered murdered—the agent didn't say. Whatever the circumstances, Steve Bechtel soon retained the services of Kent Spence, the son of famed defense lawyer Gerry Spence. Gerry Spence was noted for never having lost a case in a murder trial.

Now that he was a suspect, Steve Bechtel's pickup truck was searched by FCSO detectives, and so was the house that Steve and Amy had shared. The detectives were looking for evidence, including any DNA evidence of Amy, such as blood spatter, loose hairs, and toenail and fingernail clippings. They also looked for any diary or journal she might have recently kept. Kent Spence later referred to the detectives' search as "aggressive and insulting." FCSO sheriff Larry Matthews countered that it was just routine, and "was to gather items of Amy's in case a body was found." Matthews said later he was not surprised of how little evidence was found in the home and pickup, but he was surprised by Steve Bechtel's refusal to take a polygraph test, which would have eliminated him as a suspect. Matthews told a reporter, "These tests are commonly used by law enforcement. It's not like it's voodoo or a witch hunt or something like that."

Investigator Dave King added, "The investigation is not centered on Steve Bechtel. At some point, we need to eliminate or confirm human remains somebody may discover—that's why the search of the house and pickup."

Soon thereafter, Sheriff Matthews had a new wrinkle added to the search of the pickup and the Bechtel home. He told reporters, "There was some questionable substance found in the truck. Biological things. I'm not indicating there was anything there, but I'm not saying there wasn't either." At this point, Sheriff

Matthews and his detectives were playing everything very close to the vest. Amy's parents and siblings were, of course, disturbed by what seemed like great reluctance on the part of Steve to tell everything he knew.

Eventually Steve Bechtel sat down with a reporter from the *Lander Journal*. In the article STEVE BECHTEL ANSWERS TOUGH QUESTIONS, Steve addressed many of the concerns that surrounded him in relation to Amy. Steve started off by telling how he and Amy had met, and said that they had a "synergistic marriage." By that, he said he meant, "It's a biological term for two entities that promote each other's well-being." Steve answered questions about Amy's running habits, and said she often ran alone on trails near Sinks Canyon State Park. He also said that he and his friends tried to think where she might have been running when she disappeared. One scenario was that she ran down Burnt Gulch and back, which would have taken her a little over thirty minutes to complete. Asked if he knew she was going to run near Burnt Gulch that day, he answered that he couldn't say that to a hundred percent assurance, but he likened it to knowing that she would brush her teeth in the morning. He didn't have to see it to surmise that was the case.

One tough question was about a woman on the Loop Road on the day Amy disappeared who saw a pickup truck that supposedly looked just like Steve's pickup truck on the road that afternoon; he was supposed to have been miles away. The reporter asked if that was him. Steve answered that the woman in question had seen a pickup truck like his racing down the road on July 24. When investigators asked her about it later, she supposedly said that she was "one hundred percent sure it was Steve's truck." Yet, Steve said, "I didn't get back from Dubois until four-thirty P.M., and

I talked to two friends, Todd and Amy (Wisler), at four-fifty P.M." So, in Steve's scenario, the woman had to be wrong, since she placed the pickup she saw on Loop Road in that time frame.

Asked what he originally thought had happened, Steve said he didn't see a note around the house of why she would be gone so late, so he called the fitness center around 5:15 P.M. and asked if Amy was there. Then he called Wild Iris Mountain Sports, with the same results. Steve said he even went to Wild Iris later and asked "What's up with Amy?" He said he was casual in his questions, because he didn't want to seem like he was in panic mode. Then he added that he was "starting to get pissed off" because he thought maybe she went to visit her parents without telling him.

He said he next sat around and had dinner with some friends and then called Amy's parents around 9:00 P.M. Steve related that he was going to go out to Sinks Canyon at that point, but thought it would be a stupid idea because he could search all night in the dark and not find a thing. It was finally between 10:00 P.M. and 10:30 P.M. when he called the sheriff's office. Asked what he thought at that point, he said he thought she had hurt herself out in the woods.

Another tough question was why he refused to take a polygraph test. Steve replied, "Well, I had been answering (investigators') questions for two or three hours. One FBI guy tried to look big and tough. He said, 'I've been in the business for twenty-three years. I believe we have evidence to indicate that you were involved in the murder of your wife.' At that point, I said, 'I have no more to say to you. I want to talk to a lawyer.'" Steve added that he was very upset by this allegation, since he believed he had been very cooper-

ative with authorities. As to why he retained Kent
Spence as his lawyer, Steve said that a friend recom-
mended him.

Spence soon had a comment for reporters as well,
and said, "The FBI in their usual sensitive manner attacked Steve Bechtel when they became frustrated with
their failure to come up with any clues. They pointed
their cannons at him and accused him of being involved, when they had no evidence whatsoever."

Amy's parents and friends distributed missing person
posters in nearby national parks, hundreds of truck
stops, and every chamber of commerce in Wyoming. By
late August, the search was not only on the ground and
in the air, but clear out in space as well. The authorities
asked for photos from NASA, and even from the Russian Space Station, *Mir.* It just so happened that *Mir* had
been passing overhead on the day Amy disappeared
and had taken photographs of the Wyoming area.

Amy's case had people in the area talking about another mysterious abduction that had occurred in
nearby Riverton in April 1989. Forty-one-year-old
Kathleen Pehringer was a woman who was five-two,
weighed 120 pounds, had light brown hair and brown
eyes. As the missing person poster attested: *She was last
seen at her Riverton, Wyoming home on April 17, 1989. Authorities believe she left her residence willingly with someone
she knew and intended to be gone for a short time. There was
no sign of struggle in Pehringer's house. She has never been
heard from again. Foul play is suspected in her case.*

All throughout the summer and into autumn, false
leads of Amy being sighted came from Texas, Wiscon-
sin, New Mexico, Utah, and Colorado. It was a repeat
of what had occurred with Lisa Kimmell years before—

people believing they had seen the missing young woman, only to confuse her with someone else. On September 28, a 10K run was held in honor of Amy and to raise money for her search fund. The run was held on Loop Road in the area where she would have gone running herself in the original event.

By that point, the 10K run was officially called the Amy Bechtel Hill Climb. The race route wound up the Loop Road from Sinks Canyon State Park to Frye Lake, not far from where Amy's vehicle had been found. Steve Bechtel spoke to the gathered runners at the start line. He said, "Amy had wanted to do this race for a couple of years. She was told the only people who would show would be eight of her former track teammates." This brought a cheer from the 146 runners who had entered the competition. Then Steve concluded, "We're in this together. We know Amy's alive."

Of course, by that point, all indications were that Amy was no longer alive. And Nels Wroe, Amy's brother, and his wife, Teresa, were conspicuously absent from the race, even though Amy's parents and sisters were there. Teresa worked as the director of a center for domestic abuse, and both she and Nels were not happy about Steve's continued refusal to take a polygraph test about certain things concerning the day Amy disappeared. Nels told a reporter about some of the things he had been shown by investigators concerning Amy in Steve's journal. Nels called these things "disturbing," and said there were signs from Steve that he was jealous of Amy to the point of obsession.

Investigators began searching deep old mine shafts in the Atlantic City, Wyoming, area near South Pass. This was where the famed Oregon Trail finally topped the Continental Divide at 7,550 feet, on its long descent to the Pacific Coast. Nothing turned up in the mine shafts. The investigators also started looking at a man named Kelly McLoud, who had become infatuated with Amy when she worked as a waitress at a coffee shop. Apparently, McLoud had been on the run for seven years when he met Amy in the Laramie coffee shop. Amy got McLoud interested in running, and he entered a few races in the area. Then as he got more obsessive about her, she became uncomfortable with him. This Kelly McLoud was not in the area now, but rumor put him up in Canada.

By the autumn of 1997, Nels Wroe was particularly fed up with what he saw as Steve Bechtel's lack of cooperation with law enforcement. On Wyoming Public Radio, Nels said, "Right now, the key to finding her lies in his head. And I don't mean that in some weird, dime-store novel kind of way. He is the closest person we have to Amy. He was the closest when she disappeared."

Nels added that without knowing Steve's side of the story of what happened, "things looked scary." Most important of all, Nels said, "there were some things the FBI has presented to our immediate family that are disturbing. Steve has to answer some of these questions for us, so we can move on in the investigation." Just what the "disturbing" things were, Nels was instructed not to reveal by the FBI.

It wasn't until January 1998 that investigators learned they would not be receiving a photo from the Russian Space Station, *Mir.* Even though *Mir* had taken photos of the Wind River Mountains on the day Amy went missing, the skies had been overcast, and the photos wouldn't reveal anything of consequence. In another avenue of seeking Steve's cooperation, Amy's sisters Casey and Jenny went on Geraldo Rivera's television talk show and begged Steve Bechtel to cooperate with authorities. Even Geraldo made an on-air plea to Steve in this regard, but Steve did not follow through on the request. With a bit of irony, two weeks later, it was Steve Bechtel who had to be rescued when he had high-altitude sickness while climbing a mountain in the Wind River Range. He was helicoptered out by a rescue crew.

By February 23, 1998, the relationship between Steve Bechtel and law enforcement was more strained than ever. Investigators now revealed they could not account for Steve's location on July 24, 1997, between 2:30 and 5:00 P.M. Steve had told investigators that he and Sam Lightner went scouting some rocks to climb, up near Dubois, Wyoming, but no one had actually seen them there. And Steve said they had bought a hammer at a Dubois hardware store, but he no longer had a receipt for it. By this time, Lightner was not cooperating with law enforcement as well. Just like Steve, he refused to take a polygraph test.

Shortly after 5:00 P.M., on July 24, 1997, Steve had placed a long-distance phone call, and later through-out the evening, he was seen by various people around Lander. But his actions were not constantly observed during that period of time. When Steve finally reported Amy missing, around 10:30 P.M., to the sheriff's office, Detective King said that Steve did it "almost in a lighthearted, joking manner." King also told a reporter, "He's exercised his right to keep his mouth shut forever. Steve's actions are perfectly legal. But I can also tell you that they're an obstruction to this investigation."

To all of this, Steve's lawyer, Kent Spence, replied that Steve had been more than cooperative with authorities, until the FBI agent accused him of killing his wife. Spence said that Steve had been very specific about details of where he had been on July 24, 1997.

About the refusal to take a polygraph test, Spence declared, "Why would I ever allow a client to take a polygraph test, where they could end up with a false positive reading, and then be falsely accused of being involved in something like this?"

In March 1998, Kelly McLoud was finally located serving time in an Oregon jail. He had originally jumped bail in Paducah, Kentucky, in 1991, and been on the run ever since. Then in February 1998, he was arrested and jailed in Medford, Oregon. Authorities went out to interview him, and McLoud was able to prove that he had been on the East Coast on July 24, 1997, the day Amy went missing. Dave King had one more interesting thing to add, however. King said, "McLoud offered valuable information to us of a personal nature about Amy, and about Amy and Steve's relationship. We didn't hear anything unexpected." Just what was revealed, King didn't say.

A few weeks later, *People* magazine ran an article with photos of Amy, and a couple in Sarasota, Florida, contacted authorities. They were sure that they'd recently seen Amy standing barefoot in a parking lot in the rain, looking disoriented. Several other people also saw the same woman and called authorities with their sightings.

When these tips were checked out, however, the woman turned out to be a homeless woman from Washington, who had an uncanny resemblance to Amy Bechtel. Florida officers were quoted as saying, "From a distance, it sure looked like Amy. But when we got closer and interviewed her, it definitely was not her."

During the week of June 17 through 21, 1998, the FCSO, the Fremont County Search and Rescue Team, and the FBI conducted a joint training/search in the Wind River Mountains. It was not only a scheduled training exercise, but also a chance to look for any traces of Amy Bechtel. Once again, no trace of the young woman surfaced. And yet, something very interesting was just around the corner. In September 1997, a man had stepped out of the shadow and tried abducting another young woman. He had done it right down the road from the Wind River Mountains in Sweetwater County, Wyoming, not that many miles from Lander. Once his actions were revealed, the abduction of Lisa Marie Kimmell and the disappearance of Amy Wroe Bechtel would be seen in a whole new light. And the person that law enforcement would be looking at very carefully was a man named Dale. The same Dale who attacked Scott and Shannon Breeden in September 1997. Steve Bechtel might not have been off the list of suspects in the disappearance of Amy, but this man Dale was going to shoot way up the list as well.

8

"THAT MANIAC TRIED TO KILL US!"

Of course, on September 12, 1997, Dale Eaton was lying in the middle of a dirt road, out near the Red Desert of Wyoming, having attacked the Breedens and then having been beaten up and stabbed by them. The Breedens knew they had barely escaped with their lives, and Shannon raced the van down the road about a mile until she spotted a small group of houses and storage sheds. These belonged to a workstation for the Wyoming Transportation Department, and, luckily, there were four occupied houses at that location. While Scott and Cody stayed in the van, Shannon jumped out and went looking for help. A woman who lived in one of the houses was a security guard for the Bridger Power Plant, and she stared out her front window at an incredible sight. Standing in front of her house was a woman who was muddy, bloody, barefoot, and looked half-insane.

Going outside to see what was going on, this woman confronted Shannon; Shannon's story came tumbling out in a jumble of words. All the security guard could make out at first was that the strange woman had been assaulted by someone. She screamed about some maniac who had just tried to kill her and her family.

Shannon asked the woman for help, and the security guard called 911. Shortly thereafter, two patrol cars arrived on scene. One was driven by Officer Tibbets, of the Wyoming Highway Patrol, and the other by Deputy Sheriff David Gray, of the Sweetwater County Sheriff's Office. Gray noted later, "The woman was still wired tight. Still afraid of something."

It was hard to make out exactly what had occurred, and the officers at first thought the long-haired man in the van, holding a baby, had attacked the woman. They put him into handcuffs, but Shannon yelled, "That's my husband! Let him go!"

The officers separated Shannon and Scott, taking each one to a different patrol car. Slowly their stories seemed to meld—the couple had been attacked by someone named Dale, and they'd left that person lying on a dirt road a few miles away.

Other officers were dispatched to the area where the couple indicated they had left the attacker. When officers arrived there, they did indeed find someone named Dale, still lying in the dirt, beat up pretty badly and bleeding from a stab wound to his chest. They gave him some first aid to stop the bleeding before an ambulance arrived and transported him to a hospital.

Even hours later, it was still hard for law enforcement officers to make out exactly what had happened. At first, they thought Scott and Shannon were just a couple of vagrant "wacked-out hippies" who had attacked the man. But after a while, Scott and Shannon's stories were consistent, and the man's stories were not.

Officers learned that the man was fifty-two-year-old Dale Wayne Eaton, and his story kept changing about what had just occurred. In one tale, he said he'd picked up the couple who were having vehicle trouble, and as he drove along, he heard them whispering as if they wanted to rob him. A fight had ensued, and they'd gotten the better of him.

Soon, however, Dale started telling a more unusual story, about how he had cancer or some other life-threatening disease. When he'd spotted the couple, he decided to pick them up and start a fight with them, in the hopes they would kill him. Dale said he didn't have the guts to kill himself, so these two could do the job for him. The story went all over the place, and officers wondered if Dale was mentally unstable.

Dale started telling Detective Rich Haskell, of SCSO, "Here, lately, I've been on a real short fuse. I shouldn't be around people. I should get up and walk away. I like being by myself. It's just weird. I'm depressed about a job deal." Dale went on about the job deal, and then once again about his supposed life-threatening illness. Not much of what he said made a whole lot of sense.

When detectives looked into Dale's van, they found items that seemed to corroborate the Breedens' story. The van held a pair of handcuffs, and when asked about them, Dale said they were a sex toy. He had an ex-girlfriend who liked being restrained during sex, according to Dale. He said he wanted to sell the handcuffs and a vibrator, but he had no takers. He also related that he didn't have a key for the handcuffs, but the detectives found one on a key chain belonging to him.

Sweetwater County chief deputy attorney Anthony "Tony" Howard later said, "It was real odd. Eaton's statement was that he had cancer or a life-threatening disease and he wanted to commit suicide. He was hoping they would kill him. Suicide by stranger. He would almost seem believable at times. Mixing in lies and the truth together."

Eventually the detectives did not believe Dale Eaton's stories about what had occurred out on the dirt road, and neither did Deputy Attorney Howard. SCSO officer Sheppard wrote out a probable cause report against Dale Eaton that had multiple clauses. It mostly followed what Shannon Breeden had told them, with a few new wrinkles. Near the end of the struggle, after having been stabbed, Eaton had supposedly declared, "All I wanted was your money!" The Breedens did not believe him; they believed he meant to kill Scott and Cody, rape Shannon, and then kill her as well.

According to the report, the officers found back at the crime scene a substance consistent with blood and a .30-30 Marlin rifle, with a broken stock. Officer Sheppard noted that everything the Breedens said of the incident was consistent, while Eaton's story kept changing.

The next day, the *Rock Springs Rocket-Miner* ran an article about a family who had thwarted a kidnapping attempt and noted that *a 52-year-old Wyoming man was hurting Friday night after a Utah couple foiled his attempt to kidnap them and their baby.* According to the report, Eaton claimed to have had a clogged fuel filter when he first pulled off the road near the Breedens' van. At the end of the article, it reported that Dale Eaton was treated at Memorial Hospital of Sweetwater County and then released to the sheriff's department, which placed him in the county jail.

Two days later, the *Rocket-Miner* had the correct news that the Breedens were from California, and not from Utah. The newspaper noted that at his first hearing, Dale Eaton claimed to have a problem recalling the incident: *Eaton told the judge he had some memory problems and when asked if he wanted the statement read to him, Eaton commented he probably wouldn't understand it anyway. When asked his age, Eaton said he couldn't remember. "I think it is in the fifties," he said.*

Because of this supposed lack of memory and other statements Eaton had made previously, Deputy County Attorney Dan Erramouspe said that Eaton should be transferred to the state mental hospital for evaluation. Judge Samuel Soule suspended the case, according to Wyoming statute 7-11-301, no bond was given, and a public defense attorney was scheduled to be appointed for Eaton. Whether Dale was actually sent to the state mental hospital was not reported in the newspaper, nor in public court documents.

Later, while in the Sweetwater County Jail awaiting trial, Dale waived his rights to a preliminary hearing on December 18, 1997, and stated that he wanted his lawyer Joel Murphy to move to trial as soon as possible. Trial was set for March 23, 1998, but before that happened, Joel Murphy wrote a memo to the court that he was dropping out as Eaton's lawyer. In a very short document, Murphy wrote on January 30, 1998: *Please be advised that Joel Murphy has withdrawn from the above-captioned case and has been replaced by Scott Nelson, Assistant Public Defender.* Murphy did not give a reason why he was quitting as Eaton's lawyer.

Yet, not even Nelson and Eaton would go to trial.

Before that happened, Dale decided to take a plea deal on April 23, 1998. Dale agreed in the deal that he had not been coerced to do so, he had read the pre-sentencing report, and he did not want to make any changes to it. He agreed that he had already served ninety-nine days in jail, and that was taken into account. By taking the deal, Dale had to promise to do a whole list of things as set forth by the document. Some were even stated in archaic legal language such as, *The Defendant will demean himself in a law abiding manner, live a worthy and respectable life and have no violations of any Federal, State or Local law.* He was also to answer all questions put to him truthfully when asked by law enforcement officers, probation officers, or court personnel. He was to maintain full-time employment when released, and when not doing full-time employment, he had to perform community service.

He was not to *associate with persons of a disreputable character,* nor consume or possess alcohol, or frequent businesses where their main source of income was in dispensing alcohol. He was not to be in the presence of anyone consuming alcohol or using illegal drugs. He was to submit to a blood, breath, or urinalysis test anytime that he was requested to do so. He was to have a mental-health evaluation thirty days from April 23, 1998, and had to attend counseling sessions. He had to pay $50 to the Wyoming Victim Compensation Fund. Dale was not to contact or be in the company of the Breedens at any time.

One short sentence may have seemed inconsequential at the time, but it was to come back and haunt Dale Eaton later. It was stipulation S: *The Defendant may not own, purchase or posses any firearm or weapon.* If Eaton broke any of these conditions, his probationary status was to be revoked immediately, and he was to face further punishment, which probably meant prison time.

Eaton was extremely lucky, in that the judge sentenced him to two to five years of suspended sentence. Eaton didn't even have to go to prison, rather just a halfway house called Community Alternatives of Casper (CAC), where he was required to spend his nights in Casper, Wyoming. Eaton even got his van back so that he could go to work during the daytime. This particularly riled the Breedens, who never did get their own van back. They couldn't afford to pay the amount of money it had cost while it was being stored awaiting trial. They thought Dale Eaton had gotten off very lightly for what he had done.

CAC was a halfway house in Casper that had a structured environment for offenders, such as Eaton. Those who were housed there had to have employment, and were allowed to use their own vehicles during the daytime to drive back and forth from work. They could not stay away from CAC for the night. All in all, considering what he had done, Dale should have been pretty happy with the setup. But he wasn't, and he soon complained to friends of his in a letter.

Dale alleged in the letter that the place was making him sick, and he worried that he had caught tuberculosis there. In part, Dale wrote, *The way the sewer smell comes into the room from the septic tank when the window is open—it would fill the room so bad with sewer gas you would gag. Also I been locked in a room with four guys where if two was standing the others had to be lying down. Everyone there has a cold or something.*

Dale Eaton was a restless sort, and couldn't stay put for long. Not even if it meant getting into deeper trou-

ble later. On June 16, 1998, Eaton jumped into his van
and drove away from CAC and Casper—destination
unknown. Later, he would claim that he just couldn't
stand being confined at CAC at night with the other
people housed there, plus the "sewer smell." A lot of
times, however, he made up stories to mask the real reasons why he did something. For whatever reason
he chose to skip out, there was soon a notice sent to
law enforcement agencies about the noncompliance
of his court agreement. Warrants were arranged for
his arrest.

Dale was listed on the National Crime Information
(NCIC) computer. Sweetwater County deputy attorney Anthony Howard signed a Revocation of Probation Warrant, stating, *The Defendant Dale Wayne Eaton
is in violation of conditions of his probation in that on or
about June 17, 1998, the Defendant did escape from the
Community Alternatives of Casper.*

For weeks, not a sign of Dale Eaton appeared; then
on July 30, 1998, Wyoming Fish and Game officer Bill
Long was on a routine patrol in the Bridger-Teton
National Forest, not far from famed Grand Teton National Park. Grizzly bears had been marauding through
the area in search of food, and Long wanted to make
sure that campers were storing their food properly
so that bears could not get into the food supplies. As
the day progressed, Officer Long came upon a lone
greenish-colored van parked off Rosie's Ridge Road
in the national forest. Though it wasn't in a desig-
nated camping area, that was all right to do in national
forests. Lots of people just pulled their campers, vans,
and trailers off the roads and camped in the woods.

Just out of protocol, Officer Long noted the van's

license plate and called dispatch with it. Then he went to warn the van's owner about the bears. Officer Long thought the owner was in his late forties and seemed somewhat startled when Long showed up. The man remained nervous as Long told him about the bear problem. Long asked, "Everything all right? I'm talking to everyone in the area and making sure you have a clean camp."

The man responded, "I'm only gonna be here a little while." He refused to meet Officer Long's eyes, and he seemed to be very furtive and somewhat nervous. The man went over to his van and quickly shut a side panel door.

"No bear problems?" Long asked.

"Nope," the man replied.

"Okay, have a good day, sir."

Long didn't drive very far away. There was something just not right about this guy. Within minutes, the dispatcher called Long back with an urgent message. The registered owner of the van was one Dale Wayne Eaton and he was a fugitive felon wanted on warrants. Officer Long had the dispatcher repeat the message, and received the same results.

Officer Long called in for backup and waited, making sure that he blocked the only road in and out of the area. Within thirty minutes, two other law enforcement officers arrived. As the officers moved towards Eaton's van, they noted that he seemed to be gone, and—sure enough—within a short time, they saw him walking back on the road toward his van. The officers moved off silently through the woods, rifles drawn. They hoped it didn't come to a shoot-out, but they wanted to be prepared for any eventuality.

As they neared the van, they saw that Eaton wore no shirt, and he appeared not to have a firearm strapped around his waist. The officers moved out from cover, rifles drawn, and called out for Eaton to drop to his knees, hands in the air, and then lie on his stomach. For a moment, Dale seemed to hesitate, as if wondering if he could make a run for it. Then eyeing three officers with drawn weapons, he decided to comply with their orders.

Eaton was handcuffed, read his rights, and placed into a patrol vehicle. Soon a law enforcement ranger from Grand Teton National Park arrived on the scene as well. It was discovered that Dale had somehow managed to procure a new rifle, and had it in his van, even though he was a felon on the run. Being in violation of a weapons charge, and caught on federal property, Eaton was sent off to federal prison this time.

It all seemed rather routine and minor at the time, but Dale Wayne Eaton's statistics and data were now going to be placed into a federal criminal database. From a long, twisting path, clues and evidence would one day lead back to the abduction and murder of Lisa Marie Kimmell, and authorities would wonder what other murders Dale Eaton might have committed.

9

A ROCKY ROAD

Dale Wayne Eaton was born on February 10, 1945, to Merle and Marian Eaton. Eventually the Eatons would have eight children, Dale being the second oldest. The Eaton family moved around a lot when Dale was young, all throughout the Rocky Mountain states. Merle Eaton held a variety of jobs, mostly as a manual laborer in mining, ranching, and farmwork.

Marian was good to the children, but she suffered from mental problems, possibly schizophrenia, which got worse over time. Dale was very close to his mom, and her deteriorating condition was hard on him. He'd later call her a "good mother," but he realized at a fairly young age that she had problems beyond her control. In some ways, Dale internalized those problems, and wondered if he added to her mental illness, since he had a short temper.

Because of his combativeness, Dale made few friends in school. He was a slow learner, and seemed immature for his age. A great deal of responsibility fell upon Dale when he was young because his father often couldn't find work locally, and he would be gone for protracted periods of time. It fell upon Dale's shoulders to not only take care of the farm animals, but to take care of his younger siblings as well. He took a certain amount of pride in that, but it was also a burden for one so young.

At least Dale stuck up for his other brothers and sisters, and he was protective of them. A younger brother, Allen, had cerebral palsy, and sometimes Dale would wheel Allen to school in a little wagon. If any boys at school teased Allen about his condition, Dale was soon to pick a fight with them and probably win. He was big and strong for his age, and as time went on, other boys at school learned not to tangle with Dale.

In 1960, the Eaton family moved to Meeker, Colorado, where Merle got a job as a gas station attendant. Dale loved the region. He was always an outdoor type, and the area was filled with streams, nearby mountains, and forests. One thing he did not like was school, and Dale would later say he started running away from school and home in the third grade. Later documents, however, would show this as starting in the fifth grade. Whatever the year, Dale would say it was out of fear of being struck by his father if he came home with a bad report card. And for Dale, bad report cards were becoming a fact all too often.

It's not certain what year Marilyn O'Malley, Dale's aunt, was talking about, but she related later, "There was one time the children were playing around. And when there's several children, there's bound to be a little noise. Merle, when he came home, he expected everything to be quiet. The children were playing, so all of a sudden, Merle jumped out of his chair and grabbed his belt, and it was a big wide belt, with a buckle on it. He started beating Dale. I mean, he beat all of the kids to some extent, but I think Dale got the brunt of it. He seemed always the one who got the first and most."

O'Malley added that she never saw Merle hit his wife or daughters, but she said he often ridiculed Marian. Getting back to Dale, O'Malley recalled, "I felt so sorry for him. I was a young wife with a little child, about a year and a half old. I wanted to get Dale away from that home for a while. So I asked if I could keep him. And he came and stayed with me and my husband for a number of days. Ten days or two weeks. My husband taught him how to fish, and they would go fishing. Dale had a great time with us. I wanted to keep him longer, but his mother said that his dad had work for him to do."

O'Malley also said later that while the Eaton family was living in Meeker, "Dale was always sweet to me. His mom expressed concern for the kids, but she didn't seem to show too much affection or stand up for them. But she loved them."

Dale's mother may have loved the children, but she continued to become more and more of a problem as her mental condition deteriorated. Sometimes she was all there, and at other times, the kids had to fend for themselves. Dale would recall her having her first bad "nervous breakdown" in 1961.

One day, Dale came home from school to find a fire truck in front of the house, which they were renting at the time. His mother had just tried burning the place down. She was taken away by authorities to a mental hospital for treatment, and this had a grave impact upon Dale. Her condition became so bad that she was given electroshock therapy more than once.

For almost six months, the Eaton children did not see their mother. In those days, mental illness was viewed more with shame than as just another illness that needed medical treatment. Despite his mother's absence, however, Dale thrived in providing for the other children. He fished and hunted, often getting extra food for the table. There was nothing he liked more than going off into the woods by himself with a rifle. Dale had a real knack for living outdoors and a lot of what he learned there was self-taught.

Meeker, however, was on the other side of the Rocky Mountains, and about two hundred miles away from Greeley, Colorado, where Marian Eaton was now housed in a mental ward. The trips for Merle were becoming too laborious and time-consuming, and he moved the whole family to Greeley to be closer to Marian. Dale absolutely hated the move. Whereas Meeker had been a haven for hunting and fishing, Greeley sat upon the edge of the Great Plains and was farming country, rather than open ranching country and mountainous country.

Dale liked school even less at Greeley, and he was held back a year when he was sixteen. And it was at this age that he had his first psychiatric evaluation. It came about because a physician noted that Dale had trouble relating to others, especially classmates and adult authority figures. Dale didn't seem to have any friends at school and was a loner. In a report, he was diagnosed as being *a depressed youngster, and has serious emotional problems.* It's not clear when, but Dale was treated at the Colorado Psychopathic Hospital around this time. Just what treatment method was used was not related later in public files.

Despite this treatment, Dale started getting into serious trouble around Greeley. One time, when he was sixteen years old, he apparently needed new tennis shoes for gym class, but he didn't have enough money to buy a pair. According to one of his sisters, Dale stole either some pumpkins or watermelons from a neighbor's yard. Dale intended to sell the items for cash. When approached by the neighbor lady, a confrontation ensued, and in a fit of anger, Dale stabbed her with a knife. She recovered from her wound, but Dale was sent off to juvenile authority, cited with burglary and assault with a deadly weapon.

Dale was sent to the Lookout Mountain School for Boys, which, despite the name of "School," was a reformatory. Dale actually did well at the school, perhaps because of its regimented structure. He learned a lifelong trade there of welding, and he had a knack for it, the same way he had a knack for outdoor activities, such as fishing and hunting.

When Dale got out of the reformatory at the age of nineteen, he met a girl of sixteen whom he really fell for. She liked him as well, and they were soon together a lot. Even the rest of the Eaton kids liked this girl, and the pair got engaged. Dale, however, was out of the area all during the week, working on jobs, and only home on weekends. It put a large strain on their relationship. Being that she was so young, the girl eventually found another boyfriend and called off the engagement to Dale. He was devastated by the breakup.

The loss of his girlfriend seemed to send Dale into another round of trouble with the law. He would steal items, get caught, and be sent to jail. Put on probation, he would be okay for a while, and then get into trouble again. Eventually he wound up in the Buena Vista Correctional Facility in Colorado.

Located near the town of Buena Vista, in the beautiful Arkansas River Valley, fourteen-thousand-foot Yale

Peak towered over the prison facility to the west. But
Dale wasn't there for the view. He was housed with
about a thousand other inmates in a level-three facility for medium-risk prisoners.

In fact, throughout the 1960s, Dale Eaton was in and
out of Buena Vista several times for new crimes and
parole violations of crimes he had already committed.
Then in the early 1970s, Dale seemed to settle down a
bit. He became a member of the Operating Engineers
Union and helped build a church. He even became an
active member in the church congregation.

Then Dale married a young woman named Melody,
in 1971. He was twenty-six years old at the time, and
she was eighteen. This choice was not a good one for
either Dale or for Melody in the long run. Dale would
later say that on their wedding night she told him that
she wanted a divorce, not a very auspicious beginning
to a marriage. From day one, there was a lot of acri-
mony in the marriage, starting out with verbal arguments and progressively getting worse.

In the coming years, there would be testimony by a
witness about this volatile marriage. The witness said
under oath, "Early in the relationship, Mr. Eaton was
the primary source of support. He worked primarily
as a welder. His longest job was about a year or year
and a half. That was a long time for him. He changed
jobs frequently. He had difficulty getting along with
coworkers and got into altercations with them. Sometimes he left a job for no apparent reason."

According to Dale, Melody was fairly wild, and actually slapped him around, although he was much
bigger than she was. Dale may not have hit her back
initially, but that soon came to an end. A teenage girl
named Dixie Brewbaker would later tell authorities
what she saw of Dale and Melody and their fights,

both verbal and physical. The sudden rages that Dale could get into scared Dixie.

Dixie recalled, "My parents and Dale were friends, and I knew Dale when he worked out, at the Gas Hills Mines. Dale was fine until he lost his job at the mines. Then he and Melody moved in with us, and I was terrified of him. He would argue with Melody and he would hit her. One time, I saw him hit her [in] the face with his fist in a hallway during the day.

"On another day, I came home from school, and Melody had prepared a pork roast. It smelled differently than what my mother fixed. I opened up the oven door and pulled out the roaster. And I saw garlic cloves had been inserted into the pork. All I said was 'Mom doesn't fix it like that.'

"Dale burst into the kitchen. The evilness in his eyes, the look on his face! He looked so powerful, very controlled in what he was doing. When I saw him coming at me, it scared me to death. He grabbed ahold of me, took me over to the table, took my head and hair, and kept ramming it down into the plate that was on the table. And he said, 'Eat it, you'll eat every bit of it! You hear me? You'll eat every bit of it!' I yelled back, 'There's nothing to eat!'"

Dale began to choke Dixie with his bare hands. She recalled, "I thought to myself, 'I'm dying!' Everything was going dark. I felt like a dishrag. Powerless.

"Melody yelled, 'Leave her alone! Stop it, Dale! You're killing her!'"

Finally Dale quit choking Dixie.

"I'm going to tell my daddy!" Dixie screamed.

Dale grabbed the telephone and yelled, "Go ahead! Tell your daddy!" Then he hit her in the face very hard. She recalled, "He had a thing about the face. He didn't hit me anywhere else."

Dixie and her father filed charges against Dale, but her stepfather and mother would not. Dixie thought they were too afraid of Dale to do so. Dixie told authorities later that she was amazed that Dale didn't beat his wife to death at some point.

Dale and Melody eventually had three children, two sons and a daughter, but the years were filled with turmoil and fights. An unnamed witness testified years later, "Toward the end of the marriage, Melody became more of the primary support of the family. She took on more responsibility. She became very disenchanted with the conflict in the family and the instability of his work. He, at this time, was doing occasional welding jobs and some sort of junk business. Salvaging materials and going to flea markets. Sometimes their living conditions were quite rough. Sometimes living in a trailer without amenities."

Melody Eaton had enough by 1979, and filed for divorce, but didn't actually carry it out. She and Dale got back together, only to separate again several times, from 1979 to 1986. Finally in 1986, Melody had had enough, and she divorced Dale for good. Despite all the fights and turmoil Dale took the divorce very hard and threatened to commit suicide. He was taken in for observation at a psychiatric hospital and kept there for a while.

Dr. Linda Gummow, a psychiatrist who saw him later, testified on the stand during a trial that in 1986, "Dale was hospitalized for depression for a few days. He had actually gone to the police department about his depression and they were concerned about him. They took him to the community hospital, where they admitted him and diagnosed him with depression and thought disorder."

When released, Dale's already traumatic life took on a lonelier and bleaker existence. Dale's uncle owned some acres out near Moneta, Wyoming, off U.S. 20/26, and he let Dale live on the place. For the most part, Dale was out there alone. Moneta was only a few buildings out on a windswept plain filled with sagebrush. There were a few willows down along the streambeds, but even the streams were dry throughout much of the year. Compared to Meeker, where Dale had grown up, or even Greeley, out on the Colorado plains, the area around Moneta was sparse and bleak.

Dale's property was nothing to look at, but it did have an old 1950s bus, which no longer ran. The bus was gutted by Dale of its benches, and he made it into a living space. However, it was very spartan, to say the least, with a propane stove and small bed. There was no plumbing or electricity, and in the summer months, if Dale wanted to wash up, he would take a bath in a horse trough. When it got colder, he had to haul water into his bus and heat it on the stove. Nonetheless, Dale settled into his new existence, making money by doing part-time welding jobs and scavenging. It was a hand-to-mouth existence, and not unlike in his childhood, Dale would go out into the hills to hunt for game to supplement his meager food supply. One thing he was always handy with was a knife—for skinning and dressing game that he had shot.

Dr. Gummow testified later, "His lifestyle was very marginal, and Dale was frequently described during this time frame, and later, as not having good hygiene. There was no evidence of it earlier, but later on, he didn't bathe. Sometimes he would go into a car wash and get there in the car wash with the car and bathe himself. Sometimes he went to neighbors. He had no water on the property, so he had to go to various places to get water. His behavior became bizarre. This included his bathing, grooming, and dietary habits."

Dale would scavenge metal, used tools, clothing, auto parts, anything he could lay his hands on, to sell at flea markets. People who knew him during this period also said that Dale would steal whatever he could get away with. One man told law enforcement later, "He was always stealing stuff from farmers, the mines, the railroad—you name it. Then he'd sell it at the flea markets."

Dale basically lived a hermit's life by 1987, but he did have some elderly neighbors named the Buchtas, whom he would visit on occasion. Doris Buchta kept a journal of her daily life, and any little thing in such an isolated place made its way into her journal. Doris would mention whenever Dale showed up at their place. She didn't see him at all from January 15, 1988, to March 8, 1988. Then in March of that year, Dale came over to their residence four times. He also showed up on April 1, 1988, the day after Lisa Kimmell was most likely murdered at the Old Government Bridge.

It was also around this time, or shortly before, that Dale got a job as an "oiler" for a construction company that was doing work on Highway 20/26. Being an oiler meant that he maintained construction equipment after the road workers were done for the day. One thing was for sure—Dale knew about the Waltman Rest Stop during this time period. The work crews would often take their lunch breaks there. And Dale many times washed up there. Dale even told a woman flagger, who worked on the road construction project, not to stop at a rest stop by herself late at night, because she might be raped there. In light of what occurred to Lisa

Kimmell in that area, this was quite a comment coming
from Dale Eaton.

In the summer of 1988, Dale's teenage son Billy
started living with his father on the Moneta property,
and they went to the Buchtas seven or eight times a
month during the summer of 1988. Dale's daughter
even lived with them for a short period of time. Billy
helped his dad work around the place in his scavenging operations. And at one point that summer, Dale
did a very interesting thing. He helped Billy put new
Honda bucket seats into Billy's Ford pickup, and
Honda stereo equipment in there as well. Just where
Dale got these Honda parts, he did not tell his son.
But then Billy didn't think about that a lot—there
were bits and pieces of car parts all over the property.
There was one thing Billy would remember years
later, however, and that was the bucket seats came
from a high-end Honda, like a CRXsi.

Doris Buchta noted that on January 3, 1989, Dale
and his son went to the Salt Lake City area of Utah.
Later, Billy would tell authorities that he and his dad
stayed in Clearfield, Utah, for a couple of weeks and
then moved on to Elko, Nevada. Billy started going to
school in Elko, while Dale got a job in the area. There
was a woman who remembered Dale from this period
as well, and she even had some dates with him. She
would recall later just how dirty he could be a lot of
the time, and she nicknamed him, "Junkyard Dale."
The name fit.

Dale and Billy only stayed in Nevada for a few
months, however, and by April 1989, Doris Buchta
noted that Dale and Billy were back in Moneta. She
wrote in her journal, *Dale and Billy here—brought me 3*

pks Marlborough [sic] *cigs and sweat shirt—Just as full of BS as ever. Billy has a car of his own.*

Doris kept writing about the comings and goings of Dale Eaton, up and through 1992. She noted that he went to work in Gas Hills, Jeff City, and Denver. In April 1993, her journal on Dale ceased when she and her elderly husband moved to Casper to be closer to medical facilities.

Only later would bits and pieces surface as to where Dale Eaton was and what he was doing. In January 1994, he bought a Ford truck in Riverton, Wyoming, and he later installed a phone in Evanston, Wyoming. By February 1994, Dale bought food and gas at the Fort Bridger Travel Stop and got groceries at Sinclair. He bought auto parts all over the area for the next few months, Mountain View and Evanston among them. He seemed to be traveling west a lot in the spring of 1994, then changed direction to the north by summer, to such places as Worland and Thermopolis, Wyoming.

In the winter of 1994 to 1995, Eaton went farther afield, to Idaho Falls, Idaho, and Denver, Colorado. He was constantly on the move, doing small welding jobs, scavenging, and selling items at flea markets. Just what mayhem he may have been up to during that time would become a matter of speculation later on. Chief amongst these speculations would revolve around the disappearance of Amy Wroe Bechtel, of Lander, Wyoming. Dale knew the area well, since he had a relative living nearby. And Moneta wasn't all that far away. A lot of other people had been looked at concerning the disappearance of Amy Bechtel, especially her husband, Steve. But in the years to come, Dale Eaton would suddenly shoot to the top of the list as to who might have kidnapped her and made her disappear.

* * *

What is certain, Dale Eaton stepped out of the realm of speculation on September 12, 1997, when he kidnapped at gunpoint Scott, Shannon, and Cody Breeden. Shannon was sure Dale meant to kill Scott, and probably Cody as well. Then he would take her out into the Red Desert to be raped, and most likely murdered. If not for the desperate struggle that she and Scott had put up, she was sure he would have accomplished just that.

Dale Eaton's days of running around were almost over, after his run-in with the Breedens. He could have kept his head down, done his time at CAC, and probably slipped back into obscurity. But that just wasn't in his makeup. When he fled CAC and became a felon who had broken probation, Eaton's days of freedom were numbered. On July 30, 1998, when Officer Long and the others arrested Dale in the Bridger-Teton National Forest, he was going behind prison bars for good. But even then, his troubles were far from over. The crimes Dale had committed in the past would slowly start bubbling to the surface, and his temper would ensure that he would be in a lot more trouble behind bars. For even behind bars, Eaton would prove that he was not beyond killing someone.

10

TROUBLE WITH
THE FEDS

While Dale Eaton was in the federal penitentiary in Colorado, something occurred with former NCSO sheriff Ron Ketchum that caught everyone by surprise. Ketchum was found dead on Saturday, May 20, 2000, by an NCSO deputy. Ketchum had ended his life by a self-inflicted gunshot wound to the chest. His body was discovered next to his vehicle on Coal Mountain Road, between Casper and Alcova. Just why he decided to drive out to that area not far from where Lisa Kimmell's body had been discovered is not known.

Despite his contentious dealings with the Kimmell family, and his decision not to run for sheriff again, Ketchum was still popular in the Casper area. In fact, he was voted a county commissioner in 1999. Since he received the most votes, Ketchum became the commission's chairman.

County Commissioner Jon Campbell told a reporter upon learning of Ketchum's suicide, "I always liked working with Ron. He was straightforward and he always treated me with respect." Vice Chairman Commissioner Cathy Killen said, "He made the tedious business of the commission kind of fun. He was generally upbeat."

Of course, in the back of most people's minds was the incident of March 24, 1990, in which the hospital was very circumspect as to what had occurred. That incident made it seem that even then Ketchum had made a suicide attempt, since he was known to be very depressed at the time.

One of the hardest hit by Ketchum's suicide was Sheriff Mark Benton. He and Ron had been friends for twenty-six years. In fact, Benton had joined NCSO just thirty days after Ketchum had. They had both started as patrolmen, and then both moved on to investigators about the same time. Ketchum became a captain when Benton became a lieutenant. And when Ketchum was elected sheriff, Mark Benton was appointed as undersheriff.

Benton told a *Casper Star-Tribune* reporter, "Ron, I, and Dave Kinghorn were a tight-knit group. We did a lot of personal things together. I think he was well-regarded as a commissioner." Ron Ketchum was fifty-one years old when he ended his own life on a lonely road in Natrona County.

At his memorial service at Casper's Seventh-day Adventist Church, hundreds of mourners showed up. So many, in fact, that the sanctuary became filled, and an adjacent room was fitted with a video feed so that people in there could watch the service. Law enforcement officers from all over the area lined one wall of the sanctuary. A cousin of Ron's told the gathered people not to be angry about his suicide. She said that Ron wouldn't have wanted that. She added, "He strove for perfection in every aspect of his life." Then she spoke of Ketchum being a military policeman during the Vietnam War, and being frustrated that he couldn't give children over there hugs. The reason, he had been told by his commanding officer that sometimes children were booby-trapped with explosives.

One of Ketchum's uncles said that Ron wanted the song "Smile," written by Charlie Chaplin, to be played at Ron's memorial service. Then the uncle added that Ron wouldn't have wanted any sadness in the church. He spoke of Ron's love of the Fourth of July and fireworks. This uncle noted that Ron always set off some very elaborate displays, and added, "We'll never forget him."

The Kimmell family couldn't forget Ron Ketchum as well. They acknowledged that Ketchum had not been responsible for their daughter's kidnapping and death, but their dealings with him had deteriorated. His death left many unanswered questions in their minds about just how good a job he had done in trying to find Lisa's killer while he had been sheriff of Natrona County.

Dale Eaton was having troubles of his own that same year in the federal penitentiary in Colorado. The trouble began when an inmate named Carl Inman Palmer was assigned to a cell with Dale. Dale was basically a loner and did not like sharing his cell under any circumstances. September 3, 2001, started out like any other day in the facility, with inmates roaming around the common room, where they could watch television, play cards, or read newspapers. Carl Palmer was in the common room, while Dale was back at the cell. Dale put a piece of cardboard in the window of the cell, which was a signal that he was using the toilet and he wanted privacy.

Around 9:30 A.M., a message went out over the loudspeaker for all inmates to return to their cells for a head count. Palmer did as instructed, and either he didn't see the small piece of cardboard in the window, or he thought Dale had heard the message and knew he would be coming back to the cell. Whatever the circumstances, when Palmer entered the cell, Dale became extremely angry. Without a word, he punched Palmer in the side of his head with all his might.

In shock and surprise, Palmer asked, "Why'd you hit me?"

Dale growled back, "What the fuck! I don't come in when you're on the toilet!"

Palmer didn't say another word; instead, he collapsed to the floor. A guard called for help, and soon an ambulance was on its way. Palmer was rushed to emergency. Knowing that he was in real trouble, Dale kept asking, "Is my roomie okay?"

Palmer wasn't okay, however, and he soon died from a ruptured vertebral artery. Now Dale Eaton had a new charge against him—manslaughter, which would be tried in federal court. Yet, bad as this was, a lot worse was soon coming for Dale Eaton. And it was all tied to a small strand of DNA.

Once Dale Eaton was in the federal penitentiary, he had to give a sample of his blood for DNA testing. Unlike an ordinary citizen, Dale had no choice in the matter, since he was now a federal prisoner. This DNA sample was sent to the FBI's database—Combined DNA Index System (CODIS)—but Wyoming's own new state lab was behind on updates, since there were so many changeovers in DNA testing techniques. In fact, until recently, a lot of the Wyoming database system would not know if there was DNA in their databases that would match these with CODIS. Even though the small sample of semen on Lisa Kimmell's panties had been on file for a long time, until it was matched up with a particular individual, it was not going to help at all. And until Dale became a federal prisoner, his DNA wasn't matched up to anything concerning Lisa Kimmell.

The way this came about was that in the year 2000, Cellmark Diagnostics in Maryland created a DNA analysis of the sperm deposited on Lisa Kimmell's underwear. The analysis created a profile to an unknown male, and this DNA profile was entered into the FBI's CODIS database. Later, Bode Technology Group in Virginia ran a DNA profile of Dale Eaton's blood sample that he had to give when becoming a federal prisoner. When this was entered into CODIS, there was suddenly a "hit" between the unknown sperm cell donor connected to Lisa and to Dale Eaton. In July 2002, the Wyoming State Crime Lab got this information and passed it on to NCSO investigators.

After fourteen years of frustration, this was incredible news to the detectives at NCSO. Not once, in the thousands and thousands of tips they had received, had the name Dale Eaton ever come up in connection to Lisa Kimmell. Before going to tell Ron and Sheila Kimmell about the news, Detectives Dan Tholson and Lynn Cohee wanted to check out some things about Dale Eaton first. They went to speak with Dale at an interview room at the federal penitentiary in Colorado, and Dale told them he had heard about Lisa Kimmell in the past on television. He asked, "Wasn't she that girl who was driving to Montana?" Dale rambled on about various things until one of the detectives told him there was a match of his DNA to the dead girl. Then Dale became very quiet and didn't say another word.

July 17, 2002, began as just another ordinary day for Ron and Sheila Kimmell. Ron's parents were visiting, and Ron and his dad went out to run some errands, while Sheila visited with Ron's mom. In midafternoon, Sheila got a phone call from NCSO investigator Lynn Cohee, who was calling from her cell phone. Cohee told Sheila that she and Detective Dan Tholson would be dropping by the Kimmells' home later that afternoon. Even though Cohee tried sounding nonchalant, Sheila knew something big had to be brewing. The detectives wouldn't just be "dropping by" after driving nearly three hundred miles from Casper to the Denver area. Although Sheila tried to learn more about what prompted the detectives to come see them, Cohee said that it would be better to speak with Sheila and Ron in person at the same time.

As soon as Cohee and Tholson arrived, Ron came home with his dad. Everyone sat down, and according to Sheila, "I just blurted out, 'Okay, Ron's here! What's the news!'"

Lynn Cohee replied, "Sheila, it's good news, or at least we think so. We needed to tell you together in person, and not over the phone."

Dan Tholson chimed in at that point, "We think we know who killed Lisa. We have a DNA match."

Both Ron and Sheila were absolutely stunned. It had now been fourteen years of anguish and heartbreak, with one false lead after another. It seemed almost unreal that there might finally be a resolution as to who murdered their daughter. Finally Ron asked, "Can you tell us his name?"

Tholson responded, "Yes. His name is Dale Wayne Eaton."

The name meant absolutely nothing to the Kimmells. There had been dozens if not scores of names that had popped up over the years as suspects in Lisa's case. Dale Wayne Eaton had never been one of those names. The detectives told the Kimmells that Eaton owned property near Moneta, Wyoming, off Highway 20/26, and had probably abducted Lisa off that road on March 25, 1988. Oddly enough, the highway numbers were sometimes referred to by locals as 2/2—the same numbers the "psychic sisters" had seen in their visions about Lisa's abduction and that Agent Flickinger had noted in a report about them.

The investigators added it would take a while to obtain search warrants to thoroughly search Eaton's property, but they wanted to tell the Kimmells first about this news before they heard it from some other source. In a truly ironic set of circumstances, the Kimmells learned that Dale Eaton was now an inmate barely ten miles away from their home, incarcerated at the Federal Correctional Institution (FCI) Englewood.

11

DIGGING
FOR THE TRUTH

Before searching Dale Eaton's property, Detectives
Tholson and Cohee learned that Eaton had left a few of
his belongings at some friend's house near Glenrock,
Wyoming. Before being incarcerated at the federal penitentiary, Dale had stored things there. On July 24,
2002, the detectives did a search at the friend's property
and discovered that Dale had left three vehicles there—
a green 1985 Dodge van, a Ford F600 welding truck,
and a 1982 Ford F-150 pickup. In the vehicles, the
detectives discovered an ax, wooden club, several flex
ties, wire ties, and handcuffs. They also found nine
knives of various sizes, rope, and a blue dildo. It's doubtful that Eaton's friends knew about the more personal
items, or what he was now accused of doing, before the
arrival of the detectives. These friends had never been

in trouble with the law and were "the churchgoing type." They had just allowed Eaton to store things there in boxes while he was in prison.

After the search around Glenrock, the detectives got a search warrant from Judge Thomas "Tom" Sullins, of the Seventh District Court in Casper, to search for items on Dale Eaton's property. Two teams of investigators made their way out to the property in Fremont County, near Moneta. One team consisted of NCSO lieutenant Stewart Anderson, Deputy Mickey Anderson, and Deputy Sexton. This team searched a shed on the property that doubled as a workshop/barn. The other team consisted of NCSO deputy Tracy Warne, Sergeant John Becker, and Deputy Paula Thomason. This team began searching a trailer on the property. More detectives also went to the property, and these included Lynn Cohee, Dan Tholson, and others, who catalogued the items that were found. Detective Tholson and Casper PD crime tech Chris Reed were there to photograph the items that were seized.

Soon others were on the way as well, including NCSO sheriff Mark Benton, Undersheriff Dave Kinghorn, Coroner James Thorpen, and District Attorney Kevin Meenan. Since Eaton's property was actually in Fremont County, and not Natrona County, Fremont County sheriff Roger Millard and FCSO sergeant Roger Rizor would be there as well.

The searchers discovered that all of the structures on the Eaton property were in poor shape, especially since he had essentially abandoned them when forced into prison. The workshop/barn was filled with stray bits of junk, and the entire property had the feel of a junkyard.

Eaton had lived in a 1970s-era trailer, which he hadn't owned at the time of Lisa's abduction, but the trailer was very far gone by this point—filled with dirt, dust, cobwebs, and animal droppings. The ceiling was sagging, everything was mildewed, and the place looked a wreck. Moldy boxes of old clothes were piled in one bedroom, and in another area was a heap of wire hangers. After thoroughly searching through items in the shed and trailers, not finding anything of great evidentiary value in them, the teams headed for some man-made depressions on the property. In one area, it looked as if Eaton had begun to sink a well, and in another, there were reports he had put in a septic tank.

The work team started in on the "well area" with the aid of a backhoe operated by a backhoe operator, who would scoop out a shovelful of dirt, and then the investigators would carefully rake and sift the dirt, looking for evidence. Mostly, they found rocks and stray bits of junk from the well area. Then some intriguing items started popping up—pieces of black metal that could have come from a Honda CRXsi. They also found bits of orange/red hard plastic that could have come from taillights of a car. Then something really intriguing emerged—a hubcap with the letter *H* on it. The same kind of hubcap that was used on Honda vehicles. The work crew gave up at 6:30 P.M. because of the fading light, and the scene was taped off and guarded all night by Deputy Walters.

The next morning, work began again at seven-thirty, and after a while, it was obvious that the "well area" was not going to relinquish any more items of interest. The team's attention then shifted to the "septic tank area," and digging began there. Once again, the backhoe was utilized until the bucket started consistently scraping metal. Deputy Mickey Anderson waved his arm for the operator to stop, and Lynn Cohee ordered all digging to cease as well.

Sheriff Millard made a call for a special camera that could be dropped down a small pipe to see what was below. Captain David Good, of FCSO, arrived about 12:30 P.M. with the camera, but it didn't reveal anything that could be identified. The backhoe operator started digging again, and one bucketful brought up part of a license plate. There was a hush when the partial license plate was examined, and the investigators couldn't believe their eyes. It was part of Lisa Kimmell's Montana license plate, with LIL MISS upon it. Now there was no doubt what the investigators were onto.

Investigator Lynn Cohee called the Wyoming State Crime Lab to see if they wanted the digging stopped so that they could be on hand. Their response, however, was to keep on digging. They would come the following morning.

The backhoe was put to use once more, but before very long, the bucket kept scraping metal. Team members crawled down into the hole and began using shovels instead. As dirt was shoveled aside, more and more of a black-colored vehicle started to appear. Finally, about eight feet down, an entire car door emerged from the dirt. Detective Dan Tholson moved over to where he could read the VIN number. As he read off the numbers, one by one, Detective Lynn Cohee confirmed them. As the last number was read, all doubts disappeared. This was Lisa Kimmell's black Honda CRXsi!

Detective Cohee said later, "It's really hard to describe what happened. There was the car we'd been looking for, for fourteen years. It was very quiet. Everybody that was out there hardly spoke a word."

This was, indeed, the break they'd all been looking for. Finding a license plate was one thing. Bits and pieces of "junk" were all over Eaton's property. But an entire car, purposefully buried, was something else again. Dale Eaton was going to have a very hard time explaining why he had buried the vehicle of a dead girl with whom his DNA was now matched.

Bit by bit, other items appeared in the hole and were brought to the surface. These included one of Lisa's visors, which she had worn at Arby's, and a jar of Carmex, which she used for a rash on her legs. A small white porcelain statue of the Virgin Mary was unearthed, and a rosary and crucifix. Lisa had kept both of those items in her car. Also found was part of a road atlas and, most mysterious of all, an empty .30-30 shell casing. This was odd, since Lisa had not been shot. Perhaps Dale had fired a round near her at some point to scare her into submission. He had certainly threatened the Breedens with a .30-30 rifle. How the .30-30 shell casing had gotten into the Honda CRXsi could not be explained, and Dale would never help them out on that point.

Once again, the digging stopped around 6:30 P.M., and a guard was put on duty. When the digging began again next morning, word of what was happening out on Dale Eaton's property was already starting to get around the area. For a landscape as barren and devoid of people as the area near Moneta, several law enforcement vehicles and swarms of officers were sure to attract attention. One of Eaton's neighbors had trained her binoculars on the site throughout most of the previous day. Of course, she had no idea at the time that it was connected to Lisa Kimmell, but something awfully odd was going on out there.

Once Lisa's Honda CRX was pulled out of the ground, it was quickly covered with a tarp. But not before an enterprising film crew from Casper station KTWO was out beyond the fence line with a telescopic lens on their camera. They filmed and soon reported that a black vehicle had been unearthed and was quickly covered by law enforcement agents. They even posited that this vehicle might have something to do with the Lisa Kimmell case.

News of the secretive removal of a vehicle spread like wildfire. Soon other television stations, radio stations, and print reporters were descending upon the area. One of the first on the scene was reporter Tara Westreicher, of the *Casper Star-Tribune*. She noted investigators surrounding a ditch dug by a backhoe on property near Moneta. All that Westreicher knew at the time was *the site is located in Fremont County about twelve miles from the Natrona County line.*

When Westreicher asked Fremont County authorities what was going on, they told her to talk to the Natrona County authorities, since it was their case. When she did so, Sheriff Benton, of NSCO, only replied, "My office is investigating possible criminal activity."

Westreicher figured it must really be important "criminal activity." There were several top NCSO detectives at the scene, as well as the sheriff, District Attorney Kevin Meenan, and Coroner James Thorpen. Westreicher went to talk with people over at the small town of Lysite, Wyoming, and even the fire chief Bob Whitt there told her, "I'd like to know what's going on myself." Whitt had asked several people around the area if they knew what was happening, and they were just as in the dark as he was. The article that eventually was written by Westreicher was OFFICIALS DIG FOR CLUES IN MONETA, with a subheading, BUT ELEMENTS OF OPERATION REMAIN MYSTERIOUS.

The operations were just as mysterious by the next

day, even though reporters were starting to think along the lines of *this has something to do with the Lisa Kimmell case.* The Denver news channel began showing fourteen-year-old photos of Lisa Kimmell and talking about the strange occurrences in Fremont County, Wyoming. Equally interested were the newspapers of Billings, Montana, and Casper, Wyoming.

Tara Westreicher's article for the next day's edition was also leaning toward a connection with the Kimmell case, although she still had no official confirmation. The article was MONETA INVESTIGATION REVIVES LIL MISS CASE. It spoke of all the television film crew activity going on beyond the police perimeter, and that a film crew for Channel 2 of Casper *filmed the unearthing of a small dark-colored car.* Once again, Tara and other reporters asked what all the activity was about, and wanted to know if this was indeed related to Lisa Kimmell. All Sheriff Benton would answer was "This is a homicide case being investigated by our office. I will not confirm or deny that what we're doing here has anything to do with the Kimmell case." One thing this article brought up, which had not been common knowledge before, was that Lisa had been "sodomized" during her ordeal. Just where the reporter got that fact was not stated.

Because of the deluge of reporters, Sheriff Benton held a very short news conference, but he was as noncommittal as he could possibly be. Sheriff Benton said, "The Kimmell case is fourteen years old. It has been ongoing, and will continue to be an ongoing investigation. It is a homicide, an outstanding matter being investigated by our office. I will not confirm or deny that what we're doing here has anything to do with the Kimmell case."

By the August 2 edition of the *Star-Tribune*, there was

a headline, NO ANSWERS IN LII MISS CASE. DA Kevin Meenan made his own "neither confirm nor deny" statement, and Sheriff Benton wouldn't return any of the numerous phone calls to his office from reporters. Even Sheila Kimmell, at this point, made a "neither confirm nor deny" statement of her own, and added, "If it turns out to be the car, then we can go ahead and rejoice about it at that particular time." After so many false leads and disappointments in the past, she was not about to let her hopes get too high now.

Reporters, however, are a resourceful bunch, and one of them went to the Fremont County Assessor's Office to find out who owned the land on which all the activity was taking place. The reporter learned that the land belonged to one Dale Wayne Eaton. (Apparently, the reporter did not learn at that time that Eaton was currently in federal prison.)

Casper Star-Tribune reporter Deirdre Stoelzle spoke with ninety-year-old Doris Buchta, who had lived across the road from Dale Eaton in 1988. Buchta told Stoelzle about Dale in 1988 supposedly digging a water well on the property; she thought it was ridiculous, because as she put it, "You'd have to dig down three hundred feet to get water." Then Buchta added, "He did dig it deep enough where you could barely see the top of his head. It was a pretty damned big hole. I'm just speculating, but maybe he put a car in there at night."

Stoelzle also spoke with Dale's neighbors Grayce and Dennis Keller, who lived on the south side of Highway 20/26. Grayce said she had gotten a headache from watching through binoculars all the recent activity of the investigators digging on the property. She told Stoelzle that when the car was unearthed, it was hard to tell what make and model it was, because of all the dirt on it, and because authorities placed a blue tarp over it very quickly when it was placed on a flatbed trailer.

Dennis Keller stated, "You know what really gets me! We had the lowest crime rate in the country out here in Moneta, and now all of a sudden we're the highest, per capita." That was because there were so few people living around Moneta, and besides Dale Eaton, there was another individual from there who was serving time in prison. Keller was right—for a town with less than fifty people, two of them being in prison was a large percentage of the total population.

And journalist Tara Westreicher went to speak with Shirley Widmer, one of Eaton's neighbors, who ran the Widmer store in Waltman. Her husband was a longtime acquaintance of Dale's. Widmer told Westreicher, "People living in the area and passing through have been inquiring all day about the commotion on that property. They've been calling me since bright and early this morning asking me what was going on, and I kept telling them, 'I don't know anything.'"

Then Widmer asked a question of Westreicher, for which Tara did not have an answer. "Are they looking for a body or what?"

By the next day, reporters were going even further afield in their own digging for what was going on at Dale Eaton's property, despite Sheriff Benton's silence on the matter. Tara Westreicher was particularly busy that day. She discovered that Dale was serving a three-year sentence in Littleton, Colorado, for being a felon in possession of a firearm. (She apparently did not yet know about Eaton killing his cellmate, Carl Palmer.) And speaking again with Widmer, she also learned that "Dale used to come over here and help my husband, and then he went out to Utah or Nevada to work in a mine out there. He was gone a lot. My husband has a salvage yard, and Dale would help him out there in the salvage yard." Interestingly enough, Widmer added that Dale had some friends who lived out in Glenrock, and said that Dale had left "some items with them, and some vehicles, when he'd gone into prison." She said they came and got his "mechanics truck, pickup, and a van."

Even with all the reportage and frenzied work on Dale Eaton's property, DA Kevin Meenan would not comment on the activity. Nor would Sheriff Mark Benton. One of the more intriguing comments to occur in Tara Westreicher's reports were the following lines: *A Star-Tribune report published shortly after the discovery of Kimmell's body suggested Kimmell may have been in Fremont County before her murder. Authorities there reportedly contacted Ron Ketchum, Natrona County's sheriff at the time, to report on a suspicious incident that occurred in their jurisdiction.* According to Westreicher, FCSO investigator Bill Braddock reported that someone called the sheriff's office back in March 1988 to report "screams and saw or heard a car." Just what the screams were all about or what kind of car was not recorded.

The Denver station KMGH also picked up on Sheriff Benton's and DA Meenan's reluctance to talk about what was going on at Dale Eaton's property. The most Meenan would say was that the search warrant was sealed and the digging on the property would probably continue for another week. At least KMGH got a little more out of an unnamed investigator who stated, "It's like the killer buried a key clue to the murder, and the investigators are examining the vehicle for fingerprints and other forensic evidence."

Around that time, Sheila Kimmell was also being a little more communicative with reporters. She said,

"Until something is confirmed, all I can do is keep our hopes out there. We've been going through this for fourteen years. Until police can confirm or deny the information it's all still speculative."

One reporter asked Sheila Kimmell directly about Lisa's car being unearthed out at Moneta, Wyoming. Sheila responded, "I can't comment on that. People are drawing some conclusions that are premature." Asked how her family was doing, Sheila said, "We have our bumpy days."

Sheriff Benton was still playing all his cards close to the vest at that point, but he did tell reporters that the area around Moneta was secure, and people living there did not have to worry for their safety. Converse County deputy sheriff Jim Macormic, around the same time, spoke with *Star-Tribune* reporter Matthew Van Dusen. Macormic said that he had been out to a place north of Glenrock with Natrona County investigators who had arrived even before the digging on the Moneta property. The purpose of being there was because Dale Eaton had a friend at that Glenrock location named Schifferns. When Van Dusen spoke with Dean Schifferns, Dean said that he was surprised when the investigators showed up with a search warrant. Schifferns stated that the authorities had taken Dale Eaton's vehicles and a number of boxes that they were keeping in storage for him. The Schiffernses had also given the investigators letters that Dale had written to them. Sheriff Benton let it be known that the Schiffernses had nothing to do with the present situation out on Dale's property in Moneta, nor did they know anything about what he might have done.

KMGH turned to former FBI profiler Greg Cooper for insights on what might be happening in the case. Cooper responded that he thought that Lisa Kimmell

had been murdered by a "very organized serial killer."
Cooper added, "The burying of the car indicates not
just an attempt to conceal, but an attempt to keep a
souvenir or trophy from the crime. From my perspective, this would not be a case where you would look
at this and suggest that it was a singular event, but one
of a series by an individual who participates in these
types of crimes over a period of time."

Shirley Widmer was interviewed once again and
said that she'd just heard recently about Dale killing
his cellmate in federal prison. She related, "I was
really shocked when I heard that. But it's pretty rough
in prison. Who knows? He may have done it in self-
defense." (Which, in fact, had not been the case.)

Widmer added, "None of us think he did it." (She was
referring to the murder of Lisa Kimmell.) "He's not the
murderous type. We're trying to figure out how that car
got out there without anyone noticing. He sure didn't
do it by hand. That ground out there is like a rock."

Widmer also stated that there was so much traffic on
the highway now, compared to previous years, that perhaps no one paid any attention to Dale's digging and
covering up a car. Besides, he was always moving junk
around on his property.

By August 8, reporters were badgering law enforcement officials for more information about the secretive
affairs of Dale Eaton, and his property. In desperation
for more news, they turned to outside sources to get
some kind of clue about what was happening. One reporter turned so far afield as to ask Stanley Broskey, a
forensic scientist in Pennsylvania, about his opinions on
the case. Broskey related that time and weather were
constantly working against the investigators. Moisture
had probably destroyed fingerprint evidence and he
added, "Fingerprints are very easily smudged, and once

they're smudged, you can't see the individual characteristics." Broskey said that DNA evidence had improved
tremendously since 1988, and if the killer had left a hair
in the vehicle, that could be very incriminating.

DA Kevin Meenan was becoming so worried about
all the reporters doing their own investigations on what
might be occurring, he finally told them to "tread
lightly." In an article by Tara Westreicher in the *Star-
Tribune,* she quoted Meenan saying that he was *"troubled
by the efforts of regional news organizations in gathering
information in an important murder investigation."* Meenan
added, *"For example, let's just take Mr. Eaton. Let's say it
turns out there is stuff there that has to do with Lisa Kimmell.
By you guys contacting him, what you are doing is letting him
know about what investigators have and have not found."* In
fact, by this point, several news agencies had tried contacting Dale Eaton in the Colorado federal prison, but
he had refused to talk to them.

DA Meenan said that talking to Eaton's neighbors
and checking land records was one thing, but when
they started reporting all the rumors and innuendo
surrounding the situation, that was something else.
Meenan asked rhetorically, *"How likely is Eaton going to
talk to us? Everybody's trying to run these people down."*
(Meaning, run and find who they were and how they
were connected to Dale Eaton.) *"No one seems to care
about the potential harm such efforts could pose to the investigation. It's more than a game. It's a very serious case."* And
then he asked if they were the person who had been
killed, would they want reporters running around, contacting everyone in the area, if that would jeopardize
the case?

Nonetheless, the reporters kept at it, and Tara
Westreicher contacted Jim Clark, commander of the
Louisville, Kentucky, Cold Case Squad. Just why she

contacted him, she didn't say. Clark told her that on cold cases, "Over the years, people have a tendency to talk. Especially if the suspect is in prison and no longer a threat." Westreicher wondered if Dale Eaton had become a suspect in Lisa Kimmell's case, because someone he had talked to had essentially "ratted him out."

Finally, on August 12, 2002, authorities confirmed to the media that the car unearthed on Dale Eaton's property had belonged to Lisa Marie Kimmell. It was confirmed by NCSO that the VIN number on the car unearthed at Moneta was the same as the vehicle owned by Lisa Kimmell. Sheriff Benton, however, would not say if a tipster had led law enforcement to the site.

At a press conference, Sheriff Benton did relate, "We always hoped that from the day we found her that we would find somebody driving down the interstate to Los Angeles in the car. As a law enforcement officer, this is the kind of car that catches your attention. We never lost hope that someday someone would bring us information about this case."

Interestingly enough, for the first time, Sheriff Benton admitted that a tipster in part had directed investigators to Eaton's property about Lisa's car. Benton told the reporters that the vehicle's windows were broken when found, and that the top of the car had been six to eight feet underground when discovered. "I can't say that it was mashed down with heavy equipment, but it had been under a great deal of earth. It is dented and dinged, but I can't tell you exactly how that came about." As to what investigators found inside the car, Benton would only say that they did find some evidence.

Sheriff Benton added that investigators were now trying to locate a 1963 black Ford pickup truck that Eaton had once owned. Eaton had reportedly sold the pickup in either 1997 or 1998 to a person who may have lived in Paradise Valley. Sheriff Benton added, "We're not sure where this case will take us."

Sheriff Benton said that at the present time, Dale Eaton was only a "person of interest," and not yet officially a suspect in the abduction and murder of Lisa Kimmell. Benton then related that investigators had spent some time with Eaton at the federal penitentiary, but what Eaton had told them was "not evidentiary." Benton also stated that the Kimmell family had been "given limited information."

Doris Buchta was contacted by a reporter once again, and she said that the vehicle recently unearthed in Moneta was found in the same area where Dale Eaton had been digging a well back in the 1980s. Then she added, "Of course, that doesn't prove he did the murder. He could have buried the car for someone else."

Oddly enough, at around the same time that Buchta made her statement, a television station reported that another suspect besides Dale Eaton was still being looked at in the case. KGM noted, "DA Kevin Meenan did not return telephone calls seeking comment on that aspect of the investigation." KGM noted that there were still rumors going around that it took two men to abduct Lisa in 1988.

What authorities did reveal was that Lisa had been sexually assaulted, hit in the head, and stabbed to death. And because of this MO, the question of "the Great Basin Murders" once again arose amongst the media, wondering if Dale Eaton was the culprit for all or some of those murders. Fremont County sheriff

Roger Millard stated that his office was looking into the possibility of links between the Kimmell murder and at least two other cases in their county. One of the cases was definitely that of Amy Bechtel, and Millard said that it was a "priority unsolved case."

Talking to everyone they could find, in any way related to the case, the *Billings Gazette* spoke with Hugh Duncan, who had put up $5,000 of his own money toward a reward for the capture of Lisa's killer years before. Duncan stated, "At the time I offered the reward, I thought if we could just recover the vehicle, there would be some trace evidence or something that would lead to the murderer. The one thing that's gratifying is that there are a lot of technical tools that are available to law enforcement today that were in their infancy or didn't even exist back then. God willing, it will bring closure to the Kimmell family and this community."

Duncan also spoke to a television reporter and added, "I just thought it was a tragedy of unimaginable proportions, and nothing was happening" (as far as viable clues went in late 1988 and 1989). He was right in that regard. By the time Duncan had made his $5,000 offer on the reward, not one valid call had come in. Ironically, Duncan now lived in Glenrock, Wyoming, where Dale Eaton had stashed some of his vehicles and belongings with friends. And the dead girl Belinda Grantham had lived there before being murdered and her body dumped in the North Platte River, not unlike Lisa Kimmell's body that had been dumped farther upstream in the same river.

Duncan said that he always believed that Lisa's killer had lived somewhere in the area where she was murdered. It was doubtful in his mind that someone from out of the area would have known about the small dirt road that led down to the Old Government Bridge on the North Platte River. That road would have been hard enough to spot in the daytime, much less at night when Lisa was most likely murdered, and her body dumped into the river.

The search for Dale Eaton's former Ford pickup truck kept coming up in news reports, with law enforcement investigators looking for it because it might contain items connected to Lisa Kimmell. Investigator Lynn Cohee told reporters, "It has changed hands a couple of times, with one party who then sold it to another. They then sold it to another person, and that's the last we know of its whereabouts." The pickup truck had been painted black originally, but by the last sighting, it was white. Cohee posited that the pickup truck in question might have been scrapped for parts sometime in the previous years.

Even though the authorities kept a tight lid on most of the evidence surrounding the Kimmell case, they also used the media as a tool. The *Billings Gazette* ran a headline on August 18, 2002—TIPSTERS URGED TO CALL IN. The article spoke of Lieutenant Ron Wilson, of the Yellowstone County Sheriff's Office, telling people how important tips from the public were. Wilson said in part, *"The tip might just be the little piece we need to solve the mystery."* Then he cited how such a tip had been crucial in recovering Lisa Kimmell's buried car. He didn't elaborate exactly what had been revealed by the tip.

A *Star-Tribune* article of the same date reported on many different law enforcement officers who had been affected one way or another by the Lisa Kimmell case since 1988. Former NCSO sheriff David Dovala stated, *"Over the years I've thought about the 9,000 rumors of where the car was. It just gnaws at you, these cases that are unsolved. There's not a day goes by you don't think about those cases."*

Sheriff Roger Millard, of Fremont County, said that his office was going to look closely at unsolved homicides in his county, but not jump to conclusions as far as Dale Eaton was concerned. Getting back to the unearthed car on Eaton's property, Millard talked about what it was like when the digging was going on: *"It creates a pit in your stomach because you know full well that you've probably got what you're looking for. But at the same time you have to keep it in perspective so you do the job right."* And Undersheriff Dave Kinghorn, of NCSO, stated, *"The discovery of the car was a long time coming. The car was something that I thought we'd never see."*

Glenrock police chief Mike Colling, who had been with the Casper Police Department in 1988, agreed with Kinghorn on that point: *"It's amazing they found it! Who would have ever thought of looking underground?"* Then Collings spoke about DNA testing: *"A lot of old crimes that are in the dead file are resurfacing because of DNA testing capabilities."* This was the closest any law enforcement official, so far, had mentioned that DNA might have been the reason Dale Eaton's name came up concerning Lisa Kimmell.

A reporter for the *Star-Tribune* also talked to average citizens in the area as well. Mel Hamilton, a Casper school district administrator, who had been a high-school principal in 1988, said, "I don't know how many times I've driven by that spot at Moneta. It just points out that you never know who might be next to you. Hopefully, my students will learn to use good judgment and not put themselves in a situation where they could be abducted."

Floyd and Shirley Widmer, who owned the Waltman store, once again spoke with reporters. The Widmers said that they'd known Dale for about twenty years, and for days after the car had first been unearthed, reporters from as far away as Denver were showing up at their store asking questions. Now things had quieted down a bit, and Shirley Widmer said that she was sure Dale couldn't have been responsible for such a crime. Then she added, "I'm not even certain he was around at the time in 1988. I think the car was planted there." Just who or why someone would plant a car on Eaton's property, she didn't say. But she did note that whenever Dale took off for jobs in distant regions, his cars and sheds were always being rummaged through by strangers and vagrants.

Over in Powder River, Wyoming, the postmaster, Glenda Van Patten, told a reporter that the unearthing of the car was still a hot topic in town. She said, "God, where I work at the post office, everybody has a story to tell! Even people who have just lived here for a year. One of them even contacted the *National Enquirer* about the discovery of the car."

Of all the people contacted by reporters, none suffered more with a feeling of guilt than Wyoming Highway Patrol officer Al Lesco. It was Lesco who had pulled Lisa Kimmell over for speeding on the evening of March 25, 1988. He told a reporter that he'd been thinking about it, off and on, for every year since. Lesco said, "If I would have thrown her into jail that night, she still would have been alive today." In fact, he had been racked with such guilt that he and his wife went to pay a visit to Lisa's parents. Both Ron and Sheila told him it wasn't his fault about what had happened.

Lesco was eventually able to get over his feelings of guilt, and said, "Anything can happen at any time." And then he added one more thing concerning why Lisa might have been targeted. He said, "I wish people would stop putting license plates like 'LIL MISS' on their cars. I think that has something to do with her being abducted." In Lesco's mind, a license plate like LIL MISS was an advertisement for predators.

Up until the end of August 2002, the main theory of how Dale Eaton's name came up in relation to Lisa Kimmell was that he must have told someone in federal prison in Colorado about what he had done, and that person had tipped off the authorities. But on August 31, there was another angle on this, and the headline for the *Casper Star-Tribune* was INMATE'S DNA WOULD BE ON FILE. And just below this headline was a statement about this, INVESTIGATORS ARE MUM.

Tara Westreicher was once again digging for information, and even more than she probably realized at the time, she was right on track as far as this particular issue went. She noted that since 1997, all convicted felons in Wyoming had to submit to a blood test from which DNA was extracted and put into a file. Tara spoke with Steve Miller, interim director for the state Division of Criminal Investigation. Miller told her that just because Dale Eaton's DNA hadn't been linked to the semen in Lisa Kimmell's panties in previous years, it didn't mean there wasn't a match there. Miller explained that the old technique of DNA testing might not have picked that up, or that old files would not show a match. He then added, "They are refining techniques against the DNA database all the time. So you may have run a DNA search four or five years ago and not necessarily have gotten a hit. Now there's a new search technique that they put online this year, for example. That more refined technique would get you a hit."

Miller also noted that some of Wyoming's older DNA systems might not have been compatible with the FBI's CODIS system. If that had happened, then Dale Eaton's DNA file could have been on the CODIS system for some time, but a Wyoming database with the semen DNA sample from Lisa Kimmell's panties would not come up with a match to CODIS.

Going further afield, Westreicher spoke with Ann Atanasia, an FBI spokesperson in Denver. From Atanasia, Tara found out the CODIS system used two indexes: a forensic and an offender index. The forensic index contained DNA evidence from the crime scene, and the offender index contained DNA from convicts. It was only when these two indexes were linked, that a particular individual could be tied to a particular crime scene and victim. After CODIS identified potential hits, it was up to expert DNA analysts to either confirm or refute the match. By all her scouting around for different sources, Tara Westreicher had essentially stumbled upon the reason Dale Eaton's name had eventually come up in connection to Lisa Kimmell.

Two mysteries still remained, however. Where exactly had Lisa Kimmell been abducted, and how had Dale Eaton been able to bury her car on his property without anyone noticing? The answers to those questions were going to have to wait for a while. And so would the question: had Dale Eaton abducted and murdered women before—and after—Lisa Kimmell?

12

A NEW ROUND
OF TROUBLES

By October 2002, Detectives Lynn Cohee and Dan Tholson had accumulated numerous pieces of evidence against Dale Eaton, and it seemed as if proceedings could begin in earnest toward a trial. But October turned into November, and then December, without any word by DA Kevin Meenan to the Kimmells that he was ready to proceed. Ron and Sheila Kimmell were becoming very anxious from the lack of progress, especially since they had now waited fourteen years to get to this point.

Meenan assured the Kimmells that he would devote his full attention to their case in 2003. What really worried the Kimmells was that Dale Eaton was due to be released from federal prison in the summer of 2004. They feared if Meenan kept dragging his feet and didn't charge Eaton for the murder of Lisa, Dale could just walk out the door of prison in 2004, and disappear.

In a meeting with the Kimmells, Meenan promised them that he would have Eaton extradited from Colorado in late February or March of 2003. That time period elapsed, however, with no word from DA Meenan, and Sheila Kimmell told Meenan's assistant that if something didn't happen soon, she was going to the media about her concerns. When no charges were filed by the fifteenth anniversary of Lisa's body being found, Sheila Kimmell was primed and ready to go to the media and express her displeasure with DA Meenan. Just before that happened, however, she received a phone call from Detectives Dan Tholson and Lynn Cohee. They had just transferred Dale Eaton from the federal penitentiary in Colorado to Natrona County, Wyoming.

In headlines about the situation, a newspaper reported: KIMMELLS ANXIOUSLY AWAIT JUSTICE. MEENAN: "MUCH HAPPENING BEHIND SCENES." And just as with Ron Ketchum, there was a lot going on behind the scenes that the Kimmells weren't initially aware of.

Finally, on April 17, 2003, formal charges were filed by the DA's office against Dale Wayne Eaton for the abduction and murder of Lisa Kimmell. These ranged over many counts, including first-degree murder, premeditated murder, aggravated kidnapping, aggravated robbery, first-degree sexual assault, and second-degree sexual assault.

New information was being released to the media as well, including the facts that the wheels, seats, stereo, and gearshift knob on Lisa's car were missing when it was dug up. It was also released that investigators had spoken with Dale's son Billy Eaton. Billy related that he'd helped his father melt down four

Lisa Kimmell was a pretty, cheerful girl and a good student with an outgoing personality. *(Yearbook photo)*

On March 25, 1988 while driving from Denver, Colorado to pick up her boyfriend in Cody, Wyoming, eighteen-year-old Lisa Kimmell and her vehicle simply disappeared. *(Yearbook photo)*

In all likelihood, Lisa made it to the Waltman Rest Area in central Wyoming, or a nearby location, where she was kidnapped. *(Author photo)*

Detectives searched all over Wyoming and the West, looking for a vehicle with Lisa Kimmell's distinctive license plate, "LIL MISS."

Later, law enforcement used a Honda CRX in their attempt to find Lisa's vehicle.

On April 2, 1988, a fisherman discovered Lisa Kimmell's semi-nude body in the North Platte River. A streak of her blood was found on the side of the old Government Bridge. *(Author photo)*

Only later would Dale Wayne Eaton become a suspect in Lisa Kimmell's abduction and murder. He had many scrapes with the law, starting at the age of sixteen. *(Mug shot)*

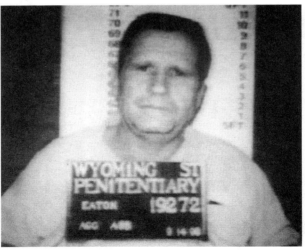

Even as a middle-aged man, Eaton could not stay out of trouble and was often in and out of prison. *(Mug shot)*

Lisa —   11-13-88
    There are'nt words to
say how much you're missed
The pain never leaves
it's so hard without you
you'll alway bealive in
me.
    Your death is my painful
loss but heavens sweet
gain   Love Always
            Stringfellow Hawke

This strange note was attached to Lisa Kimmell's grave marker
several months after her murder.

Belinda Grantham had been strangled and her body dumped in the North
Platte River. A rope had been tied around her neck, and her body was
weighed down with a thirty-pound rock to keep it from surfacing.

Not until a forensic sketch of the young woman was created did someone come forward and identify her as twenty-year-old Belinda Grantham. Just like Lisa Kimmell, she was semi-nude when found and dumped in the North Platte River.

Naomi Kidder went missing in June 1982. Her body wasn't discovered until September 1982, in a rural Wyoming county. *(Yearbook photo)*

Janelle Johnson went from Wyoming to Denver, Colorado in February, 1983. A month later her body was found after she had been seen hitchhiking in southern Wyoming. *(Yearbook photo)*

FBI profiler Greg Cooper began wondering what connection there might be to all the young women murdered in the region, whose bodies were dumped in isolated areas of Wyoming, Utah, and Nevada. *(Author photo)*

In 1993, an unidentified young woman's body was found in rural Elko County, Nevada, shot in the chest, her body "posed" by the killer. This is a forensic recreation of what investigators believed the unidentified victim might have looked like while living.

On July 24, 1997, twenty-four-year-old Amy Bechtel disappeared near Lander, Wyoming, while training for a ten-kilometer run. She was very athletic and often went running alone in the Wind River Mountains. *(Photo courtesy of Joanne Wroe)*

After disappearing underground for a quarter mile, the Popo Agi river suddenly reappears at a place called The Rise. Amy Bechtel disappeared not far from here in 1997. *(Author photo)*

The only sign of Amy's passing was one shoe print left on a dirt road near Burnt Gulch in the Wind River Mountains.

On July 30, 1998, Eaton was arrested near the Teton Mountains for being a felon in possession of a firearm. He had been living in his van on national forest land. *(Author photo)*

Acting on a tip in 2002, law enforcement detectives began digging on Eaton's property. They discovered Lisa Kimmell's black Honda buried six feet underground.

Lisa Kimmell's Honda CRX after it was unearthed on Dale Eaton's property.

Lisa's Honda CRX while it was being investigated by CSI technicians.

It was surmised that when Eaton kidnapped Lisa, he stuck her behind the front seat of his vehicle where she could not be seen before transporting her to his property.

Eaton didn't have electricity or running water on his property. He used this old tub for bathing. It was in this type of environment where he kept Lisa Kimmell for six days before killing her at the North Platte River.

Eaton's work vehicle was powerful and had a tow bar on the back, which he most likely used to tow Lisa Kimmell's Honda CRX from the scene of her kidnapping. *(Author photo)*

By 2004, Dale Eaton was on trial for his life for the murder of Lisa Kimmell. *(Mug shot)*

In March 2004, Dale Eaton received a death sentence at the main courthouse in Casper, Wyoming for the abduction and murder of Lisa Kimmell. It had taken sixteen years from the time of her death to the conviction and sentencing of Eaton. *(Author photo)*

Outside the courthouse in Casper, a statue of a cowboy looking over the herd serves as a symbol of protecting the innocent. *(Author photo)*

Not only had Dale Eaton kidnapped and killed Lisa Kimmell, but he had tried kidnapping and killing Scott and Shannon Breeden in this van. The same van was possibly spotted by a witness on the Loop Road where Amy Bechtel had gone missing in 1997. *(Author photo)*

Lisa Kimmell was laid to rest in Billings, Montana in Sunset Memorial Park. Hundreds of people, many who hadn't known her in life, went to her funeral. *(Author photo)*

Even twenty years after her death, friends and family still adorn Lisa's grave with flowers. *(Author photo)*

Honda wheels to sell as scrap, back in the 1980s, and he'd helped install a stereo and Honda seats into a pickup truck. The authorities did not believe that Billy was in any way connected to Lisa's murder. Billy had always been helping his dad on odd jobs around the property. Documents also revealed that Dale Eaton's 1963 Ford F-150 pickup truck had been tracked to Casper. The document didn't say whether anything incriminating was found inside it.

The *Rocky Mountain News* asked Sheila Kimmell about the revelations and the charges against Eaton. It reported that she replied, *"It was difficult to go over and review the information. When we actually read the charges, all eight of them, and read some of the information that hadn't been shared with us before, it was difficult. Regardless of our opinions, Mr. Eaton is still entitled to a fair trial."*

Not only was the prosecution investigating people who knew Dale, but Wyatt Skaggs and Vaughn Neubauer, of Dale Eaton's defense team, were as well. The defense team's investigator was Priscilla Moree. Things she would discover would in many ways be just as important—if not more so—in the sentencing phase of a trial, if things got that far, as they would be if Dale was found guilty. Moree spent one afternoon with Dale's father, Merle, but he was not particularly forthcoming about his deceased wife and her mental illness or his relationships with his children. There had been rumors of abuse by Merle upon Dale when he was a boy, but Moree found out pretty quickly that Merle was not going to answer anything of that nature. In fact, Merle had already told a sheriff's investigator that "Dale had a normal childhood."

This was not the picture Moree got from Dale's younger sister Judy. She not only spoke of an abusive, chaotic atmosphere when the kids were growing up, she also spoke of the violent and abusive marriage of Dale and Melody, and that they had lived in squalor. She added information about Dale's explosive temper. Yet, this cooperation with Judy was short-lived. Before long, Judy would not return Moree's letters or phone calls, and denied in public her statements that there was abuse by their father when she and Dale were growing up.

Things were just as problematic with Dale's sister Sharon. She was initially cooperative, but soon she became worried how Dale's actions would impact her and her family. Not unlike Judy, she soon would not cooperate with Moree. A third sister of Dale's, named Mary, was negative from the very beginning and would not talk about her brother Dale.

As far as Dale's brother Richard went, Moree discovered that he was fifteen years younger than Dale and really didn't know him all that well. Richard was very vague in his comments and told Moree at one point, "If that's what happened (the kidnapping and murder), my brother deserves whatever." In fact, Moree found out that Richard had spoken with an NCSO investigator, and Richard believed Dale had been responsible for another homicide.

One of the more interesting conversations Moree had was with Dale's ex-wife, Melody. This occurred over several hours, and Moree said later, "I think she wanted Dale to live just so he could die a miserable death in his cell." From the conversation, Moree got the impression that Melody was abused by him, and abused him in return. This report was shared with Wyatt Skaggs. Skaggs later declared, "The relationship was so terribly violent, so ugly, not only to her but to the rest of the kids, as well, that she would have contributed a great amount for the prosecution." Skaggs was definitely not going to be calling Melody as a witness on Dale's behalf.

Melody did indeed reveal something very ugly to Moree. She said that their son J (pseudonym) had been sexually abused by Dale when he was only ten years old. According to Melody, the state stepped in and took J out of the home and made him a ward of the state. Melody would not even tell Moree where J lived. Of course, Melody hated Dale so much by that point that it had to be wondered if the alleged molestation of J was real or not.

Moree next interviewed Billy, Dale's other son, twice in Cheyenne. Like other family members, Billy did not lend anything very helpful to Dale's cause. In fact, in one interview, Billy said that his dad was violent and would throw wrenches at his head when he got mad. The picture he painted about his father was not a very good one.

Moree had a telephone conversation with Dale's daughter, V (pseudonym). V did say she loved her dad, and he had not abused her. She had been a young girl when she stayed briefly at his place in Moneta. Even though this was favorable, V did not want to testify, and the defense was worried if she did. On cross-examination, she would have to tell about the filthy conditions she lived in while staying there. And V had told an NCSO investigator about all the abuse in the family, though Dale had not directed that at her personally.

One person who initially gave a more positive picture about Dale was a waitress named Rose, who lived in Nevada and had known Dale. When Rose and her family learned about the charges against Dale, they were shocked and couldn't believe it. Rose said that Dale had been good to her, had brought her breakfast in bed and flowers. Rose said that Dale had worked for her family in Utah, and they liked him, although he did have a fight with a coworker.

This, however, was offset by Rose's comments to law enforcement detectives wherein she told them that Dale lived in a pigsty, and that she really didn't care that much about him. She also brought up one other thing that could have been very problematic for the defense. Rose had told investigators that Dale had given her a diamond ring, which she no longer had, but this was after 1988. Lisa Kimmell was missing a diamond ring when her body was discovered.

Another avenue down in Colorado was just as fruitless for the defense. Both Moree and Skaggs went to see Vince Horn, the federal public defender in Denver who had represented Dale on the "felon in possession of a firearm" case, which had landed Dale in federal prison. Skaggs learned from Horn, that he and Eaton "didn't get along." Horn would not be a good witness, because his involvement brought in prior bad acts by Dale.

Moree interviewed Dale's former friends JoAnne and Ed Walsh by telephone. This relationship had soured, like many other relationships that Dale had over the years. The point of contention seemed to be "an item Dale had, that he shouldn't have." In other words, the Walshes thought Dale had stolen the item from them. And then JoAnne told Moree that she was afraid of Dale.

Moree began compiling Dale's work history, but this was just as difficult as the other aspects had been. Eaton never stayed with a job very long, and he was fired from three jobs for assaulting coworkers. On top of this, Dale was often self-employed and did not keep a paper trail of his activities. More often than not, he was paid in cash.

As far as Dale's medical history went, Moree learned that Dale had not been taken to doctors as a child, nor did he receive inoculations. In fact, throughout most of his life, he had no medical plan at all. The only time he had decent medical care was when he had been incarcerated.

Moree did have plenty of paperwork on Dale's time behind bars, including time in the Wyoming state penitentiary, juvenile incarceration as a youth in Colorado, and time in the federal penitentiary. Nothing in his prison history was encouraging. Dale had stabbed a woman over a stolen watermelon when he was young, had escaped from CAC, and had killed a cellmate in federal prison. All in all, it was fairly bleak as far as good witnesses that would be coming to testify on Dale's behalf in the upcoming trial.

In a prelim to the trial, on May 8, 2003, Sheila Kimmell was there, wanting to take in every step of the judicial process. Defense lawyer Wyatt Skaggs's main objections before trial were about media coverage. One of his reasons was that Greg Cooper's speculation that Eaton was a serial killer had once again been published in a local newspaper. Skaggs termed the publication of these speculations "yellow journalism," and asked for a mistrial. He didn't get one, so he then waived Eaton's rights to the preliminary hearing.

Skaggs wasn't the only one worried about media coverage. When DA Meenan learned from the Kimmells that a three-part series about ATF agent Don

Flickinger was about to run in the *Billings Gazette*, he was less than pleased. Meenan did not want some revelation published in a newspaper that might actually cause a mistrial. The Kimmells, however, were all for the article being run, because Don Flickinger had stood by them during their darkest years after 1988, when it seemed that the case might not ever be solved.

In the actual series of articles, Flickinger spoke of all the years of frustration in trying to find a viable suspect for the abduction and murder of Lisa Kimmell. He also spoke about his relationship with Lisa's parents, aspects of the psychics involved in the case, and just how far afield the investigation went.

And then Flickinger spoke of his retirement in 1995 and the things that had occurred since then. Flickinger said that after retirement he had thought of Lisa every day and often reviewed his old notes: *"I just couldn't walk away from the case."*

In retirement, Flickinger worked driving cars for the Big Sky Auto Auction three days a week. He was working on the car lot in July 2002 when he got a call from Detective Dan Tholson. Tholson asked him if he was sitting down. Then Tholson announced to him that "we got our man!"

When Tholson told Flickinger about the circumstances of the DNA test and the name Dale Wayne Eaton, the article reported, Flickinger responded, *"Well, Dan, I never heard of this guy!"*

"We didn't either!" Tholson replied.

In fact, of all the hundreds and hundreds of people who were looked at in the abduction and murder of Lisa Kimmell, Dale Eaton had never come up before the DNA results led back to him.

Flickinger said that after talking with Detective Tholson, he lowered his head and cried. Flickinger also added in one part of the article series that he believed, as Greg Cooper did, in the serial killer theory. Flickinger believed that the abduction and the captivity of Lisa Kimmell were just too well planned to have been Eaton's first time.

Flickinger drove to the Old Government Bridge, where Lisa Kimmell's body had been found. Then he drove to Eaton's property near Moneta. There was still yellow crime-scene tape strewn about the property, and the trailer where Eaton had lived was in worse shape than ever. It was filled with spiderwebs, dust, and animal droppings. Around the metal shed, car parts, oil-drilling equipment, and other debris were scattered in disarray.

Going inside the trailer, Flickinger poked through a stack of old newspaper clippings and envelopes. Flickinger later told a reporter, "This is a house of horrors! I can't even imagine what took place here."

In May 2003, Dale Eaton may have finally been charged with the crimes, but all was not right in the Natrona County DA's Office. For the Kimmells, things were about to spin out of control, the way they had with Ron Ketchum and the sheriff's office in previous years. This time, it concerned District Attorney Kevin Meenan, who was scheduled to try Dale Eaton when the trial ensued. As it turned out, by the spring of 2003, Meenan was under investigation himself. Meenan had received a settlement of $55,000 in July 1999 on behalf of his stepdaughter Micah's personal injury. He placed the money in a trust account, then apparently forged her signature. He told his stepdaughter the amount he received was only $40,000.

Worst of all, Meenan not only spent the "hidden"

$15,000, but he spent the other $40,000 as well. Then to top things off, Meenan opened a credit card account in his stepson Ryan's name and forged his signature as well. Meenan wrote checks against the credit card and let the account become delinquent. Just what Meenan was spending all the money on did not come to light.

Once this came out, DA Meenan was charged with forgery, larceny, and unauthorized use of identifying information, a false written statement to obtain credit, obtaining property by false pretenses, and unlawful use of a credit card. The Kimmells were naturally alarmed by all the revelations. The last thing they needed were more roadblocks in bringing justice for Lisa.

While this mess took place, on July 26, 2003, there was a judicial hearing of Dale Eaton's case. During this hearing, Eaton's lawyer Wyatt Skaggs wanted all the pretrial hearings closed to the public. Skaggs argued, "Much of the press coverage regarding Mr. Eaton has been horribly prejudicial and inflammatory. The press has set up camp in Casper on these occasions and has gone about town seeking interviews with virtually anybody who will talk about the matter. The difficulty in selecting a jury in this community, with all the press hoopla that has been generated, cannot be underplayed."

The media, however, was not taking this lying down, and Bruce Moats, an attorney for the Wyoming Press Association, filed his own motion to keep pretrial hearings open to the public. Moats said that open hearings were key to public confidence in the judicial system, to make sure that it ran as it should. Moats agreed that some of the sections within the hearings might be outside the scope of what the public could see and hear, but those things could be done in chambers as they arose, rather than a blanket ruling to close all pretrial hearings.

Besides the publicity of the hearings being an issue, Skaggs said that he planned to file over one hundred other motions in Eaton's defense. These would range from a change of venue request to a suppression of certain statements to exclusion of evidence, and the constitutionality of the death penalty.

By August 2003, the Kimmells were fed up with DA Kevin Meenan and his legal problems. They phoned Meenan about their concerns and wanted him off the case. Meenan tried to convince them that he could keep his problems separate from prosecuting Dale Eaton, but the Kimmells weren't buying it. They'd had their fill with Ron Ketchum in the past, and they didn't want more possible trouble down the road with Meenan. The Kimmells went to their lawyer, Mark Gifford, who was by now trying a civil case concerning Dale Eaton's property for the Kimmells as well. The Kimmells asked Gifford to contact DA Meenan and try to convince him to step aside in the pending criminal trial against Dale Eaton, and to appoint another prosecutor.

Even though Meenan seemed receptive to the idea, he still dragged his feet on the matter. Finally, in total frustration, Sheila Kimmell gave out a press release, which, in part, stated: *Given the personal complications that Mr. Meenan is dealing with at this time, we hope that he will step aside as the lead prosecutor in our daughter's case and reassign it. His personal and legal issues seem to be complex and will require a great deal of his focus and attention over an extended period of time.* She said that she hoped he resolved his own legal issues, but her overriding concern was that those issues would jeopardize the criminal case against Eaton.

Meenan was reportedly furious when this statement came out in the press. He answered back by his own statement: *I have worked very hard to keep these matters separate! We have taken every possible step to ensure that the prosecution of Mr. Eaton will continue in due course.*

One thing Meenan did accomplish was to seek the death penalty against Dale Eaton. As part of the reason for doing so, Meenan pointed to Dale's criminal past and spoke of Lisa's torture and murder as "atrocious and cruel." Meenan added, "He (Eaton) killed with premeditated malice, while engaged in committing robbery, sexual assault, and kidnapping."

And then, in a surprise to the Kimmells, DA Meenan suddenly removed himself from Lisa's case on August 4. This was not only a surprise to them, but a huge relief as well. Meenan said that Assistant DA (ADA) Michael "Mike" Blonigen would now be taking over the case against Dale Eaton. Meenan added, "Mr. Blonigen has been on this case from the beginning and is well qualified to serve as lead trial counsel." Oddly enough, Meenan's own trial was scheduled to begin even before that of Dale Eaton, which was slated for sometime in February 2004.

The defense team was already leaning heavily on having psychiatrists as their main witnesses for Eaton. Wyatt Skaggs contacted a well-respected psychiatrist named Dr. Linda Gummow, of Utah, to help evaluate Dale Eaton's mental condition. Dr. Gummow had worked on several other capital cases in the past, and Skaggs asked her to contact Dr. Kenneth Ash, of Fort Collins, Colorado. Dr. Ash was working on the mental-health issue independently of Dr. Gummow at the time. This mental-health issue would not only involve Dale, but his mother, Marian, as well.

Even though Eaton's trial was scheduled for February 2004, questionnaires were sent to 750 prospective jurors in October 2003. Both the prosecution and defense knew that a lot of potential jurors were going to be disqualified for one reason or another. One of the questions concerned whether a juror held moral, religious, or personal views that would not allow them to impose a death penalty sentence if Eaton was found guilty of first-degree murder. Another question concerned whether they had already formed an opinion about Eaton's guilt or innocence.

Dale was not helping himself when he made a statement that autumn that he would assault anyone placed in the same cell that he was in at the Natrona County Jail. In light of what he had done to his cellmate in federal prison, this did not seem like an idle threat. And when it came time in a trial for jurors to ponder whether Dale was still a threat "of future dangerousness," these kinds of statements could come back to haunt him.

By November 2003, important hearings were becoming a weekly occurrence in court, and they were, for the most part, kept open to the public. On November 15, Judge David Park made several rulings on motions. In one, Park stated that the vehicle found buried on Dale Eaton's property would be admitted as evidence. Another dealt with the blood sample drawn from Eaton for DNA testing. Defense lawyer Skaggs argued that the blood draw was an "unreasonable search and seizure," but Judge Park disagreed and stated that "a prisoner's rights are clearly diminished when they become wards of the state."

* * *

In the midst of all the Dale Eaton hearings, DA Meenan's own case was resolved in December 2003. Meenan agreed to a plea deal wherein most of the charges were dropped against him, but he would have a felony record. Along with this, he had to be booked in the county jail and submit a DNA sample. When it came time for his formal sentencing, both Meenan's stepdaughter and stepson were angrier at the judicial system and the media than they were at Meenan. In fact, they said they had never wanted the charges filed in the first place. Meenan's stepdaughter, Micah, told the judge, "In my opinion, this was never about justice for me, the labeled victim, but about making an example out of Kevin. I have felt like a victim of the justice system." She went on to say that what had occurred was a family affair, and not a crime. Micah stated that Kevin Meenan had made restitution to her as soon as charges had been filed.

Meenan's stepson, Ryan, agreed with Micah and said that it was investigators, the DA's office, and the media that had made his life "a living hell" since the day the charges became known. "All I wanted was the state and media to leave my family alone."

For his part, Kevin Meenan told the judge that the whole thing had been a "terrible judgment" on his part, and he acknowledged his guilt. He stated, "I'll make up for my mistakes, Your Honor, if you give me the opportunity and probation. I'm sorry my choices have caused such pain for so many people. If I could take it away, I would."

In the end, Kevin Meenan was given a very light sentence. No jail time, two years' probation, and no fines. But he did have to resign from his office as district attorney. The identity theft charge was suspended, but a felony charge was going to stay on his record. He had to pay $300 to a victim's compensation fund and do two hundred hours of community service.

Judge Kautz did give Kevin Meenan a verbal tongue-lashing at sentencing and said, "Society cannot tolerate conduct like this. Your actions are clearly a violation of the law. You could have left your daughter's money alone. You know, as I do, you were very capable of complying with the law."

After it was over, the prosecutor gave a short statement to reporters. He said, "Mr. Meenan will have a permanent felony record. He's lost his job. He'll probably lose his profession. He'll lose his license to practice law if the state bar treats him like every other lawyer who's ever been convicted of a felony or stolen money out of a trust account."

Around the time that all this was going on with Meenan, Judge Park made an important ruling that the trial of Dale Eaton would stay in Natrona County. Judge Park cited as a reason for his ruling that 50 to 60 percent of potential jurors polled had stated that they had not formed an opinion as to Eaton's guilt or innocence. Then, as an aside, Park added that he had preferred that the trial be held in Laramie, in another county, but that was impossible because there were no open courtrooms there in February and March 2004.

On a different point, the defense went on record as stating that they didn't mind the Kimmell family sitting in the courtroom during testimony. What they didn't want was anyone in the Kimmell family to be able to testify during the sentencing phase of Dale

Eaton if he was found guilty of first-degree murder. Skaggs argued that "their testimony would have a tremendous impact on the jury." To this, Judge Parks agreed.

As December moved into January 2004, pretrial motions were still being argued by both sides. The latest one concerned whether Dale Eaton would be forced to wear leg shackles in court. The trouble with that, as far as the defense was concerned, was that it would give the image to everyone in the courtroom of Dale as still being a dangerous man. Skaggs proposed that Eaton wear a "shock belt," a device that would create an eight-second incapacitating jolt if he misbehaved in the courtroom. Skaggs also did not want any armed deputies it the court, because they would create the same negative impression.

On the other hand, Mike Blonigen said that a shock belt wasn't enough, and he wanted leg shackles on Eaton at all times. Blonigen stated, "He has a violent criminal history." For the same reason, Blonigen wanted armed deputies in court. In Blonigen's mind, Dale Eaton had shown how dangerous he could be by the fact he had killed his cellmate in Colorado with a blow to the head. In the end, Judge Park sided with Mike Blonigen.

Something that happened around this time would not come to light publicly until after the trial, but it was a serious matter. Dr. Linda Gummow met with Wyatt Skaggs at breakfast in Capser to discuss her upcoming testimony. However, she felt very uncomfortable at the restaurant he chose because she didn't feel that their conversation was private enough. Not until after the trial, however, would she voice these concerns to anyone. And even worse, when Dr. Gummow discussed trial strategy at the public defender's office, she later characterized the mood there as "very tense." She related that Skaggs was "irritable and very snappish." Dr. Gummow learned that Skaggs had diabetes, and was not feeling well at that time, whether from a cold or complications with diabetes, she didn't know. She also would mention later that she overheard Skaggs tell a court staff member that he was not feeling well and had passed out the night before. (It would, only later, be learned that this term that he used—"pass out"—was in reference to him falling asleep almost immediately upon arriving at home, and not literally passing out. He would say, "I mean that to say I would sleep very well.") But at the time, Dr. Gummow wondered if he really had passed out, and how that would affect him as lead defense counsel in Dale Eaton's case.

Then Dr. Gummow noted that Skaggs was drinking a lot of water, perhaps to help his condition. He would state later, "Well, my mother always said, 'Drink a lot of water if you have a cold.' And at that particular point, I did have a cold. I was dehydrating, to some extent, with the cold, so I was drinking a lot of water." Once again, what Dr. Gummow thought of the situation— and what had *really* occurred—were not one and the same. All of it, however, left her uneasy, and she would describe these pretrial meetings with Wyatt Skaggs as "uncomfortable."

By February 21, 2004, jury selection was well under way for the upcoming trial, and 140 potential jurors were expected to be interviewed in the first week alone. Much of the jury selection process was held without the media present, and the reason was given "so as not to poison the jury pool." Panels of thirty were brought in at a time, and one of the things they were told was that if Dale Eaton was found guilty of first-degree murder, then they would be sequestered in a motel room while they pondered his fate in the sentencing phase. Once sequestered, they could not bring their own Bible to the motel room, but they could bring other reading material. There would be limited contact with family members while they were sequestered, and all phone conversations would be supervised.

Most of the reasons to be excused, given by potential jurors, centered around suffering financial hardship in a case that was expected to last more than a month. Others were excused in the actual process for various reasons by both the defense and prosecution. One woman personally knew Dale Eaton and was excused, and another was excused because she said she could not stand to view graphic photos of the murdered girl. A man who had a disability said that he could not sit comfortably for that period of time, and was excused.

Skaggs asked potential jurors if they could stand firm against other jurors if they felt the death penalty was not appropriate in the case, even if they were one against eleven. He also asked about their feelings regarding mental illness, and if they thought criminals used that as an excuse. Skaggs stated, "Insanity is not our defense, but mental illness will be discussed at trial."

Other parts of the questioning were held out of the presence of the media, and Bruce Moats, who was representing the *Casper Star-Tribune,* objected. He stated, "The U.S. Supreme Court has said that there is a presumption of openness in criminal proceedings, and that applies to the selection of the jury, because that is an important part of the process."

While all of this was going on, Ron and Sheila

Kimmell sat in the back of the courtroom taking everything in. DA Mike Blonigen and ADA Stephanie Sprecher did the questioning for the prosecution, while Wyatt Skaggs and Vaughn Neubauer did it for the defense.

Blonigen told potential jurors that if they were selected, they were going to have to view very graphic photos of the crime scene and autopsy. He related, "There's a great deal of violence involved in this case." Some, like the woman who was released from the first panel, stated that they could not stomach such graphic photos, and were also excused.

All through the process, Dale Eaton sat in civilian clothes, next to his defense lawyers. One reporter noted that Eaton scribbled on notepads once in a while, but mainly he seemed bored with the proceedings.

The *Billings Gazette* ran an article around this time about Janeice Lynch, the Natrona County victim-witness coordinator for felony cases. As the trial neared, Lynch spent much of her time with the Kimmell family. Lynch told the reporter, "People are hurting when they come to us. I ensure that the victim is given their rights."

Lynch helped the Kimmell family make arrangements for their upcoming stay in Casper during the trial, and went with them to every court appearance and hearing. According to the article, she helped the Kimmells sort through the varying emotions they endured during the hearings.

Lynch related, "Sometimes they (the family of a victim) just need a hug, sometimes I'm just there to listen. I'm good at keeping people on an even keel in the courtroom and helping them emotionally, while not getting sucked in myself."

Lynch related that the Kimmell family had her

phone number and could call her anytime, day or night. She noted that victims' families didn't just go through dark periods during court hearings or on weekdays, but at night and on weekends as well. On one level, Lynch dealt with the victims' families' emotional problems, and on another level, she was a travel planner and catered to their practical needs, such as airline tickets, accommodations, and places to have a meal. She also educated them about the legal system, since most people had no idea what a capital case might entail.

Sheila Kimmell said of Lynch, "She explains the court process that is so foreign to us. She is supportive, she's informative, she protects us, and she helps us wade through all the practical matters that you don't deal with when you're going through a very emotional time."

The Kimmells were also helping out the community in their own way. They went to a local chapter meeting of Parents of Murdered Children (POMC) in Casper just before Eaton's trial was to begin. In fact, they were the featured guest speakers at that meeting. The local chapter had been started by Suzanne Paschal after her twenty-year-old son had been shot to death in 2003. Among the others, there were the grandparents of a three-year-old, who had been beaten to death by a babysitter, and other family members of murdered children.

Helping with the group was Jamie Tholson, a University of Wyoming law school graduate. She had suffered her own loss when her fiancé killed himself with a self-inflicted gunshot. Tholson said, "It took me four months to get out of bed after that. We were supposed to get married, and everything was going to be perfect."

Ron Kimmell said at the meeting about the upcoming trial that he knew in years past that it was going to take a miracle for Lisa's case to be solved. And the miracle finally came in the form of DNA testing that made the link to Dale Eaton. Then he addressed a woman at the meeting named Connie Moser, who was filled with anger because there had been no resolution to a case involving her twenty-seven-year-old son who had been killed. Someone had beaten him in a parking lot and then ran over him. There were still no suspects in the case. Ron told her that for years he was filled with rage, and at different times would beat the walls with his fists, kick objects, yell, scream, and cry. He said, "Not everyone grieves the same, not everyone thinks the same, but we did learn one thing—anger is the same for every parent."

Sheila Kimmell agreed and stated, "You go through intense anger you've never understood before." Then she added that sometimes this intense anger scared friends and family. Some people told her to move on beyond it. But Sheila said, "You never get over it! There's never any closure. I hate that word!" She declared that one never got over it, but one learned how to deal with it. Some days were better than others.

Ron told Moser that he still went through the same emotions she was going through, even after sixteen years, but the emotions weren't as "raw" as they had been in the beginning. And Sheila added that they were at the meeting, in part, because they had to find some purpose in their lives for what had happened. Sheila was upset that family members of victims in Wyoming could not give an impact statement to jurors during the penalty or sentencing phases. Wyoming was one of the few states with that law. Ron did note that twenty years before, family members couldn't even sit

in the gallery during a trial in Wyoming. So things were
getting better in his opinion, and both he and Sheila
were trying to have the "Victim Impact Statement" law
changed. Then Ron said that he was determined that
"something good" had to come out of this tragedy. "It
just can't be for nothing!"

The next day, Sheila Kimmell spoke to a reporter
about how anxious the family was about the upcoming trial. She also said they were ready for things to
begin. "We're so glad we're finally coming to this
point. We're all having various difficulties with it, but
that's to be expected. I'm just gonna flat out tell you,
it's not easy!"

Just before trial began, Bruce Moats won his point
with Judge Park to unseal certain documents that
concerned pretrial motions. One of these pretrial motions dealt with two inmates who were scheduled to
speak for the prosecution. Defense attorney Wyatt
Skaggs was not happy about this unsealing of documents and said, "The media has been very good in
most cases, except for the *Star-Tribune,* who has gone
out of its way to sensationalize and stir hatred." Despite Skaggs's objection, Judge Park released the information, anyway.

If Skaggs was upset about the possibility of the two
inmates speaking at trial, he was absolutely furious
about an incident that was reported soon thereafter
in the *Star-Tribune.* A photo of a rope tied into a noose
was front and center on the front page of the newspaper. The caption beneath the photo stated, *A rope fash-
ioned like a hangman's noose dangles in front of the
abandoned trailer where Dale Eaton lived in Moneta.*

Wyatt Skaggs was outraged by the photo displayed
on the front page of the newspaper and told Judge
Park the next day in court, "It is entirely inappropri-

ate!" And then Skaggs told the judge that he believed
the photo had been "staged." In other words, someone working for the *Star-Tribune* photographer had
tied the noose and hung it there.

Star-Tribune photographer Dan Cepeda, who took
the actual photo, denied this allegation and said, "No,
we didn't stage it. That would be completely unethi-
cal. I'd never stage a photo. Why would I risk my
career?" And *Star-Tribune* city editor Deirdre Stoelzle
added, "The photograph shows the intensity of senti-
ment on the part of the person who put it there for
what has become a haunted place." Judge Park did
tell potential jurors to steer clear of articles and news
stories about Dale Eaton. And he told them if they
had seen the noose photo, disregard it.

On the second day of jury selection, Judge Park
informed the media that they were no longer going
to be able to photograph potential jurors in the hallway of the courthouse. A couple of people had complained about this and had brought it to his attention.
Up until that point, photographs dealing with the
case were fair game if they were outside the courtroom itself. Judge Park also let it be known that he
was not going to allow any photographs to be taken in
court during trial. An editor for the *Star-Tribune* was,
of course, less than pleased with this decision, and
wrote, *In a death penalty case, people on all sides of that
issue have a deep interest in the views of the jurors. Trials like
Mr. Eaton's generate considerable public interest and provide
a rare opportunity for citizens to learn about the workings
of the court.*

The jury selection process went on into days three
and four, with numerous people being excused for

one reason or another. And on day four, Vaughn Neubauer let it be known that there were possibly fourteen witnesses who would be called on the defense side. The prosecution had many more possible witnesses, numbering past forty. During his questioning, Mike Blonigen noted that the actual crimes had taken place sixteen years previously, and he asked if the potential jurors thought because of the lapse of time, it was not as important as more recent cases to seek justice. No one raised a hand.

At the end of one panel, Judge Park scolded a young man who had said that he didn't want to serve on the jury because he "wanted to get on with his life." Judge Park called the young man's attitude "abhorrent." Park was more lenient with two elderly women who did not want to serve because of their age.

On the fifth day of jury selection, Wyatt Skaggs asked if any of them were involved in a community project in Casper that was raising funds for the Kimmell family. No one raised a hand. Skaggs also told the potential jurors that in cross-examination, when Ron and Sheila Kimmell were on the stand, he would ask tough questions. Skaggs wanted to know if the panel of prospective jurors would hold that against his client, Dale Eaton. Once again, no hands were raised.

Finally, on the day the trial was to begin, March 3, 2004, forty-eight potential jurors were still in the courtroom waiting to see if they would be among the twelve actual jurors and three alternates. A little after 9:00 A.M., the prosecution and defense approached Judge Park with names of people they wanted excluded. No reason had to be given. Once this was done, a jury was selected, and it included eight men and seven women. Interestingly, one of the potential jurors who was not impaneled was Rick Tempest.

Tempest had been a former speaker of the Wyoming House of Representatives. He was disappointed not to be on the jury. Tempest said, "I thought it would be an interesting process. It's something I haven't done before. I was geared up to serve."

IV

RIVER OF JUSTICE

13

LIGHT AT THE END OF THE TUNNEL

The actual trial began at 10:30 A.M. on March 3, 2004, to a packed courtroom, although many of the people in the gallery were not ordinary citizens interested in the case, but rather journalists, investigators, and attorneys other than those connected to the trial. These attorneys were interested in seeing how the prosecution and defense would present themselves at a "big trial." Kimmell family members took up the front row directly behind the jury. Ron and Sheila Kimmell were there, along with Lisa's sisters, Sherry Odegard and Stacy Hoover, with her husband, Todd. The Kimmells brought along a long cushion, which they placed on the hard wooden bench, knowing that they were in for a long day of testimony. During a break, Mike Blonigen even patted the cushion and remarked, "Looks like you came prepared."

* * *

Mike Blonigen began his opening remarks by taking the jurors back through Lisa's life, her journey in 1988, being pulled over by Officer Lesco near Douglas, Wyoming, and her disappearance. He also talked about her body being discovered in the North Platte River, and the cause of death, as noted by Dr. James Thorpen. Another big factor in his opening statements was the note left by "Stringfellow Hawke" on Lisa Kimmell's gravestone. Blonigen told the jurors that the writing on that note matched Dale Eaton's handwriting. The biggest "smoking guns" of all, of course, were the DNA sample from the rape kit that matched Eaton's DNA, and Lisa's Honda CRXsi, which had been buried on Eaton's property.

Not far away, Dale Eaton sat at the defense table in a long-sleeved plaid shirt, occasionally glancing back at the people in the gallery. Mostly, however, he jotted down notes on a legal pad, and he kept a deadpan expression on his face, most of the time.

What was a surprise to many were Wyatt Skaggs's opening remarks. Skaggs did not deny that Dale Eaton had committed the crimes he was accused of doing. Skaggs even said, "Dale Eaton bears criminal responsibility. But there's no proof that Lisa Kimmell's homicide happened in the commission of a robbery, a sexual assault, or a kidnapping." Skaggs was trying to convince the jurors that the prosecution was asking for the death penalty—a stiffer penalty than was warranted. Skaggs kept declaring, "This was not premeditated murder!" In essence, Skaggs was almost giving up any chance that his client would not be found guilty;

instead, he seemed to be laying a framework for the penalty phase if a conviction was decided upon. Skaggs wanted to make a case early on for the jurors, that the death penalty was far too harsh for the circumstances. By admitting that Dale had done certain things, but not in a "preplanned" manner, Skaggs was hoping that eventually the jurors would vote for second-degree murder, and not first-degree murder.

The first witness for the prosecution was a very potent one; Sheila Kimmell. Obviously with Sheila, Mike Blonigen had a witness who had intimate knowledge about Lisa's life and death. Blonigen began by taking Sheila back through Lisa's early years, and the events leading up to their departure from Denver in March 1988: Lisa by car, and Sheila by plane. Sheila said that Lisa was a very organized person, and once she made a plan, she would stick with it. Sheila was adamant that Lisa would have stuck with the plans they'd made as to her route from Denver to Cody, Wyoming. Sheila related that the route would have gone up Highway 20/26 through Moneta, where Dale Eaton lived at the time.

Sheila also spoke in detail about Lisa's vehicle, the Honda CRXsi, with its distinctive license plate, LIL MISS, and that Lisa would never have picked up hitchhikers. Sheila recounted the story of when Lisa had a car accident in December 1987, and wouldn't even roll down her window all the way to speak with a road crewman because she was very wary of strangers along the road. Sheila also spoke of the moment she and her family first became worried about Lisa's absence, on Saturday, March 26, 1988, and the searches they had instituted thereafter.

Things went along smoothly in Blonigen's questioning, with no objections by Skaggs, until Blonigen asked, "Did you have any question in your mind that she would have contacted you, had she been able to?"

This brought forth an objection by Wyatt Skaggs, who declared, "Your Honor, I'm going to object. That calls for speculation."

Judge Park sustained the objection, and Blonigen rephrased his question. "Was it Lisa's habit in the past to contact you if she knew you were concerned?" Sheila Kimmell agreed that Lisa would.

Blonigen asked about Lisa's jewelry, then got into much more personal matters. He began by asking, "Prior to March 25, 1988, had you ever observed your daughter, Lisa, in a state of undress?"

Sheila said that she had. Asked when that had occurred, Sheila replied, "At the apartment in Denver, we had only one bathroom. And there would be occasions to where our bathroom schedules would overlap, and we would have to jointly share the bathroom. I had an early-morning meeting, and she had to be up very early. So I went in and I took care of my personal needs, my shower, stuff like that. And then when I was done, I went and I woke her up and let her know that the bathroom was now available. She got into the shower while I was doing my hair with my hand dryer. The hair dryer had shorted out, and it set off the smoke alarm. I yanked the dryer out of the socket and ran into the hallway. My daughter, in the shower, jumped out of that thing so fast, she didn't even shut off the water or anything, and came out dripping wet and said, 'What in the world happened?'"

Blonigen continued, "At that time, did you observe whether her pubic hair was shorn or shaved in any way?"

Sheila replied, "She was all intact."

This incident, of course, happened the day before Lisa took Sheila to the airport in Denver.

Getting to the matter of bruising on Lisa's arms and legs, Blonigen asked if the last time Sheila had seen her daughter, had she noticed any bruises? Sheila answered that she had not. To which, Blonigen added, "And you had seen her completely undressed on March twenty-fourth—is that correct?"

Sheila responded, "Just as naked as God gave her to me."

The testimony went along smoothly until Mike Blonigen began to introduce photos; at that point, Skaggs wanted a sidebar. Once out of the hearing of the jurors, Skaggs said, "Your Honor, I hate to have to go through this whole procedure every time we get up here, but I've offered time and time again to enter into a stipulation on the photographs. So I guess we're going to have to do it slowly but surely, even though I would like to see the photographs the night before so I can go through them and stipulate to them."

Blonigen replied, "If you look at the photo list, I think you can identify all of these photographs."

Skaggs replied, "Not necessarily. We've got photographs that are similar to these, but they are two or three shots of the same thing. So you don't know precisely which photograph it is."

Blonigen replied, "Well, Your Honor, those photographs will vary from time to time. And I need to lay the foundation through the witness why they are relevant, whether we stipulate to them or not. I frankly don't know why each photograph has to be gone through with Mr. Skaggs. Your Honor, I think the photographs are easily identifiable from the exhibit list."

Judge Park replied, "It's unclear to me if either of

you are asking me to do anything, or if you're just making comments for the record."

Blonigen replied, "Just making a comment for the record."

Skaggs added, "I'm not asking you to do anything, but I don't understand why we have to go through this."

That being said, Judge Park let things go on as they were, with the understanding that Skaggs would object to any photograph he didn't think was admissible as they came up, one by one.

Mike Blonigen showed Sheila Kimmell a photograph of a plaque that was recovered from the search on Dale Eaton's property in 2002. Asked if she knew what it was, she replied, "That was the plaque Lisa received when she participated in a DECA competition, where she won a scholarship for Trent College."

This drew an immediate objection from Skaggs. "Your Honor, I object on the foundation of that exhibit. He said it's an exhibit allegedly seized from a search. That needs to be done before he introduces the exhibit, and I'm going to object to the admission of this exhibit."

Blonigen responded, "A person has to identify it as being Lisa's property before it becomes very relevant for the search. You must do one or the other first."

Judge Park replied, "I will overrule the objection, subject to it being tied in."

So Blonigen offered the photograph to be brought in as Exhibit 147. Skaggs, however, objected again, saying, "It hasn't been tied in yet." Judge Park sustained the objection. Not going any further with the photo of the plaque, Blonigen asked Sheila Kimmell if she recognized the next item. She said, "That's the rosary that Lillian Howard gave my daughter when she completed confirmation for catechism."

Blonigen asked Sheila if she knew what Exhibit 149 was. Sheila replied, "Those are hats that the managers wore when they were in the work prep areas. They were required to wear those at Arby's."

Blonigen asked why Lisa would have those Arby's hats in her vehicle, and Sheila responded, "For a couple of reasons. It was required when they were in a food prep area so they would have some kind of hair control. Then, oftentimes, when the boss would come in, such as myself, if they got caught without their hat, well, they would have one handy."

Blonigen next gave Sheila a photograph of a pair of shoes and asked if she recognized the shoes. Sheila answered, "Those would be Lisa's shoes." Asked when was the last time she had seen Lisa wearing the shoes, Sheila replied, "She had those shoes on the night she took me to the airport."

Blonigen showed Sheila a photograph of two keys, and Sheila said one was an ignition key to Lisa's Honda CRX. The other was to the mailbox they had at the apartment in Denver.

On cross-examination, Skaggs knew that he had to tread carefully. Sheila Kimmell was obviously a sympathetic witness to the jurors, and any appearance of badgering her by him would backfire. Skaggs started out by asking if Lisa would pick up hitchhikers, and Sheila replied that she would not. He next asked what kind of clothing she would have taken on that trip in 1988. Sheila responded, "Her sweaters, semi–dress pants, like her Dockers or whatever. Maybe a couple of pairs of blue jeans. She wouldn't have packed heavily, but, you know, appropriate for a four-day trip."

Asked if there was a reason why Sheila would

remember the particular pair of shoes that came in as an exhibit, Sheila replied, "Because I saw her wear them on a number of occasions."

Skaggs responded, "Okay, but you understand that a manufacturer can make a number of pairs of shoes, same size, to look the same?" Sheila agreed and commented, "Well, those look identical. Whether another manufacturer made them or not, those look identical to what Lisa wore."

Skaggs tried again to make his point. "You don't know they are the specific shoes in question. They look identical?"

Sheila said, "Yes, they look identical."

Skaggs spoke of the Arby's hats and rosary, and then asked, "What else did she have in her car that you haven't seen?"

Sheila said, "I mentioned the other ring that was not located. There would have been an assortment of makeups and grooming items that she would have taken with her."

"Anything else in that car, like a lot of people carry rescue gear in their car. Extra coats, whatever?"

"I know one thing she did have was a complete collection of Pound Puppies on her dash."

"And what are Pound Puppies?"

"That was a promotion that Hardee's restaurants were running at the time. And she liked little stuffed Pound Puppies, so she made a point to collect each little Pound Puppy and put them on the dash."

"You've never seen that collection since you last saw the car?"

"No."

"What about her glasses?"

"Okay. I know that she had glasses. But she didn't

wear them around on a frequent enough basis to where I would recognize them immediately."

"You were shown a pair of frames that were recovered from Mr. Eaton's property, correct?"

"Correct."

"And you could not identify those frames?"

"Not for a certainty."

Skaggs wanted to know if Lisa had carried around any types of prescriptions with her. Sheila asked, "Prescriptions?"

Skaggs replied, "Birth control pills, anything like that."

Sheila replied, "I believe she was taking birth control pills, but that was not something she was really speaking about with me."

"Would she carry that in her car?" Wyatt Skaggs asked.

Sheila replied, "I would assume so."

On redirect, Mike Blonigen asked, "Did Lisa get those glasses after she graduated?" Sheila responded that she thought so. Asked what she used the glasses for, Sheila said, "Usually when she did a lot of reading or night driving, or when she was doing her closing work for the restaurant. Just on occasion, and infrequently."

After that, the questioning of Sheila Kimmell was over, and she stepped down from the stand.

Next up was Ron Kimmell, and Blonigen asked him questions about Lisa's early life and disappearance. But what Blonigen really wanted to get on the record was Lisa's driving plans and Ron's insistence that Lisa get gas in Cheyenne and always reset the odometer on the vehicle so as not to be surprised later and run out of gas somewhere down the road. Ron stated, "I taught her how to drive. And that was something taught to me—every time you gas up, that you zero out your trip meter so you could keep track of your mileage on your car for purposes of not having to rely on your gas gauge if something would go wrong with that. You should know how far you can go on a tank of gas just by the trip meter."

Ron also spoke of where he insisted that both Sheila and Lisa should gas up on their trips from Denver to Billings. He said, "Always in Cheyenne." As to the route from Casper to Cody, Ron stated that Lisa had been on a trip on that route before with both himself and Sheila, "but she hadn't driven then." And as to following through on plans that she made beforehand, Ron said, "It was her habit to follow through on her plans."

Getting to all the attempts at finding Lisa or her vehicle in 1988, Ron told of all the posters he'd distributed while driving on the roads around Wyoming. "I first went the back way out of Cody, and then down through Thermopolis and Shoshoni, and back the way her route should have gone. I stopped at all of the sheriff's stations along the different counties and gave posters. They took me out on some of the roads. We would get off to some of the deep ravines and you couldn't see if the car had gone down off the road. We would walk down in those."

As far as the missing person posters went, Ron said, "I put them anywhere I could put them. Stores. Anyplace. They had a description of her and the car."

Mike Blonigen moved to have a photo of the poster admitted into evidence as Exhibit 300, but Skaggs spoke up and said, "Your Honor, I would again renew my objection to the state's Exhibit 300, particularly the picture portion of the poster. The picture portion shows a live photograph, which we believe is inadmissible under *State* v. *Wiks,* and move to exclude that portion of that poster."

Blonigen shot back, "For the same reasons we outlined previously, this is relevant to their attempts to find Ms. Kimmell. It will also be relevant later, for her identification from other individuals. And we believe we will tie it in by a statement made by the defendant."

Judge Park ruled, "Based on those representations, I will receive 300." Then Park said to the jurors, "Ladies and gentlemen, Mr. Blonigen is going to show this poster around to you. You may look at that and take your time to look at it, but it's also very important that you keep track of what is going on up here. So don't become so distracted looking at the poster that you miss testimony that is coming in from the bench."

Blonigen then asked Ron Kimmell, "Did you have any doubt in your mind if Lisa had been able to respond to this publicity at that time, she would have done so?"

This brought an immediate objection from Skaggs: "Calls for speculation." His objection was sustained. So Blonigen rephrased the question by saying, "Based upon her previous habit, do you believe that Lisa would have responded?" Ron answered that he believed she would have done so.

Now Blonigen got to the main reason he wanted Ron Kimmell on the stand. Blonigen wanted to get to the matter of the "Stringfellow Hawke" note. Blonigen asked several questions about this matter, and Ron answered, "My wife called me from Denver on March 28, 1989, and she'd gotten a call from a friend of Lisa's." This immediately set off a debate between Skaggs and

Blonigen and Judge Park. Skaggs insisted this was hearsay, but Blonigen countered, "Exception, it's offered for non-hearsay purposes under *Olson* v. *State*, to explain why Mr. Kimmell took the actions he did."

"Triple hearsay," Skaggs replied.

Blonigen responded, "He received the phone call— that's why he acted."

Taking that into consideration, Judge Park pronounced to the jurors, "The information that you are about to hear concerning this phone call is not offered for the truth of the phone call. It's offered to explain why Mr. Kimmell did what he is going to describe for you. And I will overrule the objection with that explanation."

Blonigen asked once again about the phone call, and Ron Kimmell said, "My wife had received a phone call from one of Lisa's friends, who told her there was something taped to my daughter's headstone at the cemetery. My wife called me to tell me about it on the night of the twenty-eighth." Ron added that he didn't do anything about it that night, because he received the phone call around ten o'clock.

Asked what he did the next day, Ron said, "I went to the gravesite to see what they were talking about. There was a note taped there with clear cellophane-type wrapping tape. It was an extremely odd note. It was taped right on the face of the headstone, up in the upper right-hand corner."

Asked by Blonigen if he would have spotted it previously, Ron said, yes, because it was quite a large note. Ron declared that he had been out to the cemetery within the last week, and he had not seen the note then.

Blonigen queried what Ron did with the note, and he answered, "At first, I didn't do anything. I called the sheriff's office to see if I should remove it. I was

informed that I could carefully take it off. I took it off
and took it to the Yellowstone County Sheriff's Office."

Blonigen wondered how tightly the note had been
taped to the headstone, and Ron replied, "I had some
difficulty getting it off. I had to use a pocketknife to peel
up the edge so I could pull the rest of it off. I had to take
pretty good care getting if off without hurting the note.
I put it in an envelope, and I gave it to Deputy George
Jensen, at the Yellowstone County Sheriff's Office."

Blonigen showed Ron Kimmell State's Exhibit 717,
and asked if the copy of the note had been altered in
any way from the first time he saw it. Ron said that it
hadn't been altered.

Surprisingly, Skaggs had no questions of Ron
Kimmell.

The next person on the stand was Ed Jaroch, and he
basically spoke of how he had first met Lisa Kimmell,
her plans to come by and pick him up in Cody, the
moment he realized that she was missing, and then
going to see Lisa's parents in Billings. He also testified
as to when Lisa was supposed to have shown up in
Cody, and the fact she was very clear on the route she
should take from Colorado. Like Ron Kimmell, Ed
spoke about the air and ground search for Lisa and
her car, once it was determined she was missing. Wyatt
Skaggs had no questions for Ed Jaroch on cross.

The next witness was, in fact, the ghostly voice of Lisa
Marie Kimmell herself filling the courtroom. It was a
tape of her speaking with Highway Patrolman Al Lesco
on March 25, 1988. Lesco had clocked her at eighty-
eight miles per hour, and when he pulled her over and

cited her, he told her she would have to pay a $120 fine. In a soft, timid voice, Lisa was heard on the tape saying, "You want all that right now? I only have forty dollars with me." Then she asked, "Can I go to the nearest bank?"

"None of the banks are open," Officer Lesco replied.

"Um, how about a cash machine?"

"I'm not sure if there's one in town."

"And if I can't get the money?" Lisa asked.

Lesco thought she might have the money wired to her. This option wasn't tried, and Lisa followed Officer Lesco to town and tried her bank card in an ATM machine. But in 1988, a bank card from a particular bank would not work in another bank's cash machine. "It won't take my card," Lisa's voice declared over the tape.

Making a decision, Al Lesco allowed her to sign a form promising she would pay the fine when she got to where she was going. He even asked her where that was, and Lisa's voice pronounced on the audiotape, "I'm going to Cody. I was staying with my mom in Denver and I got a phone call this morning saying a friend was going into cancer surgery Monday, and, uh, and I have two days off, so I wanted to see her." Lisa gave her address in Billings and Denver; then her words on the tape stopped. Those were her last words anyone—except her killer—would ever hear again.

When the tape was over, there was barely a dry eye in the courtroom. The Kimmell family used tissues from a box that had been provided for them from the courtroom. Officer Lesco had agonized ever since he found out that Lisa had been murdered—if he'd never seen her speeding, she might still be alive today. It was, of course, not his fault, but it bothered him greatly.

* * *

Mike Blonigen asked fisherman William Bradford about what he had seen on the morning of April 2, 1988, at the North Platte River, when he had gone fishing there. Bradford testified about spotting a young woman's body in the river and then about contacting the sheriff's office. Skaggs had no questions of Bradford on cross-examination.

Detective Michael Sandfort was next, and he told the jurors how he had received a phone call on Saturday, April 2, 1988, which he took at home. He had been told that the body of a young woman had been found floating in the North Platte River, and Sandfort related how he had gone to the scene with Investigator Dan Tholson, and they arrived there about 3:00 P.M. Sandfort testified, "Just before you get to the Government Bridge, if you're going southbound, you will make a left-hand turn onto the Bolton Creek Road. There's a set of corrals there where the local ranchers gather their cattle for shipping and moving. And you have to drive down that road, maybe one hundred twenty-five to one hundred fifty yards and then turn right to get to the old bridge. The old bridge is not in use. It's just there. They have never torn it down, but that's how you get there. The far end of the bridge is fenced off. And there's just kind of a turnaround area where fishermen and hunters and people would turn around and stop there.

"The road to the bridge is dirt or gravel, and the bridge itself has the asphalt covering on it. There is blow sand and blow dirt on top of the asphalt. At that particular time, on the other side of the bridge, there was hay and cow pies. It looked like an area where the ranchers had been feeding their cows. And there was a gate at the far side of the bridge where they could move their cattle and livestock from one pasture to the other."

Mike Blonigen wanted to know in which direction the river flowed at that point, and Sandfort answered, "The river flows from south to north. There's a bend in the river, and it flows around and underneath the Government Bridge and goes down around a parking area."

Blonigen asked how far from the Old Government Bridge Lisa Kimmell's body had been found. Sandfort replied, "By the crow flies, from the bridge to where her body was found, about eight-tenths of a mile. By the course of the river, a mile and a quarter, something like that."

Blonigen asked if there were any rural roads that ran directly from Moneta to the Old Government Bridge area, and Sandfort said that there were several. Sandfort added, "One of them would be the Gas Hills Road, going south from Waltman to the Dry Creek Road. You would be coming from south of Alcova, almost to Independence Rock."

Blonigen wanted to know how far it was from Douglas, where Lisa had been stopped for speeding, to Casper. Sandfort replied that it was approximately forty-two miles. Blonigen then asked if there would have been any way for Lisa to have gotten from Douglas to the Old Government Bridge by 9:40 P.M., and Sandfort said no. In fact, Sandfort had driven this route himself, and said, "I found that it would take forty-five minutes, plus or minus a couple, depending on how fast you were driving from Casper. Since Lisa got her citation for speeding, I would think that it would probably slow her down to just over the speed limit. And I was taking that forty-five minutes from the McDonalds in Douglas just to Casper. You could add another forty miles to that to the Government Bridge."

Blonigen handed Detective Sandfort several photographs and asked him to explain to the jury about them. Photo 404 depicted an area of the North Platte River where Lisa's body had been found. Sandfort said, "There's a gravel bar that comes out from the west side of the river, and that's an area where a lot of fishermen fish, because it's a good place for the fish to spawn and feed."

Blonigen asked if Lisa Kimmell's body could be seen in the photo. Sandfort replied, "Yes, in the distance. About thirty-five to forty yards out into the river itself, and probably in about fifteen to eighteen inches of water."

The next photo was a closer view of Lisa's body, as was photo 406. Blonigen had the jurors pass the photos around and look at them. Along with these was photograph 401, which was a close-up of Lisa's body. Blonigen told the jurors to look at the photos, but also to stay focused on the testimony. As the photos were passed around, various members of the Kimmell family in the gallery wiped away tears from their eyes.

Blonigen wanted to know what Sandfort did after photographing from a distance. Sandfort said, "We went out into the water and took more photographs of the victim's body in place. And after we felt comfortable with the amount of photographs, then we removed the body from the water out onto the shore."

Blonigen asked if Lisa's body had been caught up on any obstruction, and Sandfort responded, "No. It was just hung up with the arms dangling and the legs dangling on the rocks in the shallow part of the river."

Blonigen asked, "At the time, did you know basically what you were looking at?"

Sandfort replied, "I suspected it at that time. But it was not confirmed."

"You've seen bodies that have been in water for substantial periods of time?"

"I have. Approximately fifteen to twenty drowning victims."

"How can you describe the appearance of this body at the time you observed it?"

"This was a fresh body. It had not been in the water long, or did not appear to have been in the water long. In my experience, bodies that have been in the water a lengthy period of time—"

At that point, Skaggs jumped in and said, "Your Honor, I'm going to object to this, unless it's qualified. He's not an expert witness."

Blonigen responded, "Your Honor, he's just saying what he observed. He's not claiming to be a medical doctor or anything else."

Judge Park declared, "Objection is overruled."

So Blonigen started again. "You indicated the body appeared to be recent. 'Fresh,' I think, is the word you used."

"That's correct."

"And could you explain why you came to that conclusion?"

"It did not have the white, waxy color to it. Again, in my experience, bodies that have been in the water for a long time get almost like a wax bean look to them. And that one did not have that color. It still actually had human flesh color, if you will."

Blonigen asked if Sandfort had participated in the removal of Lisa's body from the river. Sandfort said that he had, and during his testimony, he was still emotional about what he had seen there so many years before. Sandfort noted that Investigator Kinghorn was in charge of the operation, along with Dr. Thorpen, who was the coroner. Sandfort also noted that when the body was taken to the shore, they all noticed several stab wounds to the chest area. Blonigen asked if he recognized the body at that point, and Sandfort replied, "From the posters that had been posted in truck stops, in the mini-marts, and everything else, I recognized the body to be that of Lisa Kimmell."

Blonigen wondered what Sandfort's job was after the body was pulled to shore, and Sandfort replied that he was to find the "dump site," where the girl's body had been deposited into the river. From past experience, he started looking at the bridges, the old one and the new one, as possible sites where she had been thrown into the river. Sandfort added, "The new bridge, because it was so well-traveled, and there was so much traffic on it, we didn't think there would be a good place [for the body to have been dumped]. But the old bridge would be a good place to start. We checked both bridges, but there was nothing found on the new highway bridge."

Sandfort noted that he was in charge of checking the Old Government Bridge, along with Patrolman Frye and Sergeant Means, of the Wyoming Highway Patrol. They started looking at the Old Government Bridge about 4:00 P.M. Mike Blonigen asked, "When you went to look at the Old Government Bridge, was the fact that the body had been found midstream significant to you?"

Sandfort replied, "Yes, it was. That time of year, the river—"

Skaggs objected again. "Your Honor, I'm going to object to that. The question was 'Was it significant to you?' The answer was yes. And now he's expounding on that. He's answering a question that wasn't asked."

Before Judge Park could rule on the objection,

Blonigen said, "I'll simply follow up with a different question."

Judge Park said, "All right."

So Blonigen asked, "Why was it significant to you, Mr. Sandfort?"

Sandfort answered, "That time of the year, the water runs fairly low. We'd not had the spring runoff yet. So you can tell where the main channel of the river is, by looking into the river itself."

"And in the main channel, would there be enough water and current to carry something downstream?"

"Yes."

"What happened when you and Mr. Means and Mr. Frye arrived at Government Bridge?"

"I parked on the north end of the bridge, on the Casper side of the bridge. Sergeant Means parked on the south side of the bridge, and then we started walking toward each other along the downstream side, or the west side of that bridge. Patrolman Frye went to the other side of the bridge, which would be the upstream side of the bridge and started walking toward the south. Sergeant Means was walking toward me. We were probably forty or fifty yards apart. And he pointed at the bridge and said, 'Here it is.' I immediately went there. And there was a large pool of blood on the downstream side or west side of the bridge."

Blonigen queried, "What do you mean by 'large'? How would you describe 'large'?"

Sandfort replied, "Probably the entire area was maybe six feet wide, or the length of the bridge. And then maybe a foot and a half out from the concrete curb on that downstream side of the bridge."

"Now, by six feet long, was the entire bloodstain six feet long?"

"No, no."

"You're referring to an area, then?"

"An area, yeah. The actual blood spot was, well, there were actually two of them. One on either side of a drain."

Blonigen then showed Sandfort a photograph of the bloodstain, and Sandfort agreed that was the way things looked on April 2, 1988. Blonigen had Sandfort use a Sharpie ink pen to highlight the area in the photo he was talking about, and Sandfort circled the area. Blonigen then asked if Sandfort and the other officers scouted around the bridge for other evidence. Sandfort said that they had, and these officers included himself, both of the mentioned highway patrolmen, Detective Dan Tholson, and Sheriff Ketchum, who had arrived on scene. They started on the beginning of Bolton Creek Road and worked their way to the bridge, looking for anything that might be significant. These included cigarette butts, beer cans, and, as Sandfort put it, "anything that might have been involved in this crime."

"Did you find any other items of significance outside of the area you've discussed with us?"

"No."

Blonigen got Sandfort to tell more about the bloodstained area, and Sandfort said, "There was a large amount of blood that had run down the outside of the bridge, both on the concrete structure itself and down about five and a half or six feet into an angle iron section that goes to the inside of the bridge that helps support it. There was blood that had run down the concrete and was on the outside of a rail."

Mike Blonigen wanted to know what the condition of the blood was when he looked at it, and Sandfort said, "It was fresh blood. It was crisp. It was clean. There was no dust on it. It had not feathered out. By feathered out, what I mean, once it is exposed to water, it tends to bleed to the outside. There was no indication it had been exposed to any kind of water at all."

Blonigen asked if that was true for blood that had dried, but had later been exposed to water, such as rainfall. Sandfort replied, "Yes. There was no separation of the blood. I'm not scientific, so I don't know how to explain it. But the blood will separate into levels. There was no separation of the blood."

This was all important material for a timeline. If the blood was fresh, then Lisa Kimmell's body had not been at the Old Government Bridge very long by the time her body was discovered. And if that was the case, then she had probably been held captive and sexually molested on Eaton's property for a number of days after March 25, 1988, when all sightings of her being alive ceased.

Blonigen showed Sandfort a photo marked 410 and asked him what it depicted. Sandfort said, "That would be the bloodstain in the center area on top of the concrete pylon, and in the shadow of the larger pool of blood. Just to the north of that, there's a drain hole. And there was blood there that had gone into that."

Blonigen asked, "From all of your observations at that time, did it appear that Ms. Kimmell's body had been dumped off that bridge?"

"Yes."

"Did you ever find any other location that would suggest the body had been placed in the river anyplace but Government Bridge?"

"No."

"Now, I've noticed on some of the photographs we'll look at today, there is actually a date of '89, instead of '88. Can you explain why that is?"

Sandfort testified, "The camera that we had at that time had what was called a 'data back' on the back of it. And when you would be at the crime scene, you would have the strap around your neck. And there were three little knobs on the back of this, on the lower left corner, that set the date. And big-thumbs me, every time I picked it up, I would click that. That's why the date is wrong."

Blonigen wanted to know if after observing the bloodstains, had he processed any of the evidence? Sandfort replied, "Yes, we did. Myself and Investigator Tholson began by what is called 'trace taping' the top of the concrete. Trace taping, it's a clear tape, kind of like you would seal a package up to ship at UPS. And you lay it down, you smooth it out, pick it up, and lay it down and smooth it out. What we're trying to do is pick up any kind of fibers or hairs or anything like that, that might be left at the scene on or near the concrete. Concrete is an abrasive, and clothing like wool or anything like that might leave minute traces on the concrete."

Blonigen asked if an individual was hit with a hammer, would there sometimes be head hair left at the scene? Sandfort agreed that was correct. Blonigen then asked if he remembered seeing any head hair that day, and Sandfort answered no. Then Sandfort added that he didn't know how the testing went later. His job then was to pick up any trace evidence in the area. Something might contain head hair, but he wouldn't actually see that at the time.

At that point, Blonigen went through a list of items that Sandfort had obtained from the bridge. Number 417 was blood and dirt collected from a large pool of blood. Number 418 was a sample from the other side of the blood pool.

Blonigen asked him if they'd found anything else besides blood at the bridge. Sandfort replied that they'd seen some kind of light-colored fluid on the north side of the bridge, up against a curb. They thought it might be saliva and a mixture of blood together, so they collected it, and it became an item marked 419. Number 420 was a blood scraping from the rail on the outside of the bridge, about five feet down from the deck. Items 421, 422, 423, and 424 were also blood scrapings from various parts of the bridge, while 425 and 426 were blood samples from the railing, and 427 another mucus or saliva sample.

Mike Blonigen asked if there was any other evidence of a person who might have been in the area of the blood, around the time it was left there. Sandfort replied, "There was a partial footprint, or what looked like a footprint, which we illuminated with a flashlight. It was just to the north and east of the saliva. It was also within inches of where the body was deposited into the river. We tried to do a plaster cast of it, where you mix plaster of Paris and pour it into the area. It was our best shot, but it wasn't particularly productive."

Blonigen then asked what difficulties they had processing fingerprints. Sandfort said, "I wouldn't have a clue how old that bridge is, nor how many coats of paint [are] on it. The paint, the primer, and the silver color it originally was had chipped off. There was a lot of rust on the rail. We did our best. We tried to get latent prints, but we didn't get any."

Blonigen wondered if the concrete area would be a good place to get fingerprints, but Sandfort answered, "No, the concrete is like sandpaper. The oils from the skin is what makes the latent print. And I don't believe there's ever been a case in history where you get a latent print off of concrete."

At that point, Skaggs objected, saying, "That last part wasn't called for."

Judge Park overruled him.

That being done, Blonigen now approached the judge, along with Skaggs, and Blonigen said outside the hearing of the jurors, "Your Honor, I would also like to enter into the record a stipulation as to the blood samples, that these items were properly handled and a chain of custody established. They were properly collected, maintained, and duly transmitted to the Wyoming State Crime Laboratory by the Natrona County Sheriff's Office."

Skaggs replied, "Your Honor, this is the beginning of a stipulation in a series of what I call 'chain stipulation.' There have been a series of chain stipulations dealing with the blood evidence, which was collected, and, of course, tested several different times, moved around from laboratory to laboratory. We have been provided several different copies, several different times, with various parts of the chain. We were able to reconstruct the chain. We determined that due to the nature of the defense, and also due to the fact that the chain appeared to be solid, as far as we could tell, that requiring the state to prove a chain of evidence on the blood samples would be unnecessary, time-consuming, distract from the defense, and generally unneeded. So we elected to enter into a series of stipulations with the state. It was done at our behest, as a matter of fact."

Blonigen chimed in, "Both sides have thoroughly gone through the chain and it is well documented. I also can perceive of no difficulties in the chain." That being said, Blonigen announced that he was done questioning Detective Sandfort.

On cross-examination, Wyatt Skaggs handed Sandfort a copy of his report, and said, "Sergeant, you and

I have had occasion to meet before. As a matter of fact, I didn't recognize you this morning, it's been so long. But I want to ask you a series of questions about your investigation on that particular day at the bridge. Now, you indicated that it had rained some previous days before that?"

Sandfort replied that it had, and said that had occurred a couple of days before Lisa's body was found. So Skaggs asked Sandfort where he lived, and Sandfort replied in Casper. Skaggs then got Sandfort to agree that if it rained in Casper, it may not have rained out at the Old Government Bridge.

Skaggs asked if Lisa's hands had been in contact with the bottom of the riverbed, and if the body had run along rocky surfaces and the sandbar for a ways, before coming to rest. Sandfort agreed that the body was facedown at the time they found it. Skaggs then asked, "After the body was dumped in the water, it was probably facedown from there on out, until you found it, correct?"

"That is the normal position of drowning victims," Sandfort agreed.

"Okay, so she would have floated facedown, with her arms dangling, correct?"

"No evidence of that, but I would assume so."

"When you took the body out, you were very careful to treat it in such a way that no further marks or injuries would occur to the body—isn't that correct?"

Sandfort agreed that was so.

"And the reason for doing that is so that nothing happens to the body that was placed there artificially by the investigation. You indicated that the body looked fairly fresh. It did not have a waxy look to it?"

"That is correct."

"You didn't have occasion to measure the water temperature, did you?"

Sandfort replied, "I did not myself, but I do believe it was done that day."

In fact, someone had measured the river temperature that day, and Skaggs told Sandfort that the temperature of the water that day was forty-four degrees, as noted by Dr. Thorpen. Skaggs also got Sandfort to admit that the river water was very cold that day, something he knew, because Sandfort had waded out into it. Sandfort also agreed with Skaggs's assessment that a body will decompose more quickly in warm water, and stay "fresh" in colder water. Then Skaggs said, "Drowning victims sometimes develop a waxy look when the body starts getting older. But you're aware that Ms. Kimmell was not a drowning victim?"

"Yes."

"Okay, so you had occasion to write out a report on this matter?"

"Actually, it was tape-recorded, and then it was transposed from the tape recording."

"And you have a copy of that report in front of you?"

"Yes, sir."

"And that was written out shortly after your investigation, was it not?"

"Within several days, I would think."

"And it's accurate, is it not?"

"As accurate as I can—"

"I know you don't want to answer that question, because you're afraid I'm going to hit you with an inaccuracy. Be that as it may, it was accurate to the best of your recollection, correct?"

"Yes, the best of my memory and what I recorded at the time. My thoughts."

At this point, Skaggs started zeroing in on the fact

that Sandfort had said many things in his answers to Mike Blonigen's questions during direct testimony that were not in his initial report. Skaggs asked, "You did not indicate in your report the condition of the body, did you?"

"I do not believe so, but I would have to look through it."

"It would have been on the first page, I think. And I note that you didn't get the stab wounds and those sorts of things you reflected on in there either. But right now, I'm talking about the fresh condition of the body, as you testified to. That wasn't indicated in your report, was it?"

"It was not."

"And then you indicated that after you assisted in the body recovery, you had occasion to go back to the Government Bridge, where this blood had been, and you had a van?"

"Yes, we had a van."

"Now, before you reached the bridge area, a highway patrolman drove across the bridge and parked on the other side?"

"That would have been Sergeant Means, yes."

"Then you walked out onto the bridge, so did Sergeant Means. And you kind of met about halfway in between and saw the blood?"

"Yes."

"Then you walked back to the van and drove out onto the bridge with your van?"

"That's correct."

"And had there been any other cars across the bridge related to the investigation prior to the time the highway patrolman drove across?"

"Not that I'm aware of."

"You did not do any kind of photographs with respect to any kind of tire tracks, did you?"

"The bridge is real hard. There's no notation of tire tracks on the bridge."

"Listen to my question. Two cars had already driven on the bridge related to the investigation. So if there had been tire tracks there before, they might have been obliterated by either one of those two—isn't that true?"

"Yes, there—"

Skaggs cut Sandfort short before he could answer further. Skaggs said, "Now, you also had occasion to examine the blood, which was on the bridge, correct?"

"Correct."

"You said the blood appeared to be fresh blood?"

"That is correct."

"Referring to your report, did you indicate that the blood that you saw was fresh, on the report?"

Sandfort looked at his report and replied, "I do not see where I made that notation."

"Did you make any notation on your report that the blood did not appear to have been splayed out as a result of rain, or anything like that?"

"I don't believe I did."

"Did you make any indication on your report that there was no dust on the blood?"

"I don't believe I did either."

"Those are all things you remember from the scene, but you didn't put them down in a report, correct?"

"I remember them from the scene and seeing the photographs."

"So that's what you remember from looking at the pictures?"

"No. That's what I remember."

"Did you write in your report that you looked for cigarette butts, beer cans, anything that could possibly relate to this scene? In fact, you didn't indicate specifically looking for hair, did you?"

"I don't believe I did."

Skaggs now got to the blood that had run down the side of the bridge. "If you were to go to the edge of the bridge abutment and drop something down into the river, a pebble down into the river, it would contact the railing, would it not?"

"It might. It might not."

"Well, it's fairly apparent that when the body was dumped into the river, that it contacted that railing—isn't that true?"

"That's correct."

"As a matter of fact, in your report, you note that the body may have become hung up on that railing—isn't that true?"

"Yes, I did."

"Now, as to the saliva, was that sent in to [the lab] right away, or a long time after the investigation on the bridge?"

"That, Counsel, I cannot answer. I just collected it at the scene."

"Okay. In the plaster cast of the footprint, you attempted to cast it. Did you actually get a cast?"

"We did get a cast, but there is nothing discernible on that cast itself."

"Whatever happened to the cast? I've never seen it."

"I would not know."

Skaggs had scored some points by alluding to the fact that Sandfort had said many things on direct that had not been written down in his report. Skaggs hoped to put doubt in the jurors' minds as to whether Sandfort was now "remembering things" to help the prosecution—things he had not originally noted at the crime scene.

* * *

To counter this effect, Mike Blonigen, on redirect, addressed this matter. He asked Sandfort, "How would you describe your memory of this particular crime?"

Sandfort replied, "This, in a law enforcement career, was a traumatic experience."

Skaggs piped up and said, "I'm going to object to that, Your Honor. That is nonresponsive."

Judge Park overruled him, and Sandfort continued. "It remains vivid in your mind. Several of the crime scenes that I have investigated remain vivid in my mind. A quick glance at a report brings things back crystal clear."

Blonigen asked, "Whether you put it in your report or not, could you clearly see in the photographs that the blood had not been disturbed?"

"Yes."

"Could you clearly see in the photograph there was no dust in the blood spot?"

"Yes."

Getting to the van driving onto the bridge, Blonigen asked why it had been driven so close to the crime scene. Sandfort answered, "Our crime scene van has all our equipment. Instead of making trips back and forth, we parked the van fairly close to the scene."

Blonigen then asked if the van had been stopped short of where the blood was found. Sandfort replied, "I stopped short of the crime scene itself."

"Even though you didn't observe any tire tracks, after you and Mr. Means had been at the bridge, did you observe whether your vehicles left any tire tracks?"

"We did not leave tire tracks."

"Mr. Skaggs asked you about the body striking the rail or getting hung up on the rail. I'm going to hand you a photograph, which is number 415. And that's where we have these three arrows with the blood spots. Do you recall that?"

"Yes, sir."

"Those blood spots appear to have been produced by a drop from a height?"

Skaggs jumped in and declared, "Your Honor, I'm going to object. That calls for speculation."

Judge Park agreed and said, "Sustained. No foundation for that at this point."

So Blonigen rephrased the question. "In your training and experience, have you become familiar with what certain bloodstains appear like when they are deposited in particular matters?"

Sandfort replied, "In our training, there are high-velocity blood impacts and low-velocity impacts."

Blonigen asked, "And if blood or any other liquid, for that matter, falls from a height and hits a smooth surface, does it leave a different sort of mark than something being dragged over something?"

"It does. And then it depends on the angle at which it hits the surface, as to what direction the blood will go."

"Do the blood spots you see there appear to have come down from a height or been spread across a surface?"

"They appear to have come from a height, a simple drop."

"You talked about there being rocks along the river bottom, where Lisa's body came to rest. You went out there and actually assisted in the removal of the body— is that right?"

"Yes."

"How would you describe those rocks you folks were going over?"

"It's a gravel bar, so they are larger and smaller. It's

deposited material or sediment from the fleshing and the river flow itself to get [to] that area."

"Are they slick rocks? Smooth?"

"I would say, most are smooth because of the water."

"What we call river rock, if you do landscaping?"

"Yes."

Blonigen ended at that point, but Skaggs had a couple more questions. One was that Sandfort didn't claim to be an expert on all the types of river rocks in the North Platte River. There could be smooth ones, rough ones, sharp ones. Sandfort agreed that was so. Then Skaggs said, "You indicated in your report, and also your investigation indicated, that apparently the body had been lifted up over the curb and fallen off the side and hung up on the rail down below. Isn't that what you put in your report?"

"Yes."

"Okay. And even though there are no blood smudges on the railing down below, [it] doesn't mean that the body didn't come in contact with that railing, does it?"

"No."

Skaggs wanted to leave an impression in the jurors' minds that Sandfort's story kept changing in order to benefit the prosecution. Whether he accomplished that with the jurors remained to be seen.

Mike Blonigen next had Lieutenant Dave Kinghorn on the stand, to bolster what Sandfort had said, and also to relate his version of what had occurred upon discovering Lisa Kimmell's body in 1988. Kinghorn testified that he had been on call for the coroner's office on April 2, 1988, and he was also a deputy sheriff for the Natrona County Sheriff's Office. When he got the phone call about a body being found in the North Platte River, his duty that day was as a coroner's investigator. Asked what that meant, Kinghorn replied, "To assist Dr. Thorpen in the investigation on a coroner's side of the case."

Kinghorn related all the things he saw when he first arrived on scene, including the other officers there. Blonigen handed him a photo numbered 401— a photo of Kimmell's body—and asked if it accurately depicted what he saw that day. Kinghorn answered that it did. As to the position of the body, Kinghorn stated, "It was facedown in the stream. The head was pointing downriver, or toward the north. It was right at the surface of the water, but basically submerged."

Like Sandfort, Kinghorn noted that the water there was about eighteen inches deep, and Lisa's body had become hung up on a gravel bar in the river. Kinghorn then spoke of the pink panties and blue socks being the only clothing on Lisa's body. He also noted that the day was "sunny, clear, and springlike warm."

Kinghorn spoke of loading the body into the coroner's vehicle, and after that, he briefly became part of the search for evidence on the Bolton Creek Road. Kinghorn also noted that as soon as Lisa's body had been rolled over, there were apparent stab wounds to her chest. After his brief stint searching for evidence on Bolton Creek Road, Kinghorn said that he and Dr. Thorpen drove Lisa's body to Bustard's funeral home in Casper. The body was then photographed with the clothing on, and then photographed with the clothing off. Kinghorn spoke of looking for trace evidence and finding a couple of hairs on her stomach that did not appear to have come from Lisa.

Since the panties and DNA were so important to the

case, Mike Blonigen said, "I hand you the item I marked as State's Exhibit 603 and ask you if that appears to be the pair of panties that was removed from Ms. Kimmell's body that day?"

Kinghorn agreed that it was. Then Blonigen asked what had happened to the panties after they were removed. Kinghorn replied, "They would have been taken to the sheriff's office and logged in to evidence."

Blonigen asked, "Was their condition changed in any way upon collection? Did they remain in that condition?"

Kinghorn responded, "I can't answer that. They were turned over to Undersheriff Benton."

"And subsequently logged in to evidence?"

"Right."

"Was their condition changed at all by removing them from the body?"

"No."

Blonigen then got to the condition of Lisa's watch, and this momentarily caused confusion in Kinghorn's mind. He was shown item 634 and asked what time was on the watch. Kinghorn answered, "Ten after four."

This was Blonigen's mistake, and he quickly made light of it by saying, "Ah, I see that with age (his age)— and now I have my glasses. I handed it to you upside down. Now orienting the watch correctly, could you tell us what time is on it?"

Kinghorn answered, "It would be twenty minutes to ten."

"And is there a calendar or A.M./P.M. indicator on this watch?"

"No, there is not."

Kinghorn then answered questions about the sexual assault kit that had been used upon Lisa Kimmell's body, and stated that Dr. Thorpen had done the actual collection of evidence and did the sealing.

Mike Blonigen handed State's Exhibit 602 to Kinghorn and asked what it was. Kinghorn replied that it was a checklist of everything collected for the rape kit. Asked what was in that particular rape kit, Kinghorn replied they were blood samples, combed pubic hairs, pulled pubic hairs, six vaginal swipes, four anal and oral swabs. Kinghorn said that once the kit was sealed, no one opened it before it reached the lab.

Blonigen got back to the foreign hairs collected from the stomach of Lisa Kimmell's body. He handed State's Exhibit 607 to Kinghorn and asked what it was. Kinghorn replied that it was a clump of hair he had found on Kimmell's stomach, which he removed by wearing rubber gloves. He had put this into an evidence envelope, sealed it, and it was treated the same as other evidence. Blonigen had Kinghorn speak briefly about his role at the autopsy, saving the main questioning of that event for Dr. Thorpen.

On cross-examination, Skaggs first asked if Kinghorn had ever taken the temperature of the water in the North Platte River. Kinghorn said that he had not done so. Asked if anyone had done that, he replied that he didn't know. Kinghorn did admit that a "core body temperature" was done on Lisa's body after it had been recovered. Skaggs asked if Kinghorn knew the exact time the body's temperature had been taken, and he said he didn't know, but he agreed that it would have been after 5:30 P.M.

Skaggs then stated, "You were very careful to roll the body over in the water, correct?"

Kinghorn agreed that was the case. Kinghorn

also agreed that they were careful when placing it on a backboard, and then into a body bag. This led to Skaggs's next question about the foreign hairs found on Lisa's stomach area. Skaggs asked, "When you recovered the body and placed it in the body bag, you did not observe the hairs that you observed the subsequent day, did you?"

Kinghorn replied, "Actually, the hairs were observed that night. And no, I did not at that time observe the hairs."

Skaggs asked if the first time the hairs were observed was at Bustard's funeral home, and Kinghorn replied that was correct. Skaggs then noted that the body bag itself was a coroner's body bag, and asked if Kinghorn knew who maintained that body bag. Kinghorn replied that he maintained it.

Skaggs queried, "You didn't use a brand-new body bag at that particular time in 1988—is that correct?" Kinghorn answered that the bag used would have been a brand-new plastic bag that Lisa Kimmell's body would have been placed into, and then that was put inside the canvas-type bag.

"So the canvas-type bag is not a new bag?"

Kinghorn agreed that was so.

Skaggs next queried, "Was that bag inspected prior to the time that it was used to place the body into it?"

Kinghorn said he didn't recall, but it would have been a normal procedure to do so.

Obviously, Skaggs wanted the jurors to believe that the foreign hairs discovered later on the body's stomach area might have come from anyone who had been placed in the canvas body bag prior to that point.

Skaggs next got to the bruising found on Lisa Kimmell's wrists and ankles, and noted that the bruises were not observed until two days later, after the autopsy.

Skaggs asked, "You had not noticed it in the autopsy?" Kinghorn said that was the case.

"Now, the fact that you saw the bruising on that day does not in any way indicate that the bruising wasn't present two days earlier, does it?"

"No, it does not," Kinghorn replied.

It is not certain what Skaggs was getting at here, except perhaps to put in the jurors' minds that if Kinghorn and the coroner missed the bruising aspects for two days, what else had they missed?

Dr. James Thorpen was next to take the stand, and before he did so, he had spoken to the Kimmell family members in the gallery and warned them that much of his testimony would be very graphic, and the accompanying photos even more so. Even with this admonition, the Kimmells decided to stay. After all these years, they wanted to find out definitively how Lisa's life had ended.

Dr. Thorpen testified as to his qualifications by saying he had attended Johns Hopkins University School of Medicine, and then worked at St. Luke's and the Children's Hospital in Denver. From there, he'd moved on to joining the Central Wyoming Pathologist Group for the Wyoming Medical Center in Casper. He had been elected coroner of Natrona County in 1982, a post he had held ever since.

Thorpen was only on the stand briefly on Thursday. He detailed a small portion of his autopsy report and related that Lisa Kimmell's body had shown that her pubic hair had been shaved about six or seven days prior to her death. Sheila Kimmell had already testified that she had seen her daughter naked on March 24, 1988, when the fire alarm in their apartment went off, and Lisa had "intact" pubic hair. The implication was that her killer had shaved off Lisa's pubic hair as part of his sexual fantasy.

Dr. Thorpen's testimony resumed the next morning at nine-thirty, March 5. He spoke of the bruises and abrasions on Lisa's wrists and ankles, arms and legs, noting that he thought they had been caused by hemp or nylon braided rope. These bruises and abrasions had shown up after her body was embalmed, a situation that did happen on occasion. Thorpen said, "In my opinion, they represented binding marks," and he added that she had most likely been tied up throughout most of her captivity. There were also bruise marks at the bases of Lisa's thumbs, consistent with someone who had been forced to wear handcuffs for a prolonged period of time. In Thorpen's opinion, Lisa had been raped repeatedly during her captivity. The rapes had been of a "violent nature," according to Dr. Thorpen.

As far as Lisa's body temperature went, it was forty-six degrees Fahrenheit when discovered, and the water temperature of the North Platte River had been forty-four degrees that day. Only her fingertips had shown any signs of wrinkling. The best estimate Dr. Thorpen could give was that Lisa had been killed thirty-six to forty-eight hours before being found. That would have meant sometime between late March 31 to April 1, 1988. Since her watch had stopped at nine-forty, the most likely time of death had been 9:40 P.M., when it would have been dark. At 9:40 A.M., it would have been much more likely that someone could have seen Eaton there, by driving down the highway on the new bridge, or spotted by a fisherman on the river.

Dr. Thorpen noted that Lisa had been fed some kind of beef stew shortly before her death. Blood tests proved she had no alcohol or drugs in her system at time of death. Just before her murder, Thorpen surmised that her hands had been placed in front of her body and been handcuffed together. They had remained that way for some time, perhaps an hour and a half between the ride from Eaton's property in Moneta and the conclusion of the drive at the Old Government Bridge. Her hands had suffered a sort of "rigor" even before her death from the lack of her being able to move them.

From blood evidence and autopsy evidence, Dr. Thorpen speculated as to what had occurred when Lisa was killed. She was apparently marched out onto the span of the Old Government Bridge and told to stop. She most likely was looking away from her killer at that point. The killer hit her in the back of her head with a blunt instrument, possibly a hammer. He did it with such force that it caused a four-inch fracture at the back of her skull. Dr. Thorpen surmised that this blow probably did not kill Lisa instantly, but it would have left her unconscious and unable to move. She would have bled out within two to six hours without medical attention.

Her killer did not wait for that, however. He turned her over and stabbed her in the chest five times, hitting vital organs every time. He was skilled at what he was doing—not once did he nick any of her ribs. The killer also stabbed Lisa once in the upper abdomen, and the stab wound pierced her heart. In Dr. Thorpen's opinion, she died within seconds of being stabbed. The stab wounds were all 5.5 to 6.5 inches in depth, and three of them had actually gone in far enough to reach her spine. Lisa lost so much blood at the bridge, that both Dr. Thorpen and Tom Bustard were unable to draw any blood from her body on the night of April 2, 1988. Thorpen had to wait until the autopsy the next day to do so.

All during his testimony, graphic photos of the stab wounds and autopsy were shown to the jurors. The jurors did their best not to reveal any of the photos to the Kimmell family, who were sitting close by in the first row of the gallery. Some photos of the stab wounds, however, were held up in front of Dr. Thorpen so he could explain them to the jurors, and the Kimmells could see those very well. Despite these grisly revelations, the Kimmells were determined to sit throughout Dr. Thorpen's testimony to finally find out exactly how Lisa had died. For years, they had been bombarded with rumors, speculation, and innuendo. Now they were finally hearing the unvarnished truth.

Dr. Thorpen also noted that Lisa had suffered a broken hip, but this had most likely occurred when her body had been dumped over the side of the bridge and hit a guardrail down below the roadway part of the bridge, before splashing into the water.

On cross-examination, Skaggs got to one main point he wanted the jurors to hear. Skaggs asked Dr. Thorpen about whether Lisa Kimmell had been able to feel the stab wounds after being hit in the head. Thorpen admitted she had probably felt nothing after that blow. Skaggs then asked, "She did not suffer at all—is that correct?"

"That is my opinion," Thorpen replied. "No defensive wounds were found on her body, that would indicate that she had put up a fight while being struck in the head or being stabbed."

Of course, Skaggs did not ask if Lisa Kimmell had suffered both mentally and physically while being held captive and sexually assaulted by Dale Eaton.

Dr. Thorpen's testimony had been graphic and emotional for jurors and gallery alike. By contrast, the next witness's testimony was almost surreal by comparison with its past moments captured in time. The witness was Chris Reed, and she was the audio/visual technician for Natrona County. While the video of the search of Eaton's property was shown, Reed pointed out to jurors what was taking place. Reed had done the videotaping during the search of the property, trailers, outbuildings, and the actual unearthing of Lisa Kimmell's car. Reed discussed the condition of the dilapidated full-size mobile home and smaller trailer, and described them as being "in poor condition." That was putting it mildly. They had been filled with dirt, cobwebs, rodents, and insects.

Reed also noted, "There were piles of dirt scattered around. A lot of digging had taken place on that property over the years." What exactly Dale Eaton had been looking for, or burying, was hard to say. But one area of dirt dug up next to a white pipe sticking out of the ground was crucial to the case. It was right next to the small trailer, most likely in the area where the old school bus had been, where Lisa had been held captive. As jurors watched in rapt attention, they saw investigators digging deeper and deeper into the soil. The investigators went down six feet, eight feet, ten feet, twelve feet, until they attached cables to a black battered Honda, which had been buried underground. Then the vehicle was raised carefully to the surface. The vehicle was covered with dirt inside and out, and its windows were smashed.

Once it was lifted to the surface, the vehicle was quickly loaded onto a flatbed trailer and covered with a tarp. Reed explained that the vehicle was then taken to Casper, where it was thoroughly inspected for any evidence. She said, "Dirt, moist cold conditions underground, and the length of time the car was buried destroyed any chance of recovering fingerprints on the car. The VIN number on the car, however, matched that of the vehicle owned by Lisa Marie Kimmell. And the Montana license plate LIL MISS had come out of the same area as the car."

Just as important as Lisa Kimmell's vehicle being found on Dale Eaton's property was the DNA testing by two forensic labs. In some ways, it was even more important. Dale could have said that he had buried the vehicle on his property to help out a friend, but it was much harder to explain why his semen was found on the body and on the panties of the dead girl.

Two DNA experts testified for the prosecution, one being Kim Clement, a DNA analyst with Bode Technology Group of Virginia. Clement testified that another person besides Dale Eaton having the same DNA profile was 1 in 240 quadrillion, a mathematical impossibility, since there were only roughly 6 billion people on earth. A quadrillion is a million times larger than a billion.

Three areas of Lisa Kimmell's underwear that appeared to have semen stains on them had been cut out and eventually sent to the labs for testing, along with vaginal swabs from her body. The DNA from the semen connected a direct line from Lisa Kimmell back to Dale Eaton. Cellmark Diagnostics of Maryland, independently of Bode Technology, came back with the same results—Dale Eaton was the donor of the semen.

Wyatt Skaggs in cross-examination questioned the DNA analysts' techniques and how they arrived at their results. And Robin Cotton, of Cellmark, admitted that when tests were run on November 29, 2000, that a hit came back about an unknown male as the donor. The profile generated by Cellmark was entered into the FBI's CODIS database, and it wasn't until July 2002 that the Wyoming State Crime Lab notified investigators that a blood sample taken from Dale Eaton matched the DNA profile compiled by Cellmark Diagnostics.

It wasn't the DNA analysts, however, who were the main point of contention at trial that day. As the matters of RFLP, PCR, and STR analysis were discussed at length, it was noticed that one juror, in particular, appeared to be nodding off during testimony. Testimony of DNA evidence can often be lengthy and tedious for a juror. The jury was dismissed for the afternoon, and an emergency motion hearing was convened between Judge Park, Wyatt Skaggs, and Mike Blonigen. They all knew that something as vital as a juror not staying awake during testimony could lead to a possible mistrial, or serious complications when the case was reviewed by an appellate court. With that in mind, the "sleepy juror" was excused from further service, and an alternate took her place.

Up until Tuesday, March 9, Dale Eaton had conducted himself in court quietly and respectfully at the defense table. Scribbling on a notepad or gazing at witnesses, he showed almost no emotion most of the time. But when an inmate named Joseph Dax began to testify, Dale became extremely agitated.

Judge Park made an interesting comment to the jurors even before Dax began to speak. Park said,

"Ladies and gentlemen of the jury, this gentleman who is about to testify is in confinement. Because he's incarcerated, he's under the guard of a deputy, who is in the courtroom. That deputy is here solely because of Mr. Dax, and has nothing to do with Mr. Eaton."

That out of the way, it was learned that Dax had been in an adjoining cell to Eaton at the Natrona County Jail, in April 2003. Dax had been convicted of conspiracy to commit aggravated burglary; then later, not unlike Dale Eaton, Dax was serving time in a federal prison for being a felon in possession of a firearm. Dax's troubles began in 1991 when he was convicted of burglary in Crook County, Wyoming, and then he was convicted in 1996 for receiving and concealing stolen property. It was for this 1996 crime that Dax had been in the Natrona County Jail from April 3 to April 8, 2003.

While in the Natrona County Jail in 2003, Dax said, he had been in F Pod, which was an area where a lot of prisoners went before being transferred elsewhere. While Dax was there, Dale Eaton had been housed in a cell right next to his.

Mike Blonigen asked, "Do you see Dale Eaton in the courtroom today?"

"Yes, I do," Dax replied.

"Could you identify where he's sitting and what he's wearing?"

Dax pointed at Dale sitting at the defense table and said, "That guy over there."

At that point, Dale came unglued. Without warning, he shouted, "You f***ing don't know me! Why in the hell are you talking and pointing to me?"

Everyone was momentarily stunned by the outburst. Judge Park regained his composure and ordered Eaton to sit quietly at the defense table and not respond to anything witnesses said. Judge Park stressed that another outburst would not be tolerated. Eaton finally simmered down, but he was still clearly agitated as Dax answered Mike Blonigen's questions.

In fact, Blonigen took time to ask, "The gentleman that just spoke?"

"Yeah," Dax replied.

If Blonigen was trying to be ironic, he could have hardly used a more appropriate word than "gentleman." Dale was obviously not conducting himself like a gentleman at the moment.

Blonigen got Dax to talk about how much time a prisoner in F Pod could spend outside his cell during a day, and Dax said, "They give you about an hour out. They call it 'flag,' where you can walk around and go out and shower and use the phone."

Blonigen asked if while Dax was in F Pod, he had any conversations with Dale Eaton. Dax replied, "Quite a few, actually. Roughly maybe five or six."

Blonigen wanted to know if Eaton had told Dax that he was a suspect in a homicide, and Dax said, "Basically, yeah." Asked to expand on this, Dax responded, "There were numerous different conversations with him, but the first one was that he told me that it was something to do with CAC. Then he said that they had discovered some car out on a property. The first time we talked about it, he didn't give out much information."

Blonigen wanted to know if Dale had given out a theory of why the authorities were searching for a car on his property. Dax replied, "I'm not sure if it was the first or second conversation, but he told me about the property out there a little bit. It was his uncle's property and it was passed down to him. He didn't tell me where it was. He said that when he'd first gotten the property, all that basically was there was a camper, and he did some improvement on it and put up a shed.

He couldn't figure out something about this car. How they found it. He wasn't sure if some guy out in Colorado had said something about it, or if they had just found this vehicle by accident."

Blonigen asked, "So he was worried about some fellow in Colorado telling them, or something?"

"Supposedly, yeah," Dax replied.

Blonigen asked if Dax had ever seen Dale with a newspaper article in F Pod. Dax said, "One time, I did. I didn't see the article, but he had it in his hand when he was complaining about the article. It was about the car. He was saying a lot of aspects of it were, well, he thought they were trying to get him to admit to something. Or he didn't believe they had a lot of evidence and they were just trying to get him to admit to something. He didn't elaborate on what was in the article. He was kind of covering up his speaker when he was saying that."

Blonigen wanted to know what speaker Dax was talking about, so Dax replied, "They have a little speaker in every room. Sometimes the officer will call down on it and say, 'Get your shoes on and get ready to go.' And they can talk to you. And there's a little button you can push to contact wherever an officer is."

Blonigen asked Dax what else Eaton had to say, and Dax responded, "He called me over to his cell, and he'd heard I had a federal sentence. And he asked about my federal sentence and how much time I had. And that's—"

Neubauer jumped in at that point and said, "Your Honor, I'm going to object to that."

So Blonigen skipped to a different point, asking about what Dax had directly said at the time. Dax stated, "I was talking about my stuff, and we both were basically kind of talking about our age and not having a whole lot to lose in our lives, and stuff. And he talked about the property out there and the improvements that he put on it. It was [about] that time he had that newspaper article and he was kind of upset about it. That is when he kind of closed up the speaker and he started talking to me a little bit about it. And he said, 'You know, it's kind of funny how things happen in life. You don't mean to be in a situation, and all of a sudden, you're in a situation.' He started talking about this girl being a really nice girl. Out of the blue, he kind of said that she was helping him out. He didn't say what she was helping him out for. He said she was giving him a ride."

Blonigen asked if Eaton had ever told Dax how he and the girl had met. Dax said that no, he hadn't. Then Blonigen asked what happened after the girl gave Dale a ride. Dax replied, "Well, it was kind of weird. They were just driving along and talking. And he asked her if they were going to have dinner later. Just kind of teasing her. And he said he could see she started getting nervous, as if she was acting high and mighty. And he kind of reached down and put his hand on her leg, and made a comment, 'You don't date older guys?' She kind of freaked out and slammed on the brakes, and they went over to the side of the road. She was screaming and yelling, and telling him [he] was lucky to even be having a ride, and he shouldn't be acting like a weirdo. Then she said he could get out and just start walking."

Blonigen asked what Dale's next remarks had been. Dax replied, "He said that he wasn't going to get out in the middle of nowhere. He said that he got pissed off and basically just told her he wasn't getting out. She was still mad. She started to get out of the car and he didn't want to let her get out right there. So he just reached over and grabbed her. Everything just kind of spun out of control. He said that at that point he didn't have anything to lose. Then he looked over at me and said, 'Well, what would you have done?' And I didn't really know what to say to this guy. I mean, I probably would have just let her get out of the car or gotten out of the car myself. Then he said, looking back on it, 'I kind of wish I would have done the same thing. But I wasn't getting out of the car, and I wasn't letting her get out of the car, and that was it. Right then and there, I took ahold of her. There was no turning back. I knew I had to do her right there.' But he knew whatever was going to happen couldn't happen right there. And he was still making a point to me about if she hadn't been so high and mighty, a lot of this wouldn't have happened. It was weird, it was like he was trying to make me believe that he was justified in what he did. And I'm sorry, I wasn't buying it."

Blonigen asked if Dale indicated that he had sexual contact with the girl at that time. Dax said, "Yes. He said that nobody was even going to miss her, and that—I don't know if I want to say this—but basically that she was a lousy lay."

There was an audible gasp in the gallery and an immediate objection from Neubauer. "Your Honor, I object! This is not responsive!"

Blonigen chimed in and said, "It is responsive, Your Honor."

And then in an odd moment of solidarity, Joe Dax agreed with Blonigen and said, "Yes, it is."

Judge Park looked temporarily surprised by Dax's response, and then told him, "Mr. Dax, that's my decision."

All Dax said to that was "Okay."

After things simmered down, Judge Park overruled the objection, and Blonigen went on with his questioning. He asked once again if Dale had indicated that he'd had sex with the girl, and once again, Dax answered, "He said she was a lousy lay."

This brought another objection from Neubauer. "Your Honor, I object to that answer! It is highly inflammatory, and I ask that it be stricken from the record!"

"Overruled," Judge Park declared. And then he said, "Ladies and gentlemen, that statement is offered to you solely for the purpose of Mr. Blonigen's question, which was to indicate whether or not—and once again, it's up to you to evaluate the testimony—if Mr. Eaton had any sexual contact with Ms. Kimmell."

Blonigen then asked Dax, "Did he ever tell you he killed this girl?"

"No. Uh-uh," Dax replied.

"Did he ever tell you what happened, besides what you've told us about the incident on the highway?"

"No. They took me out. They transferred me out to Torrington Jail the next day."

Blonigen wanted to know if Dax told anyone about the comments Dale Eaton had conveyed. Dax replied, "I was in Torrington for two days and I told my federal attorney. Sometime later, I was interviewed by the police about this. Quite a while later."

Blonigen asked if Dax had also spoken to Dale's defense team about this, and Dax said that he had.

On cross-examination, Vaughn Neubauer said that Dax had just indicated in his testimony that he'd had five or six conversations with Dale Eaton while they were both at the Natrona County Jail. Dax said that was correct. Neubauer then noted that Dax had only been in F Pod at the jail from April 3 to April 8, 2003, so how could he have had six conversations with Dale in that period of time when they were only let out into a general area one hour a day. Dax said the number was five or six times, but he couldn't remember exactly.

Neubauer then handed Dax a paper entitled Defense Exhibit E, which was Dax's felony record. Neubauer asked Dax if it was accurate, and he said that it was. Neubauer wanted the exhibit introduced as evidence, but Blonigen spoke up and said, "Your Honor, I would object. It's not proper subject of impeachment. Under rule 609, impeachment can only be had on the nature of the conviction, the place, and the date. Contents of the exhibit exceed rule 609."

Neubauer countered, "I disagree. Under *Rivera*, the sentence received is relevant."

Blonigen came back with, "609 is merely impeachment. It is not substantive evidence."

Judge Park declared, "I agree with that remark. So based on that, I'm going to refuse Exhibit E. But that does not preclude you from discussing those under the rule."

So then Neubauer went about it in a different manner. He said, "Without an exhibit, Mr. Dax, you have to admit that you have a long, serious felony record, do you not?"

Dax replied that he did. So then Neubauer said, "And now you are facing some very serious time. You've already received some very serious time—fifteen years on your federal sentence, and you got twenty to twenty-five years on your state sentence, correct?"

Dax stated that was correct. Neubauer then asked him, "You've testified that the deal in the federal case was part of a drug investigation, correct?"

"It was, yeah."

"In that drug investigation that you were testifying in, you were hoping to get this deal on your federal sentence, correct?"

"Correct."

"That testimony you gave in January 2003, correct?"

Dax became upset now, because Neubauer seemed to keep pushing this point, and Dax replied sarcastically, "I've already answered that twice. I said yes."

Neubauer didn't back down and said, "Is that right?"

"Correct," Dax replied.

"Had you ever cooperated with the government, as far as testifying in a criminal trial, before that testimony in 2003?"

"Never."

"But you're hoping for a deal out of that testimony (about Dale Eaton) you gave in 2003?"

"Yeah. It's pretty much going to amount to a couple of years."

Obviously, Neubauer was trying to show the jurors that Joseph Dax had never tried making a deal when he had served small amounts of jail time in the past. But when he got fifteen years on one sentence, and twenty to twenty-five on another, he started fishing around for some deal to make. The impression Neubauer wanted to leave in the jurors' minds was that Dax had read about Dale Eaton in a Casper newspaper, knew that Eaton was in the cell next to him, and then concocted a story about Dale having conversations with him about the abduction of Lisa Kimmell.

On redirect, Blonigen asked if Dax knew how much of his state time and federal time were concurrent. Dax said that they were concurrent, so that both would be done at about the same time. And Dax said, "Even if I didn't get any sentence reduction in the state court (the present case), it's virtually pointless."

The impression Blonigen wanted to leave with the

jurors about Dax was that he came forward about Dale Eaton, not because he wanted a reduction in time, but because he knew it was the right thing to do.

Dax's testimony had clearly upset Dale Eaton, and he was still agitated by the next witness on the stand, Alice Kardonowy. In 1988, she had been a flagger/laborer on a road construction project on Highway 20/26, between Waltman and Hiland, Wyoming. In that capacity, she met Dale Eaton, who also worked for the construction company as an "oiler." Essentially, Eaton would grease and fuel the road construction equipment in the evening when the operators had quit work for the day. He did this on scrapers, trucks, and backhoes.

The Waltman Rest Stop was about the only facility in the area where the workers could wash up, use restrooms, and have lunch at a picnic table. Mike Blonigen asked Alice if she had ever been to Dale Eaton's place while she was working on the project, and she said yes. Asked if she had seen any digging or holes on the property when she was there, Alice replied, "Yes. He told me while I was over at his place that he was digging a well. Hand-digging a well on one side of his trailer, and he had a septic system he had just put in on the other side of the trailer."

Blonigen asked if Dale had ever taken Alice out to an old ranch near his property. Alice responded, "Yes. I really don't know the exact location, just that it's between Moneta and Hiland. About fifteen miles south on the highway."

Once Alice Kardonowy started talking about this ranch, Wyatt Skaggs interrupted the testimony and said, "Your Honor, may we approach the bench?"

He was allowed to do so, and the conversation that

took place was outside the hearing of the jurors. Skaggs said to Judge Park, "At this particular point, I would object to the testimony about this as being totally irrelevant. This place is not owned by Mr. Eaton. It doesn't have any connection whatsoever to Mr. Eaton other than her testimony that he used to take her to visit there. We don't have any time as to when it was done. We don't have any linkage as to what the relevancy would be with respect to this case. He's going to want to introduce pictures of this place and we have never seen the pictures before today. We never even knew about this testimony until today. I would object to this particular statement about going to another place that I don't even know about."

Skaggs was obviously worried that Alice Kardonowy was going to reveal something to the jurors about a trip to an old ranch near Hiland and what Dale might have done or said there. Blonigen, however, shot back to Judge Park, "Your Honor, Ms. Kardonowy looked at some old pictures she had, and she gave these to me at eight this morning. And I promptly gave them to Mr. Skaggs and told him about it. It is relevant, Your Honor, because this is a relatively remote location, directly off of 20/26, within the defendant's knowledge near the time period in question. And I would cite *Taylor* versus *State*—not all circumstantial evidence is DNA or a smoking gun. Sometimes it's little pieces. And this shows access to a place immediately off the route Ms. Kimmell would have been traveling at or near that time or place, and shows he was familiar with that location."

Skaggs countered, "There is no connection with Mr. Eaton at all with this particular place, no connection other than he showed it to her. It doesn't establish circumstantial evidence. She doesn't even know when it occurred. And she doesn't know whether or not he knew about it during the spring of 1988."

Blonigen argued, "She said this happened in the '88 to '89 period. That's very close in time. And that gives us a fair inference that he would have known about it then."

Judge Park thought about all of this, and finally told Skaggs and Blonigen, "Okay, I'm going to excuse the jury. And we're going to do this out of the presence of the jury, and I'll decide whether it can be brought in, in front of the jury."

That being said, Judge Park then addressed the jurors by saying, "Ladies and gentlemen of the jury, if you'll excuse us, the bailiff will show you back to the jury room, and we'll call you back when we need you."

Once the jurors were gone, Blonigen asked Alice Kardonowy some questions while only the defense, prosecution, and judge were in attendance. Blonigen asked Alice if she had worked on the highway project in 1988 and 1989, and she said that she had. Blonigen wondered when Dale had shown Alice the old ranch about fifteen miles from his property, and she thought it had been in June, probably in 1988. Skaggs jumped right in and said, "Well, Your Honor, she originally said 1988 or 1989. Now she's specifically saying 1988."

Judge Park responded, "You'll get a chance to cross-examine, Mr. Skaggs."

Blonigen continued, "Did Mr. Eaton ever tell you how he was familiar with this property?"

Alice replied, "I had mentioned that my brother had talked about a place that was real historical and really neat. And Dale said he knew where it was and he would show it to me. And he did. And it's a very beautiful place.

He took me there, and I have no clue as to how exactly to get there, except for just the general direction."

Blonigen asked what general condition the place was in, and Alice said, "It's a totally abandoned old ranch. A historical-looking place. I think it was on a private ranch road."

On cross, Wyatt Skaggs asked if Alice Kardonowy had gone into the ranch buildings, and she replied, "Yes, all of the buildings."

Skaggs queried if she saw anything out of place there. Alice said, "They were just old buildings, except for the way they were built. Everything is really unique. The bunkhouses had stoves in the middle of the rooms, and the stoves could slide over, and there were hidden rooms underneath them. It was supposed to be a place that was part of the Wild Bunch." (She was referring to Butch Cassidy and the Sundance Kid and the Wild Bunch, who were known to operate in the area.)

Skaggs asked, "Did you see anything out of order in those buildings, like blood, signs of a struggle, human hair, anything like that?"

"It's a dirty old condemned—"

Skaggs cut her off. "I understand that. So the answer is no, correct?"

Alice said that was correct.

Skaggs asked, "You indicated the first time that you met Dale Eaton in the summer of 1989 and 1990."

Blonigen jumped in and said, "I'm going to object to that. She said it was 1988 and 1989."

Judge Park looked at the testimony so far and replied, "That is correct, Mr. Skaggs."

Now things became very contentious between Wyatt Skaggs and Alice Kardonowy. He kept saying that she indicated a time period anytime in 1988 or 1989, while she kept insisting that she was now sure it was in the late spring of 1988, only months after Lisa Kimmell had been murdered. In fact, it got so bad, Skaggs said, "This is just a cross-examination, Ms. Kardonowy! Am I being unfair to you in any way?"

Blonigen jumped in and said, "Your Honor, I'm going to object to that."

But Skaggs responded, "She's being real aggressive, and I would like to know why!"

Judge Park told Skaggs to continue, so he asked Alice Kardonowy, "Now, did you meet Dale in the middle of summer?"

Alice replied, "In the middle of construction season. I'm not sure which month."

Skaggs kept trying to pin her down as to the exact time when she had first met Dale Eaton, and she responded, "It was after we started the job in April. That's all I can remember. I'm sure he started about a month later."

Skaggs kept hitting on this point of when she had first met Dale, and a very irate Alice Kardonowy said, "I don't know what the problem is! It was in the middle of construction season, whatever time that was!"

Skaggs looked deeper into his records and asked, "Do you remember talking to Lynn Cohee on August 21, 2002?"

Alice answered, "I talked to a person from that office. I don't know when or with whom."

Skaggs added, "Do you recall telling them that you didn't remember if it was 1988 or 1989?"

At her wit's end, Alice responded, "As I just told you, yes!"

* * *

Finally Blonigen and Skaggs made their final arguments to Judge Park on this issue. Blonigen reiterated that Alice Kardonowy's testimony placed the incident very close in time to Lisa Kimmell's abduction and murder, and that it proved that Dale Eaton knew back roads in his area. And according to Blonigen, this proved that Dale could have taken back roads to the Old Government Bridge on the North Platte River when he transported Lisa there to be murdered.

Judge Park finally ruled, "I'm going to sustain Mr. Skaggs's objection. I think that it does come as a surprise to him. He hasn't had a chance to make any inquiry or check out this property. And it is so circumstantial that it doesn't seem to be relevant."

Wyatt Skaggs was nearly as upset by the next witness as he had been with Alice Kardonowy. Keith Kerr was a power company worker in 1988, who spoke of Eaton installing his own power line and pole on the Moneta property. Kerr testified, "He (Eaton) advised me he had access to a backhoe and could install the power line himself." Kerr also spoke of overturned dirt on various portions of the property, where there had been digging. As to the power pole in question, Kerr testified that he was surprised that Eaton had planted the power pole so far away from his residence. The implication that Blonigen wanted to make was that the power pole, as the septic tank had been, were just ruses by Dale as to his real intention—burying Lisa Kimmell's Honda CRX. According to Blonigen, Dale wanted his neighbors to think all the digging on the property was about water and power, when, in fact, he was burying the dead girl's car. A car that had been described in all the local newspapers and on television news programs.

* * *

The next witness caused Dale to become agitated once again. It was none other than his own son Billy Eaton. Billy was now thirty-one years old, but he'd been a fifteen-year-old while living with his dad on the Moneta property. When Mike Blonigen asked Billy to identify Dale Eaton at the defense table, Billy said, "That's my father." Billy told about how he had been enrolled in Shoshoni High School from late August 1988 until January 2, 1989. During that time, he was living with his dad on the Moneta property. Asked what things his dad had on the property, Billy answered, "Some cars, a school bus, some poles, and, I think, a camper." Blonigen wondered if Billy knew of a metal shed on the property at the time, and Billy said, "There were poles there. The building was put up afterward. Dad was working on it (the shed)."

Asked who lived on the property then, Billy said that he did with his dad, "and my sister, for just a little bit." Blonigen questioned him about any holes that Dale was digging, and Billy replied, "He was digging a well." Asked to expand upon this, Billy said, "It was toward the southeast corner, I guess."

Asked if there were any other buildings on the property, Billy said no, then added, "There was a building across the street. I don't know if he had access to it. It was on the south side of the highway." Billy said that it was on the Buchtas' side of the highway, and he never went into the building. Asked why not, Billy stated, "Pretty much I was told to stay away from it."

"Who told you to stay away from it?" Blonigen asked.

"My dad."

"Now, was there some discussion about your dad saying he would find a vehicle for you?"

"No. No discussion."

"Okay. That wasn't a very good question. Let me ask this—I take it, like any kid that age, you wanted to have something to drive—is that right?"

Billy said, "Actually, I had a pickup."

"Where did that pickup come from?"

"My uncle Darrel."

"And what kind of pickup was it?"

"It was a '62 or '63 Ford F-150."

"What kind of condition was it in?"

"It was in really good condition. It had been redone."

Blonigen asked if Billy was familiar with Honda vehicles, and Billy said that he was and had been, even at the age of fifteen. Then Blonigen said, "After you moved to your father's place, did you see anything that appeared to have come off a Honda?"

"Seats and a radio," Billy responded.

Blonigen asked if Billy would describe those seats, and Billy replied, "They were black bucket seats, with kind of some pinstripe lines through them. I figured they were from a Honda, because I knew Honda seats. That's kind of what they looked like."

Getting to the stereo, Billy said, "The AM/FM cassette player had about a two-inch pocket under that for storage of tapes. And the AM/FM cassette lid said Honda on it. The console kind of wrapped around. It would have wrapped around the shifter on the floor of the Honda. We cut that off so we could put it in the pickup."

Blonigen asked who had cut it down, and Billy said that he and his dad had. Moving on to some aluminum wheels that Billy had seen on the property, around that time, Billy said they were Honda wheels, and he knew that they were, because they had the Honda *H* logo on them. "They had a teardrop sort of look to them.

Those kind were on CRXs and a top-of-the-line Accord at that time. Pretty similar wheels."

Asked what had happened to those wheels, Billy said that his dad had melted them down. Blonigen wanted to know if his dad melted down other items on the property, and Billy responded, "We melted down stuff like wire and sold it."

Blonigen questioned Billy about the vehicles Dale had owned back in 1988. Billy replied, "He had a '79-ish club cab Dodge dually (two rear axles), and a '72-ish International Travelall. The Dodge was his welding truck. It had a welding machine, toolboxes, and gin poles on it."

Asked what a gin pole was, Billy said, "Just something to hoist parts up in the air or whatnot."

Blonigen asked, "Were either of those vehicles capable of pulling a small Honda?"

Billy answered, "Oh, sure."

Moving in a different direction, Blonigen asked, "Was there any running water on the property?"

"No," Billy replied.

"Any electricity?"

"No."

"When you were living there, did you ever see your dad convert a vehicle into a septic tank?"

"I did years and years before we lived in Moneta. Over by Glenrock."

On cross-examination, Wyatt Skaggs asked Billy Eaton, "We met once before on a cold December morning. Do you remember that?"

"Yes, sir," Billy replied.

"Did you have any problem with that?"

"No, sir."

"You're acting rather nervous or hesitant now."

"No, I'm okay."

"So we had a nice conversation then, did we not? It was not confrontative, or anything?"

"No. It was fine."

Skaggs asked Billy if the larger trailer house had been out at his dad's Moneta property in 1988. Billy said that it had not been. Then Skaggs said, "You talked before about living conditions out there, and you described them as 'kind of old-timer living.' Correct?"

"Yeah."

Skaggs asked what he had used to take his baths in at the time, and Billy replied, "In a horse trough."

"And you had to use the restroom outside?"

"Yeah."

"And your sister had to take a bath in this horse trough?"

"Yeah. Once in a while, she would go over to Doris and Buck's."

"And that's where if you really needed to shower or something, that's where you went?"

"I don't ever recall myself going over there and showering, but I know my sister did."

"That property, there was a lot of dirt blowing around?"

"I suppose. It's a long time ago."

"Well, that's what it's like out there in the summertime. Not real pleasant, is it?"

"I don't really remember it being all that bad. I was pretty young. It was kind of fun."

"I guess 'camping out' would be a way to describe it?"

"Pretty much."

Skaggs questioned Billy about the building across the highway and asked, "You said you were instructed not to go in it by your dad. Do you recall saying that?"

Billy responded, "I'm pretty sure I was told that I was not supposed to go around that building. And I believe the reasoning was—"

Skaggs cut him off before he said another word. "Well, I didn't ask you what the reason was."

Billy said, "Okay."

Skaggs then asked, "You don't know what was in that building, correct?"

Billy answered, "I don't know if anything was in that building."

Moving on to the hole in the ground, Skaggs wanted to know if there was anything in the hole at the time Billy saw it. Billy replied, "No."

"And there was no backhoe around there?"

"No, there was not."

About the Ford F-150 pickup, Skaggs asked if it was actually Dale who had driven it to the Moneta property from Darrel's place. Billy said that he didn't know, and then added, "He (Dale) kind of did what he wanted."

"And your father had quite a lot of junk lying around the place?"

"Always."

Then Skaggs said, "It was kind of a junky old pickup, correct? It wasn't really a pretty pickup?"

This irritated Billy, and he answered, "Well, if that's the opinion you have, fine! But it had a brand-new paint job. It was a very nice pickup!"

Skaggs quickly added, "At that particular time. But have you seen it since it was recovered?"

"Yes, I have."

"And it's not very pretty now, correct?"

"I'm not impressed."

Perhaps at that point, Skaggs thought it was best to let things stay as they were, and he ceased his questioning.

* * *

Mike Blonigen had a few more questions on redirct. He asked if Billy got to know the country around Moneta a little bit when he was there, and Billy said that he had. Blonigen wondered, "How would you describe the country out there?"

Billy replied, "Oh, sagebrushy. There's kind of canyons, creeks, willows, here and there."

Blonigen asked, "That water hole—there was never actually water in it, correct? Just a big hole?"

"Right."

"And when you saw those Honda parts at the time, how did they look to you?"

"Pretty new. Very new."

A woman named Mary, who worked at the Community Alternatives of Casper while Dale Eaton was forced to stay there under the terms of his plea deal for assaulting the Breedens in 1997, took the stand. Even more than this, Dale had been friends with her husband, and she had known Dale since 1989.

Mary testified that Dale began asking her out after she and her husband had separated for a while. She refused to do so, even when Dale gave her son one of his trucks. She described it as an odd gift to give someone "when they were courting." Dale was persistent, however. He gave her a ring, a coat, and a pair of red gloves, all to no avail. She still steadfastly refused to go out with him.

Mary described Dale as someone who rarely showered. Dale had also told Mary, while staying at CAC, his version of events with the Breedens. Dale once again used the story that he assaulted the couple so they would grab the rifle and kill him. He said that he was suicidal at the time, but he was too chicken to kill himself.

Then he told Mary something very disturbing. He said to her back in 1991 never to stop at a rest stop when she was alone. He declared that a woman on her own doing that could be raped and then killed. This was the closest Dale alluded to what probably had occurred to Lisa Kimmell in 1988 at the Waltman Rest Stop.

Corporal Lynn Cohee, of NCSO took the stand on March 10 and explained one item of evidence after another to the jurors. Cohee held pieces of a taillight from the Honda that had been dug up on Dale Eaton's property, and placed them next to blown-up photos of a taillight being unearthed. The actual item and the photos from 2002 matched. She said the taillight items had been discovered near Eaton's "water well hole." Cohee did the same thing with actual bumper pieces from the Honda, and photos of the bumper pieces being unearthed in 2002. These matched as well.

Photos of investigators unearthing the car in 2002 were shown to the jurors, and Cohee explained that the bulk of the car had been ten feet or more underground. Dale would have needed a backhoe to bury the car that deeply. One photo showed that the vehicle keys had been left in the car. Personal belongings of Lisa's were discovered within the buried car as well. These included a pair of shoes, a few Arby's visors, eyeglass frames, and a rosary she had hung from her rearview mirror. On direct examination, Sheila Kimmell had identified all those items as belonging to Lisa.

* * *

On cross, Lynn Cohee admitted that other personal items of Lisa's were never found, including her suitcase, extra clothing, cosmetics, and her wallet. There was one question, however, that Skaggs may have wished he had not asked. It was about a jar of Carmex found in the vehicle. Lisa Kimmell had used Carmex for a rash on one of her legs. Perhaps Skaggs wanted to prove by the date on the Carmex container that it could not have been sold by the time Lisa was murdered. If so, what was that Carmex doing in her buried car? But Cohee had been able to track down the coding date of when that batch of Carmex had been made, and it turned out to have been before Lisa had been murdered.

Detective George Jensen testified next, mainly to address the issue of the "Stringfellow Hawke" note left on Lisa Kimmell's headstone. Jensen recounted how the note had been handed over to him by Ron Kimmell, and it had not been altered in any way. Next to address the mysterious letter was an expert in handwriting analysis, Jim Broz.

Jim Broz, who had been one of the initial NCSO investigators on Lisa Kimmell's case, was now living in Denver and working for the United States Mint. Broz was by this time a handwriting expert, and he testified that since 2002, he had been given 137 handwriting samples that Dale Eaton had penned. Broz noted their particular punctuation and the incorrect spelling of various words. He also noted similar stroke marks on certain letters, both in Eaton's handwriting samples and the "Stringfellow Hawke" note. In both cases, there were also a mixture of words that were printed and in cursive style. In Broz's opinion, Dale Eaton had written the "Stringfellow Hawke" note.

* * *

When Eaton's defense lawyers did not cross-examine Broz, Dale became irate once again. He shouted at his lawyers, "I can prove where the fuck I was that day, and you guys won't do nothing!"

Once again, Judge Park admonished Eaton to be quiet and to control himself. In fact, there was a hearing outside the presence of the jury later in which Dale Eaton was told to conduct himself quietly at the defense table and not interrupt the testimony of witnesses.

Following Broz came ninety-one-year-old Doris Buchta, who had been Dale Eaton's neighbor in 1988. She had kept a journal during the spring of 1988, and penned various entries of the key dates of March 25 to April 2, 1988. On being called to the stand, Blonigen asked her to state her name. Doris turned toward Judge Park and said, "I can't hear. He has to speak louder."

Judge Park leaned toward Doris and said in a loud voice, "What's your name?"

"Doris," she replied.

"And your last name?"

"Buchta."

That being accomplished, Blonigen asked, "Did you ever live in Moneta, Doris?"

This brought another look of consternation to Buchta's face. She turned around and said to Judge Park, "I can't hear him!"

Judge Park repeated the question in a loud voice, "Did you ever live in Moneta?"

"Yes," she responded.

Since this was getting nowhere, Blonigen asked Judge Park if he could approach the witness stand

and be closer to Doris. Park agreed that he could. Meanwhile, Doris, who had been fiddling with her hearing aid, finally got it working correctly, and announced, "All right. I got my hearing aid in."

Once she had the hearing aid working properly, Blonigen asked her if she had kept a diary, and Buchta said she had done so for thirty years, including the year 1988. When Blonigen asked her if she remembered everything she had written down in 1988, Doris replied deadpan, "I don't even remember what I did yesterday."

The gallery burst out laughing. Blonigen had to keep moving closer and closer to Doris to be understood, even with her hearing aid working properly. Finally Judge Park asked, "Ms. Buchta, how old are you?"

She replied, "Ninety-one and a half."

Blonigen asked, "I've put some green arrows there on an area (a blown-up section of her diary). Do you see those?"

"Where is the green arrow?" she replied. "I don't see a green arrow."

Judge Park leaned over and pointed to where it was. "Right there," he said.

Doris replied, "Oh, it's so big I couldn't see it."

This brought forth another round of laughter in the courtroom.

At this point, Wyatt Skaggs spoke up and said it would be okay if Mike Blonigen actually moved onto the witness stand right beside Doris Buchta. Blonigen did just that, and with the aid of a magnifying glass and flashlight, he pointed out the entry from March 24, 1988.

By this time, Doris Buchta had practically become a one-woman comedy act. She stared at the writing and said, "Where am I? Oh, right here. *I got the mail and burned all the papers.* My, how exciting!"

The gallery cracked up again.

Doris went on, "*Had breakfast*. What does that say there? *I watched a guy?*"

Judge Park told her, "It says 'quiz show.'"

"Oh, *I watched a quiz show*. Yeah. That's the only thing I watch on television. *Helped,* um, *Buck helped,* um, *my husband Buck helped Eaton. Dale Eaton worked on the car,* and so forth. That's Thursday, March twenty-fourth."

Blonigen pointed out an entry from April 1, 1988, and had her read it. Doris said, "*I didn't feel good that day*. How about that? And Dale. Oh, yeah. *Dale visited.*"

Blonigen asked, "So Buck and Dale were busy that day?"

"Yes."

Before having Doris Buchta step down, Judge Park asked Wyatt Skaggs if he had any questions for her. Skaggs turned toward Doris and asked, "Do you remember me?"

"Yes," she answered.

"I have no questions," Skaggs said.

Then, perhaps mixing up Wyatt Skaggs with Mike Blonigen, Doris said, "I thought you did a good job."

"Pardon?" Skaggs replied.

So she said it again: "I thought you did a good job."

At a loss at how to respond to that, Skaggs said, "Thank you very much. I hope you are doing well. Are you doing okay?"

"Fine," she answered.

Skaggs added, "You still got that sense of humor."

Unable to hear this, she turned toward Judge Park once again. Park said in a loud voice, "He said you still have a good sense of humor."

Doris smiled and replied, "Might as well be dead if I don't have!"

The gallery burst out laughing again, and Judge Park laughed with them as well.

NCSO detective Dan Tholson took the stand next, and Tholson was there to testify about more evidence found on Eaton's property, and to tie up loose ends in the prosecution's case. He showed ten slides of bloodstains left on the Old Government Bridge when Eaton allegedly murdered Lisa Kimmell before dumping her body into the water. Tholson spoke of the weather conditions on April 2, 1988, and the freshness of the blood that was found. The freshness of the blood seemed to point to the fact that Lisa had not been murdered until March 31 or April 1, adding strength to the claims by the prosecution that she had been held captive and sexually tortured from March 25 until she was killed.

Tholson also testified that when Lisa's Honda was unearthed, the trip meter read 215.8 miles. If Lisa had filled up with gasoline in Cheyenne, as her father had instructed she always do before driving to Montana from Denver, then that would have put her vehicle near Moneta, Wyoming, when she and it were taken on March 25, 1988.

With Dan Tholson, the prosecution called its last witness and there was a recess for a day while the defense decided whom among their fourteen witnesses they would call on Friday, March 12. On Thursday, March 11, Mike Blonigen spoke to reporters and said, "The trial is moving along. I always thought we could finish this quicker than the total time set for it. But we do anticipate some evidence from the defense on Friday. Nothing is set in stone."

Asked by a reporter if he thought the state had proven its case against Eaton, Blonigen replied, "I think, with very minor exceptions, we got in the evidence we wanted to get in."

On Friday, March 12, before the jurors even came into the courtroom, Wyatt Skaggs presented a motion that Judge Park pronounce that Dale Eaton should be acquitted because some of the charges against him constituted double jeopardy. On top of that, Skaggs also contended that the state had not proven some of the many areas they were charging against Eaton, especially in regard to premeditation of murder or sexual assault. Skaggs declared, "There's no evidence it (sex) was done without her consent." This immediately brought forth gasps from the gallery. To them, it seemed almost blasphemous to even entertain the thought that Lisa had consented to have sex with Dale Eaton.

As to the other issues, Skaggs said that there was no proof of kidnapping. Then he added that it was the prosecution's own witness Joseph Dax who had stated that it was Lisa who had given Dale Eaton a ride on her own volition. Skaggs added there was no proof of robbery before Lisa was killed. To that point, Skaggs said, "We believe the robbery falls outside of the homicide, because her property (the Honda CRX) was not taken until after her death."

In rebuttal, Blonigen argued that the pattern of the stab wounds showed a "deliberate and premeditated" attempt to kill Lisa. In the end, Judge Park denied all the defense motions, saying that it was up to the jury to decide guilt or innocence of Dale Eaton.

The jury was brought in, and Wyatt Skaggs called only one witness from a list of fourteen possible witnesses. The witness was Dr. Daniel Spitz, a forensic pathologist from Tampa, Florida, and Skaggs spent a great deal of time asking Dr. Spitz about his background, education, and training. It was tedious and lengthy, but Skaggs may have been wanting to place in the jurors' minds that Spitz was more qualified than Dr. James Thorpen, the state's medical expert witness.

For the most part, Spitz said that he agreed with Dr. Thorpen's findings, but he disagreed on several key points. By this point, the defense was not even pretending that Eaton was innocent of killing Lisa Kimmell, what they were trying to do was show that it did not come up to the standards of first-degree murder. One key disagreement between Dr. Spitz and Dr. Thorpen was that Spitz did not believe that the marks on Lisa's ankles and wrists were necessarily made by rope. He said the marks appeared to him to have come from someone who had "grabbed or held" her. That theory could lead to "impulse" rather than "premeditation." Also, Spitz testified, "the small abrasions and contusions on Lisa Kimmell's arms and legs were common in bodies recovered from moving water."

Spitz also disagreed with Dr. Thorpen, who had said the killer had carefully avoided striking Lisa's ribs when stabbing her. Spitz testified this could have been a factor caused by luck, as much as anything else. And Spitz testified that Lisa was not necessarily murdered at the Old Government Bridge. He said, "I would have expected a wider distribution of blood at the bridge, had she been killed there." His theory was that her body had been placed in some kind of wrapping material, like plastic tarp, and her body dragged across the bridge roadway and then dumped into the river.

On another issue, Spitz stated that since there were no defensive wounds found on Lisa, he doubted she had been struck in the head before being stabbed. Spitz argued that someone would throw up their arm to protect their head from any kind of blow. He concluded that the head wound she suffered either came from when she had been stabbed and her head hit a curb on the bridge, or when her body was dumped over the side and hit a railing.

And as to how long Lisa's body was in the water before being discovered, Spitz said that no one could tell. He said that Dr. Thorpen's estimate of thirty-six to forty-eight hours was just a guess at best. According to Spitz, it could have been much longer than that. This was important, because the prosecution contended that Lisa had been trussed up and sexually tortured for six days before being killed. With Spitz's contention, Lisa might have been held for six days, three days, or one day before being killed.

During cross-examination, Spitz admitted that Lisa might have been restrained by ligatures during her captivity, and that those sorts of things happened during a violent sexual assault. But Spitz would not give ground by saying that her killer had intentionally missed her ribs when stabbing her. That was the prosecution's theory, and matched well with Eaton being familiar with knives and skinning and cutting open animals he had killed while hunting.

In the end, Dale Eaton did not take the stand in his defense. It was now up to a jury to decide his guilt or innocence. And because the defense had all but admitted that Eaton had killed Lisa Kimmell, it was basically boiling down to how many extra charges the jurors would find him guilty of, which might bring the death penalty in the penalty phase.

On Monday, March 15, closing arguments began, and Mike Blonigen gave an overview of the case to the jurors by using evidence and testimony of witnesses. He declared that Lisa Kimmell had been "held for days in sheer abject terror. No one except for Dale Eaton will ever know for sure when and where each of the crimes occurred. What is known is that Eaton put a lot of thought into how Lisa Kimmell's abduction would end. Both she and Eaton knew exactly how this was going to end. She had to know. And it doesn't matter in which sequence the events occurred. The state only has to prove that they occurred as part of a continuous transaction. It doesn't matter if the murder is first, last, or in between."

As evidence of Eaton's total control over Lisa Kimmell during the time he had her in captivity, Blonigen pointed out that Dr. James Thorpen had said that Lisa's pubic hair had been shaved six to seven days before her death. Blonigen stated that Eaton kidnapped her, sexually assaulted her, and then killed her—all of that being part of the "continuous transaction." That was why there were multiple charges against Dale Eaton, and not just a murder charge. According to Blonigen, because Dale Eaton had kidnapped, robbed, and sexually assaulted her, it made his crime a first-degree murder. Blonigen declared, "He had choices to make, and Dale Wayne Eaton chose, with premeditated malice, to end this young girl's life."

* * *

For his part, Wyatt Skaggs left no doubt that the defense was not even trying to say that Dale Eaton had *not* killed Lisa Kimmell. Skaggs even declared in his closing argument, "There is no question my client kept, sexually assaulted, killed, and disposed of Lisa Kimmell's body. Dale Eaton did it." However, Skaggs told the jurors, what had been done did not add up to first-degree murder. Skaggs argued that the kidnapping, robbery, sexual assault, and murder were not all part of one continuous transaction. There were gaps and unrelated events in the total amount of time that had passed. Then Skaggs said, "There is plenty evidence of malice in this case, but premeditation is lacking."

Skaggs attempted to bolster this last comment by saying it was possible that Lisa Kimmell had been struck in the head very shortly before being killed. Quick enough for Dale Eaton not to plan it, but rather a spur-of-the-moment action. By making this point, Skaggs seemed to be backing away now from Dr. Spitz's testimony that Lisa Kimmell might have suffered the head wound, not from a hammer blow, but by striking her head on the pavement or bridge, after being stabbed and dumped in the river.

Skaggs also contended that the prosecution had not proven that Lisa had been killed at the Old Government Bridge. She could have been killed at Eaton's property and then dumped into the river later. Why this was important was Skaggs' effort to deny there had been a stream of continuous events from day one. And it attempted to show there had been no premeditation on Dale's part by taking Lisa all the way to the Old Government Bridge, knowing that he was going to kill her there. In essence, Skaggs contended that he didn't have to prove these theories. It was up to the prosecution to disprove them beyond a reasonable doubt.

Skaggs even attacked the DNA evidence collected and analyzed by the state. He alleged that the two labs Cellmark and Bode had very different results in their findings. Skaggs also contended that the DNA samples taken from Lisa Kimmell's panties never proved that there wasn't a second man who had raped her. If there had been a second individual involved, then it could not be proven beyond a reasonable doubt that it was Dale Eaton who had actually killed her.

Wyatt Skaggs also declared that Eaton had not written the "Stringfellow Hawke" note, nor had he placed it on her grave. And Skaggs tore into Joseph Dax's testimony, calling him an opportunistic liar who testified to have his sentence reduced in prison. Skaggs said, "I contend Joe Dax is a flat-out liar. He never talked to my client. That was a preposterous story, and it just didn't happen."

On rebuttal, Mike Blonigen refuted Skaggs's contentions, one by one, and added rhetorically, "Where is the lack of intent? Dale Wayne Eaton killed because he wanted to kill. He chose not to extend mercy to this girl."

With closing arguments over, the jurors were ushered out of the courthouse and sequestered at a motel until they reached a verdict. There they could be kept safe from talking to the media, the public, and even their own family members. What they could not be kept safe from was their own foolishness. The jurors had gone to deliberate on Friday and quit doing so at around suppertime. They did not reconvene for deliberations until Monday morning.

It was on Monday morning a juror revealed to the other jurors that he had gone out to the Old Government Bridge over the weekend. This was in direct violation of Judge Park's admonition not to do any investigating on their own, but to only consider evidence that came in during trial. Judge Park had not just told them this at the beginning of the trial, he had made that admonition at least twice a day, all during the trial.

This could have derailed everything and led to a mistrial. When the other jurors found out about this, they were in shock. They immediately informed the court of what had happened. Everything now hung in the balance as to whether a mistrial would occur. If so, the present jurors would be dismissed, a new set of jurors picked, and the whole thing would have to begin once again.

Judge Park took into consideration all that had occurred. Eventually he declared there would be no mistrial, because the other jurors had acted with great promptness about alerting the court to the problem. They had not been "tainted" by the errant juror's ill-advised investigation at the bridge. That juror was summarily dismissed, and an alternate was put in his place. The deliberations would go on.

By 5:00 P.M. on Tuesday, March 16, there still was no verdict by the jury, so once again, they broke deliberations for the evening. On the morning of March 17, they were back at it again, and at around 2:00 P.M., they announced they had a verdict. As the Kimmell family hurried to the courthouse, they were met on the steps by a crowd of reporters, snapping their photos and filming them for the television news stations. The Kimmells had nothing to say to them at that point.

* * *

The jury members filed back into court, and when they were seated, the clerk of the district court read the verdict on the various counts against Dale Wayne Eaton. One by one, there was the word "guilty"—guilty of premeditated first-degree murder, guilty on aggravated kidnapping, guilty on aggravated robbery, guilty on first-degree sexual assault. There were guilty verdicts, as well, on robbery, sexual assault, and kidnapping all during the commission of a murder—charges that could get Eaton the death penalty in the next phase. The only count not addressed was second-degree sexual assault, because the jurors had already found him guilty of first-degree sexual assault.

Dale Eaton listened to the verdict, showing no emotion at all. That was not the case with the Kimmell family. They wrapped their arms around each other, and as the guilty verdicts came in, Sheila placed her head on her husband's shoulder. The family was quickly ushered out of the courtroom and made no comments to the media waiting outside, reserving their comment until after the penalty phase.

There were several court observers, however, who commented upon the jury's verdict. One of these was Dora Westbrook, of Casper, who had watched most of the court proceedings. She told a reporter, "The jury had no other choice in the matter. He (Wyatt Skaggs) admitted that Eaton was guilty."

Skaggs had no comments to make at that time, but Mike Blonigen answered several of the reporters' questions. Blonigen said he was happy with the verdict and predicted the penalty phase could last several days. He added, "The penalty phase from the state's point of view will be based largely on the testimony already produced at trial. But there will be a few witnesses."

One of the prosecution witnesses slated for the penalty phase was Shannon Breeden, the woman Dale Eaton had tried kidnapping in 1997. She was in Casper now and ready to blast Dale Eaton for what he had done to her and her family.

14

LIFE OR DEATH

Thursday, March 18, 2004, witnessed another packed courtroom as proceedings got under way in Dale Eaton's penalty phase. The day began by attorneys on both sides arguing about what evidence from the guilt phase had opened doors to other revelations about Dale Eaton that the jurors could now hear. It was a fine line between an accounting of who Dale Eaton really was and discussing what he had done besides the abduction and murder of Lisa Kimmell. Much of these things the jurors didn't know, and the prosecution definitely wanted those matters in, while the defense wanted them kept out. In the end, Judge Park excluded as being too inflammatory much of what the prosecution wished that it could get in.

In his opening statement in this phase, Mike Blonigen spoke about the penalty phase and conviction, and that the aggravating factors in the case outweighed the mitigating factors. He said that Dale Eaton should receive the death penalty. Blonigen listed the aggravating circumstances, one by one—the murder was especially atrocious and cruel, unnecessarily torturous to the victim; the murder was premeditated and purposefully committed while Eaton was engaged in the crimes of kidnapping, robbery, and sexual assault. Eaton was previously convicted of a felony involving the use of threats and violence. Any one of those factors under Wyoming law could get Dale the death penalty.

Blonigen declared, "A killing is a bad enough thing. But when it goes beyond murder to torture, it's not on the same level. Particularly when the torture, mostly mental, goes on for days and involves three of the most serious offenses known to man. Dale Eaton has some issues. But how does that weigh against the offenses? They're excuses, rationalizations, and explanations. A full measure of justice is required in this case. In Dale Eaton's case, that is death."

Wyatt Skaggs, for his part, said that Dale Eaton accepted and respected the jurors' verdict of guilty in the guilt phase. Then Skaggs said that Eaton's life had value, and he spoke of how a person was a product of his home environment. Skaggs talked of his own happy family and contrasted that to the family Dale had grown up with. Dale's mother had severe mental illness, and Skaggs called Dale's father a selfish drunk who severely abused Dale as a boy. Skaggs further declared that Dale's father had dined out on steaks, while his wife and children stayed at home eating bologna sandwiches.

Skaggs declared, "Dale never had a chance, ever in his life, that we had. He was poor and moved around a lot, suffering from mental illness." It was that mental illness, Skaggs declared, that had caused Dale to abduct and kill Lisa Kimmell. Then Skaggs argued, "Dale's issues are not excuses, but are reasons to spare his life. His mental impairment at the time of Lisa Kimmell's death was so profound, he wasn't of sound mind, and therefore not deserving of the death penalty." Even though Skaggs had not put on a case earlier that Dale Eaton was mentally incompetent, the thrust of his argument now was that Dale had suffered from mental illness for so long, his judgment was badly impaired during the days he held Lisa Kimmell captive and decided to end her life.

Because of Judge Park's restrictions, Mike Blonigen could only go so far with his witnesses in this phase. His first witness was Shannon Breeden, and she couldn't go into depth about what had occurred to her and her family at the hands of Dale Eaton. What she was able to say was that Eaton had tried abducting them on September 12, 1997, near Wamsutter on Interstate 80. Shannon was also able to point at Dale Eaton in the courtroom and say the man at the defense table was the person who had done those things to her.

Shannon Breeden may not have been able to say much on the witness stand, but she certainly vented her feelings to newspaper reporters after she was excused. She told them, "I think it's appalling that Eaton's family can get up there and cry and talk about him as a little boy and how they loved him, and 'poor, poor Dale.' But I can't tell the jury that he had a gun to the head of a five-month-old. But I'm not reliving something that resulted from my getting harmed. I'm reliving the fact that I survived something where we got away. So that's great! It was a victory! I'm still mad. I've got all this anger. He's a sick son of a bitch! I didn't realize how pissed-off I was until coming here. I think this has been a long time coming. I'm just really relieved to know that he's not out killing people."

Asked what she thought about the possibility of Dale Eaton receiving the death penalty, Breeden replied that she was generally opposed to the death penalty. But in Eaton's case, she said, "Dale has slipped through the cracks so many times that the only way I'm going to be relieved is if he dies."

Then Breeden added that she had communicated through sign language to her four-year-old son, Cody's younger brother, because that boy had a hearing impairment. She told the boy that she would have to be going away for a while to a trial, and that Cody had survived an attack when he was only a baby. Breeden related, "In sign language, he said, 'Mommy is going to help the police lock up a monster.' I couldn't have said it better myself."

Wyoming State patrol officer J. B. Tippits testified briefly about the Breeden abduction by saying, "At first, what we perceived was that this guy (Eaton) had been assaulted by some wacked-out hippies. Then we discerned that he (Eaton) was the instigator of the attack."

Not much information by anyone concerning the Breeden incident could go very far in the penalty phase. Officer David Gray said of Shannon Breeden right after the attack, "She was still wired tight. Still afraid. Obviously, she knew she had been fighting for her life."

Sweetwater County chief deputy attorney Tony Howard recalled, "At first, it was difficult to distinguish attacker from victim. Dale Eaton was seriously injured, and the Breedens were distraught but unharmed." Then Howard said, "It was real odd. Eaton's statement was that he had cancer or some life-threatening disease and he wanted to commit suicide, but didn't have the guts to do it. Suicide by stranger. Fortunately, Eaton made our job easier by making a quick confession."

Because of the restrictions placed in this phase by Judge Park, not allowing in "inflammatory statements" about Dale Eaton's past crimes and alleged crimes, the prosecution rested after only those few witnesses made their brief statements.

If Mike Blonigen called very few witnesses, who spoke for only a short time, that was not the case with the defense. In fact, the penalty phase was the defense's main battleground, having conceded during the guilt phase that Dale Eaton had committed the crimes against Lisa Kimmell. The first witness on the stand for the defense was Fort Collins, Colorado, psychiatrist Dr. Kenneth Ash. And just as with Dr. Spitz, Skaggs spent a great deal of time explaining to the jurors about Dr. Ash's credentials as an expert witness. These included his schooling, general and specialized psychiatry, and training in addictive behavior.

Dr. Ash testified that he had read Dale Eaton's medical reports and had interviewed Dale for twelve hours in person. Dr. Ash had asked Eaton about his childhood, teen years, and adulthood. Ash said that in Eaton's medical records, there was one constant— he suffered from severe depression. In fact, Ash declared that Eaton's depression was so profound as to cause brain damage. He defined this brain damage as "occurring in the hippocampus area of the brain, which is especially important in terms of stress regulation, memory, and new learning."

Asked about Dale's living conditions at Moneta, Dr.

Ash testified, "Mr. Eaton was living in the most abject of circumstances. He had lost his marriage, lost his family. He had lost his welding business. He had lost a home that would have cost about two hundred or three hundred dollars a month in Cheyenne, and was now living in a bus by himself. He was isolated, essentially from friends, and he was isolated from family. He was in poverty. He was able to manage to feed himself by scavenging cans out of garbage dumps and selling them for money at grocery stores."

And then Dr. Ash added a new twist to when and where Lisa Kimmell had been abducted and murdered. Or what had happened to her, at least according to Dale Eaton. Dr. Ash testified that in his interview with Dale, Dale had spoken about specifics of what had allegedly occurred back in 1988. Just what Dale said was at great variance to the story Joseph Dax had told during the guilt phase.

Dr. Ash said that Dale Eaton had told him that on the evening of March 25, 1988, he had gone to town and phoned his ex-wife. The main reason Eaton had done so was because he wanted his kids to spend some time with him during Easter break. According to Eaton, his wife just laughed at him and replied, "Those kids aren't even yours!" Then she let Dale know that she was now with another man. Eaton left town in an agitated, frustrated, and dark mood.

What occurred next showed just how far this version of events varied from the one that Eaton had supposedly told Joseph Dax.

Skaggs: *I want to ask you precisely how this homicide came about. Essentially he (Eaton) had gone into town, and made the phone call, right?*

Ash: That's correct.

Skaggs: And did he encounter Lisa Marie Kimmell?

Ash: Yes, he did.

Skaggs: And where did he encounter her?

Ash: Mr. Eaton said he encountered Lisa as he was driving toward his land.

Skaggs: Okay. And she was parked alongside the road, then?

Ash: Her car was parked there. And when he got there, he felt someone was again breaking in and robbing his bus. (According to Eaton, this had happened before.) And so he was angry. He was already in an angry state, but he got angrier. He felt that Lisa was not alone. That there were other people there.

Skaggs: Did Mr. Eaton confront Lisa Kimmell with a gun?

Ash: Yes.

Skaggs: Could you please explain what happened?

Ash: Well, he had a gun, took it out, and walked her up to his car. He realized that she was alone. So then he proceeded to take her down to his bus. And he said that the moment he started taking her down to his bus, that he knew he was in trouble.

Skaggs: And did he have an occasion to keep her?

Ash: He kept her there. He said, for a few days. During that time he kept her there, he said to himself he was not going to be alone at Easter. He kept her there and forced her to have sex with him. He was, during the entire time, ex-

*pecting the police to come at any moment. He
was thinking whether to let her go, or whether
to keep her. And then he decided that he was
too afraid of what would happen to him if he
let her go.*

Skaggs: *So what happened next?*

Ash: *What happened after a couple of days, and
this part is not exactly clear, he decided he was
going to kill her. And he walked up from
behind her and hit her in the back of the head
with a pipe. She fell to the floor unconscious.
He realized her heart was still beating. And
then he proceeded to stab her until her heart
stopped beating.*

Skaggs asked how Eaton had disposed of Lisa's
body, and Ash replied, "He said he had some plastic
material from old mattress wrappings and that he
wrapped up her body in that and then put her in his
car and took her to the bridge. He said, 'This probably sounds screwed up, but she wanted to be home
with her family for Easter.' So he took her to the river
and threw her in. He said he knew there would be
fishermen that would find her."

By now, nearly everyone in the gallery was crying—
the Kimmell family, most of all. Eventually they were
led out of the courtroom by Janeice Lynch so that
they could sob uncontrollably without interrupting
the testimony.

It was hard to say if Dale Eaton had told the truth
about these series of events, part of the truth, or just one
lie after another. He had tried changing details of the
Breeden abduction to put himself in the best light with

authorities in that incident. And the prosecution still believed that Dale had driven Lisa to the Old Government Bridge and killed her there. As to whose story was true—Dale Eaton's, Joseph Dax's, or neither—was hard to tell.

A break was taken in the proceedings, while the various lawyers and Judge Park discussed how much of Dr. Ash's testimony could be used by the jury as mitigating evidence. When cross-examination began, Blonigen declared that Dale Eaton had played the mental-illness card, time and time again, when he got into trouble with the law. In a sense, Blonigen began lecturing Dr. Ash about Eaton's previous bad acts by saying, "He's become skilled at fooling the specialists who evaluate him, hasn't he?" Dr. Ash disagreed with that premise.

Blonigen asked Dr. Ash, "When he spoke to you, Mr. Eaton described a fairly miserable life at the time of early 1988. Is that a fair statement?" Dr. Ash said that it was. "Were you aware that he was, on a frequent basis, visiting his neighbors?"

"At that time in the spring?"

"Yes."

"No," replied Dr. Ash.

"Okay, for instance, did you know there was a little old lady across the way who kept a diary?"

Dr. Ash responded, "I was aware of the people across the way. I had thought that they were getting involved with each other after that (the captivity and murder) happened."

"Okay, well, let's talk about that then. Because Mr. Eaton basically told you, he holed up and didn't leave unless he just had to?"

"Yes."

"That's not an overstatement, is it?"

Dr. Ash said, "That is not an overstatement."

"So if she (Doris Buchta) has a note that Dale visited on March eighth, and paid the taxes on the adjoining property, that would seem somewhat inconsistent with what he told you, wouldn't it?"

Dr. Ash asked, "How much were the taxes?"

Blonigen responded, "Well, I guess that's inconsistent two ways. He was going out and seeing people. That would indicate that, right?"

"Well, he had a hard time getting out and seeing people."

So then Bloningen asked if Dr. Ash knew that Dale had visited the Buchtas on March 16, 1988. Ash said no. Dr. Ash had the same response when asked if he knew that Dale had also visited them on March 22 and March 24 of that year. Blonigen asked, "This depression persisted after March twenty-fourth, did it not, during this supposed period of horrible isolation?"

Dr. Ash replied, "In my opinion, and from what I've been told, yes."

"Were you aware he visited the Buchtas again on April first?"

"No."

"And he went over and visited them for six hours on April eleventh. That doesn't sound like he's keeping himself in isolation, does it?"

"No, it does not," Ash responded.

"So he's maybe not quite as isolated as he led you to believe?"

Dr. Ash said, "There are more visits than I was aware of."

Blonigen asked, "Did they (the defense team) ever give you that journal to look at?"

Dr. Ash said no.

What was glaringly missing in Doris Buchta's diary

were visits from Dale Eaton to the Buchtas from March 25 up until April 1. It was during that period, the prosecution contended, that he was keeping Lisa Kimmell captive and sexually torturing her.

Blonigen even poked holes in the defense's argument that Dale was nearly destitute, when, in fact, he had welding jobs and owned three vehicles.

Blonigen asked, "In listening to your testimony it sounds as if Dale Eaton's reporting played a very important role in your conclusions. Is that an accurate statement?"

Ash replied, "It was an important part, yes."

Blonigen once again stressed that Eaton only claimed mental illness when he was in a jam. And in one psychiatric evaluation concerning psychosis, Eaton had scored off the chart. That would only happen if somebody was faking psychosis, not someone who was truly psychotic, according to Blonigen.

Dr. Ash repeated that it didn't appear that Eaton had been lying to him.

On redirect, Skaggs attempted to do some damage control about Dale's so-called isolation at Moneta. Skaggs asked Dr. Ash if seeing the Buchtas every couple of weeks caused him to change his mind about Eaton's isolation. Dr. Ash responded, "A visit every couple of weeks is actually more visits than I had in mind that he was making. If that's all the contact with people during that time, that's still pretty isolated."

Skaggs said that Dale may have had contact with people over at the Waltman store as well, and asked if Dr. Ash still felt Dale was isolated in Moneta. Ash declared, "He gave a picture of being very isolated. Very alone. Very depressed."

* * *

After Dr. Ash's lengthy testimony, Dale's elderly aunt Betty Ferrins took the stand. In fact, when she spoke, it was one of the few times Dale showed any emotion. He covered his eyes and cried when Skaggs asked Ferrins if she wanted Dale to die. She cried out, "No! I don't think Dale was in his right mind when he did this."

Dale's elderly uncle had little to add for the defense. He spoke of Dale and his siblings having to eat bologna sandwiches, while Dale's dad went to town and had a steak. Another example of "abuse" was when Dale's dad allegedly hid a box of candy in his car, because he didn't want the kids to have any. One thing glaringly absent from the mitigation phase was that neither Dale's brothers or sisters testified on his behalf.

Two neighbors and friends of Dale's also spoke briefly about him, and said they didn't want him to die. Compared to many such death penalty cases, there were very few people speaking up for the person on trial.

Last on the list of defense witnesses was Dr. Linda Gummow, a psychiatrist from Utah. Once again, Skaggs asked her about her credentials, the way he had done with Dr. Spitz and Dr. Ash. Dr. Gummow spoke of Dale Eaton's mother being hospitalized with chronic schizophrenia, one of Dale's brothers committing suicide, another brother with anger issues, and Dale's father being an alcoholic. She had interviewed Dale over a two-day period and evaluated his mental-health records, diagnosing him as someone who suffered from a major depressive disorder and low IQ. Dr. Gummow told the jurors, "Dale Eaton's condition has been a lifelong struggle for him. There is a history of depression and mental illness in his family."

Then Dr. Gummow declared that the prolonged severe depression caused moderate to severe brain damage for Eaton. She claimed that at times this led to "great emotional disturbances, even dementia." Gummow said that Dale's failed marriage was a major factor in his slide toward deep depression. In fact, Eaton told her that on their wedding night, his new bride had told him she wanted a divorce. From there, things didn't get any better, according to Dale, even though they stuck out the marriage for sixteen years.

Dale told Dr. Gummow that his dilapidated trailer and bus at his Moneta property were his "hideouts," and he said, "I needed to get away from people." Gummow said that Dale was so depressed during this period that he seldom bathed or kept up his appearance. Gummow related, "He was known to bathe at a car wash or at friends' houses. His few friends would take their own food when they went to visit him. Dale's idea of dinner was to throw frozen venison into a dirty frying pan and eat it with his hands."

In the interview, Eaton claimed that a big part of his depression stemmed from his feelings of guilt that he might have caused his mother's mental illness to get worse. And he also felt guilty about his brother's suicide. He told Dr. Gummow that he owed his brother money, which he never repaid. Dale worried that financial problems might have caused his brother to kill himself.

Dr. Gummow showed the jurors a slide presentation of how a normal person's brain looked and functioned. This presentation included slides of MRIs and positron emission tomography (PET) scans. Then she showed how a dysfunctional brain looked. Interestingly enough, she never showed any MRIs or PET scans of

Dale Eaton's brain, but rather photos from textbooks on the subject.

Dr. Gummow testified, "Usually, most depressed people have multiple family members who either have psychiatric conditions or depressive disorders. The major depressive disorder is considered to be a brain disease that impacts the brain transmitters and brain communication. It's exacerbated or worsened by social factors." Dr. Gummow said that Dale had most of these factors, including an early onset of child abuse and his mother's severe mental illness.

Dr. Gummow added that people with major depression were far more vulnerable to stressors than those who did not suffer from it. She then referred to the severe psychiatric disorder of Dale's mother, the alleged abuse by Dale's father, anger issues of one brother, and the suicide of his brother Darrell. Dr. Gummow said, "I believe Dale Eaton has moderate to severe brain damage, and that depression is linked to his behavior. A person with milder depression is not going to lose control. Some people have good family support that helps them develop techniques or coping styles to manage the difficult feelings associated with depression, but Mr. Eaton did not have anyone to help him deal with irrational feelings associated with his illness. His lifelong psychiatric disorder caused extreme emotional disturbance, inability to conform his conduct, and extreme duress in March and April 1988, the time of the Kimmell homicide."

Dr. Gummow testified about Dale's son Billy speaking about his father. She noted that Billy said that his dad, during the time he spent with him, was very unstable. They lived four or five different places in one year's time, and Billy was dragged from school to school. Billy also spoke of his dad being very controlling, and he wanted to get away from him as soon as he could.

As to Dale's relationships with women, after the divorce from Melody, Dr. Gummow said, Dale didn't have any relationships except for one woman in Nevada. And even this woman ridiculed Dale, calling him "Junkyard Dale." Dr. Gummow added, "I should mention, during the time period of Lisa Kimmell's death, Mr. Eaton had been a freelance welder, but he lost his welding truck. His credit rating was down, and he basically never worked more than ninety days at a time, anywhere, after that. When I talked to him, he couldn't even remember his major employers. He went from one job to another job to another."

Asked by Wyatt Skaggs if she worried that Dale Eaton had tried to fool her in the interview, Dr. Gummow said no. Gummow stated, "I found him to be ninety-five percent truthful and proficient at remembering. There was no malingering on Mr. Eaton's part."

Mike Blonigen on cross grilled Dr. Gummow on all aspects of her testimony. He asked how she could accurately assess Eaton's mental state at the time of the abduction and murders; after all, sixteen years had passed since then. Dr. Gummow stated her long experience in psychiatry, and reading the mental-illness reports taken by others on Eaton over the years helped her come to her conclusions. Blonigen pointed out that most of the reports concerning Dale came from his own statements about his life. And they mostly came when he was in trouble with the law. Blonigen declared that Dale's statements were helpful to his cause to appear to be mentally ill. All of these reports by Dale varied as to his work history and early years. Blonigen contended that Dale made things up as he went along. Mike Blonigen admitted that Eaton's IQ was low, but that it still fell within the normal range.

Blonigen wanted to know how much she was being paid, and Dr. Gummow responded that it was $5,000 in Eaton's case. Then Blonigen named numerous cases in which Gummow had declared that the defendants were mentally ill. Blonigen said, "It's real interesting that you find something for everyone." This brought an immediate objection from Wyatt Skaggs, which was sustained by Judge Park.

Mike Blonigen contended that Dale Eaton didn't have brain damage in 1988 at the time of the abduction and murder of Lisa Kimmell. Blonigen said Dale might have sustained brain damage later, when he tried abducting the Breedens and they beat him in the head with a rifle. Asked if that was the cause of Eaton's supposed brain damage, Dr. Gummow said, "It could have been mild, but not moderate."

Blonigen was saving his biggest "punch" for last. He asked, "You said you always checked things out carefully—is that right?"

Gummow replied, "I try."

Blonigen wanted to know what kind of impact Dale's brother Darrell Eaton's suicide had on Dale. Dr. Gummow replied, "I never specifically discussed that with him. I don't know whether it was still bothering him or not."

Blonigen looked at the chart Dr. Gummow had created and had shown to the jurors. He noted that it stated that she had spoken with Dale Eaton about it, and Dale seemed to still have been quite upset about the suicide at the time of Lisa Kimmell's murder. But there was something off here, and Wyatt Skaggs must have sensed it—sensed it enough to speak out. "Your

Honor, excuse me! Actually, the suicide of his brother, I don't think happened until after—"

Skaggs was cut off in midsentence by Mike Blonigen, who observed, "That's not what her chart says."

In fact, Wyatt Skaggs must have blanched when he saw what was written on Dr. Gummow's chart for the time she had for Darrell Eaton's suicide. It didn't help matters when Dr. Gummow suddenly spoke up and said, "It was '87, is my understanding." (She was referring to the time of the suicide.)

Mike Blonigen knew he was onto something very explosive. He asked Dr. Gummow, "Did you consider the suicide of his brother a significant event in his life and his mental state in 1988?"

By now, even Dr. Gummow seemed to realize something was amiss. She answered, "I have no way to evaluate that."

Blonigen asked, "Did you do anything to confirm whether that information was accurate?"

Dr. Gummow replied, "It was mentioned in reports. That's where I got the date from. I didn't get it from Mr. Eaton."

"So you were standing up there with this time chart and said that one of the most significant events in Dale's life before the homicide was the suicide of his brother Darrell—is that correct?"

"That was my statement, yes."

"And that was listed as occurring on January 1, 1987—is that correct?"

"That's an approximate date. I only had the year. So when I have something like 1/1/87, it means that I didn't know the exact date, and I put in the year."

"Both you and Dr. Ash talked about this being an event that was affecting him at the time of the homicide, as part of his depression—isn't that true?"

"No, I didn't testify to that."

"Well, Doctor, did you ever bother to get a death certificate?"

"No."

Blonigen brought forth a document and said, "I would like to show you Exhibit 1003, a simple thing to check on. A very simple thing to check on."

"Not for me," Gummow replied. "I'm not an investigator."

Blonigen then said, "Doctor, what day did Mr. Eaton's brother commit suicide, from the document?"

She replied, "October 10, 1988."

"Well after the Kimmell homicide—is that true?"

Dr. Gummow first looked stunned and then angry. She finally responded, "That's true."

Mike Blonigen asked that Exhibit 1003 be introduced as evidence.

Wyatt Skaggs appeared to be just as stunned as Dr. Gummow by this revelation. He declared to Judge Park, "I object to that, Your Honor!"

Blonigen responded, "Well, Your Honor, I'm sure he does, but it directly impeaches, and it is a certified copy of a regularly kept public record."

Judge Park responded, "It may be a certified copy, but the doctor has not testified that this suicide was a factor that she weighed in her diagnosis."

Blonigen replied, "I disagree. On her direct testimony, she testified that it was a very significant event."

Skaggs jumped in and said, "I disagree with that, Your Honor!"

Blonigen interjected, "Well, are they saying his suicide is not related to the homicide in any way, or his state of mind?"

Skaggs declared, "That's exactly what we're saying."

It had not seemed that way during Dr. Gummow's

direct testimony, and even if there was a reversal on that strategy now, the damage had been done. It appeared that if Dr. Gummow had not spent enough time making sure that her facts were correct on this important matter, then what else in her testimony wasn't correct as well?

Moving on, Blonigen said, "What we have is someone who suffered a divorce and decided to kill a young woman!"

Skaggs objected, and Judge Park sustained the objection, but it was a bell that could not be "unrung" as far as the jurors were concerned. Dr. Gummow, the defense's main witness, had just been made to look foolish on a key point. Either she had not checked her facts, or Dale Eaton had lied to her about the date of his brother's suicide. Either way, it drew into question everything else she had testified to previously.

After this stunning revelation about Darrel Eaton's suicide, Wyatt Skaggs tried to do some damage control by calling Investigator Lynn Cohee to the stand once more. He had her talk about information she had gathered where Dale Eaton and his father had gotten into fights when Dale was young. And Cohee also spoke of some friends of Eaton's who liked him. But after the fiasco with Dr. Gummow, this was little help for the defense. Cohee was the last witness for the defense, and then both sides made their closing arguments.

The arguments were basically a reiteration of things they had already said at trial, driving home points they wanted the jurors to take away with them to deliberation. Wyatt Skaggs listed mitigating circumstances that could give Dale Eaton a life behind bars rather than death. He spoke of Dale's father and alcoholism and alleged abuse, and of Dale's mother's schizophrenia, which put her in the hospital. Skaggs said, "Dale Eaton's own mental illness affected his capacity to appreciate the criminality of, and rendered him unable to conform, his actions to the law. Whatever happens today, Dale Eaton is not going to walk free. Don't do what Dale did. Don't do that!" Then Skaggs reminded the jurors it only took one of them to grant life rather than death.

Mike Blonigen in his closing arguments had no sympathy for Dale Eaton or his alleged mental illness. Blonigen said, "What he did to Lisa Kimmell in the five days before he decided to kill her is unforgivable. Some murders must be regarded as different from other murders. What your verdict says will reflect what this murder means. Dale Eaton can mask his cruelty behind psychiatrists and tears. But don't be fooled. He wasn't content simply to kill. He played 'catch me, if you can' for the next fourteen years. Dale Eaton knew what he was doing and took five torturous days to do it."

At 11:45 A.M., on March 19, the jurors began to deliberate. They all agreed that they wanted to work on Saturday, March 20, as well. If Dale Eaton was able to read the local newspaper that day, he might have had pause to think about an article in it. The *Casper Star-Tribune* had an article CAPITAL CASES HARD TO DEFEND. The reporter spoke with Len Munker, a retired public defender. In fact, Munker and Wyatt Skaggs had defended Mark Hopkinson, the last man in Wyoming to have been executed, in 1992. Hopkinson was the only person in the state's history to be executed in spite of the fact that he had never wielded the murder weapon that ended the lives of Jeff Green, Vincent Vehar, and two members of Vehar's family. Hopkinson was convicted of ordering the murders, and though he claimed innocence to the very end, he was executed by lethal injection.

Munker told the reporter in the article that after hearing about Wyatt Skaggs's closing argument in Dale Eaton's case, and lack of defense witnesses, he would have gone about things very differently. Then Munker admitted, "Such cases as these are hard for his attorney to defend because they are often working with uncooperative clients." Munker said that he would have brought up the aspect of mental illness much more during the guilt phase, and essentially not conceded Eaton's guilt so easily. That being said, Munker agreed that he didn't know what kind of dynamics went on between Wyatt Skaggs and Dale Eaton. Munker declared that defendants in death penalty cases were often unstable personalities. "They often refuse to divulge all the relevant information. For an attorney to defend somebody, it's necessary that he knows the good stuff, as well as the bad stuff."

Munker added that many times the client would become angry with the defense attorney for trying to elicit more information, while the attorney would become angry at the client for making his task so difficult. Munker related, "Often the client wants the impossible done."

Munker did note that jurors in death penalty cases were under a lot of strain as well, and remarked about the Eaton case losing two initial jurors during the trial. "People don't like sitting on death penalty juries. It's harder now to get jurors for such cases than it was twenty years ago."

* * *

The jurors on the Dale Eaton case did work on Saturday, March 20, and around 3:00 P.M. let a bailiff know that they had come to a decision. The Kimmell family, who was staying nearby, were informed and rushed to the courthouse. Once again, they were met by a barrage of questions by reporters on the steps of the courthouse, but they said nothing.

When the jurors were ushered into the courtroom and took their places, there was an absolute hush of expectation. The jury foreman passed their verdict to a court clerk, who handed it to Judge Park to be reviewed. That done, Judge Park handed the note back to the clerk. In a voice amidst the absolute silence, the court clerk read the decision: *"Death for Dale Wayne Eaton."*

Dale sat entirely emotionless on hearing the verdict. The Kimmell family, by contrast, cried and hugged each other, then hugged the prosecution team.

On leaving the courthouse, the defense team had nothing to say to reporters. And the Kimmell family declined to comment at that time as well. Mike Blonigen did talk to reporters briefly. He said that the Kimmell family would hold a press conference on Sunday morning. Then Blonigen added, "They were satisfied with the verdict. They do believe it's fair." Asked how he felt about the verdict, Blonigen stated, "It's no small thing to ask for a man's life. I did so, however, because I believe it was the right thing to do, and the jury agreed."

If the Kimmell family said nothing when the death sentence was pronounced upon Dale Eaton, on Saturday, March 20, they were more than open on Sunday, March 21, at a press conference. Not only were the

Kimmells there, but Mike Blonigen was as well. He thanked his own staff and NCSO investigators as well. Blonigen said, "Mike Sandfort, Jim Broz, and Dan Tholson built a foundation. We might not have known it for fourteen years, but they did everything that made what has happened here possible." Along with these, he thanked Lynn Cohee, Assistant DA Stephanie Sprecher, victim witness coordinator Janeice Lynch, and state crime lab technicians.

Ron Kimmell told the gathered reporters, "For our family, the words 'thank you' are very inadequate to express our gratitude to so many. We had no jurisdiction to help us when we learned that Lisa was missing, nearly sixteen years ago, and we turned to you for help. Without exception, you were here for us from the very beginning of this tragedy and stayed with us for these many difficult years."

Then Ron thanked the reporters for doing a difficult job of reporting the facts without being sensationalistic or invading their privacy. Ron said that they had treated him and his family with "concern and respect."

Ron then thanked the investigators as a whole, and Sheriff Benton, Dr. Thorpen, Don Flickinger, Lynn Cohee, and Dan Tholson, in particular. Ron declared, "They were there for us in our times of deep despair. Even during the times we felt hopeless, after many years had passed, they never gave up."

He said that to some degree the trial had opened old wounds, but that the family had pulled together and made it through sometimes very painful testimony. Ron also acknowledged, "There will be an emptiness that lingers from her absence."

* * *

Sheila Kimmell also profusely thanked all the investigators and prosecution team. She said, "They sacrificed family, friends, and personal time for months preparing for this trial. They wanted justice for Lisa, for our family, and for you, the concerned citizens who have suffered from Dale Eaton's actions." Sheila gave particular praise to Janeice Lynch for her "practical support and emotional support."

Lisa's sister Sherry thanked the jury for sticking with such a difficult and stressful case. She said, "They (the jurors) painfully endured a glimpse of Lisa's tragic death. We're certain they had to deal with many of the same inner conflicts we have had, as they decided Mr. Eaton's fate." Then, surprisingly, Sherry even thanked the defense lawyers, by saying they had a difficult job to do and did it to the best of their ability. "We respect them for performing their civic duty. We know that wasn't easy for them."

Lisa's sister Stacy told the reporters, "I'd like to thank the community. We are so humbled and touched by the generous kindness that has been extended to our family during this very trying time. It seems as though a legion of angels was dispatched to brace us and embrace us, to give us strength and to get us through each agonizing day. It is true that Casper cares."

At that point, the reporters began asking the Kimmell family questions. One question was "What was Lisa like?"

Sheila answered, "Lisa was an extraordinary young

lady. She was kind, independent, motivated, and a daughter to be truly proud of."

Ron added, "She was wise beyond her years."

Sherry responded, "At sixteen years old and eighteen years old, you know, you always have that sibling rivalry and fighting. I wish I still had the opportunity to become friends with her. Stacy and I, we talk every day."

Then the family recalled one of the most agonizing points during the trial. They said that occurred when they discovered one of the jurors had gone out to the Old Government Bridge to do his own investigation, after being warned repeatedly not to do so. The Kimmells said they couldn't bear to think of having the trial start all over again from scratch with a new jury.

Another tough part of the trial was when crime scene and autopsy photos were being passed amongst the jurors. Sheila said her family realized the jurors were trying hard not to show what the photos depicted, and her family appreciated it very much. Then she added, "We had seen some of the photos, but not the really graphic ones. I can only equate being at the trial to the initial eight days when we were looking for our daughter."

Asked what they thought of the verdict on the death penalty, Sheila replied, "We are the kind of people who could not intentionally hurt anybody, let alone kill anybody. But we think justice has been served."

And then Sheila revealed that she had first met some of Dale Eaton's family members when she had gone to his trial in Colorado, where he was charged with killing his cellmate. Sheila told the reporters, "I can say they are truly and genuinely wonderful people. Dale Eaton's actions were his own. My heart goes out to them. They have become victims too."

Asked where they went from here, Sheila responded with one word: "Home!"

The Kimmell family may have been going home, but that was only for a short duration. In May, there would be a formal sentencing of Dale Eaton, and at that time, they would finally be able to speak directly to him during a Victim Impact Statement. Before that happened, however, there was a hearing, because the Kimmell family wanted to present at the formal sentencing a DVD of Lisa's life, which also contained music. Judge Park made a ruling that the visual part of the DVD could come in, but not the accompanying music. His reasoning was "We have to be careful this doesn't turn into a memorial." Even at that point, Judge Park had one eye on the future. He realized that an appellate court would be looking at this phase, as well as all aspects of the guilt phase and penalty phase.

In May 2004, the formal sentencing took place to a once-again packed courtroom. Judge Park spoke directly to the Kimmell family and said, "Prior to your making your statement, I would like to make a comment. During the trial, which you attended, and many of the pretrial proceedings that you also attended, you had to listen to some terrible things. And you all sat there, maintained your dignity. Your ability to experience what you had to hear and see is a comment not only on your devotion to your daughter, but in your courage. And I acknowledge that."

Judge Park then addressed the family's unhappiness of not being allowed to present the audio portion of the DVD to be heard by the court, and by Dale Eaton in

particular. Park explained that the Wyoming Supreme
Court (WSC) and federal courts would both be looking
at every detail of this phase and all the other phases of
the trial. Park stated, "My mission since this case was
assigned to me was to ensure that whatever verdict was
ultimately reached would withstand the scrutiny, and, in
part, this was done by my attempt to meet every proce-
dural and substantive safeguard."

That being said, Judge Park had a surprise for the
Kimmell family. He said that Wyatt Skaggs had withdrawn his objection to the music and audio being
played with the DVD, and they could do so if they
wished. The relief on the faces of the Kimmell family
was apparent for all to see.

The entire family walked forward to a podium and
stood together as a group. Sheila spoke for them all
and said, while looking directly at Dale, *"Mr. Eaton,
through the course of this trial, you have learned more about
Lisa, but you really don't know who Lisa Marie Kimmell was."*

Sheila told Eaton that Lisa had been born in Covington, Tennessee, on July 18, 1969, and was named
Lisa Marie because that was a wish of Ron's mother to
have a granddaughter with that name. Ron's mother
often referred to her as "my little Miss Lisa Marie,"
and that was how the nickname of Lil Miss began.

Sheila told Eaton that Lisa was independent, inquisitive, creative, and smart from an early age. She was a
good student and began part-time work at an Arby's
restaurant when she was only fourteen years old.
When Lisa turned sixteen, she wanted a water bed,
and bought one on credit, always paying on time or
ahead of schedule. By the time she turned eighteen,
Lisa was able to buy her own Honda CRX without a
cosigner, because her credit rating was so good. Sheila

said that her own mother had commented, "Lisa is a thirty-year-old disguised as a teenager."

Sheila stated to Eaton that Lisa was a daughter, a sister, a granddaughter, a niece, and a friend. She was a good employee and motivated to excel at whatever she did. Despite those qualities, she was also naive in certain regards, and had an innocent quality about her. Sheila said Lisa was loved by her family, and that she loved people and animals. *"Lisa loved life. Lisa loved to be in love, and to be loved."*

Then Sheila told Dale Eaton about all the "what ifs" that might have occurred if he had not brutally murdered Lisa. Sheila spoke of what might have happened if Lisa had taken certain career or college paths—what if she got married, what if she had children. Because of what Dale Eaton had done, no one would ever know. Sheila declared that Lisa was not his only victim. Her family and friends were victims, all the law enforcement agents who had to deal with the case were victims, the community at large were victims, and so was Dale's own family. *"They have cried many tears because of you and for you. They have wept for us and wept with us because of what you did to our daughter. They will bear the undeserved stigma of shame of your actions, though it is not of their doing, and our hearts go out to them."*

Sheila said the people in the gallery—observers and media alike—were not there out of a morbid curiosity, but rather because they also grieved for Lisa and her family. She acknowledged their support over all the intervening years from the time that Lisa's body was discovered at the North Platte River to the present.

Then Sheila pronounced: *"Mr. Eaton, your crime against Lisa Marie Kimmell wasn't an accident or error in judgment. It was evil! Can we ever forgive you? The answer is no. How can we forgive someone who has never asked for*

*it? We are not vindictive or cruel people. You made the deci-
sion to abuse your God-given gift of free will. Even if you were
to ask for forgiveness and take responsibility for what you
have done, we maintain and pray that you will be punished
to the maximum extent in your present life. We know God
will honor that, and we know that God will also deal with
you in the hereafter."*

Sheila began the DVD of Lisa's life, and she told
Dale Eaton to pay very close attention to it. Everyone
in the courtroom did, many of them quietly crying.
Dale, however, just stared at the defense table and
showed no emotion at all. When asked by the judge if
he had any comments before being formally sentenced, Dale just shook his head no.

Judge Park signed Dale Eaton's death warrant, and
tacked on an additional life sentence, plus fifty years,
just in case the death sentence was somehow overturned at a higher court. Even though Dale's execu-
tion date was set for June 25, 2004, everyone knew
that was a remote possibility. There were sure to be
legal challenges on many aspects of what had tran-
spired over the previous months of trial.

Once again, there was a crush of media on the courthouse steps. And this time, Dale's sister Judy spoke to
them directly. She said she was there to speak for her
father, two other sisters, and a younger brother. They
were ashamed of what Dale had done, and she was
angry at the defense team for portraying their father as
an abusive alcoholic. Nothing was further from the
truth, she said, and she thought Wyatt Skaggs's arguments in that regard had been cheap shots at her
father. She also was angry that her mother's mental
problems had been used by the defense to excuse what

Dale had done. She said, "She was a wonderful and caring mother, and we loved her dearly."

Asked by a reporter what she would tell her brother Dale if she could, she answered, "I would tell him I loved him. But he took away a life. What he did was not right. His actions were his own."

All the proceedings of Dale Eaton's case in Wyoming's Seventh Judicial District Court were now over, but his legal battle to stay alive was not over by a long shot. Because of certain things that had occurred in the trial, and the defense team's strategy, the court's decision to put him to death was not a slam dunk. Good legal minds would be at work to overturn the death sentence, and they began working on it in earnest.

Beyond this issue was also a civil court case wherein Dale Eaton would lose his property. And the recipients of this property would be none other than Ron and Sheila Kimmell. And several more things concerning other young women victims in the Great Basin and throughout Wyoming would turn up after the sentence. One of these that had looked as if Dale Eaton might have been the perpetrator would spin off in an incredibly different direction, to another serial killer. Another would be linked to a copycat killer, and yet a third and fourth would come full circle and point at Dale Eaton as the killer.

15

END OF THE LINE

Besides the criminal trial against Dale Eaton, Ron and Sheila Kimmell also took him to court in a civil trial. They were seeking restitution from him for the death of their daughter. In April 2004, they won this case and were granted a judgment of $5 million by district court judge Thomas Sullins.

Sheila told a reporter for the *Star-Tribune* that she knew that Dale Eaton didn't have that kind of money. She then related, "There is no profit in this for us. He has nothing of value. But we want to strip him of everything he does have. It's the principle of the matter."

Even more important, the Kimmells were granted ownership of Dale's property out at Moneta—the property on which he had raped and held captive their daughter. Sheila said about this that they were going to demolish everything there that had ever been owned by Dale Eaton. She declared to a reporter, "We do not want the property to stand as an evil, haunting reminder of what happened to our daughter."

In the summer of 2005, the Kimmells had their wish carried out. The Fremont County Fire Protection District did the actual burning of the sheds and dilapidated trailer on Dale's property. Fire Chief Craig Haslam told a reporter for the *Billings Gazette* that they would be part of a training exercise. He said, "We felt we could help the Kimmells out and benefit us by doing some training."

The Kimmells were also going to have the rest of Dale's junk hauled away. Sheila said, "I don't want to see so much as a tire rim there."

The Kimmell family hadn't heard the last of Dale Eaton, however. With a new team of lawyers, Eaton sent an appeal against his death penalty sentence to the Wyoming Supreme Court, and it was much more than a forlorn hope. The new team of lawyers consisted of public defender Kenneth Koski, senior assistant appellate counsel Tina Kerin, senior assistant public defender Marion Yoder, senior assistant public defender Ryan Roden, and appellate counsel Donna Domonkos. They had a lot of ammunition stemming from what had occurred at Dale Eaton's guilt phase and sentencing phase of his Seventh District Court trial. To many, inside and outside the judicial community, Wyatt Skaggs's admission of Eaton's guilt very early in the trial seemed a risky gambit at best, and "bad lawyering" at worst. This new team of lawyers was going right down that avenue calling it "ineffective assistance by counsel."

In fact, they had a whole laundry list of issues stemming from the trial, any one of them being quite damaging if the WSC agreed with them. Not unlike the fact that it only took one juror to not vote for death, it only took one issue agreed upon by the WSC to have the decision by the jury thrown out. Either a new trial would commence, or Dale Eaton would be given a life sentence instead of death if the prosecution decided not to try once again for another jury trial. The very lengthy list of issues contained the positions: Ineffective Assistance of Counsel, as well as Hostility/Prejudice/Bias Toward Eaton at Guilt/Innocence phase, Juror Misconduct, (wrongful) Admission of Evidence, Incomplete Record, Prosecutorial Misconduct, Cumulative Error—and all those were only in the guilt and innocence phase. There were also many other points the new defense team was challenging.

The Wyoming Supreme Court had to look at each issue, one by one, and hear the arguments by Tina Kerin, chief for the defense, and the chief counsel for the prosecution position, senior assistant attorney general (AG) David Delicath. In fact, all the issues were studied and argued for years; the WSC did not render decisions on each and every one until August 18, 2008. And as noted, if the WSC found for Dale Eaton in even one small instance, then the whole trial might have to be done over again.

The WSC decision by 2008 had a summarization of the basic crimes Dale Eaton was charged with and convicted of, and also a summary of everything that had occurred from April 2, 1988, when Lisa Kimmell's body was found by the fishermen in the North Platte River, to the point when Dale received the death penalty. It retold about the DNA testing that linked Eaton to the crime, and also the two theories put forth by witnesses that linked Dale to Lisa, one coming from Joseph Dax and the other from Eaton's own words to Dr. Ash.

* * *

After the introduction, the WSC decision got down to the issues, one by one, the first being "Was Eaton incompetent during trial and the proceedings in this court?" As the supreme court noted, *This issue ranges far and wide in the briefs, but at this juncture we intend only to address the initial premise, that Eaton was not competent to stand trial.*

The WSC cited Wyoming law that stated, *No person shall be tried, sentenced or punished for the commission of an offense while as a result of mental illness or deficiency, he lacks the capacity to comprehend his position, understand the nature and object of the proceedings against him, conduct his defense in a rational manner or cooperate with his counsel.* And then the WSC noted, *Our concern is whether or not Mr. Eaton was competent during the time he actually stood trial. If he was not, then we would be compelled to reverse and remand and direct the proceedings could only commence once Eaton was declared competent.* In other words, if Dale had not been competent during his trial in 2004, then a new trial would have to start all over again if Dale was found to be competent in 2008. This would have been devastating to the Kimmell family.

So the WSC went back through court records to see if Dale Eaton seemed competent back before his trial of 2004. They found that at his arraignment on June 6, 2003, Dale was asked if he suffered from any mental disability or learning disorder. His attorney answered on Dale's behalf, saying, "I'll respond to that particular question, Your Honor. We, on this particular point, believe that he understands sufficiently enough to be arraigned. We are having him examined by mental-health professionals. We've not got the results of those examinations yet. And so we're not able to totally answer that particular question. But we do desire to go forward with the arraignment at least today, reserving the right, of course, to change the plea later on."

When this issue was heard again on October 2, 2003, Judge Park askéd defense counsel, "All right, Mr. Skaggs, one last point. There was a discussion that Mr. Eaton, for lack of a better word, was being interviewed for possible consideration of not guilty by reason of mental illness or deficiency. Are you still evaluating that prospect?"

Skaggs answered, "Well, Your Honor, the question that you asked is improper. We didn't necessarily have him interviewed for purposes of not guilty by reason of mental deficiency or illness. We did have him interviewed for a number of different reasons, competency being number one, of course. The second thing was to develop possible mitigating circumstances in the penalty phase. At this point, we have no inclination to enter a plea of not guilty by reason of mental illness or deficiency. We have no interest in continuing the case by doing that sort of thing."

The WSC even noted that Dale Eaton at his trial never brought up the contention that he was incompetent to stand trial, nor did his defense lawyers. And neither one of them contended he had been too mentally ill at the time of the crime as to not understand what he was doing. The WSC also noted that the defense did not want Dale to be checked by a state-appointed examiner, because they felt that it would produce expert testimony that was contrary to what they wanted to present at trial. Judge Park had even brought up this issue before trial. Judge Park said to the defense, "All right, I have one other concern that's come up. I don't think it has been raised before, but it is troubling. It arises because of the case out of Gillette where the [state] supreme court ruled that the judge should have ordered an evaluation of the client. Now there's testimony that Mr. Eaton has troubles with his memory. So I guess I want the counsel, well, both of you, to inquire of him to his memory problems."

Wyatt Skaggs responded about the incident that the judge was speaking of at the moment, "He (Eaton) indicated that he remembered this incident quite well."

Judge Park said, "Okay. You know, I'm concerned that that's going to come back to haunt us all at some later date. So, I guess, I'm not asking for submittals at this time, but I want the parties to be prepared to address that, whether the court now has an obligation to order an evaluation of Mr. Eaton, given those difficulties that have surfaced."

Mike Blonigen replied, "Your Honor, I don't believe they do. Even if he had a complete lack of memory, that would not be a lack of competency under case law."

Judge Park responded, "Might be inability to assist his counsel."

Blonigen said, "The courts have ruled on this specifically. In fact, Mr. Short (a defense lawyer) had a client on a vehicular homicide some years ago who complained because of the accident, he couldn't remember anything that had happened. And Mr. Short raised exactly that issue. And it was litigated, and our research shows that it does not qualify as to the competency the court refers to. So I think even the claim of a lack of memory would not make him incompetent."

Wyatt Skaggs joined in. "Absolutely! I totally agree. I totally oppose any attempt to have his (Eaton's) competency looked at, because I can assure the court I have done that."

* * *

The WSC next brought up the issue of Joseph Dax's testimony concerning the moment that Dax pointed toward Dale Eaton in the courtroom, and Dale had an outburst. Dale was now claiming through his new attorneys that his outburst in court during Dax's testimony showed that he was mentally ill, and not able to help in his defense. In fact, Dale claimed his being in the courtroom during those outbursts may have hurt his own cause and swayed the jurors to vote for death later on. In the new defense's words: *This irreparably prejudiced his own case in the eyes of the jury with his unseemly behavior.*

The WSC noted that the first outburst had occurred when Joseph Dax was asked to identify Dale Wayne Eaton and pointed at him at the defense table. Dale had shouted out, "You fucking don't know me! Why in the hell are you talking and pointing to me?"

The WSC said that because of this outburst, it was taken up in chambers after Dax was done testifying, and the jurors were not present. Judge Park asked Dale Eaton about this outburst, and Dale replied, "I was mad because of the fact that this morning, the guy didn't even know me. I'm supposed to have talked to him, then everybody that has come in so far sat there and lied about me. And they (Eaton's defense attorneys) haven't done nothing about it! It's, I mean, my own son come in and you can tell someone taught him, well, led him along about it, because all of a sudden he knows what is all in a CRX. And the only Honda that I had was after he done left and went back. I had a Honda back there three or four years ago. Before I got in trouble. I had a Honda in that Moneta. They (the defense lawyers) keep telling me to write stuff down as I remember it. I write it down, and they never use any of it!"

Judge Park then told Eaton about how a direct examination, cross-examination, and redirect were done in courts, and did he understand about those things? Eaton replied, "They explained some of it to me."

Judge Park asked Dale if he was dissatisfied with his attorneys, and if he wanted new ones. Eaton replied, "Let's just go on with it," which was a statement deemed to be that he did not want to get rid of his attorneys Wyatt Skaggs and Vaughn Neubauer.

Another outburst, of course, had come when Jim Broz testified about the note from "Stringfellow Hawke" on Lisa Kimmell's grave marker. Broz claimed that the handwriting was the same as Dale Eaton's. Eaton had then shouted out at his attorneys, "I can prove where the fuck I was that day, and you guys won't do nothing!"

In chambers afterward, Wyatt Skaggs explained that he was not able to get an expert handwriting analyst to state that it was not Dale Eaton's handwriting, and he did not want to put Dale on the stand to explain that it was not his handwriting. Putting him up there might open a lot of doors the defense did not want opened.

The WSC looked at all of this, and noted that the defense attorneys on many occasions explained the court proceedings to Dale Eaton. The WSC also ruled that the outbursts by Eaton were just that—outbursts by an angry man, and not a sign he was too incompetent to understand what was going on around him in court.

Now came a real possibility that the WSC might find exactly what the new defense of Dale Eaton was looking for: *ineffective assistance of counsel.* The WSC noted that Dale Eaton had been represented by the capital case attorney of the Wyoming Public Defender's System, Wyatt Skaggs, as well as a second attorney from the public defender's staff in the Second Judicial District, Vaughn Neubauer. These two were assisted by an "experienced legal investigator." The WSC added that Wyatt Skaggs had considerable experience in handling murder cases in general and death penalty cases in particular. The second-chair counsel, Neubauer, however, did not have experience in death penalty cases, and, in fact, not very much experience in major felony trials. The WSC was now relying heavily on hearings held by the district court on this very issue over five days in June 2005. That hearing had produced a transcript 1,178 pages long, much of which the WSC now reviewed for the purposes of ineffective counsel. And the WSC stated, *Our paramount consideration is whether, in light of all the circumstances, trial counsel's acts or omissions were outside the wide range of professionally competent assistance.*

Right off the bat, the WSC noted that Wyatt Skaggs told the jurors that Dale bore some responsibility for the kidnapping and murder of Lisa Kimmell. And the WSC admitted the reason that Skaggs had done so was: *The express goal of the defense team was to save Eaton's life, and the first step in that process was to avoid a verdict of first degree murder. The path to that goal included Eaton's admission of some guilt, so as to avoid the "I didn't do it, but if I did, I am very sorry I did it," defense.* By admitting some guilt, the defense hoped to present some mitigating evidence at the penalty phase persuasive enough to convince at least one juror to spare Dale's life.

Within this framework, the WSC addressed a part of Wyoming law that stated, *Counsel at all stages of the case should make every appropriate effort to establish a relationship of trust with the client, and should maintain close contact with the client.* And then the WSC added that Wyatt Skaggs admitted that he was *unable to develop a working relationship with Dale Eaton, and that was also true of the mitigation specialist,* who happened to be a woman. She even declared that after one meeting with Dale Eaton she quit, because "he frightened her." In a remand hearing, both Skaggs and Neubauer declared how hard it was to work with Dale Eaton to present a defense. And yet, all that being said, Dale Eaton had signed a document before trial that stated, *I, Dale Wayne Eaton, do hereby give permission for my counsel to pursue, as a trial strategy, the lesser included offense of second degree murder in the Lisa Marie Kimmell case. I understand that by doing so, my counsel will admit to the jury that I face some criminal responsibility in this case, but not for first degree murder.*

Dale Eaton's appeal now was that *the defense theory was unrealistic and it conceded guilt to first degree murder.* Eaton contended that Dr. Ash's statements on the stand further eroded his chances of being found guilty of second-degree murder. The WSC, however, stated that juries were people with independent intellect, and the defense theory was as *good as anything we can think of, given the circumstances of the case.* And the WSC noted that the appellate lawyers had not come up with a more compelling theory that they would have presented.

There was an appeal now that there had been no challenge by Skaggs and Neubauer to the DNA evidence. Eaton's new lawyers said that the original defense team had never hired an independent expert of their own to challenge the DNA findings. The WSC, however, stated that Skaggs had challenged some of the DNA technicians, but *the effort was tempered by the reality that the DNA was checked and double-checked and pointed to Eaton as the individual who deposited semen on Ms. Kimmell's clothing.*

Then there was a challenge on *failure to know the applicable law.* This went to a challenge that Skaggs and Neubauer did not sufficiently know the law regarding death penalty cases. The WSC said that the challenge overstated the case, and cited *Bullock* v. *Carver—While counsel may be unaware of certain aspects of the law, that circumstance does not necessarily equate with deficient performance. Counsel may be unaware of applicable law and his performance can still meet the* Strickland *standard.*

There was a challenge on *concession of guilt without Eaton's consent.* The WSC disagreed and pointed to Dale signing an agreement that he knew his defense lawyers were going to use a certain strategy to try and get the jurors to vote for second-degree murder instead of first-degree murder. Part of that plan was for an admission that Dale Eaton had abducted and killed Lisa Kimmell, but they contended it had not been premeditated. The new lawyers argued Skaggs went way beyond Dale Eaton's intent in the signing of this document. In his closing argument, Skaggs admitted that Dale had committed kidnapping, robbery, and sexual assault, they said. These, of course, could all lead to a death penalty if and when Eaton was convicted. The challenge was that Skaggs should have never admitted to those things. Those were matters that the prosecution had to bring up and prove, and they didn't need any help from the defense on the matter. Yet, the WSC reiterated that Skaggs had done what was required in *Boukamp* v. *State: present a plausible defense to both first degree and felony murder.* And the WSC stated, *If there were better theories, they have not been called to our attention nor have any occurred to us. Defense counsel's strategy was not such a leap beyond what was contemplated by the concession of some guilt, so as to make defense counsel's strategy the functional equivalent of a guilty plea and to render counsel's assistance ineffective.*

Another issue was that the defense team had not secured a change of venue from Natrona County, even though there had been a great deal of publicity about Lisa Kimmell there ever since her body had been discovered at the Old Government Bridge in 1988. The defense had tried, however, to have the trial moved to Albany County, Wyoming, where both Skaggs and Neubauer lived at the time. This attempt at a change of venue to Albany County was dropped, when it became apparent that no courtroom was going to be available for the trial.

It was also cited that the defense had made no study to show that having the trial in Natrona County was detrimental to their client, and even the WSC acknowledged that the *Casper Star-Tribune* had run a great many articles about Dale Eaton. The WSC added, however, that there was no state law that a defense had to conduct a study that a certain area was inimical to their client receiving a fair trial. And they added a Wyoming homily: *It has been said that Wyoming is a unique place, where Wyoming's highways make up Wyoming's Main Street.* In other words, through the media, a Wyoming resident who got the *Casper Star-Tribune* in Laramie, Sheridan, or any other town or city, was just as aware of the case as was a resident in the Casper area, where the actual trial was held eventually.

There was a challenge on *failure to object to instructions.* The WSC agreed that jury instructions were very important. And the WSC said they gave great latitude to district courts in how they instructed jurors from case to case. Wyoming law had to be adhered to, but both the prosecution and defense could present their theory of why and how the crime occurred and just how harshly the perpetrator should be punished, with all aggravating and mitigating circumstances included for a juror to help them decide.

There was a challenge over "Jurors' Instruction Number 27": *You are instructed that to occur in the perpetration of a felony killing must occur in the unbroken chain of events compromising the felony. The time sequence is not important as long as the evidence point to one continuous transaction.* This was, as Mike Blonigen had contended, that Eaton could have killed Lisa and then robbed her, or robbed her and then killed her. It didn't matter in what sequence those things had occurred. And once again, the WSC said that defense counsel had not been ineffective in respect to the jurors' instructions in the guilt/innocence phase about this issue.

There was even one section in the challenge that stated: *The foregoing arguments, in combination, demonstrate that Eaton was abandoned by defense counsel.* In effect, this meant that both Skaggs and Neubauer had washed their hands of Dale Eaton at some point. The challenge stated that because Eaton admitted he was depressed, uncooperative, and a difficult client to manage, the defense counsel simply abandoned him to his fate. Once again, the WSC did not agree with this contention.

Dale Eaton also cited "twelve instances" where the district court had "prejudice or bias" against him. In effect, he was saying that Judge Park held those things against him and he didn't have a chance at a fair trial. One instance, according to Dale, was that during the guilt/innocence phase, the judge brought up matters concerning the penalty phase about whether he should be put to death or not. Eaton contended this unfairly hurt him when only guilt and innocence should have been decided. Another incident was during voir dire, when the judge would not let his counsel inquire into a juror's understanding of depression. Another centered on a juror who wanted to know more about child abuse. A more glaring one during voir dire, according to Eaton, was when a potential juror was not excused when he uttered, "I'm a black-and-white guy. I have to be shown things before I lean either way." This person also expressed, "An eye for an eye, but, of course, that would make everyone blind." Eaton thought that Judge Park should have excused this person for cause right away.

And then there was one issue that was so odd, it's not even certain why Eaton found it so objectionable. One potential juror kept calling defense counsel, "sir," while answering questions. This happened eight times. Judge Park commented, "I appreciate you're trying to be polite, but it isn't necessary to call him 'sir' every time." Perhaps Eaton thought that Judge Park was trying to tell everyone that Wyatt Skaggs was not worthy of being called "sir." His reasoning was obscure at best.

Last but not least, Eaton said Judge Park showed bias when he told Dale to "calm down" during one of his outbursts. According to Eaton, the jurors heard this and it influenced them against him.

The WSC related, with perhaps a bit of cynicism, *In summary, Eaton contends that just about every ruling the district court made during voir dire and the guilt/innocence phase that was adverse to him demonstrated a prejudice against him.* The WSC said they had looked at all the transcripts very carefully and found no prejudice or bias on Judge Park's part.

The next issue was potentially very explosive, and, more than most, seemed to have a good shot at leading toward a mistrial: *juror misconduct.* This was, of course, about the juror who had gone to the Old Government Bridge on his own, and then went into deliberations and told the others he had been out there. Even the WSC acknowledged that this juror's actions had *created a significant crisis in these proceedings.* And it also acknowledged that death penalty cases were *different than other felony cases.* That being said, they also cited that *a defendant is entitled to a fair trial, but not a perfect trial.* The WSC said that although the juror's conduct created a crisis, everything possible was done by the district court to salvage the hard work that had already been accomplished.

What had occurred was that the jurors had begun deliberations on the guilt/innocence phase on Monday, March 15, then at 9:55 A.M. on Tuesday, March 16, the judge called all the attorneys into his courtroom about a problem that had just come to his attention. Judge Park put before them, "The jury members have a serious concern about one jury person that openly admitted going out to Old Government Bridge to investigate and form an opinion about the tire track evidence presented during the case." Then Judge Park called in the juror who had gone there. This juror admitted that he had gone there, but his comments to the others had not been very prolonged or in depth. Then the judge had the jury foreperson called in. This foreperson related that the matter had actually been a matter of "substantial discussion," and that nine out of eleven other jurors expressed serious conern about it.

It was decided very quickly that replacing the errant juror with an alternate was essential. Wyatt Skaggs also let it be known that he needed time to consider a mistrial motion. Judge Park heard Skaggs's argument for a mistrial and said that further inquiry of the jury was needed under the circumstances. It was agreed by all parties that the general timeline for the incident had taken a certain path; the jury began deliberations at 2:05 P.M. on March 15, and retired for the day at 5:00 P.M. The jury resumed deliberations at 9:00 A.M. on March 16, and the note came to Judge Park at 9:45 A.M. that same day. At that time, Judge Park told the jurors to cease deliberations.

The eleven remaining jurors were brought in to speak with Judge Park, the prosecutors and defense team. Juror number 1 said she could put aside the errant juror's comments and begin new deliberations with a new juror relying only on evidence presented at the trial. Juror number 2 said the same, but juror number 3 was more of a problem. Initially he did not think he could put aside the comments made by the errant juror and it would influence him in further deliberation. A great deal of time was spent with this juror, and he finally agreed that he could put aside the comments and start deliberations anew with an alternate juror being brought in.

The remainder of the jurors said that they could put aside the comments, and at the end of those, Wyatt Skaggs once again made a motion for a mistrial and also a motion that juror 3 be released for another alternate. Judge Park denied both motions. This was very thin ice, and the WSC looked at this issue very carefully. Eventually they ruled, *We conclude that Eaton was not prejudiced by the errant juror's misconduct and that the district court adequately addressed all of the concerns raised by that misconduct.*

Another potentially damaging issue was the testimony of Joseph Dax and Dale Eaton's outburst in the courtroom in response to it. It was noted that Joe Dax had been incarcerated with Dale Eaton at the Natrona County Jail between April 3, 2003, and April 8, 2003. Of course, Dale Eaton claimed he had never spoken with Joseph Dax, and that Dax was only in court helping the prosecution because he wanted his own sentence lessened. One of the most damaging things Dax had said in testimony was Dale's alleged comments about having sex with Lisa Kimmell: "I don't think anyone will miss her. She was a lousy lay." This had brought an immediate objection from Vaughn Neubauer, which was overruled. But Judge Park then said to the jurors, "Ladies and gentlemen, that statement is offered to you solely for the purpose of Mr. Blonigen's question, which was to indicate whether or not Mr. Eaton had any sexual contact with Ms. Kimmell."

The essence of Eaton's challenge now was that the statement was so "inflammatory and prejudicial" that its admission by Judge Park required a reversal of his conviction. The WSC, however, cited Wyoming law: *Evidence that points to guilt is, by its very nature, prejudicial.* The WSC said that Dax's comment went to the heart of the crime: Dale Eaton had kidnapped Lisa Kimmell, sexually assaulted her, and murdered her. And then on thin ice, indeed, the WSC added, *We agree that the prosecutor used poor judgment in allowing it to be a part of his case, a crucial case for the Kimmell family, for the citizens of this state, and for Eaton. The district court might well have disallowed its admission because all parties knew it was coming and the objections were made well in ad-*

vance of its telling. The WSC, however, ruled that Judge Park had admonished the jurors that they were to use the statement only to decide if Dale Eaton had sexual contact with Lisa Kimmell. Because of that admonition, the supreme court did not agree with Eaton's challenge. It was a very close thing, and had Eaton won the challenge, just as he had hoped, his conviction would have been overturned.

Eaton lost on that issue, but there were still plenty more where he could win a challenge. The next in line were the photos shown by Dr. Thorpen on the stand. Exhibits 632 and 633 were particularly grisly autopsy photos. The WSC noted that they were of the stab wounds, bloodred in color, and very detailed as to the entry wounds. Part of the challenge was that Dr. Thorpen had actually gone into the jury box with the photos and personally showed them to the jurors. At the time, however, the defense made no objection to this unorthodox presentation. The WSC noted that because there was no objection at the time, they now viewed this under the *plain error standard*. The plain error standard said that Eaton had to show this had been a clear and unequivocal violation of law, as shown by *Lopez* v. *State*. The WSC said the challenge did not meet that standard.

There was an issue of *prosecutorial misconduct*, according to Eaton and his new lawyers. This centered around Mike Blonigen's statement that from the time she was kidnapped, Lisa Kimmell must have known what her fate was going to be, and this was mental torture. The WSC said that this was a fair argument, since Lisa Kimmell had been kidnapped, held captive for a number of days, and been bound with rope during that period of time. They even went so far as to state: *Ms. Kimmell was handled roughly, bound and raped during her captivity.* The WSC declared that Mike Blonigen's statement was within the bounds set by court precedents.

All of those challenges only covered the guilt/ innocence phase. There were a whole list covering the sentencing phase as well, and Eaton especially hoped to have his sentence overturned because of one error or another in that phase. Starting with voir dire, the new lawyers contended that it was *so poorly done by the defense team that the penalty imposed must be remanded for a new sentencing trial.* They said that the biases of individual jurors were never properly explored by Skaggs and Neubauer, even when the biases were obvious. And through his new lawyers, Eaton stated, *The defense team failed to exercise the customary skill and diligence that a reasonably competent attorney would provide.* The new lawyers went even further, stating that even if the defense team was not incompetent, Judge Park had a duty to explore the biases of the jurors during voir dire, and had not done so.

The WSC looked at this voir dire phase and noted that potential jurors had been brought in, in large groups. The WSC said they scanned these transcripts very carefully, looking for errors, a process that covered hundreds of pages. After all that, the WSC stated that Judge Park had done a *creditable and evenhanded job of overseeing the process.* They denied this challenge as well.

Once again bringing up the testimony of Dr. Ash and Dr. Gummow, there were challenges that Skaggs and Neubauer had failed to alert these two about key areas of concern. One was the fact that both Skaggs and

Neubauer knew about Doris Buchta's journal before Dr. Ash took the stand. Because of this journal, it was contended that Dale Eaton was not as isolated as Dr. Ash believed, and it left him open to damaging cross-examination by Mike Blonigen. Things became even worse with Dr. Gummow. One glaring error, in the minds of Eaton's new lawyers, was the failure to provide Dr. Gummow with the correct date of the suicide of Dale Eaton's brother Darrell. And very damning was the fact in a posttrial hearing before a lower appellate court, Dr. Gummow had used this statement about Wyatt Skaggs: "Trial counsel was not organized and helpful." And trial counsel was "irritable, shaky, and not in good health." The new lawyers put it this way about the key testimony during the defense side of the sentencing phase: *There was over-reliance on two ill-prepared doctors, mixed in with family members who tanked and gave the jury no coherent mitigation story.* Because of this, the challenge stated that not a single mitigating factor was found by even one juror in the sentencing phase.

The WSC looked at the prosecution's rebuttal of these allegations and noted that they said that Skaggs and Neubauer had used their investigator to find family and friends, acquired medical and mental-health records of both Dale and his mother, and had Dale interviewed and tested by two experienced psychiatrists. It wasn't for lack of trying in this phase by the defense, the prosecution contended. If the jurors had found no mitigating factors in the sentencing phase, then that went more to Dale Eaton's character and the crimes he had perpetrated than to a lack of effort by the defense.

Then the prosecution pointed out that aside from a schoolmate's report that Dale had been bullied by another student in elementary school, and that Dale

sought some counseling in 1986 at the hospital in Torrington, Wyoming, there wasn't much else the defense could have brought in. The WSC agreed that
these two instances would hardly have swayed the
jurors in their votes for mitigation.

The challenges about Dr. Ash and Dr. Gummow
were very serious concerns, and the WSC looked into
this very carefully. The WSC reviewed all of this in the
light of the legal standards and analytical model set
forth in several cases, including *Strickland* v. *State* and
Burger v. *Kemp*. In part, they noted that ineffective assistance by a counsel had a performance component
and a prejudice component. The components were
generally a mixed question of fact and law. In the performance component, the challenger had to show
that the defense lawyer made errors so serious as to
not be conducting himself up to professional standards. And in the prejudice component, the challenger had to show that the performance was so
deficient in practice it affected the sentence.

The WSC reviewed the opening statements by both
the prosecution and defense. In the prosecution opening, they noted that Blonigen said he expected the defense to talk about Dale Eaton's life history and
depression, but that these things were not enough to
overcome the aggravating circumstances of Dale's
crimes. Wyatt Skaggs did, in fact, review Dale's life history and mental problems, and said they were a big
factor in who he was, and that Dale Eaton's life had
value and should be spared. It was toward this life history of Eaton—of which the new lawyers said the original defense team had done such a poor job—that WSC
now turned their attention.

WSC agreed that much of the defense evidence in
this phase came through their expert witnesses

Dr. Ash and Dr. Gummow, and not through family and friends of Dale Eaton's. Dr. Ash had said he spent twelve total hours interviewing Eaton and had read his medical records, including those from the Colorado Psychopathic Hospital when Dale had been sixteen years old. From these, Dr. Ash stated that Dale's depression went far beyond mild depression to a state of clinical depression, which could cause brain damage. Dr. Ash also charted Dale's IQ as being somewhere in the eighties to low nineties.

WSC also reviewed Dr. Gummow's background as an expert witness and all the notes and studies she had done concerning Dale Eaton. In one of Dr. Gummow's reports, she noted that Dale *had a strong emotional attachment to his mother, who was reported to be a good mother, who cared for her family and did the best she could until she started to have mental health problems around 1961.* Dr. Gummow said this had a profound effect upon Dale. WSC even took into account an exchange between Dr. Gummow and Mike Blonigen on this issue:

Blonigen: *Was she (Dale's mother) hospitalized more than once?*

Gummow: *Yes. Multiple times. And Mr. Eaton believed that he was responsible for his mother's mental-health problems.*

WSC looked very hard at the issue of Dr. Gummow being wrong about the date of Dale's brother Darrell's suicide. She had flatly stated that it had occurred sometime in 1987, when, in fact, it had occurred in October 1988, after Dale had kidnapped and murdered Lisa Kimmell.

There was a very viable possibility of the trial being

overturned, stemming from the testimony of Dr. Ash and Dr. Gummow, the two key expert witnesses in the sentencing phase. In fact, for all intents and purposes, Dr. Ash and Dr. Gummow *were* the defense's mitigators at the sentencing phase. If the jury did not believe them, or found them to be ill-prepared, then the chances that the jurors would return a death sentence against Dale increased dramatically. The problem with Dr. Ash had been that he did not know about Doris Buchta's journal. Asked after the trial in an evidentiary hearing about these matters by the appellate court, Wyatt Skaggs answered that he believed showing that journal to Dr. Ash was not relevant. "Mrs. Buchta's living three hundred yards away across the highway did not mean that Eaton was not in isolation. I think the jury understood he was very isolated there." During this hearing, even Dr. Ash stated about Doris Buchta and her husband, "If that's all the contact Eaton had with people at that time, that's still pretty isolated." WSC agreed that the defense had not been in error or had shown ineptitude in this matter.

The situation with Dr. Linda Gummow was potentially more damaging. She had been made to look a fool on the stand when she stated that Darrel Eaton's suicide had been in 1987, when it had been in October 1988, after Lisa Kimmell's murder. In an appellate hearing, Dr. Gummow was asked by Eaton's new lawyers if she felt "beat up" during Blonigen's cross-examination of her. Dr. Gummow stated, "Not particularly." WSC agreed and said that this incident, while egregious, was not significant enough to cause a mistrial.

As far as the jury instructions in the sentencing phase went, WSC said the challenge *boils down to this: The defense team offered good instructions, but they did not vigorously pursue the use of those instructions*. Once again,

Eaton was claiming that his lawyers had caved in to the prosecution's wishes, and the instructions finally settled upon by both sides *did not create a comprehensible scheme for guiding the juror's decisions.* In fact, Eaton's new lawyers said the instructions were inconsistent and contradictory. So WSC looked at those instructions under the plain error standard. After doing this, they found that none of the instructions were contradictory or did not meet the plain error standard.

There were plenty of challenges to Mike Blonigen's closing remarks, one of them being that Blonigen never should have uttered, "Don't let Mr. Eaton attempt to hide the enormity of his crime in a veil of psychiatrists and tears." The contention was that Blonigen was asking the jurors to ignore a possible mitigating circumstance and not even consider it, when by the jury instructions, they had to consider it. WSC said this was fair argument and fell within the bounds of a closing argument.

As to Blonigen's comments, "He (Eaton) simply finds young women alongside the road a convenient target," the new lawyers said this constituted a comment on future dangerousness, something that could not be considered by the jurors. But WSC ruled that not only did Joseph Dax's statements point to this, but so did Dale Eaton's own self-report to Dr. Ash about how Lisa Kimmell had given him a ride. And on a different issue, there was a challenge that Blonigen contended that Eaton had "blamed" the victim for the things that befell her. WSC said this was a fair argument, since in Dr. Ash's testimony and self-report by Eaton, he had found Lisa Kimmell on his land at night and thought she and others were there to rob him. So whatever befell her later on, in Dale's mind, was justified.

* * *

There was a challenge that the state had somehow suppressed evidence that was discovered in Dale Eaton's school bus taken from his property at Moneta. That challenge contended it might have led to someone else who kidnapped and raped Lisa Kimmell, not Dale Eaton. This point concerned some blood found in a drain of the bus. But WSC noted that this blood sample was very small, and nothing definitive was ever determined from it. The challenge was that if the bus had not been destroyed by authorities, new evidence might have turned up from that blood. This was also a roundabout way of getting at the original defense's contention that Dale Eaton had killed Lisa on a spur-of-the-moment whim on his property, and not at the Old Government Bridge. This theory would have made it second-degree murder, since it could have been done without forethought, and thus not first-degree murder. If that was the case, then no death penalty should have ensued.

WSC said there was no suppression of evidence by the state, and the defense was the first to have knowledge of the bus. Then in a scathing comment, WSC wrote, *We deem it a leap over a giant chasm to speculate that, even if it could be established that the bus was Eaton's, the presence of blood in the drain would result in a different verdict at the guilt/innocence stage.*

In conclusion, WSC asserted that a death penalty sentence had to ensure a meaningful judicial review, which safeguarded the process. They said they had done this by reviewing all the transcripts and all pertinent material. In the end they stated they were satisfied that all the evidence supported the jury's findings with respect to t

additi

had imp

passion, p

Then they

the district court,

a new trial. The c

purpose of vacating th

setting a specific date for

dering this decision,

Judge Park's court to pick

to be put to death by lethal

After hearing about the Wyom... Supreme Court decision on Dale Eaton's appeal, Sheila Kimmell told a reporter for the *Billings Gazette* that she had mixed feelings about it. She was frustrated by how long it had taken for the judicial process to get that far, but glad that at least that hurdle had been overcome. Sheila then said she wasn't sure if she would go to see Dale Eaton executed, but she would consider it if it would help encourage him to confess about other young women he might have murdered. She said, "I want those families to have a measure of peace." There was one other reason as well. Sheila said, "It would be his last chance to ask for forgiveness," especially of his own family members. Sheila acknowledged, "They were victims of his crimes too."

Epilogue

There were four cases, in particular, that would have widely different outcomes by the year 2008. Two would lead directly away from Dale Eaton to other killers and surprising conclusions, while the other two would come full circle right back, pointing toward Eaton as the murderer. The first case was one of "the Great Basin Murders," in which Eaton had remained a suspect for so long because of his journeys into that region, and the things he had told people while living there.

As former FBI agent and profiler Greg Cooper had noted, three out of ten unsolved Great Basin murders seemed to have been committed by the same perpetrator. The female victims had been shot in the head and then possibly posed in isolated areas in the form of a cross. Cooper used his years as an FBI profiler to look at these crimes, including an initial three-step criteria:

1. The steps taken to ensure the success of the crime.
2. Steps to help protect the identity of the killer.
3. Steps to help effect the killer's escape.

Cooper then utilized more steps to filter the profiling, starting with victimology. This concerned the lifestyle of the victim, where they lived, shopped, and did recreational activities, which could include everything from hiking to going to bars. He wanted to know the possibility that the victim and killer knew each other. If a victim was abducted and killed in an isolated area, that tended to point more to death by stranger. If she was killed in the relative safety of her residence, the first people who had to be looked at were husband, boyfriend, or people with whom she was close.

Cooper looked at the possible initial contact site, if that could be discerned. Was this a place where the victim had a routine, or a onetime visit to the area? And as to the actual murder site, the five *W*'s had to be asked: who, what, when, why, and where. If the disposal site was different than the murder site, what made the disposal site attractive to the killer? Did the site help the killer escape, or was it a place where the victim had been dumped as quickly as possible?

Physical injuries to the victim were important. It made a difference if the victim was shot at a medium distance or short distance. Even more personalized were stab wounds, especially if they were inflicted upon the face, breasts, or genital area. And did the killer stab more often than was necessary to kill the victim? Was it, in essence, "overkill," a sign of a rage killing that might be personally aimed at the particular victim or females, in general?

If there was a sexual assault, was it vaginal, anal, or oral, or was it a combination of those factors? Was a foreign object involved, and did the perpetrator ejaculate on or in the victim? Was sexual torture involved?

Then there was the category of the killer acting in an organized or disorganized manner. An organized killer would make attempts to cover up his identity and hide the body. A disorganized killer would leave the body where it lay, and do very little to hide what he had done. Cooper noted that in the two types of individuals, an organized killer would generally carry out organized activity in his everyday life. This type tended to keep a neat work area and residence, whereas the disorganized killer was sloppy and had a messy residence.

The risk level of the victim had to be taken into account. Was the victim a prostitute, alcoholic, drug user, or hitchhiker? This elevated their risks. This had to be looked at with caution, however. Lisa Kimmell had only elevated her risk level by driving on a lonely road at night, a road she did not know well. Otherwise, she led a relatively risk-free life.

While Greg Cooper initially thought there might be a link between Lisa Kimmell's murder and the three other Great Basin murders he studied, the more he researched the case, the further he backed off from that theory. Even though Dale Wayne Eaton was in the area of the murder victim in Millard County, Utah, around the time she died, it was Cooper's investigation into aspects of that crime that led him to a startlingly different conclusion. He began to surmise that the female in Millard County was the victim of another wanderer, not unlike Dale Eaton, who just happened to be one of America's most prolific serial killers—Robert Ben Rhoades. Cooper eventually related the information he had gathered to the sheriff of Millard County, and it led to some very surprising revelations.

Robert Ben Rhoades was a professional long-haul truck driver in the 1980s. Rhoades drove all over the United States, and basically eluded notice by law enforcement because of all the jurisdictions he passed through. It wasn't even detected until an incident in Arizona in April 1990 that women's bodies started showing up along the routes he drove. On that date, Arizona Highway Patrol officer Mike Miller noticed a big rig parked on the shoulder of Interstate 10. Thinking the truck driver might have broken down and needed assistance, Miller pulled his cruiser over and walked toward the truck. As he approached the truck, Miller was stunned when he looked into the cab's window and saw a nude female tied up with restraints in the sleeper part of the cab. The trooper also discovered the truck driver there, a man who was identified as Robert Ben Rhoades.

Rhoades tried talking his way out of the situation by saying that the woman who was bound was consensual about the situation. It was just their way of having kinky sex, he said. Patrolman Miller didn't buy it, and soon discovered a loaded .25-caliber automatic pistol. Trooper Miller handcuffed Rhoades and placed him in the police cruiser, but little did he know that Rhoades had a handcuff key and almost escaped. Miller was able to recapture Rhoades, restrain him again, and waited with him until backup arrived.

When other officers arrived, the nude female was rescued and she turned out to be Lisa Pennal. Her English was not good, but she managed to convey that she had accepted a ride with Rhoades at a coffee shop. Pennal said that she had later fallen asleep in the sleeper area of the cab, only to wake up with her wrists and ankles tied in restraints. Rhoades then proceeded to undress her, whipped her, attached spring-type clips to her nipples and vagina, and sexually tortured her.

While in custody, Rhoades still tried to claim that the situation with Pennal had been consensual, but his story began to break down as more and more of her statements jibed with the pornographic and sexual assault items found in his truck. When Rhoades's home in Houston, Texas, was searched, the officers found handcuffs, spring-type clips, a dildo, and various items of women's clothing. He also had photographs of young white females in various poses while they were nude and seminude.

Then in September 1990, the decomposed body of Regina Walters, only fourteen, was found in Illinois along one of the routes that Rhoades had driven. Walters and a boyfriend started hitchhiking from Texas, and were probably picked up by Rhoades. Walter's boyfriend's body was eventually found near El Paso, Texas. Regina Walters, it was determined, had been killed by manual strangulation.

A clearer picture of Robert Ben Rhoades began to appear after he pled guilty in September 1992 to the murder of Regina Walters. He was born in Council Bluffs, Iowa, in 1945, and had few problems in school. Rhoades even played football on the school team, wrestled, was in the boys glee club, a choir, and French club. Then he got into a few scrapes around this time for fighting and tampering with a motor vehicle. In 1964, Rhoades enlisted in the U.S. Marine Corps, and, interestingly, his father was arrested that same year for performing lascivious acts upon a twelve-year-old girl. His father committed suicide after being arrested.

Rhoades was soon in trouble himself, and discharged from the Marine Corps in 1968 after committing a robbery. He attended college for a short while, but dropped out, tried becoming a police officer, but didn't make the cut. Eventually he ended up becoming a long-haul truck driver. It was during his truck-driving days that his penchant for picking up young female hitchhikers, torturing them, and killing them began. Rhoades's first "kill" was thought to have occurred in November 1989.

None of this might have led back to the unsolved Millard County, Utah, case, had Greg Cooper not started looking into the truck routes that Rhoades had traveled during the 1980s and 1990s. One of those routes led right through Millard County on Interstate 15 in the time period when Millard County's Jane Doe had been murdered. It was this information and more that Cooper passed on to the Millard County sheriff, and for the first time, Rhoades started being looked at as her possible killer.

It wasn't until 2003 that the female victim in Millard County was finally identified. She was twenty-four-year-old Patricia Candace Walsh, of Seattle, Washington. In 1990, she and Scott Zyskowski began hitchhiking from Washington State to Texas. What was pieced together later was that Rhoades probably killed Zyskowski and dumped his body near El Paso, Texas, early on; then for the next six days, he sexually assaulted and tortured Patricia Walsh as he drove west. Finally tiring of this, after days of abusing her, Rhoades killed Walsh and dumped her body in rural Millard County.

In February 2005, charges in the Fourth District Court of Utah were filed against Rhoades for murder in the first-degree and aggravated kidnapping. The first-degree murder charge could bring Rhoades the death penalty. And two months later, Millard County sheriff Ed Phillips and two of his investigators drove to Illinois and picked up Rhoades. Phillips had a few interesting things to tell a reporter about the drive back to Utah with Rhoades. Phillips said, "Rhoades was hard to read because he was so guarded. He had a macho persona." Rhoades had fought the extradition from Illinois, but this matter was out of his hands, and there was an agreement between the governor of Utah and governor of Illinois that he should be extradited.

Meanwhile, the murder case of the woman whose body had been dumped off Interstate 15, near Mills Junction, in Juab County, Utah, took a whole different course that involved neither Dale Eaton nor Robert Ben Rhoades. In fact, it may have been a "copycat killing" when the killer read about Millard County's Jane Doe case of the previous year. The victim turned out to be Barbara Kaye Williams, of Florida, but no missing persons report on her even surfaced until 1997. Williams had left Florida in 1990, and the unknown female's body had been discovered in Juab County, Utah, on March 22, 1991. Apparently, Williams had moved to Salt Lake City, Utah, in 1990, and then pretty much fell off the grid. It wasn't until 1995 that Agent Bill Goote, of the Florida Department of Law Enforcement (FDLE), started looking into old unsolved cases in his area. This went on for several years, until Goote found out about the "unknown woman" in Juab County, Utah. More time passed and finally Goote contacted Sheriff David Carter in Juab County. Carter said, "Goote let us know that our unidentified body and the missing woman could possibly be the same person. He said the weight, size, and physical characteristics of both the body and the missing woman led him to think they could be a match."

Fingerprint testing was eventually done on the body and it matched that of Barbara Williams. And by now, Barbara's former husband, Howell Williams, was being looked at as the main suspect. Deputy Justin Kimball and Millard County detective John Kimball went to Florida and spent three days there. Justin Kimball also went to Tucson, Arizona, around this time, and he may have looked into aspects about the Robert Ben Rhoades case. Whatever he found seemed to make Justin Kimball look once again at Howell Williams, and not Rhoades, as Barbara Williams's killer. Finally, on March 3, 1999, Howell Williams was charged with the murder of his ex-wife, Barbara Williams, and he was extradited to Juab County, Utah.

There was potentially another family that may have been a victim of Dale Eaton's crimes, and in the summer of 2008, evidence of that possibility came to light in a very strange way. A journalist was looking into the disappearance of Amy Bechtel, and because he happened to be in the Waltman area, he stopped in at the Waltman store where Dale used to hang out and even lived for a while behind the shop in his van. The journalist started talking to a relative of the store owner, and the man remembered Dale Eaton very well. They, of course, talked about the Lisa Kimmell case, and almost as an afterthought, the journalist asked if Dale might have been responsible for Amy

Bechtel's disappearance. The answer from the man who knew Dale Eaton came as a complete surprise to him: "Yes, it's a real possibility. He was pissed-off about something that Thursday. He took off in the afternoon and didn't come back for several days." Of course, Amy had disappeared on a late Thursday afternoon in 1997.

Then there was another surprise. The man took the journalist out back, and sitting amongst hundreds of junked cars was Dale Eaton's green Dodge van. The same Dodge van that Dale had tried kidnapping the Breeden family in. In fact, a very similar green-colored van had been spotted by a woman on the Loop Road outside of Lander on the day Amy Bechtel had disappeared. The woman recalled the van heading west, the direction of Moneta. This woman also recalled a young woman at the wheel of the van, looking very distressed. Of course, in 1997, Dale Eaton had forced Shannon Breeden at gunpoint to drive his van, and she, too, had been "distressed" while doing so. If not for her quick thinking and brave action, she and her family might have simply disappeared in the Red Desert, where the rivers disappear beneath the sand.

The journalist eventually contacted Amy Bechtel's brother, Nels Wroe, about the things he had learned. Nels was so impressed by these revelations that he told the journalist that the tip "was a good one, with teeth in it." Nels added that he was forwarding this information to the FBI. Obviously, Nels wouldn't have done so if he didn't think the new information had some validity. Not unlike the Kimmells, Amy Bechtel's family had received information over the years—everything from Amy's husband had killed her, to the possibility of Native Americans from the Crow Reservation.

By this time, the journalist wasn't alone in thinking that Dale Eaton had to be placed high on the list of people possibly responsible for Amy Bechtel's disappearance. Tony Howard, the former DA of Sweetwater County, who had prosecuted Dale Eaton in the Breeden abduction case, agreed with that assessment. When the journalist phoned Howard, the former DA thought that Eaton "looked good" for the abduction of Amy Bechtel. And then Howard recalled the disappearance of other young women in Wyoming, including Janelle Johnson, Kathleen Pehringer, of Riverton, and Belinda Grantham. In all those cases, Dale Eaton was still high on the list of possible suspects.

Former FBI profiler Greg Cooper also agreed with Tony Howard about this, and when he received news about what the journalist had uncovered, he told the reporter, "I think you're onto something."

Perhaps even more incredible was the fact that Elko County Sheriff's Office detective Dennis Journigan started looking once again at that county's Jane Doe case of 1993. In the spring of 2009, Journigan decided to use cutting edge technology at Isoforensic's lab in Salt Lake City, Utah. Detective Journigan sent them a small sample of the 1993 victim's hair. Isoforensic lab did an oxygen isotope analysis of the hair sample and determined that the victim had been twenty-seven or twenty-eight years old when murdered. Even more importantly, they were able to determine through isotope analysis that she had lived in Starr Valley, Wyoming during the seven months prior to her death. Isoforensic could do this because of the water she had drunk there became part of her DNA makeup, even down to the hair on her head.

Detective Journigan was amazed at these results. He had recently learned that none other than convicted murderer Dale Wayne Eaton had lived in the Starr Valley area during that period, and Dale, of course, had lived in Elko as well. Detective Journigan was so impressed by this new information concerning the 1993 Jane Doe, that he sent the Isoforensic information on to the Natrona County Sheriff's Office. A very small strand of hair was suddenly placing Dale Wayne Eaton in the cross hairs of evidence to a 1993 Nevada murder of a young woman.

As 2009 progressed, one thing was certain for Dale Eaton—if he didn't come up with some kind of deal on other murders he had committed, then he, in essence, was a "dead man walking." His vehicles were gone, his property was gone, and his family was gone, for all practical purposes.

All he had left was a tiny cell and a ticking clock in the background, ticking off the remaining minutes of Dale Eaton's life.

GREAT BOOKS,
GREAT SAVINGS!

When You Visit Our Website:
www.kensingtonbooks.com
You Can Save Money Off The Retail Price
Of Any Book You Purchase!

- **All Your Favorite Kensington Authors**
- **New Releases & Timeless Classics**
- **Overnight Shipping Available**
- **eBooks Available For Many Titles**
- **All Major Credit Cards Accepted**

Visit Us Today To Start Saving!
www.kensingtonbooks.com

MORE MUST-READ TRUE CRIME FROM PINNACLE

MORE SHOCKING TRUE CRIME
FROM PINNACLE

Lethal Embrace   0-7860-1785-6 $6.99/$9.99
Robert Mladinich and Michael Benson

Love Me or I'll Kill You 0-7860-1778-3 $6.99/$9.99
Lee Butcher

Precious Blood   0-7860-1849-6 $6.99/$9.99
Sam Adams

Baby-Faced Butchers 0-7860-1803-8 $6.99/$9.99
Stella Sands

Hooked Up for Murder 0-7860-1865-8 $6.99/$9.99
Robert Mladinich and Michael Benson

Available Wherever Books Are Sold!

Visit our website at **www.kensingtonbooks.com**